GOD
DES
SES

GOD DES SES

NINA MILLNS

**SIMON &
SCHUSTER**

London · New York · Sydney · Toronto · New Delhi

First published in Great Britain by Simon & Schuster UK Ltd, 2023

1 3 5 7 9 10 8 6 4 2

Simon & Schuster UK Ltd
1st Floor
222 Gray's Inn Road
London WC1X 8HB

Simon & Schuster Australia, Sydney
Simon & Schuster India, New Delhi

www.simonandschuster.co.uk
www.simonandschuster.com.au
www.simonandschuster.co.in

A CIP catalogue record for this book is available from the British Library

Hardback ISBN: 978-1-3985-1830-8
Trade Paperback ISBN: 978-1-3985-1831-5
eBook ISBN: 978-1-3985-1832-2
Audio ISBN: 978-1-3985-1838-4

Typeset in the UK by M Rules
Printed and Bound in the UK using 100% Renewable Electricity
at CPI Group (UK) Ltd

MIX
Paper | Supporting
responsible forestry
FSC
www.fsc.org
FSC® C171272

In memory of the 72 people
who lost their lives in the Grenfell fire

For all the Ayeshas
. . . and their Yazes

PROLOGUE

Ayesha kept low and crept slowly around the lake, making sure to keep the others exactly on the opposite side. She moved when they moved. Her soaking body trembling uncontrollably, her teeth chattering violently, she tried to calm her panicked breathing and keep herself concealed in the darkness of the country night. When they were just over a quarter of the way around, there was a chilling scream of triumph. Ayesha froze; her stomach sank. She could just make out the silhouette of a finger against the night sky pointed directly at her. A beam of cold light locked onto her. Then another. Someone ululated. More voices joined in and then they ran at her.

Ayesha pelted away, back into the thick dark of the forest. But they were much closer now. Two figures sprinted with intense determination in Ayesha's direction. She didn't need to look behind her. She felt their intent and heard their rhythmic breathing as they closed in on her. What would happen when they caught her? How far would they go? She had no idea anymore where the line was. She knew they weren't fully themselves, but even as themselves she was now terrified of what they were. How had she got them so wrong? How could Yaz do that, join them, help them hurt her? Surely there was some mistake. She thought of turning, trying to reason with them, snap them out of this savage intoxication. But she didn't dare slow down. Instinct told her to keep running. Maybe for her life.

GODDESS,

WE CANNOT WAIT TO WELCOME YOU TO THE PARTY OF
THE YEAR / CENTURY / GALAXY — ALL IN THE NAME OF
CELEBRATING OUR BELOVED QUEEN GODDESS INDIA.

LOCATION: THE MAJESTIC RHODES-WOODHOUSE ESTATE
LOCATED DEEP IN THE HEART OF OUR GREEN AND
PLEASANT LAND.

A FEW FRIENDLY 'FEEL FREES' AND
'FAUX PAS' TO CONSIDER:

DO . . .

—> ADOPT A WHEELBARROW; BECOME BESTIES WITH A
WILD MUSHROOM; TALK TO THE STARS; HUG A CONSENTING
TREE; TAKE A TRIP OUTSIDE YOUR BODILY LIMITATIONS;
DISCARD YOUR HUMAN DRESS AND DON YOUR DEITY'S
ATTIRE; DANCE LIKE THE UNIVERSE IS WATCHING AND SING
LIKE THE ANGELS ARE YOUR BACKING VOCALS.

DON'T . . .

—> BE A SLAVE TO YOUR PATRIARCHAL CONDITIONING;
INFEST THE SACRED SPACE WITH MAN-MADE MATERIALS,
INGREDIENTS, BELIEFS AND SYSTEMS; DISRESPECT THE
CIRCLE AND ANY WITHIN IT; HARM THE BODY, EMOTIONS
OR SPIRIT OF ANOTHER GODDESS.

**DO NOT WALK ANTI-CLOCKWISE AT ANY TIME OR
ENTER INSIDE WITH SHOES.**

BLESSINGS AND LOVE,
INDIA AND CLEMMIE x

¨ INDIA'S GODDESS RETREAT ¨
ITINERARY

ARRIVAL
AURA CLEANSING

THE DESCENT OF THE GODDESS
THE FIRST TRANSFORMATION

CEREMONY OF CUPS
THE FORMING OF THE CIRCLE

SHEDDING OF THE HUMAN FORM
THE SECOND TRANSFORMATION

FORAGING THE FEMININE
THE THIRD TRANSFORMATION
RETURN TO THE CIRCLE

THE BUILDING OF THE ALTAR
IN HER IMAGE

THE REVELATION
THE FOURTH TRANSFORMATION

THE FUSION
RETURN TO THE CIRCLE

THE ULTIMATE OFFERING

CARRIAGES

CHAPTER ONE

JULY 2018

Saturday 1.00 p.m.

The windows were down – they had to be. It was hot. If she switched on the air-con, the ancient red Peugeot 206 would protest wearily and slow down even more. They were cruising along an A-road heading out of London at a modest 47 mph. Not because Ayesha was a cautious driver, but because when the speed hit 50, the car began to shake and she wasn't sure it would make it all the way to Buckinghamshire.

She wasn't sure the willy-shaped cake would either. She pictured the bright pink icing slowly melting in the boot, maybe leaking out onto the pink sashes she'd had made specially – the ones that said 'Hen Do Krew' on them. She'd paid extra for them to spell it with a K. Extra cash she didn't have, to print a sparkly K onto what she had thought would definitely be a winning addition to this exclusive gathering. But with every mile they clocked up, Ayesha was realizing with growing shame that she'd got it wrong. Again.

She glanced at the passenger seat where Yaz was sitting.

'She's gonna hate the pink stuff, isn't she?'

Yaz glanced back and grinned from behind her round sunglasses.

'Yep.'

'I shouldn't have bought all the willy stuff either.'

'Nope.'

Ayesha let this sink in.

'I might just leave it in the car when we get there, suss the vibe first,' she said breezily, knowing already that none of it would make it out of the boot at all.

'Good shout.' Yaz turned back to watching the suburbs fly by.

It was the latest email, which Ayesha had read this morning when she was already on her way, that had made it painfully clear how wrong she'd got it, firmly asserting that they were not, under any circumstances or on any platform, to refer to it as a hen do.

India had been very specific about this, and the message was relayed to the select group of guests through Clemmie, India's old school friend, who had taken charge of the arrangements and the emails.

Remember Wonderful Ones: This is a <u>Goddess Retreat</u> and should be referred to as such. Come adorned in an outfit that befits your deity status, use language that respects and honours our Queen Goddess: India.

It was Clemmie's family house they were heading to – a location that Google Maps showed as a blank, green expanse in a shire of blank green expanses. Ayesha hadn't met Clemmie, but India had told them she was a yoga teacher, a ritual birther and a baroness.

She had scrolled through Clemmie's Instagram profile – an endless palette of pastels and sunlight, smoothies and foraged greens, earthy powders in mortar and pestles. Clemmie with her sandy-blonde locks and white teeth laughing over organic produce, smouldering under crimson capes, looking piously respectful in mystical temples . . . And more recently, enticing hints of what was to come this weekend: an up-close detail of the empty eye of a Venetian mask intricately patterned with feathers, gold and royal blue . . . Layers of fairy lights decorating a table laid with goblets and wild berries . . . A perfectly messy pile of patterned fabrics . . . Flames and drums . . . Body paint and glitter . . . Bunting made from sari offcuts . . . Hula hoops . . . A ukulele.

The giant inflatable penis balloon might have also been a mistake. It flailed about like an enormous moshing jellyfish, bashing against the back windows, the front seats and, every now and then, caught the side of Ayesha's head. It also managed to never be in time with the music playing on the stereo – a detail which was slowly driving Ayesha insane.

She had been so sure that these fun accessories would be in keeping with the glitter and the hula hoops, that as the resident comedian of the group it was her duty to bring the LOLs. But she could see now the gaping chasm between

Clemmie's tastefully curated decor and her own cheap, offensive tack.

Ayesha tried to stop her brain from automatically adding up the cost of the hen do paraphernalia that would never see the light of day. It was her own stupid fault and she'd just have to write it off. End of.

She tried to focus on Yaz nodding to the music next to her, mercifully on the beat. It was Lauryn Hill's *Miseducation* album. She cranked it up. The car protested slightly.

Another bash to the side of the head. Yaz turned to her again.

'So which actual goddesses are invited to this thing?' she asked.

'Well, there's India, of course, and Clemmie,' Ayesha replied. 'Frankie ... and where Frankie goes—'

'Joni follows.'

'Yep.'

'What about Jessica?' Yaz ventured.

Ayesha paused before replying. 'I mean, she was included in the emails so ...'

Yaz's eyebrows rose over her dark glasses.

'I thought you said there was ... beef.'

Ayesha sighed sadly. She thought of Jessica, that proud, cold, hurting woman who had come to mean so much to her and hoped that she would find a way to allow herself to be included in this gathering. She was, after all, an original member of the group, or 'the collective' as they called it, and they had worked so closely together, fought for a better world even, until ...

She shrugged.

'I mean, she did drop us all in it on live TV that one time, but apart from that . . .'

'Yeah, there was that,' Yaz agreed, amused at the memory of that disastrous day. 'So how come she's on the guest list?'

'Well, the thing is,' Ayesha rubbed her forehead. 'I think her beef is more with Frankie than India . . .'

Yaz waited for further explanation. It didn't come.

'Cool. Cool . . .' Yaz said eventually turning away again, just to turn back almost immediately.

'What about me?'

'What do you mean?' Ayesha asked.

'Why have I been included in this . . . exclusive circle?' Yaz asked. 'India's got bare followers. She knows everyone. Except me. She doesn't really know me.'

'Yes she does,' Ayesha insisted.

'She's *met* me, sure,' Yaz agreed. 'But she doesn't *know* me.'

Ayesha could tell Yaz was working hard to get things straight in her head. These women, the different dynamics and allegiances, it was all still relatively new to Yaz. What she knew Yaz would never mention was how desperate Ayesha had been to have her there. Yaz was booked and busy. Yaz had enough friends and family. Yaz did not check for these girls, this scene, their vibe. But she'd taken one look at Ayesha's pleading face and told her to pick her up at eleven.

Ayesha sighed. 'She wouldn't shut up about you. Both of them – Clemmie and India insisted you come.'

Yaz raised an eyebrow.

'Rah, I'm in demand you know. These posh girls are gagging for a taste of Yaz. Not surprising really.' She slunk lower in her seat and used a single finger to push her sunglasses closer to her face with a flourish.

Ayesha giggled.

'So, where are you in the pecking order at the mo?' Yaz enquired from her new, reclined position.

Ayesha tensed, but kept her eyes on the road.

'It's not like that.' Ayesha countered, 'I mean, it's cool. Mostly.'

Her mind whizzed through the complex interconnections within this small, exclusive friendship group. It was something she did several times a day, trying to keep on top of it all, desperate not to commit any more indiscretions. And now there was Clemmie – and Yaz – to incorporate into this complicated, charged dynamic. She sighed.

Yaz watched her carefully.

Ayesha took her eyes off the road momentarily to glare back at her.

'We're going, aren't we?' she said, with more than a hint of barb.

'All right, easy.' Yaz raised a hand in submission, then looked back out of the window.

Lauryn's voice rang out loud and clear in the silence, counselling them not to be a hard rock when you're a gem, reminding them that respect was a minimum. Yaz left it for a while, let the music work its magic. Then she tried again.

'So, this Clemmie person. Is she maid of honour or ... what?'

Ayesha thought for a moment.

10

'I've got a feeling such labels are beyond us goddesses,' she replied.

Yaz smirked.'But you know my girl reeeally wants the job,' she countered. Ayesha glanced back mischievously.

'She's certainly putting in the hours . . .'

They chuckled at this. The balloon joined in, bouncing around with glee.

Ayesha felt them both relax again, ease into their effortless way, and a wave of relief washed over her as it always did when it was just the two of them.

Yaz.

Ayesha. Loved. This. Woman. From the tip of her thick dark crew cut to the very bottom of her pristine footwear. If she could spend the whole weekend cruising around with her, listening to Ms Hill on repeat and catching jokes like only they knew how, she would want for nothing more. But they'd been summoned. By the notable India Baxter-Wright no less, and you didn't say no to India.

Yaz considered for a moment. Then,

'Clemmie . . . What's that short for anyway?'

Ayesha glanced away from the scorching tarmac to make sure Yaz was ready for this.

'Her email signature reads Clematis Rhodes-Woodhouse.'

'Are you shitting me?'

'Nope.'

'Did you just make that up? That's good . . .'

'Nope. That's her name.'

'Shit. These posh girls have *all* the surnames,' Yaz mused.

'It'll take an hour just to do the introductions,' Ayesha added.

'Ha!'

They watched the last few high-rises whizz by to be replaced by immense concrete warehouses, an IKEA megastore, followed by mock-Tudor semi-detached houses, blackened by the smog from the traffic that zoomed by their doorsteps twenty-four hours a day. Now Lauryn made way for Little Simz, her familiar British flow a fitting salute to the final signs of their beloved city.

Yaz turned to Ayesha once more.

'Clematis ... Isn't that what your skanky ex-boyfriend gave you?'

Ayesha nearly crashed the car.

They were well past Zone 6 now. Out of the M25 Circle Of Safety. Old Mother Peugeot seemed to be advancing with increasing reluctance, Simz's album had finished, and even the shiny, inflatable bellend seemed to be headbutting them with less gusto.

Other road users overtook them with increasing frequency and aggression. The hot, fume-filled air blew noisily in through the windows but did nothing to alleviate the discomfort of the day. Ayesha's thick curls, washed and treated with heat and product so they would be goddess-ready this morning, sat heavily on her neck and shoulders and her favourite baby pink tracksuit bottoms were making the inside of her legs prickle with sweat. The tight white vest top that hugged her thick curves mercifully allowed her upper body some air. It also exposed her skin to the sun glaring aggressively in through the windscreen. But Ayesha was determined not to complain about the weather. England got a maximum of, like, ten days sunshine every year and she was not about to hate on it. Besides, her olive-brown skin didn't burn easily and she only got cuter as she tanned. Fact.

Though this year had been extreme. For weeks temperatures had soared way above average causing scenes of unhinged hedonism as day after day of scorching sunshine roasted Brits into an edgy trance.

She glanced at her friend sitting in her black jeans and vest combo, contemplated with envy her short hair, the breeze it afforded the nape of her brown neck.

She focused back on the road. Here they were – Yaz and Yeesh – on a road trip. Listening to—

Ayesha pressed play again and Ty's 'Wait A Minute' filled the car. Yaz smiled, bounced her shoulders to the upbeat tempo as the demented balloon failed, once again, to catch the rhythm.

Ty, Yeesh and Yaz. Cruising down the M40 at a cool 47.

Ty, Yeesh and . . .

'Yaz?'

'Hmm?'

'How come my nickname sounds like a Nineties American sitcom catchphrase? *Yeesh!*'

'It's better than an exotic sounding piss. Sorry guys, excuse me, I'm just popping out for a quick Yaz . . .'

They were off again.

'Maybe that's what they call a wee in Buckinghamshire. They don't piss, they Yaz.'

The two friends chuckled raucously at their own jokes, and then quietened down. As they turned off the motorway onto country roads, brick gave way to field, grey ceded to green.

Yaz opened her mouth to speak and then shut it again. She looked straight ahead. Ayesha couldn't see her dark brown eyes under the shades but she could tell that she still wasn't sure what to make of this whole new scene they had been pulled into. It was heady and fabulous and right-on and full of intense characters. It had afforded them both new opportunities and, most importantly, a chance to finally work together. But the effort it took to hold so many strong personalities together was beginning to show. Cracks were forming and, if Ayesha could see them, it was only a matter of time before Yaz did too. Tensions and resentments had grown in the dark unspoken spaces between the glamour and sisterhood, and deep down, Ayesha was sure that it was all somehow her fault.

Ayesha gritted her teeth. She summoned India's radiance to her mind, the effortless way she drew you to her, commanded spaces, projects, people. She tried to remember Frankie's incredible commitment and passion to The Struggle, the years she'd spent tirelessly driving change for them all, and what an honour it was to be a part of that struggle, to stand beside this living luminary. And Joni, whose ruddy-faced grin, dad jokes and endless cups of tea had made her feel instantly at ease. These were her friends, her allies. They'd achieved so much together in such a short space of time. And ultimately, this was about coming together to celebrate India, maybe to spark new ideas, new projects they could all be a part of. And hopefully Jessica would be there. So she had to be there too.

Yaz turned to her with new energy.

'Do you reckon you get your comedy genes from your dad's side?'

Ayesha thought of her long-absent dad who was endlessly On The Road, chasing the next gig, the next laugh, the better spot. She remembered how her clowning had saved her from moments charged with the promise of violence and marvelled at how she had managed to form a joke at the same time as being so terrified and tiny and so very alone. But maybe better to take after *him* than *her*.

She shrugged.

'I dunno. Makes sense, I s'pose ... Yours are obviously from your nan.'

'*I do not know what you are talking about,*' Yaz replied in her nan's Indian accent. '*Stop talking this nonsense and dressing in your father's clothes. Enough. You will die alone. I promise.*'

Ayesha's jaw dropped. She cracked up.

'That's actually really dark!'

'Tell me about it,' Yaz replied. 'That's granny love for you ... Blesses you one minute, prophesizes your death the next.'

'I never met either of my nans, so ...' Ayesha shrugged, let her thought trail off.

She felt her friend's gaze on her and kept her eyes on the road. Ayesha's fragmented, dysfunctional family was a topic they'd talked through many times over. Yaz, on the other hand, came from a loud, warm, messy, never-ending clan of aunties and cousins and grandmas who Yaz brought to life with her impressions and anecdotes. A way, Ayesha knew, to bring her in on the joke and the family. But also to bring everyone else in on it too. This was Yaz's superpower, the thing that had launched her career and saw her go from strength to success to sold-out comedy show. No one quite did what Yaz did the way she did it and it was a delight to witness. Yaz seemed to have burst onto the scene knowing who she was and what she was about. Even when they were young and not yet fully honed, Ayesha remembered the impression she'd made on her when they had first met at school. Yaz seemed to have appeared fully formed and funny as hell even then, and had barely noticed the faltering, confused young Ayesha until they drifted into the same friendship group – a mix of girls finding safety and joy in each other.

'It must be your inner goddess, then.' Yaz concluded. 'That's where you get your skills from.'

'You reckon?' Ayesha asked with amusement.

'Yep. She's an absolute joker,' Yaz confirmed.

'I reckon she is.' Ayesha contemplated her inner goddess for a moment. 'Hot though, too.' She considered her own full breasts, her substantial backside, the curves she was so proud of.

'Of course.' Yaz agreed.

'Kick-ass.'

'Goes without saying.'

'With a wardrobe full of fabulous dresses and bling,' Ayesha concluded.

'Sure.' Yaz was grinning warmly.

Ayesha glanced at her friend.

'What about your inner goddess, Yaz?'

Yaz took a breath.

'My inner goddess likes to wear black, gender-neutral clothes and no make-up and if anyone comes near her with anything pink or floral, she will deck them.'

The penis balloon thunked against the side of Ayesha's head, punctuating Yaz's pronouncement.

'What about willies?' Ayesha ventured.

'I don't mind the occasional willy.'

'Noted.' Ayesha nodded. 'How about a dress?'

Yaz glared at her friend.

'If you try to put me in a dress, *you will die. Alone. I promise.*'

They made their way along the final stretch of country road. Waves of endless foliage branched inwards, a sky free of concrete frame. But the greens were parched, yellowed or darkened, the air thick with quivering heat. And the stark expanse provided no shade, no respite, nowhere to hide. Ayesha tried to take a couple of deep breaths. She had left the stress of her city life behind, for a weekend at least, to live it up with these living, breathing goddesses. She'd hoped the fresh air would alleviate the chronic tightness in her chest, but it didn't seem to be doing the trick. Yaz had also gone quiet. They'd switched the music off a few miles back when it had become too incongruous with the setting. Now they drove in silence, contemplating the distance between the constant but familiar hustle of their beloved metropolis and these new, unknown ends.

'You have arrived at your destination,' the phone blurted out abruptly. Ayesha slammed on the brakes. They looked around, but there was nothing there. No signpost, no mansion, no destination. Just the narrow road flanked by high hedges on both sides.

'Back up a bit.' Yaz suggested.

Ayesha reversed a few metres.

'Stop. There.' Yaz pointed to a rusting metal gate which disrupted the long line of hedgerow. Ayesha tried to position the car as close to the hedge as possible and then pulled up the temperamental handbrake. She left the motor chugging as they both got out of the car, taking their time, relieved to have a chance to stretch their legs, feel a breeze. Yaz leaned on the gate. They peered beyond it at the faint track that started at the foot of the gate and meandered further into the land beyond. Two overgrown grooves only just visible through the grass and weeds, created by vehicles that must have once driven through. It disappeared into a thick forest and there was no sign of human life or any sort of building. The two women stood staring at the dusty trail and into the deep, dark foliage beyond. There seemed to be two contrasting climates before them – the buzzing heat of the intense summer that scorched the edges of the hardiest of weeds, and the frigid depths of the murky, lush forest. Despite the heat beating down on her, Ayesha shivered. She glanced over at Yaz whose brow was furrowed, then turned back to check the map on her phone again. It insisted that this was the spot. Yaz was looking around the gate now, searching either side for a latch, a buzzer. She started to fiddle with a rusty chain wrapped loosely around a post.

'I reckon we can just lift this off,' she called over her shoulder. 'We might get tetanus or rabies or something, but at least we'll make it to the party.'

'Hold up,' Ayesha called, looking at the map on her phone, 'there's a turning further up. Let's follow it round and see if there's another entrance.'

Yaz let go of the rusty chain. It clunked stiffly against the gate. They got back into the stifling car and set off again along the road.

Ayesha turned left and then left again.

'What about down there?' Yaz pointed to a well-manicured private road that seemed to lead into the heart of the green blob on the small screen. Ayesha turned in. A hundred metres down, they came to a stop in front of a gleaming dark iron gate. The black bars towered over them and ended two metres above with a swirl and a flourish, out of which protruded a series of sharp ornamental spears.

Yaz looked at Ayesha. 'Is that to keep us out or in?' she asked with alarm.

'Either way, it's extra,' Ayesha concluded.

'*You have arrived at your destination,*' her phone repeated.

Ayesha switched it off.

The gate was flanked by two stone pillars connected to a high wall that ran deep into the trees and bushes on either side. They climbed out of the car and peered beyond the gate at a gravel pathway leading into more trees and foliage. Eventually, Ayesha noticed an incongruously modern buzzer to the right of the gate. She pressed it. A pause. The two women looked around uncertainly.

'Hello?' A sing-song voice tinkled out of the speaker moments later.

'Hey! It's Yaz and Ayesha.'

'Welcome goddesses! You made it. Through the gate and follow the path.'

There was a click and a buzz. With a metallic screech, the heavy iron bars slowly began to swing open, the spearheads conceding ground. They got back in the car and drove down the lane into the dense greenery.

CHAPTER TWO

MARCH 2017

Ayesha sat in the middle of the packed venue as Yaz took to the stage, her signature black jeans and vest hugging her lanky frame, her thick hair cropped short, her footwear box-fresh. No make-up, just shitloads of confidence and charisma.

She was the opening act. Ayesha had seen her name on the bill, a bill Ayesha was keen to get booked on herself, and had come down – partly to watch her do her thing, partly in the hope there might be a chance to bump into her, catch up maybe, after all these years.

Ayesha recognized her instantly, almost called out to her, but caught herself in time, unsure what kind of reception she would get, wondering whether Yaz remembered her at all. Plus she had already launched into her set.

Yaz opened with a bit about how her increasingly blind grandma kept mistaking her for the Grim Reaper and then did an impression of Grandma asking her why she insisted on dressing like a boy and who would marry her if they kept thinking she was the rickshaw driver.

Before she knew it, something had bubbled up and out of Ayesha. And she was laughing, really laughing, and as Yaz's act built, so did Ayesha's hysteria. Tears were streaming down her face at Yaz's impressions of her Indian aunties and the clash of generations and cultures. She'd never seen anything like it. Her technique was on point, gently drawing the mic stand back in as she hit them with her final gag, placing the mic in the holder as she shouted her own name and bid them goodnight.

Something else had bubbled up in Ayesha too. That old longing, so familiar, to be close to this funny, formidable woman again. They had stomped the streets of West London with their little crew of teenage misfits, supposedly causing all sorts of mischief, but looking back, it was harmless, blissful, carefree, girl fun. When they left school, they drifted apart, but Ayesha had looked her up every now and then, quietly comforted by the memory of that precious friendship which represented the happiest moments of her life.

Yaz was charming London with her unique content and style. Ayesha's trajectory had been humbler but steady. She hadn't so much charmed as relentlessly returned until she'd carved out enough regular bookings on the circuit to be a jobbing comedian, and worn down Simon with terrible puns DMed to his Twitter account until he'd agreed to be her agent. But Yaz made it look so effortless, despite the graft Ayesha knew she must have put in to make it seem that way.

She wanted to hang with her. She wanted to laugh with her again. To be seen by and with her. But Yaz had already left the building by the time Ayesha managed to get through the crowd to the backstage door.

A few months later, Ayesha finally ran into her at the Cat's Back.

The Cat's was an institution. A legendary old cabaret club in the heart of Soho that had survived the changes the area had seen over the years. Ayesha remembered that a good decade ago, when she was just starting out, it had been flanked by a sex shop and a strip club – now it was an Itsu and a Costa Coffee. But it was still standing, and getting onto the bill was a rite of passage for any stand-up comedian.

Ayesha had appeared countless times at their open mic nights hoping, as so many did, that it would lead to a proper booking. Years of late nights and drunken debauchery with Stan, the original owner, at the helm. He was a kind-natured old diva who would don a frock every full moon and do a turn on his own stage to everyone's delight. He was ancient now, and he limited himself to DJing after the final act had done their thing. He'd been playing the same Pet Shop Boys followed by Abba followed by George Michael followed by the dance remix of 'I Am What I Am' for the last fifteen years, but in fairness, Ayesha thought, he had added a Britney Spears song to his repertoire last summer.

The club was now officially run by his 'business partner', Andrew. Andrew loved show business. He also hated

23

comedians. A very different character to Stan, Ayesha had once been unlucky enough to be accosted by him when he was drunk and at a loose end towards the end of a Tuesday night. He regaled her with stories about the famous people he'd rubbed shoulders with – most of them, incidentally, now in rehab or doing time for sexual misconduct. After a good hour of talking at her, he'd finally paused long enough to ask her what she did and if she was anyone famous he should know about. Ayesha took her chance and introduced herself as a comedian, hoping the hour she'd just spent listening attentively and gasping dramatically at all the right moments would earn her a spot. But as soon as Ayesha mentioned the C-word, Andrew went quiet and with a look of disgust, turned and walked away without another word.

So, running a comedy club was a bit of a challenge for Andrew. He seemed to square this circle by having someone else on the door who would deal with the only thing worse than a comedian – the general public – and then managed the line-up himself by saying as few words to the acts as he possibly could.

Still, to Ayesha's astonishment and her agent's relief, he'd called. She was in.

She arrived a bit later than planned. She rushed in, and there was Yaz talking to the woman on the door. It was the assured yet warm stance, the confidence and sparkle that emanated even from the back of her, that confirmed to Ayesha it was Yaz. She was looking at a piece of paper that Ayesha guessed was tonight's line-up. Andrew was hovering behind the receptionist watching Yaz with dis-approval. He took in her short, thick hair, her brown skin and her effortless charisma with a sneer he wasn't working very hard to hide.

Ayesha strode towards the three of them, enthusiasm bubbling over into clumsiness, and almost stumbled. They looked up in alarm.

'Hello! Hi! How are you?' Ayesha tried to address all of them at once.

Yaz raised an amused eyebrow.

'How can I help?' said the woman behind the tiny desk at the door.

'So I'm actually one of the acts tonight. My name's Ayesha Jones.'

'Ayesha ... Ayesha ...' She ran her finger down the names. 'Ah yes. There you are. Ayesha. Yep. You're on early in the first half. You've still got an hour or so ...'

'Great! Thanks.' She turned to Yaz. 'Hi, I don't know if you ... I'm—'

'Yeesh! Shit girl, it's you.' An easy smile spread across Yaz's face as she recognized Ayesha. Ayesha flushed with joy.

'Yep,' Ayesha replied. 'Long time.'

'Loooong time,' Yaz affirmed. 'You doing this too? Comedy?'

'Yeah,' Ayesha shrugged. 'I am.'

'Seen,' Yaz nodded.

They stood gazing at each other warmly, Ayesha trying to tone down her enthusiasm, taking in the fact that this was happening, they were meeting again.

'I've seen you perform,' Ayesha managed eventually. 'Brilliant. You're just brilliant.'

'Thanks sis,' Yaz replied. 'Looking forward to seeing you do your thing too.'

She wondered briefly what Yaz saw. A shorter, thicker, curvier figure than her own, skin a few shades lighter, more olive in tone. Hair almost as thick but curly, very curly, and scraped, worked and tamed into a tight ponytail, edges gelled down, framing a face that was still prone to breakouts even in her early thirties. Her pastel blue tracksuit bottoms and white vest top hugged just enough to accentuate her curves, the matching blue hoodie zipped halfway down her chest. Her favourite white trainers had seen better days. Ayesha was suddenly aware of how scuffed they were; she wished she'd given them a once-over with a wet wipe before heading out. She smoothed the back of her hair self-consciously, hid one foot behind the other.

'No. No. No. No. No.' A voice cut sharply through their moment.

They both turned to see Andrew with the line-up list in his hands.

'Sorry. No.'

'Are you all right there?' Yaz ventured.

'I'm sorry, but there's no way we can have both of you on,' Andrew explained.

'But our names are both down—'

'Well, yes, but how was I to know you were both ...'

'Both ... ?' Yaz's eyebrows shot up. Andrew doubled down.

'... I'm sorry, it's just not going to work.'

'And why's that exactly?' Yaz challenged.

Andrew rolled his eyes, sighed.

'Look. I'm not going to spell it out. It's bad enough we have to make sure there's a woman on every bloody bill, but I can't have two ...'

They waited. He faltered.

'I dare you to finish that sentence.' Yaz glared at him. The receptionist stuck between them stared at the floor, desperately trying to disappear.

'Look,' Andrew tried again. 'I've seen your act before, Jazz—'

'Yaz.'

'Sure. Some people at least think you're funny so you can stay, but the other one. Look, come back on Tuesday, okay?'

Yaz kept her eyes locked on him.

'We're both on the bill, Andrew. We're both going to do our set.'

Andrew stared back at her coolly.

'You know what?' he said, handing the paper back to the flustered doorwoman. 'I don't actually care. There's only space for one of you tonight, so sort it out between you.'

He sauntered off, head held a little too high. They watched him leave. The receptionist continued to contemplate the floor intensely.

'Look, it's no problem. I could actually do with a bit more practice so Tuesday sounds great.' Ayesha's face flushed a hot red, mortified at causing a scene. The thought of upstaging Yaz in any way, being the reason she lost out on a gig, was unbearable. 'And he's right, Yaz. You're brilliant. I'd love to watch you again.'

Yaz turned to Ayesha. She had a fire in her eyes Ayesha remembered from long ago.

'You know what?' she addressed the receptionist loudly, without taking her eyes off Ayesha, 'You're down two acts tonight, coz we're out.'

Ayesha looked at her in horror.

'B-but it's the Cat's Back. You can't just—'

'Watch me.'

Yaz slung her backpack over her shoulder and strode out, yanking Ayesha with her.

The cold London air hit Ayesha's burning face. She gasped. Had she just walked out on a career-defining gig? I mean sure, the guy was a sexist, racist nonce-lover, but it was a paid gig.

'Oh my god. Did we just do that?' Ayesha exclaimed.

Yaz turned to her, eyes wide, and burst out laughing. So Ayesha burst out laughing too. And they doubled over outside the venue in the chilly Soho night, gusts of steam escaping from them as they shrieked with laughter at their comedy careers trickling down the plughole.

'Drink?'

'Yep.'

They stayed out till 3 a.m. Ayesha remembered laughing and laughing, just like they had done all those years ago. Yaz did impressions of Andrew, impressions of the woman stuck between them, clearly mortified and looking like she was willing herself to just vanish. Ayesha's stomach hurt, her eyes were bleary with tears and she was very drunk.

They staggered to the bus stop guffawing and recounting the story over and over, adding details, exaggerating the anecdote and the night's events, until the night bus arrived and took Ayesha on the long journey back to West London – Yaz travelling south.

Next morning, Ayesha found herself giggling again before she'd even opened her eyes. Her phone beeped beside her.

Did he actually call me . . . Jazz???

Ayesha and Yaz never found themselves on the same bill, but they went to each other's gigs and established themselves as a team of sorts. Yaz worked up this new bit about Jazzgate, as they now called it, and although she never mentioned the name of the establishment or the manager, everyone knew who she was talking about. She did, however, mention Ayesha's name, and if she was in the audience a few people would turn to look at her – this special friend of Yaz's who had witnessed the very story she was telling – and Ayesha's cheeks would flush and she'd giggle as Yaz put on Andrew's voice once again, mispronouncing her name, followed by the mic-drop moment when they both stormed out, and her reflecting on how she'd probably just flushed both their careers down the toilet.

That was indeed how Ayesha's agent saw it.

'What the hell were you thinking, Ayesha?'

'Hi Simon. Great to hear from you. So actually it's a funny story because—'

'Fucking hilarious I'm sure. Andrew has blacklisted you from the Cat's Back before you've even played a gig there. Quite an achievement. Are you laughing? I hope you are.'

'No, but the thing is—'

'Are there any other bridges you'd like to burn as I attempt to forge a career for you?'

'Well, I mean, that's a bit harsh—'

'ANY OTHER BRIDGES AYESHA?'

'No Simon.'

'Good. The Copa. Next Wednesday. Be nice.'

On Wednesday Ayesha got ready for the gig in good time and set off promptly, early even.

It had been a tough day, harder than usual and Simon's rage replayed in her head as she hauled herself up and out of her basement flat. She felt chastened, determined to make amends. She couldn't stand anyone being angry with her, especially not the one person who might be her ticket out of this area. So she pushed through the darkness that could so easily consume her, kept her eyes on the punchlines, the comedy, the laughter. Kept it relentlessly light.

Ayesha usually took the long route to the bus stop, but in her rush to be early she found herself heading straight past the spot she was always so keen to avoid – just down the road from her flat. Her heart slumped as she crossed the street to avoid the outstretched hands holding leaflets she didn't want to read. The pain-filled faces of the relatives, still seeking justice so many months later. She crossed back to avoid the memorial that had been created by the remaining community in the wake of The Tragedy, the candles still kept burning, the flowers tended to even now. The cameras, politicians and media vans were long gone, but it still attracted some strange characters: Sometimes a tourist looking for an 'alternative' London landmark, taking selfies surreptitiously – preferably with the charred remains of the building in the background; often a preacher with a makeshift megaphone; always a woman who insisted she'd been in the building when it caught fire, died and come back to life; and in the last few days, a man dressed in green pushing a shopping trolley with an old hi-fi system. He'd parked up in front of the preacher and the professional survivor and blared out Irish folk music at a deafening volume.

She knew the moment to look away as she passed the building, blackened from the outside in. She always made sure she was focused on her phone, angled away from the horrific spectacle, still too painful to fathom, until she was well out of the area. It was too much. There was never an end to the noise, the grief, the gaping charred hole left in her community. The people she'd known, their sisters, cousins, friends. Lost in a way that she couldn't bear to think about. So she kept moving, left the area whenever she found an excuse to, avoided the people, the place, the pain. And today there just weren't enough miles she could put between herself and that.

The bus inched its way from west to east. Ayesha had nabbed the prime seat – front right on the top deck. She propped her feet up on the ledge as she ran through her new material. It always excited her, this journey. Sure, she had to allow almost two hours to get across London in time, plus it meant waiting at the bus stop in all sorts of weather, but she didn't mind. Not if it meant getting back to those ends, where it was all happening, far away from West London and the decades of memories that cohabited with her, permanently residing outside every corner shop, at the entrance to each estate, in the nooks of pubs and crannies of community centres. This place that was both her haven and her hell. The only home she'd really known, the only place and people she belonged to, but also the setting for so many transgressions, aggressions, violations. Ayesha had received it all – the devastating kindness of foster mums, the joyous and fleeting siblinghoods, the watchful neighbours and protective elders. The well-placed perpetrators, the casual acts of violence, the daily horror of being out in the world on your own with no net or shield and the ravenous ones who were waiting to feed on this.

But she kept it light. Always.

She felt her load lighten as they passed through the postcodes, felt her prospects expand the further east she reached. She looked out at the people here, the smart, fresh souls, oblivious to, and uncontaminated by, the grief on the other side of their city. The fashion was different down this way – something Ayesha tried to emulate with varying success. She noticed the effortless way they moved. Belonging there. Going somewhere.

The excitement often teetered into yearning. The yearning often threatened to become despair. As the years went by, the chances of affording the move to this side, of integrating herself with this new breed of Londoner seemed to dwindle, the toll of the two-hour journey hitting her harder each time. But she kept on keeping on.

The venue was packed. An old working men's club that had been transformed into a trendy variety club when the area had started coming up. It had been rebranded as The Copa by the new owners, who still kept the option of a pint of Light And Bitter on the menu as a nod to the old working lads who had frequented the establishment for decades and who were now priced out. The new clientele, the young, hip twenty-somethings, often ordered those same old men's favourite for novelty's sake, wrinkled their delicate noses up at the strong taste, sipped it tentatively.

Ayesha waited in the tiny backstage area with the other acts, most of whom she'd met on the circuit before. The lights went down and the chatter subsided. The music kicked in and the compère for the night took to the stage, warming the crowd up, asking them questions and talking up the acts that were to follow. There were two comedians on before the interval. Ayesha knew them well. Solid guys who'd worked the circuit for a while, cut their teeth up in Edinburgh too. Ayesha was on in the second half. She could have sat out front and watched the first half like she usually did, but tonight she wanted somewhere quiet and dark where she could just *be* until it was her turn. She was the only woman on the bill, and the only non-white person too. Again. She tried to shake it off and run through that middle bit one more time.

The first two acts came back offstage in turn, both pumped.

'It's a decent crowd tonight guys. Should be a good one.'

Their elated faces geed her up a bit. She started to psych herself up, warming up her talking muscles and going over the opening lines, the adrenaline beginning to work its way through her body.

Then the music kicked in and the compère was back on. The crowd had had a few drinks by now and the chatter was warmer, more relaxed.

'Everyone had a good break?' the compère enquired. 'Did you all do a wee-wee? I suspect some of you might have even had a beverage or two … Naughty … It is a school night y'know.'

Guilty titters from the audience floated through to Ayesha backstage.

'We've got a great second half coming up for you kids, but let's have one more round of applause for the acts so far! Weren't they great? You all laughed – I heard you. Even at the risqué material – especially at the risqué material! So I hope the #MeToo brigade isn't in tonight because otherwise we're in serious trouble. The shit will hit the fan, folks. There's shit flying about everywhere at the moment, isn't there? It's a literal shitstorm. I mean, every man in the world seems to have been accused of, I don't know, touching their gran on the shoulder in 1982, or picking up their work colleague's pencil and handing it to her two summers ago. I swear, before I got to this gig tonight, I had to chuck out ninety percent of my material in case I got accused of sexually assaulting someone with my jokes.'

Laughter.

Ayesha frowned, the adrenaline turning sour in her stomach.

'You can't say anything anymore! So, I've made a list of things I think are still okay to make jokes about and I've started to write down some ideas ... Bear with me ...' Ayesha heard the rustle of paper. 'Here we go ... Crumpets! Are they still okay to talk about? How about street lamps? They're pretty shady ... No? Okay, hold on ... Let's try basil. That's a funny sounding herb, isn't it? Basil ... No? See? That's all I've got left! There's nothing funny left! I'm out of jokes guys.'

Ayesha listened to the warm response from the audience. Raucous laughter. Louder applause. A defiant whoop. She suddenly felt very tired. She looked around the cramped backstage room at the others for an ally: one guy laughed and clapped, another was busy running through his set in the battered mirror nailed to the wall, seemingly oblivious to this tirade. She shook her head, tried to figure out how she was going to adjust her opening bit, get everyone back onside. Save the vibe.

The compère continued.

'Well, seeing as I'm out of material, let's bring someone on who's still got some left. Ladies and gents, put your hands together for Ayesha Jones!'

And with that, she made her way to the mic.

The stage seemed a lot smaller once she was on it, the lights a lot brighter. Ayesha could hardly see the audience. Maybe a good thing. But the atmosphere hung thick in the bright, coloured lights. She wasn't sure how the hell she was going to get through this, but she'd had a lifetime of practice.

As she'd told Yaz many times, 'Tough crowd? Try my primary carers.'

Yaz often called out this shit in her act, speaking out about what it was like to start every gig with a mountain to climb in less than a minute. As a woman, a minority woman at that, you started at the bottom of the Funny Ladder before you'd said a word. Your job was to convince these paid-up ticket holders that you were indeed worth the entrance fee in your first few sentences so they could relax and let you make them laugh. And now the compère had added the small extra obstacle of global sexual violence to really get the crowd on side.

Ayesha took a breath, tried to channel her inner Yaz and, before she could think too much, she launched into it.

'Wow, what an introduction. Thank you Phil. Luckily, I have a solid ten minutes on street lamps so buckle up people cos it's about to get really politically correct up in here ...'

She heard a few tentative titters, and mercifully felt the audience begin to relax, so she reverted back to her original material.

36

'Let me tell you a bit about me. My name's Ayesha and I've been working the circuit for a few years now. Fun fact, it actually runs in the family because my dad is also a comedian . . .'

Ayesha was into her opening bit now and she could tell she was wresting back control.

'That's right. He does stand-up. And it makes for an interesting approach to parenting . . . He didn't really have any idea how to talk to a growing girl such as myself, his daughter, so he kind of resorted to this weird metaphor that involved associating everything that happened to me with his life On The Road. It kind of became his slogan. You got good grades at school? It's just like that high you get off the crowd when you're On The Road. You're not feeling so good? Try three weeks non-stop gigging On The Road. You started your period? It reminds me of this time when I was On The Road . . .'

More laughter. Ayesha let herself sink into Cruise.

And then.

'Like when you're fucking!' A voice rang out from the audience.

Ayesha stopped mid-sentence.

'. . . like what . . . ?' she asked the darkness before her.

'Fucking! You deaf cow. I said fucking.'

There was a gasp from the audience. Heads turned, searching for the source of this interruption, then back to her, waiting for her response. Ayesha felt her mind fumble for words outside of the tight script she'd practised over and over.

'Well that's a big word, mister. Did you just learn it?' she quipped.

Nervous titters passed around the room. She strained her eyes trying to look beyond the lights for the culprit.

'Is that why you just had to randomly call it out in the middle of my set?' She addressed the anonymous voice. '*Fucking! I can say fucking*! I mean, that's a whole two syllables, well done.'

More laughter.

'Ah, you're not even funny,' came his drunken, slurred reply from somewhere at the back of the room.

This time Ayesha didn't miss a beat.

'You know who hasn't got even one laugh tonight? You. Your material, if I may, needs some work. So why don't you just let the professionals get on with it?'

'You're not even fit,' came the riposte. 'What's the point? Where are the men? Bring the lads back on.'

Ayesha felt her heart thumping as the adrenaline flowed around her body. She took a breath, let go of her tightly rehearsed set, let her mind go blank. She felt that part of her take over, the muscle she'd honed with years on the circuit, let the impulse and the words just come.

'Well make up your mind. All you could talk about a minute ago was how much fucking I was doing and now apparently I'm not fuckable. I'm having trouble keeping up and I'd really like to get back to entertaining these lovely people who have paid good money to hear a professional—'

'Calm down love, it's just a bit of banter.'

And with that, something just gave.

'Banter? Banter … ? What even is that?' Ayesha took the microphone out of its holder, leaned forward. 'What is banter? I genuinely don't know. It's not really a joke, is it? It's not actually funny. We comedians don't make a professional living out of telling well-structured banters. So what does that word mean? It seems to me, Prick – can I call you that? Too late, I just did – it seems that the word banter has become a way for pricks like you to say any old misogynistic, racist, homophobic bullshit and as long as you do it with a wink and a nudge it's okay cos it's *"just a bit of banter"*. But here's the thing, Prick, that's not how comedy works. You actually have to make people laugh for it to work. And that's literally what I'm up here trying to do. I'm trying to do my fucking job. So would you take your foot off my neck and let me get to the end of my fucking set?'

There was a pause. And then, mercifully, applause. But Prick wasn't done. He stood up this time and she could just make out a clumsy, swaying figure in the dark leaning forward to attack once more. But Ayesha wasn't done either.

'What is it this time?' She sighed with despair. 'I *am* fuckable now. I'm *not* fuckable. You want the men back on? Babes, I hate to break it to you but I've heard it all before. All your material. It's been done. And while I'm listening to this second-hand, upcycled dross, I'm *still trying to do my job.*' Ayesha hit each word of the phrase with an accentuated rhythm, paused, then continued before he could formulate a response. 'I arrive on stage after a whole rant about how women have collectively killed the vibe for everyone by finally speaking up about the horrors we've been silently dealing with since forever, when all we've been trying to do is quite literally live—'

'Here we go. Not another one—'

'Yes! Another one! Me fucking Too. Of course, me too. Because I don't know a single woman this horrific shit *hasn't* happened to – and I *still* manage to salvage the fucking vibe and make you laugh and it's *still* not enough. What more could you possibly want? Tell you what, why don't you do us all a favour – take your banter and shove it up your own arsehole cos let's be honest, it's the only way you're gonna get a laugh tonight.'

She got off the stage somehow. There was a lot of noise – mostly her own blood pumping furiously in her ears. Lights, then darkness, the heat of the venue, the chill of the night. She got home somehow. Got into bed. Slept.

Ayesha woke up late, her mind blissfully blank. She felt hungover but couldn't recall why. She rolled out of bed, did a wee, opened the curtains, yawned and switched on her phone. As it came to life she took the four strides into her kitchenette and popped a crumpet in the toaster.

There was a half-metre space between the bed and the small, square table that was pushed up against the wall. She liked to think of this as the dining area. That's why she didn't do work on it. It was strictly for mealtimes. There was a fold-out chair either side that kept a precious corridor of space free for her to be able to pass between the bed and the dining area, and a plant pot on the tabletop that took up most of the surface space, but which Ayesha insisted on keeping. She looked over to the far side of the room where her kitchenette was, the tiny bathroom off the tiny hallway that led to her front door. This was her studio flat. The same place she'd been living in since she was sixteen and the council had given this foster kid her own home. She remembered what it felt like when her key worker had unlocked the door and she'd stepped inside for the first time. She couldn't fathom what she would do with so much space. It felt scandalous to give one person so much. She'd spent much of the first few days in a foetal position on the floor between the bed and the window, terrified of all the space she was being asked to take up.

Now, in her thirties, the walls often felt like they were inching in. She could hardly breathe some days and she needed to escape the flat regularly just to get some air. She was beginning to worry it wasn't all paranoia. Over the years she had been living in the neighbourhood, building after building had been discovered to be riddled with asbestos. Some of them, after intense campaigning from tenants' associations, were stripped, floor by floor, of the toxic material. Some were demolished altogether, using it as an excuse to disperse the locals to the suburbs and make space in this prime location for new builds, new locals. Fairer. Richer. Gentler folk. But some still stood, quietly, surreptitiously, retaining their poison in the very walls. And then, on the outside, there was the cladding.

Hers wasn't a high-rise, but as she passed through the streets the locals called Grove, there they stood, the last survivors of the Great Gentrification that had swept across their ends. One now a blackened, derelict shell. It was too much. The pain, the horror, the rending apart of families, the confusion of classes. So many of her friends had been shipped to remote locations over the decades — a few hadn't made it out of the building in time.

It was getting harder and harder to keep upbeat, funny, keep her head above the mire of pain and panic that threatened to consume what was left of the community. And that was Ayesha's thing. Her superpower. The thing that had got her through every transition, from one foster home to the next, where she charmed her new family, blindsided the older kids, kept the darkness out. But the area was full of toxic material, no good for stand-up. And Ayesha desperately wanted out. So she kept busy, writing, plotting, planning, rehearsing her way out of there.

She was adding a generous layer of butter to her crumpet when her ringtone blurted out the opening to M.I.A's 'Paper Planes'. She turned back to the bed and grabbed the phone.

'Ayesha. Simon. I have no fucking words. You are done.'

Ayesha tried desperately to understand what was happening.

'What? Simon, I—'

'—and if I have anything to do with it, you will not work again in this city.'

'Hold on, I can explain—' But she wasn't sure what she could explain.

The line went dead. For a moment she was struck by the fact that it was probably the longest call she'd had with Simon, then the severity of what he'd said hit her again. She stood there, mind reeling. Gradually, confusion and hurt were replaced with horror as yesterday's gig came back to her, piece by agonizing piece. She felt a strong need to heave.

'Oh my god, Simon. I'm so sorry ...' she said into a dead line.

Her legs went weak. The words she'd yelled into the mic the night before repeated and repeated in different orders around her head. Ayesha cringed and cringed some more.

'No, no, no, please no.'

She crawled to the bed and covered herself in the duvet. She felt like she'd been punched in the stomach but, oddly, like *she'd* been the one to do it to herself, over and over. Right in the gut. And then the tears came. Deep sobs welled up and out as the years of hustle and grit, the desperate optimism and endless gigging were made meaningless, just like that.

There seemed to be something inevitable about it all. Of course she would go and fuck it all up. Lose the only agent she'd ever had. Get herself literally blacklisted from venues. Of course.

The walls inched in, the air felt thicker. This was her lot. As it had been for years. Why couldn't she just be grateful, like she had been the first time she'd heard she'd made it to the top of the housing list? Why did she think she would ever leave this place? This tiny flat? This neighbourhood? How many long bus trips across town did she really have left in her? It was cute to have flirted with that lifestyle for a while, but who did she think she was to really belong there? It was a joke. She was a joke. The only real joke she knew. She lay there immobile, grieving the little taste of a different life she had been thrown before it was snatched back, the blow to the gut making it hard to breathe.

A while later, the phone rang again. It was on the floor. She didn't pick it up. She didn't move from under her duvet. She didn't think she could. It rang some more. Eventually, Ayesha reached out and turned it off. She slept.

She woke up at some point in the afternoon, the relief of oblivion swiftly replaced by a sinking feeling as the reality of her situation dawned once again. She lay staring at the ceiling, her mind unable to fully focus, until eventually she reached over to her phone to check the time. It was switched off. She pressed the button on the side and waited. A few preliminary pings. An incongruously perky buzz. There were several missed calls from Yaz. Ayesha felt a surge of shame. How could she explain all this to her? What would it mean for their friendship? What did they even have in common if they weren't the two brown girls on the circuit, doing their thing? Then followed a pang of resentment. This was Yaz's influence. Ayesha would never have had the guts to speak like that if she hadn't been hanging around Yaz so much. She was naturally compliant and apologetic about everything.

Where had this outburst come from? Who did she think she was? Not Yaz, and not one of those white lads.

And then the phone lit up. It was Yaz calling again. For a moment Ayesha considered not answering, but she needed her friend, more than ever, even if it meant facing her disappointment too. She steeled herself, the tears already welling up, and answered.

'Yeesh. Where the fuck have you been?' Yaz demanded immediately.

'I'm sorry Yaz, I had a bit of a rough—'

'Mate, I've been calling all morning. Have you seen this shit?'

'What shit?' Ayesha asked weakly.

'You haven't ... You haven't even seen the video?' Yaz asked.

'What video, Yaz? You're scaring me,' Ayesha pleaded.

'Okay. It's all good. I'm sending you a link now. Call me back.'

Yaz hung up. Ayesha's phone pinged a few more times. She stared in stunned silence at it. Then a message came through from Yaz. She opened the link. Pressed the play icon. Waited.

'... *Why don't you do us all a favour, take your banter and shove it up your own arsehole ...?*'

The words that had been swirling around in her head all morning repeated on the small screen in her hand. And there she was, mic in hand, gesticulating angrily, a dangerous spark in her eyes. Ayesha. On the stage. Having the rant of her life. But why was she watching it now?

Oh god. Someone had filmed it. They'd filmed her melt-down and put it online.

She was over. She felt her insides sink. It was out there, for everyone to watch over and over. Simon wouldn't have to do a thing. Ayesha was cancelled.

Her eyes automatically moved from the video down to the comments below.

Who does this crazy bitch think she is?

That's why women shouldn't be allowed a mic when they're on their period.

I hope they got their money back.

Give her a good seeing to. That'll shut her up.

Die.

The phone buzzed in her hand, Yaz's name mercifully obscuring the rest of the comments. Ayesha answered.

'Yaz, what have I done?' Ayesha wailed. 'I've messed it all up. All of it. I can't believe I said those things—'

'What are you talking about, Yeesh? You smashed it. You're everywhere. Everyone's talking about you,' Yaz gushed, her words loud and fast and insistent.

'Yaz, I read the comments. They're crucifying me. I don't know what I'm gonna do. I can't leave the house. I feel sick,' Ayesha sobbed.

'What? What are you reading? Did you read the first three

trolls and then give up? Sis, they love you. Celebrities are atting you. Ayesha – YOU'RE TRENDING.'

Yaz finally convinced her to look again and hung up. She was right. The video had been shared tens of thousands of times already. On Twitter, every woman with a blue tick seemed to be sharing it with comments like,

I couldn't have put it better.

Thank you for speaking for us all.

Someone give this woman her own show.

Preach sis.

T.H.I.S

Ayesha watched, mesmerized, as the number of shares increased by the second, her heart racing. She sank to the floor in a stupor as waves of conflicting emotions washed over her. She had no idea what to think.

The phone was beginning to erupt in sporadic electronic farts, the noises of the different alerts combining into an unholy cacophony as it tried to keep up with the constant influx of connection. Ayesha was completely overwhelmed.

And then her email pinged once more. Not knowing where to start, she opened the latest one.

Hi Ayesha

I hope you're okay. It must have been quite an intense

few hours. I hope you're remembering to eat, breathe, hydrate – that sort of thing. Like everyone else, I watched the video and I was really impressed. Proud, in fact.

It would be great to meet.

Frankie Roberts

CHAPTER THREE

JULY 2018

Saturday 2.10 p.m.

The manicured greenery of the private lane quickly morphed into a wilder, thicker wood on either side as Ayesha drove into the grounds. Ancient trees towered over them, forming a frigid, dense climate of their own. Thick layers of canopy above reached over the road and blocked out the heat and light of the summer sun. It turned chilly and dark. Ayesha could see nothing but row upon row of these silent sentries to either side, behind them, and closing into a dark point ahead of them. Ayesha's throat constricted. Even in the largest council estates, amongst the tallest high-rises, there were glimpses of sky between the brutalist concrete blocks. Here, nothing. She was about to switch on the headlights, but then the deep emerald curtain ahead slowly began to open up as if at the start of a show on a West End stage. Ayesha breathed deeply as it parted to reveal an immense stately house of grey stone, with latticed windows framed with heavy wooden beams. At its centre, a thick oak door, and to the right of the door, a white metal pole that stretched the height of the building, at the top of which a tired Union Jack hung drowsily in the airless heat.

The two friends glanced at each other, each one searching the other's face for the right response. At a loss, they turned back to the scene before them.

As the little red car inched forward, the aged mansion loomed ever higher, dominating the skyline. It almost seemed to lean forward as it scrutinized this new, humble arrival with suspicion. The central section stood in a squat, rigid oblong, its dark windows reflecting none of the dazzling sunlight, giving nothing away. To the right of the building, Ayesha glimpsed the beginnings of some sort of extension, simpler in style and comparably modest in its dimensions, leading round the side of the grounds and out of sight. The effect was a strange one. She was both awed by the sight of the main section, and discombobulated by this extra addi-tion, which made the scope and bearings of the place even more unfathomable.

'Rah,' came the quiet exclamation from her usually verbose friend. 'It looks like a movie set. One of those where bare white people wear corsets and lipse each other on the DL.'

They fell back into silence.

Ayesha suddenly became very conscious of the car, silently cursing the chug-chug of the arthritic engine.

The gravel path opened into a wide expanse where several cars were already parked. A figure stood in the doorway. As they pulled up, they saw it was Frankie, her familiar grinning face bringing some comfort to Ayesha. She was relieved to see Frankie was wearing her signature Doc Martens, baggy jeans and even a long-sleeved jumper, despite the heat. A casual goddess. She was holding two champagne flutes filled with bubbles.

'Goddesses, you made it,' she announced sarcastically as the car came to a stop. 'Get used to this.'

Yaz and Ayesha stepped out of the car and graciously accepted the drinks. The cool, fizzy liquid was a welcome antidote to the afternoon sun. They were relieved to finally be out of the suffocating little metal container, but Ayesha felt a new tension between the person she was with Yaz and the person she was with these other women and wondered how she could be both at the same time.

Behind them the drive curved away and back into the thick, dark foliage, the gate through which they had come, and the road beyond, concealed somewhere behind it. In front of them, the exterior of the manor seemed to absorb all sunlight, leaving no trace on the ancient grey stone. Behind Frankie, the front door was ajar, revealing an even darker interior.

Ayesha searched Frankie's face carefully for any signs of resentment or anger. Their last meeting had ended civilly enough, but there had been an unmistakable tightness in Frankie's smile as she bid Ayesha goodbye, a tightness very similar to her final farewell with Jessica – the only other person who had openly defied her.

Frankie's short mousey hair was streaked with grey, and the faint lines at the corners of her eyes and mouth were accentuated in the bright sunlight. Her pale skin, dotted with the odd mole, made her look somehow more vulnerable in the intense glare. The tops of her ears were already beginning to pinken. But thankfully not with anger. Ayesha let herself begin to relax as Frankie watched them sip the bubbles with satisfaction.

'So your trusty old banger made it all the way.' Frankie quipped, taking a couple of steps towards the Peugeot.

Ayesha remembered the pink paraphernalia inside with a jolt. She had concluded, on the journey, that Frankie wouldn't find these symbols of phallic dominance and pink gendering acceptable or fun or even amusing. None of them would. And she'd only just survived her last transgression. She was an idiot for letting herself relax so soon. Ayesha shot a look of alarm at Yaz, who sipped her bubbles quietly and watched with amusement. Ayesha took a step sideways, blocking Frankie's view of the car.

'Just about!' she replied, and gestured at the building with exaggerated enthusiasm. 'And look at this! Do we need to master a secret handshake to get through the door?'

Thankfully, Frankie hesitated and turned back towards the house, a smile of approval at Ayesha's sarcasm spreading across her face.

'Of course you do,' she confirmed. 'And the virgin will be

sacrificed at midnight while we all wear our standard cloaks and masks. You have brought them, haven't you?'

Frankie glanced back at the Peugeot, then at Yaz.

'Sure,' Yaz said brightly. 'We brought the standard ones and the special editions, just in case.' Ayesha laughed with relief.

'Just the weather for cloaks and masks,' Ayesha added.

Ayesha hooked her arm through Frankie's. Frankie awkwardly accommodated this sign of affection and allowed herself to be led back towards the entrance.

'No but really, it's so good to be here,' Ayesha gushed. 'I can't believe this is our home for the weekend!'

Yaz stifled a smirk and followed them. Frankie smirked back.

'It's . . . pretty full on, all this.' Frankie gestured to the vast grey tomb they were about to enter. 'I mean, could it be any more of a symbol of the pale, male and stale?'

Yaz glanced at Ayesha. She'd made it clear to Ayesha that she wasn't a fan of these soundbites Frankie often spoke in, and which Ayesha had recently started to repeat.

'Clemmie's printed out copies of the itinerary for the weekend,' Frankie continued, oblivious. 'In case we thought we'd be able to get away with deviating from the schedule she already emailed us.'

'Oh wow,' Ayesha exclaimed, 'I thought she had requested we don't print out any of the directions or info? Something about gratuitous tree appropriation . . .'

There was a snort behind them. They both turned to look at Yaz.

53

'Was ... that not a joke?' she asked.

'I don't think Clemmie makes ... jokes,' Frankie replied.

'Good job we do that for a living then,' Yaz said sarcastically.

'Ha!' Frankie retorted with amusement. 'Just FYI, I'm planning to get increasingly sloshed on all the expensive booze lying about and plot the downfall of the patriarchy in between hugging circles,' she told Yaz. 'It's the only way I reckon I'll get through it all. So if anyone wants to join me ...'

Yaz raised an eyebrow.

'Well, I don't plot revolutions on weekends, but a quality drink sounds good.'

A wave of relief and gratitude flowed through Ayesha as they stepped into the leaden shadow of the entrance.

CHAPTER FOUR

OCTOBER 2017

'One of the main criticisms of the people who have spoken out about what happened to them is that they didn't fight back. The amount of times I've heard someone on TV – educated, seemingly intelligent people – say things like, "Why didn't she just get out of there? Why didn't she run away? If I was in her position I would have fought with every breath I had left ..." I think what these people are referring to are what we understand to be the two responses we have when we find ourselves in critical danger. Even animals seem to respond with either fight or flight. But there is a third reaction that we don't often hear about: freeze. A freeze response is a very common reaction to a mortal threat. If someone's reaction to the very real threat of sexual violence – especially by someone with a lot more power than you, someone just plain bigger than you, or someone you thought you could trust – is to freeze, then that is a perfectly normal, clever thing to do in order to save your own life. In fact, there are several other responses to life-threatening situations we *don't acknowledge enough: fawn, friend, fake, flirt, even. Whatever it takes to survive. This is a crime often witnessed only by the perpetrator and the victim. So now we've finished blaming the victims, shall we get back to focussing on the perpetrators?'*

Ayesha had watched Frankie's videos with awe, working her way through them diligently in preparation for their meeting. Frankie had been shouting about this stuff for a long time. Her speeches on *the silent epidemic plaguing our world* were several years old. But it wasn't just Ayesha rediscovering them – a new wave of women trying to make sense of this fresh era of revelations that hit them every time they checked their media feed, trying to comprehend their own experiences, their own trauma, outrage, was making Frankie's viewing numbers soar.

Frankie was outspoken and angry. Frankie wore Doc Martens, a nose ring and a crew cut. Ayesha did not own any Doc Martens and she now wished she'd had her nose pierced, even though in her mind it accentuated her ethnicity – made her look like she'd just stepped off The Boat, and also unemployable. But it was too late to pierce it now. Ayesha was standing on the doorstep of Frankie's North London house for the first time and ringing the bell.

She wasn't really sure what she was doing here. Frankie had been vague in her invitation, using phrases like *meeting of minds* and *intersectionality,* which Ayesha thought might be the title of a Prince album. But nothing about the last forty-eight hours made any sense, so Ayesha tried to go with it, let herself be swept along, all the way to North London.

Frankie opened the door. The mousey brown crop, the piercings, the boots, the pale skin – all there in real life in front of Ayesha.

'So are we hugging, shaking hands, high-fiving? Your shout.' She grinned at Ayesha.

Ayesha froze. So many options were terrifying for someone who had no idea what they wanted for breakfast most days. Ayesha was also certain that she would pick the wrong one. This was clearly a test of some kind and she would fail at the first challenge. The seconds ticked by. She forced herself to answer.

'Let's hug it out.' And they did, awkwardly, but it was a hug, nonetheless.

'Come in,' Frankie said.

Ayesha stepped into the hallway. Rustic wooden floorboards stretched out and into unknown rooms beyond the entrance and up the bare wooden staircase to the first floor. On the walls hung framed pictures of Frankie over the years, arm in arm with a series of activists, politicians and celebrities – mostly from the Nineties; articles from newspapers; honorary degrees. Ayesha started to make a mental list of all the famous people she was now just one degree of separation from. And then an image of herself standing by Frankie – arm in arm even, like the others – framed and placed among such esteemed company crept into her mind, maybe with a fist in the air? She shook her head gently and tried not to giggle nervously.

Frankie stood in the centre of the hallway, a lopsided grin

on her face. Ayesha compared the Frankie before her to the pictures behind her. She was older now, the flecks of grey and the fine lines revealing the years of commitment and activism. Behind her hovered an even paler woman with striking red hair, slim and perfectly turned out, and younger by about ten years. She looked permanently cold somehow, her skin so light it seemed almost blue, her expression just as frigid. Ayesha felt the warmth drain slightly from her own amiable smile and wondered how the woman had appeared so silently by Frankie.

'This is Jessica,' Frankie announced. 'She's the real deal. A woman who brings her lived experience to the cause. I'm hoping we'll all be working closely together very soon.'

'Great!' enthused Ayesha, although she didn't quite understand what that meant. 'It's good to meet you, Jessica. Any ally of Frankie's must be sound.'

Jessica managed a smile of sorts.

'Ally. Wow, you're already using the lingo,' she retorted condescendingly. 'You'll fit right in.'

'Thanks,' Ayesha said uncertainly, surprised the introduction had taken such a strange turn.

Loud, stomping footsteps made them all turn towards what Ayesha thought might be the direction of the kitchen. A woman in her late twenties with cropped sandy hair and a ruddy, friendly face bustled in, her hand already outstretched towards Ayesha.

'Ayesha! Yes! It's you, like proper. In the flesh, live and direct!' she gushed, pumping Ayesha's hand enthusiastically.

'I'm Joni. And I'm psyched. Honestly. I must have watched that video twenty times. Fifty. You smashed it mate.'

Ayesha tried to keep up with the sudden change in temperature. Her face reddened. Her raw, uncensored outburst was even more excruciating to contemplate in the presence of these women.

'Ah thanks,' Ayesha replied. 'I don't usually rant like that, FYI. Bit of a one-off really. Probably best not to watch it too many times . . .'

There was a silence as Ayesha trailed off, then Joni spun around.

'Tea! And biscuits. For you soldiers, while you plan how to smash things up and build it back up again, better.' She turned back to Ayesha. 'I'm not really here. I'm just . . . refreshments and morale.' She grinned cheekily, glanced at Frankie and was gone.

Ayesha wished she'd stayed. Joni's Essex twang, her homely bustle, baggy jeans and cheeky banter had thawed the spacious, chilly Edwardian home. She looked back at Frankie and Jessica. Frankie's status as a living legend and the circles she moved in placed her firmly on a pedestal several levels above Ayesha. And Jessica, still frozen, her auburn hair coiffed and set, a gentle wave reaching over one shoulder, directed a piercing gaze right back at Ayesha. Eventually, Ayesha had to turn away.

'Right,' Frankie said. 'Through here, where all the plotting and scheming happens.'

Frankie led them into the living room. A well-worn sofa

with plenty of battered cushions spoke of years of discussion and organizing, decades of activism and campaigning. Late nights putting the world to rights. The three women sat down, and Joni tiptoed in with refreshments then tiptoed out, glancing once at Frankie before disappearing into the kitchen.

'So,' Frankie began, 'The plan is to form a gang of like-minded, kick-ass activists to share resources, organize, support each other while we do our work.' Ayesha nodded solemnly. Jessica sat stiffly on the edge of the sofa, listening intently.

'Let's be real for a moment,' Frankie continued. 'Speaking out about this stuff can be pretty brutal and also lonely. It's important to have a team of allies you can call on.'

Ayesha looked from Frankie to Jessica, still perched on the edge of the sofa. She tried to contemplate her as an ally. Jessica turned her gaze on Ayesha once more and something seemed to pass between them. What was it? A spark, an instance of recognition? Ayesha felt exposed somehow, forced to look away once more.

'There are a lot of opportunities flooding in at the moment,' Frankie went on, 'Media appearances, comment, that sort of thing. I want to make sure you're ammoed up before you go into battle.'

Ayesha tried to keep up as Frankie continued.

'And which battles are those?'

Jessica's clipped, clear voice cut like a sharpened blade. Frankie stopped, looked at her, blinked.

'There's only one battle, Jessica,' she replied. 'The illusion that our struggles are separate, individual, is perpetuated just to keep us from uniting. One unified cause.'

'And is that one unified court case too?' Jessica asked. Ayesha looked from one woman to the other.

'It could well be,' Frankie countered. 'There are a number of ways of seeking justice, but if we don't collectively fight for a fairer justice system, it won't make any difference whether you go it alone or not. The result will always favour the interests of the patriarchy. That's why we need to look at the bigger picture.'

Jessica stared at Frankie intently. Frankie met her gaze with determination. Eventually Jessica turned away and Frankie pushed on.

'In all the time I've been speaking out about this stuff, there's never been a moment like this. It would be foolish to use it just to further one individual's interests.' Frankie turned to Ayesha who automatically sat a little straighter. 'There will be all sorts of requests for personal information, personal stories – what I call trauma porn. Be very careful who you talk to, however attractive they and their deals are. Collectively we can set boundaries, make choices, keep it safe, contained. There are lots of awesome humans keen to join us, but we start small, make a splash and then expand to make waves.'

Frankie paused, looked at Ayesha expectantly. Jessica's eyes were also fixed on her. It took Ayesha a moment to realize they were waiting for her to respond.

'Wow,' she began, 'I mean, this is great! Really amazing. I just ... You do know that I'm not ... I just tell jokes. I don't *speak out* like you guys do. I just had a shit gig that escalated a bit.'

Frankie sighed and looked at Ayesha with a hard, defiant gaze, 'That gig was activism of the highest order, Ayesha,' she said solemnly. 'Make no mistake: you are one of us.'

Ayesha felt a jolt of surprise at this proclamation, but it was soon replaced by a feeling of relief. She hadn't quite been asked, but it seemed to have been decided that she was now *one of them*. Maybe it was the cuppa Joni had discreetly placed in her hands, but with it also came a warm glow which rose inside her despite the coolness of the room. A part of her, a very old part, was very tired and she thought that, just maybe, she might be allowed to rest here.

Ayesha found herself beaming at the two women. Frankie smiled back. Jessica managed another grim smirk.

An hour later, Ayesha found herself back in the hallway, elated but also dazed and even more unsure. Apparently, she'd just joined some kind of group. She wasn't sure how or why, but Frankie just seemed so sure. Of everything. And Ayesha was sure of nothing. Not her career, or her future, let alone her present. And definitely not her past. Of what had happened that night and everything since. She hadn't asked for any of it, and she once again found herself watching her life take a turn she hadn't expected or chosen. But surely this was a good thing? Something to cling onto, someone to anchor herself to who would help navigate it all ...

She had hoped to say goodbye to Joni too, but she had

disappeared somewhere upstairs and didn't come back down. Another awkward hug with Frankie and a nod from Jessica. It was her face that Ayesha saw last as the door closed, her jaw set, her eyes glaring fiercely.

She was halfway down the road when it hit her.

She had to pause and put her hand on a brick wall to steady herself. Something from deep inside her gut escaped from her mouth. Something long-buried and suddenly unearthed. A sob unlike any other. And another. And another.

She didn't understand it, but Frankie's determined face, Joni's good-natured smile, and even Jessica's piercing look – this more than anything – had floored her somehow. Because there was a sense that here, finally, maybe the darkest, most abandoned parts of her – the least funny - could be known, seen even, and included.

Ayesha stood there, gripping the wall until the convulsions subsided and she could walk again.

'Sounds intense,' Yaz said levelly, as they perched on the wall outside her family home. The loud voices of at least three generations of cousins, aunties and grandparents drifted out of the front window, adding warmth to the chilly, grey afternoon.

'It was a lot,' Ayesha admitted. 'But in the best way. Frankie's crazy connected, and she's got all these plans. And she wants me to be like a founding member of this new group.'

'Founding member? Did she say that?'

'Yeah. Well, not exactly. But basically, we're the OGs. We get to shape it, create it from scratch and kind of dictate the narrative—'

'Dictate the what now?' Yaz frowned at her friend's new turn of phrase.

'Yaz man, this is serious stuff,' Ayesha reasoned.

'Exactly, so why are you – a comedian – getting involved?'

Ayesha hesitated. How to explain to her friend that feeling, that moment, what it meant to her?

'Because ... it means something,' she said weakly.

Yaz pursed her lips. But she knew her friend well.

'Okay,' she conceded gently. 'Just make sure you really are shaping the ... narrative. Yeah?'

''Course.'

CHAPTER FIVE

JULY 2018

Saturday 2.15 p.m.

'Pretty sweet operations base for the revolution, eh?' grinned Frankie as she led them inside.

Ayesha blinked several times to adjust to the twilight of the interior. She did some quick calculations and figured that the hallway alone was bigger than her entire flat. She looked down at the bespoke mat under her feet, itself taking up more space than her kitchen table. Wellington boots mixed with crocs and a single deck shoe were scattered by the door. Beyond the mat, wooden floorboards, richly varnished, each half a metre wide, covered the rest of the floor, leading to a staircase that zigzagged up to a level beyond. Several doors stood ajar to each side, a thick heat seeming to emanate from them. Despite the spaciousness of the interior, Ayesha felt stifled once again, as if she was back in her stuffy little car.

Joni was next to greet them. She appeared in the hallway from somewhere beyond the stairs, wiping her hands on a tea towel. The cheeky sparkle in her eyes and her natural warmth put Ayesha at ease immediately.

'You made it!' she said. 'Come here, you legends.' Joni grabbed Ayesha and Yaz, one in each arm, in a strong bear hug. 'How was the trip?'

'A bit like Coachella, if it was set in a dodgy mobile sauna on the A41,' quipped Ayesha.

She thought she saw Yaz frown. There was a pause, then Joni snorted and pushed her away playfully.

'That's good, that is. Who was headlining, Athlete's Foot and the Verrucas?' She winked and glanced at Yaz, then Frankie.

'We did actually almost end up spending the weekend in some dodgy field,' said Yaz.

Ayesha nodded.

'Really? How come?' Joni frowned and smiled at the same time.

'Our phone map sent us to some random gate at the other end. You must have ended up there too if you put in the same postcode?' Ayesha nodded to Frankie's car parked near her Peugeot.

'Random gate?' Joni looked at Frankie. 'No ...'

Frankie raised her eyebrows in confusion.

'Our trip was pretty smooth,' she added. 'No wrong turns for us.'

'I reckon Google maps is racist,' Yaz blurted out. 'It sent us the wrong way on purpose.'

Ayesha looked desperately at Joni and Frankie. It was the kind of joke she and Yaz made all the time. If it had been just the two of them, she would have added an extra bit and they would have riffed for a good five minutes on how satnav was really invented by Nazis. But the other two women looked at them both blankly.

Joni attempted a laugh. Eventually, she nodded at their glasses.

'More bubbly?' she suggested and produced a bottle from somewhere behind her. Ayesha and Yaz held out their glasses eagerly. Joni filled them generously.

'Tough crowd,' Yaz murmured to Ayesha as she took a sip.

Ayesha took a big glug from the freshly filled flute.

'I could get used to this,' she said loudly and brightly to everyone.

Frankie smiled.

'You are merely being welcomed in a manner befitting your goddess status,' she said in a heightened, sarcastic tone as Joni topped her up too.

'Sure, whatevs. Cheers.' Yaz downed half the glass in one and looked up and around at the interior. 'This is serious money. Old money.'

'It's bloody huge, mate,' Joni added conspiratorially. 'We put our bags in one of the bedrooms upstairs, but I've got no idea how I'm ever gonna find it again. Especially after a few drinks. But apparently it doesn't matter cos there's that many rooms, you just crash wherever you find yourself at the end of the night.'

'And I could basically move into the library permanently,' added Frankie. 'It's perfect for plotting the revolution.'

'Franks, behave,' said Joni playfully. 'We're here for India, so put on your best goddess face and get with the programme.'

'Look, I've already hugged, like, four people in the space of an hour,' Frankie reasoned. 'I'm as down with the programme as the laminated schedule says I should be!'

Joni shook her head at Frankie but couldn't resist a grin. She watched them make light work of the top-up and collected their empty glasses as they heard a creak. They all looked up. A woman's pale bare feet appeared at the top of the staircase. Her body and outfit were revealed in stages as she descended. A rich maroon dress that was made of Indian sari fabric but cut in a style that suggested the 1920s with a headpiece to match. Her messy blonde hair was gently tousled, and her toes were adorned with toe rings. Ayesha recognized the golden locks and the well-bred skin from the selfies Clemmie had posted on her Instagram page. She also recognized the look. The white skin in brown people's traditional clothing.

Yaz glared at Ayesha, her eyebrows raised. Ayesha glanced back at her and then quickly away, but she'd caught the look in Yaz's eye – a mix of amusement, surprise and disapproval at Clemmie's take on an Indian classic. Ayesha widened her smile till her cheeks hurt.

'Ah! Our Eastern goddesses have arrived. Ayesha. Yaz. I'm Clemmie. Welcome.' She took the final steps towards them both and gazed at them intensely, the warmth of her words of welcome not quite reaching her eyes.

'Clemmie! It's so good to meet you. Thank you so much for having us. It's such a beautiful place,' Ayesha gushed. Yaz raised her eyebrows at her friend once more, but this time her amusement and surprise were aimed directly at Ayesha. Ayesha kept her eyes firmly on their host.

'Not at all,' replied Clemmie, 'You are so very welcome.'

Clemmie inspected their faces carefully. Ayesha looked back at the flawless skin, the glossy golden hair, the pale blue eyes scrutinizing her with a cold fascination while her pink mouth smiled. The moment lingered. She could feel Yaz meeting Clemmie's gaze with equal scrutiny, while Ayesha continued to smile desperately, willing this strange moment to be okay. Finally, Clemmie inhaled deeply and calmly broke eye contact. She reached into a hidden pocket within the folds of rich, delicate material on her person and took out a small glass bottle. She lifted it high and sprayed twice above each of their heads. Ayesha felt Yaz flinch next to her. As the moisture descended on them, she inhaled a musky mix of essential oils.

'Let us rid you of all traces of the city,' Clemmie intoned. 'The smog and the glare and the concrete. The hustle and bustle. The man-made materials. The plastic particles that penetrate our very pores. The noise. Leave it all behind. Arrive anew as the natural goddesses you truly are.'

Ayesha's mind wandered back to the cheap neon parapher-nalia in the car. She willed it to disappear.

'Your auras are cleansed,' Clemmie confirmed. 'Your beings are blessed. Shoes off please!'

Ayesha rushed to take off her Air Maxes and place them by the other shoes on the mat. As an afterthought, she slipped off her socks and stuffed them in her shoes. Yaz followed suit. Ayesha noticed how both her and Yaz's crisp kicks were at odds with the well-worn country footwear they were placed next to, their unnatural brightness a stain on the earthy hues of their surroundings. She felt her feet expand and breathe with relief at being liberated from their bulk. She also felt suddenly more vulnerable. She glanced at Yaz, whose unshod brown feet made her also seem exposed somehow.

Clemmie nodded with approval.

'Is there Wi-Fi?' Yaz asked bluntly.

Clemmie blinked in surprise, then to Ayesha's relief, she smiled.

'This is a protected space, a purified atmosphere,' she said. 'I wouldn't dare tell anyone what to do, but I would encourage you to switch off as much as you can bear it. And certainly no electromagnetic radiation in the circles. Okay?'

'So ... No Wi-Fi?' Yaz asked.

With a whisper of silk, Clemmie turned around and headed through an entrance on the left.

'Our Queen will be gracing us shortly. She's just perfecting her look,' Clemmie announced over her shoulder, ignoring Yaz's question. 'Now just one more goddess to join us and the circle will be complete,' came the final words before she disappeared.

Ayesha looked at Frankie and Joni and quickly surmised that it must be Jessica who hadn't arrived yet. Frankie sipped her bubbles and did not make eye contact. Joni pursed her lips together in an almost smile. Ayesha was keen to see her friend, but also extremely anxious about how this would all work. Frankie was clearly not ready to forgive and forget, but perhaps Clemmie and India were closer to Jessica than she realized. Perhaps they would be the ones to bring her in, make her feel welcome once again. They had, after all, been generous enough to invite her.

Ayesha tried to think of when she'd last seen Jessica. Tried to remember when their last call had been. Another of their late-night marathons that had lasted hours. Something about them seemed taboo, a betrayal of sorts, but she couldn't explain why, or who exactly she was betraying. She also couldn't explain why she hadn't told anyone about them. But recently even those had stopped. She felt a pang of guilt, hoped that this weekend she'd have the chance to make it up to her.

Ayesha realized they'd been standing in silence for a while. It was awkward. Yaz looked from Ayesha, to Frankie, to Joni and back again. Ayesha hoped desperately she wouldn't crack another one of her jokes or mention the beef with Jessica.

Eventually, Joni cut through the silence.

'Apparently numbers are very important for this thing,' she said sarcastically. 'As well as the state of your chakras, the wellness of your aura, and which direction you move around the sacred circle. I just know I'm gonna fuck up first

71

and probably jinx the entire wedding or something because me and my murky chakras went West instead of East.'

'Not if I fuck up first!' Ayesha retorted and laughed a bit too loud. Yaz jumped slightly. The silence settled once more.

Joni turned to Frankie, who sipped her drink quietly. She looked back at the others.

'Tour?' she suggested hopefully.

Joni led them up the stairs, chatting away about the size of the place, the gluten-free, low-carb vegan snacks she had spotted, and the giant pot bubbling on the aga that she called 'Clemmie's cauldron'.

They arrived on a landing at one end of a corridor that stretched out ahead of them. The windows along the left side looked out onto the front drive and Ayesha could see her battered old Peugeot parked next to the other cars, the sun glaring off the hot metal. To her horror, the string of the willy balloon was just visible in the window. She cringed and looked away. Opposite the wall of windows was a wall of doors, four to be exact, and Joni had already opened the one that was furthest away. They followed her in.

It was a vast room with a deep plush cream carpet and hand-woven rugs placed on top. Thick wooden beams crossed the ceiling and an antique desk and chair were placed next to the door to the ensuite bathroom. A king-size sleigh bed was positioned in the middle of the room, facing the windows on the other side. Ayesha walked tentatively across the room towards the latticed windows, her feet sinking pleasantly into the layers of carpet, and looked out at the view to the back of the house. Below, a stone patio led to a lawn which segued into a wilder field that led to a forest of large, ancient oaks and maples. Beyond them Ayesha caught a glimpse of blue: some kind of water? A lake maybe?

The women paused for a moment, taking in their surroundings. Frankie sighed loudly and dramatically as she dropped into a chair and put her heavy boots up on an antique dresser, sipping directly from the bottle of bubbly she'd carried up with her. Ayesha and Yaz involuntarily gasped at the outdoor footwear on pristine carpet. Joni giggled.

'If she tried that shit in my mum's house she'd be wearing that boot *in* her backside,' Yaz whispered to Ayesha.

But Ayesha wasn't surprised. Frankie had a very specific code of conduct and boundaries, but Ayesha had noticed that she could be quite fluid with her interpretation of other people's rules. She was, after all, a professional rebel.

'We bagsied this one when we arrived and India's got the one at the other end. But there's a whole other level too!' Joni enthused as she headed back out and beckoned them to join her. Yaz and Ayesha followed obediently.

Frankie took one more indulgent swig before joining them. Joni pointed at the doors next along from theirs.

'That's Clemmie's room and that's where India's staying, and this . . .' she pointed to a doorway which turned out to be the entrance to another staircase, '. . . is the servants' quarters.'

'The servants' quarters? Is that where they're putting us

up?' Yaz murmured to Ayesha as they followed Joni up the cramped steps to the floor above.

'You haven't seen it yet, it might be . . . nice,' Ayesha tried.

Yaz glared at her all the way up the stairs.

The rooms were longer and narrower and filled with single beds, but still comfier and more luxurious than anywhere Ayesha had stayed before. One room had five single beds, each with its own bedside table and vintage lamp. It had the feel of a luxurious dorm in some kind of magical boarding school Ayesha must have seen in a movie. Another room had three beds and a dresser with a mirror. The third was similar. It took Ayesha a moment to register that she was suddenly breathing normally for the first time since they had arrived. Deep, welcome, fresh breaths. She could handle a room this size. And more importantly, despite it being much smaller, it was cooler than the others. The little window at the far end had been left open, and the stifling heat from the lower floors seemed not to reach up here. Despite her reservations, Yaz had already slung her bag onto one of the beds and Ayesha followed suit. Frankie grinned, giving the room a quick once-over.

'This reminds me of your flat share, JJ,' Frankie called to Joni. Joni popped her head in the room and looked around.

'Ha! The old attic above the pub,' Joni exclaimed. She turned to the others. 'There were five of us, all working in the bar downstairs and sharing the rooms upstairs,' she explained, seeing their blank looks, 'It was . . . intimate. All the other staff seemed to come and go and get younger and younger. I'd been there six years before this one bowled in and ordered a pint. And then another. And another ...' She poked Frankie playfully.

Frankie almost managed a bit of a flirt with her girlfriend. 'And look at you now, lady of the manor,' she exclaimed.

'Too right,' replied Joni. 'I've gone up in the world ...' She winked at them.

Frankie gave the bedside table an experimental tap and then headed out.

'Come on, we've still got the grounds to cover,' Joni said in a mock-dramatic voice as she followed Frankie. They descended the narrow staircase, Ayesha close behind, turning to beckon Yaz down too.

Back on the first-floor landing, Ayesha glanced out of the window. The sun glinted off the metal roof of her car, blinding her for a moment, but then she spotted once more the telltale string of the balloon just in view through the side window. She'd have to find a way to get back out there and get rid of it. Hide it all. Maybe even dig a deep hole somewhere in this vast estate and bury it where no one would ever find it. She contemplated the wide selection of neon plastics she'd brought here that would never ever decompose, however deep she buried them.

She felt again the thickness of the muggy air as she descended the stairs and found herself slightly panting. She longed to rush back up the servants' staircase and stand in the cooler, smaller room, gulping in the fresh air.

Just then there was a click and the door next to the

staircase opened. Ayesha, Yaz, Joni and Frankie all turned to see India step out. She was dressed in layers of rich silk, each layer a contrasting colour of complex Eastern patterns and rich shades. Her feet were bare but adorned with dark red nail polish and toe rings, tiny bells strapped around her ankles. There was a slit on one side of the fabric revealing her left leg up to the middle of her bronzed thigh. Her head was wrapped in equally rich layers of fabric and gold coins dangled from it, framing her face. One hand, also carefully bronzed, was covered in elaborate mehndi designs. The other sported a hefty diamond ring. She looked at each face in turn.

'Goddesses.' She beamed.

Ayesha felt a surge of gratitude and awe. India was a vision. She floated towards them, extending her sun-kissed arms and inviting them all into a group hug. The women came to her and stood together in a circular embrace. India to Yaz's right, Frankie to her left, beyond her, Ayesha between Frankie and Joni. A lump of emotion began to form in Ayesha's throat. How the hell had she ended up surrounded by this calibre of legends? In this dream house? The whirlwind of the last few months seemed to suddenly settle and culminate in this moment of perfection. She breathed deeply and tried to remember that she belonged.

After a while, India gracefully stepped back, the bells around her ankles tinkling gently. They all seemed to be gathering themselves again. Joni wiped a tear away. India gave this all space, nodding slowly and looking at each of the women in turn. The coins framing her face matched her hazel eyes, occasionally flashing in the daylight, accentuating the smattering of freckles on her skin, the flecks of gold in her irises. She observed them as they observed her with emotion and admiration.

All but Yaz, who had stiffened somehow. Ayesha had sensed her friend's discomfort on her periphery, and she turned to her now and watched her fully take in India's costume.

'Did you rob a gypsy or something?' Yaz suddenly blurted out.

India's head snapped around in surprise. There was a pause which felt like an eternity to Ayesha. Then India's face softened.

'I believe the correct term is Traveller,' she responded levelly.

Mercifully, Frankie burst into laughter. This made Joni giggle, and then India's face broke into a satisfied smile.

Yaz looked over at Ayesha expectantly. Ayesha wasn't sure what she was meant to be thinking or feeling. She turned back to India and suddenly saw her through Yaz's eyes. The outfit that had seemed to accentuate India's mystique a moment ago appeared now to sit unnaturally on her frame, the colours not quite working with her complexion, even with her meticulously cultivated tan.

But Ayesha was in no position to comment. More than anything, she was relieved that India had received them – her – so warmly. As with Frankie, Ayesha was even less sure of India's feelings towards her. She knew she needed to find a moment, as soon as possible, to speak to India privately, to explain, clear the air, before the weekend really began.

She shook her head and suddenly India looked sublime again, as she always did. Ayesha's mind whirled. Maybe she should be offended. But there seemed no space for that in these moments of magic India created. She tried to placate Yaz with a knowing look, and then turned to India and beamed intensely at her. It was exhausting.

'You look beautiful,' she gushed. India turned briefly to her, a cold smile appearing and disappearing almost immediately. Ayesha's heart sank.

'Let us descend and join the rest of our clan,' India announced, returning her gaze to Yaz.

And with that, the goddesses traipsed down the stairs, several pairs of bare feet making irregular rhythms on the runner, the occasional creak of ancient floorboard accentuating their progress downwards. Ayesha tried to catch up with India, hoping to pull her aside, but she remained just out of reach.

They walked through into a spacious kitchen where Clemmie was bent over a large green metallic contraption that had steam emanating from it. Ayesha guessed this was what an Aga must be. Clemmie turned and straightened up as India made her entrance. She began to clap. The other women took their cue and soon they were all applauding India.

Ayesha looked to Yaz, this time mirroring her confusion. What was happening now? Why was everyone clapping India? A dangerous spark passed between them, a glint of amusement that threatened to boil over into uncontrollable giggling. This time it was Yaz who mercifully took the lead, pointedly breaking eye contact with Ayesha and enthusiastically joining in with the clapping. Ayesha swallowed her laughter and solemnly followed suit.

India stood beaming, soaking it in. It lasted longer than Ayesha expected, and her hands started to smart, which made her clap with even more determination. Finally, Clemmie brought it to an end by raising her hands.

'Our Queen Goddess has descended to Earth,' she announced. 'Let the celebrations begin!'

There was a burst of activity. Joni joined Clemmie at the Aga and took up the wooden spoon she had been using to stir the pot. 'Clemmie's cauldron', Ayesha thought, remembering Joni's quip from earlier. As Joni stirred, Clemmie watched, commenting quietly and giving instructions. To Ayesha's left was a huge fridge that almost reached the ceiling, and next to it, a smaller fridge which sat snugly under the marble countertop. Frankie opened this, revealing a neat line of champagne bottles inside. She pulled one out and popped it efficiently.

Ayesha was relieved to see India take Yaz's arm and lead her into the dining area beyond. Yaz glanced momentarily in Ayesha's direction and then gamely let herself be led away.

Ayesha nodded encouragingly at everyone for a few moments and then took her chance. She walked backwards out of the scene, still smiling, out of the kitchen, into the hallway, and headed to the front door.

It was still ajar, letting a sliver of stark sunlight into the dark interior. She didn't stop to put her trainers on but ventured out barefoot, experimenting with this new bohemian vibe, and also keen to do this as quickly as possible. She tried to ignore the sting of the baking gravel on her sensitive soles as she headed towards the car. In her haste, she reached out to the car door without thinking and yelped. It was scalding hot. She turned around to see if anyone had heard her, but the sounds of activity wafted out of the front door undisturbed. She pulled at the handle more carefully this time and as the door opened, the stifling heat of the interior hit her. She flinched, then pushed on, reaching over the driver's seat into the back for the balloon. But it bobbed away playfully. Ayesha gritted her teeth and tried again. It was more awkward than she'd expected. Her car was a humble 3-door, which meant trying to pull the balloon diagonally through the middle of the car and out through the driver's door. The balloon did not co-operate. She leaned in further, wrestling with its impossible buoyancy, her backside hanging out of the car door, the heat and the exertion causing her to break out into a sweat. She yanked at the curly string and the balloon hit her in the face, but before it could bob away again, she grabbed at it, wrapping an arm around the floaty phallus with determination.

'Well, that's one way to get your kicks.'

Ayesha twisted around in alarm to find Yaz laughing at her. Ayesha had one leg on the car seat, one arm gripping the headrest and the other embracing the buoyant bellend, the string wrapped around her neck.

'Fucking help me,' Ayesha growled.

'What are you trying to do?' Yaz enquired between chuckles.

'Get rid of the fucking thing,' Ayesha replied with frustration.

'Where?' Yaz asked, trying to suppress more laughter.

Ayesha looked around wildly. For a moment she contemplated just letting it go and watching it float up high into the sky. But then she took in the numerous branches of the grand old trees that the floating willy could get stuck in on its way up and reconsidered.

'Just ... let's ... just ... chuck it in the boot.'

Yaz helped Ayesha guide the balloon out of the car and gently disentangled her from it. It caught the sunlight with such a harsh dazzle it blinded them both for a moment. Yaz flinched and retrieved her sunglasses from the top of her head.

They opened the boot. A stifling pocket of heat was released into their faces. They peered in at the contents.

'Bloody hell,' Yaz exclaimed with disgust.

The pink sashes had lost their lustre. One had wilted into the willy cake which had melted to the point of oozing out of its cardboard box and onto the rest of the sashes. The ink of the special 'K' she had paid extra for had begun to run and was now mixing with the escaped icing. There was also a half-drowned willy wand slowly succumbing to its sticky fate. It was a hot, plastic, pink mess. A cheap neon car crash. A crime scene that was so disturbing, it was hard to look away.

'Oh god. What was I thinking?' Ayesha groaned, both repulsed and mesmerized by the carnage.

'Sis, your boot is trashed,' Yaz said helpfully.

'Yep, thank you,' Ayesha replied. She sighed with frustration, frazzled and hot. 'Let's just shove the balloon in with the rest of it and pretend all of this is not here.'

But the cheerful, cheeky, helium-filled phallus had other ideas. It evaded them several times, bobbing gleefully just out of their reach, bumping off every corner of the boot and generally making things difficult.

Ayesha growled with exasperation, her face even redder, her skin even sweatier.

Yaz doubled up with laughter once again, and then tried to recover when she saw Ayesha's angry face.

'Okay. Okay. Just ... let me,' she offered.

Ayesha stepped back and let Yaz wrestle the balloon into the boot. Then she remembered the other thing she had come out to do.

She took a few steps away from the car, took out her phone, scrolled through her recent calls and hit a number. Nothing. She looked again at the screen and noticed the words No Service in the top left corner. Wi-Fi. She needed Wi-Fi. She also needed for this to be sorted asap, and for the others not to know a thing about it. She waved the phone around desperately. Nothing. She sighed and took a step back. One precious bar appeared, and she froze in place. Moving as little as possible, she tried the number again. After a moment of silence, she heard the ring tone with relief. A crackle and then an answer.

'Hello, Hen Men?'

'Oh hi. Er, I actually ordered a stripper—'

'Hello?'

'Hi! My name is Ayesha and the thing is—'

'What was that? You're breaking up,' said the voice at the other end.

'Sorry, I'm just out somewhere . . .' Ayesha craned her neck a few inches higher. 'Is that better?'

'Yep, just about,' the Hen Men receptionist replied. 'Wherever you are, don't move.'

'Okay!' Ayesha was on her tiptoes. 'So the thing is,' she continued, 'I ordered a stripper to come to my friend's hen do and basically we don't need him anymore.'

A sigh. 'Okay . . . Can I take some details please?'

Ayesha gave the particulars and the deep voice at the other end sighed again and did some tapping.

'Now this was out in . . . Buckinghamshire?'

'Yep. That's the one,' Ayesha confirmed.

'Okay, well the thing is, it's really late notice . . .'

A tap on her shoulder. Ayesha shrugged it off and tried to listen.

'Yep. No, I totally understand.'

Another tap. Ayesha turned around and Yaz indicated the car, closed and with no balloon in sight. Ayesha nodded.

'We will have to charge I'm afraid,' said the voice on the phone.

Yaz nudged her again and signalled for the car keys. Ayesha felt around until she found them in the pocket of her tracksuit bottoms and handed them over.

'Of course. Of course,' Ayesha replied down the phone. 'If you could just make sure he doesn't come. That would be great. I'm really sorry. Thank you.'

She hung up, sighed, trying once again not to think about the amount of money she had just wasted on bespoke hen do accessories and cancelled strippers. She looked up at her grinning friend and then burst into laughter so sudden and intense she couldn't catch her breath. Yaz guffawed with delight. And that was it.

The hot pink mess of her boot, wrestling with the flying willy, the money lost, the spontaneous clapping, the aura cleansing, the impossible politics of it all. And the two of them stuck here together trying to roll with it. They were both doubled over now, tears streaming down their faces, a hundred jokes overlapping in their heads that didn't even need to be told.

Finally, they gathered themselves. Ayesha wiped her face and straightened her outfit.

'Okay. Let's do this,' she said with conviction.

Yaz's grin faded. She looked reluctantly back at the dark interior of the mansion and then at her friend. Ayesha's face was determined, imploring. Yaz rolled her eyes.

'Sure. Let's get back in there and frig some chakras,' she replied.

They headed back in.

Ayesha looked up at the grand building as they entered and thought she caught a glimpse of a figure, pale and still, watching from a window on the first floor. The sun glinted off the glass and blinded her for a moment. Yaz looked over at her with a grim expression and Ayesha refocused, urging her friend inside.

CHAPTER SIX

NOVEMBER 2017

Frankie's plan picked up pace fast.

Ayesha found herself travelling to North London several times a week for what Frankie called media training and collective consulting. Then there was the campaigning, the awareness raising and the public appearances.

Frankie had instructed Ayesha to forward the influx of emails she received for personal requests and appearances, and Ayesha was more than happy to let Frankie make sense of it. She hated saying no, but she couldn't possibly say yes to them all, so Frankie did it on her behalf, on everyone's behalf.

Joni created social media pages, positioning their group as the go-to team for #MeToo comment, and a week of targeting an exhaustive list of media connections established them as just that. Soon the requests were flowing in with Frankie and Joni fielding them all, organizing the schedule of appearances and passing it on to Ayesha and Jessica.

One day they were being interviewed for the *Evening Standard*, the next day making a video for an online news channel, then an early start on a morning TV show. The world was hungry for content and comment, and they were the ones to deliver it – just as Frankie had envisioned.

Sometimes it was Ayesha and Jessica, sometimes just one of them, but always with Frankie there ensuring the interviews were contained and safe. Joni was chef, security and roadie all in one, keeping them fed and watered, getting them there early and sniffing at the interviewers with a protective glare.

Ayesha had no time to take stock of it all, but after so many years of banging on doors which remained firmly closed, it was bizarre and wonderful to be wanted so intensely that someone else had to manage it all for her. And that someone else was none other than the legendary Frankie Roberts.

And then there was Jessica.

Ayesha had looked her up too. Jessica's name produced a rich result of articles and blogs, mostly lifestyle stuff that she had written, and a smattering of professional photos in a muted but stylish array of blouses, all showing her with her trademark glare. But the earlier pictures were different. The uncompromising stare into the camera was full of spark and ambition. Hope even. Ayesha could see the year where it changed into a cold defiance. The year she had become a survivor. Jessica had shared publicly that she had experienced sexual violence just before the global avalanche of revelations had started. She had written a series of eloquent and carefully worded articles which began with the myriad ways such violations ruined your life, and in recent pieces began to critique the system and power structures that facilitated these violations and violators. Ayesha could see how cautious Jessica had been with her words, brushing over, but never naming the institution, person or establishment she was referring to. She also noticed that, unlike her lifestyle articles which featured in broadsheet newspapers and high-profile magazines, these new articles were largely self-published, blogs, or at best, appeared in grass-roots feminist press collectives.

But now, alongside Ayesha and Frankie, she was mainstream once again. Ayesha imagined that it had started with an email similar to the one she had received. That Jessica had watched Frankie's videos just as she had done and felt seen, understood, represented. And that Frankie had offered to give her a proper platform for her story, a movement to be a part of, a chance to come out of the cold and back into the centre of things.

Jessica was articulate and fierce and on message. She was glamorous and coldly charismatic, if not exactly likeable. For the first few weeks she barely spoke to Ayesha. They would sit silently in the journalist's office or stand in the wings of the TV studio waiting to be called, and Ayesha found herself desperately trying to fill the silences with terrible jokes and weak observations about the decor until even she gave up.

But when Ayesha finally quietened, the unthinkable happened. Jessica started to speak.

They were in a green room in the back warren of yet another

studio, waiting for their segment to be recorded. As usual, Frankie had accompanied them to the studio that morning and then had broken off to talk with an exec about a more ambitious future segment. Joni had popped her head in through the door and given the space a once-over before heading out again. A runner had brought them chilled water and coffee a while ago. Ayesha had let hers congeal in the branded mug. Jessica had done the same. Ayesha sat on the standard-issue green room sofa. She felt dazed, a familiar state now that she found herself in constant motion. She knew that soon she would have to shake it off, assume her new public face once more, switch it on for the cameras, so she allowed herself this moment of quiet vagueness. She hadn't realized how long they had been sitting quietly until Jessica spoke.

'Why don't you ask for tea?'

It took a few seconds for Ayesha to take in that Jessica was talking to her. She turned to her with surprise, her eyes a wide question.

'You don't drink coffee, so why don't you ask for tea?' Jessica repeated.

Ayesha blinked, trying to understand how she had got it wrong again, which piece of etiquette she hadn't been privy to while she had been desperately trying to be as obliging as possible.

'I ... don't know. I don't really mind,' she shrugged amiably.

'Yes, you do,' Jessica countered, seemingly annoyed. Ayesha's stomach contracted, her mind suddenly racing to find the right answer.

'When Joni makes you tea, your face lights up like it's Christmas,' Jessica explained. 'So you do mind. Why don't you just tell them to make you tea instead of coffee?'

'They ... don't really ask,' Ayesha found herself saying. 'They always say the same thing, 'Coffee?' And they're already halfway out the door, so it's just easier to ...' She shrugged, glanced over at the mug holding her frigid drink. 'Joni asks,' she continued. 'She asks what I'd like to drink and how I like it. So I tell her.'

Jessica watched her carefully, then sat back ever so slightly, seemingly satisfied with this explanation. A surprisingly comfortable silence settled for a moment.

'Plus, I hate the branded mugs,' Ayesha suddenly added. 'It's just a bad vibe to drink your tea out of.'

Jessica's eyes sparkled with amusement.

'A good mug is important,' she agreed.

Ayesha felt her shoulders relax, her stomach unclench. She had passed the test, made it to the other side. She realized how tense she usually felt around Jessica. How she was in a constant state of low-level alert when she was in her presence, which was pretty often these days. Now that the scrutiny had been alleviated for a moment, she tried to pinpoint what it was about Jessica that had this effect on her. It wasn't just her perpetually glacial persona that made things difficult. Ayesha realized she felt somehow exposed when she was around her, like she could see straight through Ayesha's act. A strange familiarity, as if Jessica knew there was something more real, raw between them.

This only made Ayesha double down on the small talk. And the jokes. Anything to keep that piercing look from really hitting its mark. But recently she'd just been too tired, too overwhelmed to keep it up.

'That's the first time you've actually expressed an opinion about something.'

Ayesha was jolted out of her introspection. She focused on Jessica once more. Despite the personal comment, her expression seemed warmer somehow, a softness around the eyes.

'I'm always expressing an opinion!' Ayesha insisted defensively. 'That's literally what we're here to do.'

Jessica dismissed their shared mission with a tired wave of her hand.

'Not that stuff. I mean personal stuff. Like an actual personal preference for something,' she explained. 'It's a good thing,' she added, almost kindly.

Ayesha frowned. Was that true? Looking back, she realized that she often had no idea what she preferred. She looked over at the mug again, saw Jessica's on the opposite side of the coffee table, also holding a full cup of stale coffee.

'What about you?' Ayesha countered.

'Hmm?' Jessica raised her eyebrows.

'You got the coffee too. But you haven't drunk it,' Ayesha challenged.

Jessica's eyes narrowed slightly. An air of mischief Ayesha hadn't seen before danced in them.

'I like watching it congeal,' she said.

* * *

'Course I watched it. I always watch your stuff,' Yaz said.

'Did you hear when they tried to ask a personal question and I steered it back to the statistics?' Ayesha asked.

'Yeah, I think so.'

'It's this technique Frankie taught us in media training. You have your three key points and whatever they ask you, you find a way to bring it back to the key message.'

Yaz nodded.

'It's a bit like if a heckler tries to interrupt your set and you've got to steer it back to where you left off,' Ayesha explained enthusiastically.

She yanked the skinny jeans up her thighs and over her backside. The material fit snugly over her curves with just enough give for her to move freely, breathe easy. She always went for the Spanish brands. They seemed to accommodate a thick thigh and an ample posterior better than the British ones. Yaz didn't have that problem. Her long legs, slim torso and flat butt fit into any UK high street brand with ease. The pastel palettes and shades of blue that swamped the market didn't quite work with her rich, brown skin, but she opted for black most days so she bypassed that conundrum with ease.

'Jessica smashed it too,' Ayesha continued. 'I think we've found a flow now. We kind of bounce off each other. And Frankie was really happy, so ... We've got three more confirmed for next week.'

'That's what I'm talking about,' Yaz said with approval. 'Sis, your profile's getting so big I'll need to call your people just to book in a cotch.'

Ayesha giggled.

'Well, that makes two of us. Booked and busy,' she replied.

Ayesha looked at her friend and felt something new. For the first time in their friendship, she felt like something of an equal. Yaz never dwelt on her success or talked much about her busy schedule, but she had appeared in two write-ups that week alone as the 'freshest face in comedy'.

'Ain't nuttin' fresh about this old mug,' she'd quipped to Ayesha when she'd called to congratulate her. 'Just cos they've only just clocked I exist doesn't mean I haven't been out here hustling for years. But I'll take the exposure, cash the cheque and keep it moving.'

Yaz's next three gigs had sold out and she was booked well into the new year. Now, so was Ayesha. But with one big difference.

'... *Cash the cheque and keep it moving.*' Ayesha's stomach had sunk a little, even as she had murmured her agreement. Some cash, or a cheque even, would be nice. She had turned down three well-paid gigs that month because of the intense schedule Frankie had imposed, and her bank balance had taken the hit. But that was just part of the journey, what you had to do to raise your profile so the big deals could flow in. She was just in that tricky middle bit where she'd outgrown her usual pay bracket and was moving into a much more lucrative one. She just needed to hang on and keep hustling. And there was also something much more important now. The Struggle. Ayesha had been brought into a Movement. A Global Movement that was changing the world. For someone who had spent the best part of her life feeling like the perennial outsider, she now found herself part of something huge. She belonged. And you couldn't put a price on that.

She lifted her chin a little higher, looked at her friend a little straighter.

Yaz sat by the open window and blew easy smoke rings into the night. She nodded to the music which filled her room – 'Battle' by Wookie – and waited for Ayesha to finish getting ready. Yaz had donned a fresh black T-shirt and given her trainers a once over with a wet wipe. Then she'd sparked up the slim, streamlined zoot she'd prepared earlier and relaxed while Ayesha applied the finishing touches, fastened an extra chain around her neck, put in her hoops, and continued with the debrief. Yaz nodded and gently waited for her friend to be done with the day's report, quietly assured that she would return to her.

Whenever they both had a weekend night free of gigs, this was their ritual. Ayesha had woken up only an hour ago. She'd rushed back from the interview and slept for two hours. At 8 p.m. her alarm had woken her and she'd headed over to Yaz's, still dozing on the bus. But now, the garage beat claiming her body, a glass of rum and Coke in her hand and her bestie by her side, the weariness subsided and she found herself replenished.

Ayesha nodded to herself in the mirror, surveyed her outfit one last time, and dance-walked over to the window. Yaz passed her the zoot and she inhaled deeply. With the exhale Ayesha let go of the day's events. Frankie and Jessica and

Joni and the bright lights of the studio, the tightly rehearsed words, the key messages, the lost gigs and elusive cheques all loosened their grip and floated away as the fragrant smoke dispersed into the night air. She turned to her friend, her eyes finally focussing on her, them. Yaz looked back with patient, warm eyes. And now 'Battle' segued into 'Flowers' which mixed into 'A Little Bit Of Luck'. Gun fingers automatically raised in homage. Lips pouted. The music rose and rose, the intensity escalated as the production climbed higher, anticipating the inevitable drop. The two friends looked at each other wide-eyed, they held their breath and waited, and then at the same time brought their hands slamming down.

But it was a bar too early.

They both looked at each other with shame as four beats later, the drop they had anticipated actually dropped. They both fell about laughing.

'Come,' said Yaz with a jerk of her head. They headed out.

They took the tube south. Brixton station was the last stop and they let the flow of the crowd lead them up and out into the street. The neighbourhood that incorporated Windrush Square and Electric Avenue, that had witnessed the riots of 1981, 1995 and 2011, had changed dramatically. The heads lining the escalators were fairer, the skin lighter, the food stalls and music venues blander. But there were pockets down the far end of Coldharbour Lane, and that corner between Brixton and Peckham, where the brown and black people, the first- and second-gens, the diaspora of London, still communed. Ayesha and Yaz worked their way along the line and into the club, the bass line greeting them with a reverberation that shook off the outside world and demanded they be present only to this moment, this beat. They found their spot on the dance floor and looking into each other's eyes, shocked out to a collective rhythm that the whole club was locked into. It was a thing of beauty, a transcendence, a soul-satisfying catharsis. The DJ segued into the infamous opening to Ms Dynamite's 'Boo' and the crowd hit a new high. Exclamations of recognition and appreciation were thrown into the air and the beat rose and rose. For the second time that night the two friends looked at each other wide-eyed with expectation. The beat rose further, the intensity building once again, the precision and genius of the production commanding the very breath of the crowd and then, at the same time, they both slammed down their hands. The whole club followed. This time right on the drop. For the second time that night, the two friends burst into laughter, but this time it was with elation, not embarrassment. Ayesha never felt so free, so carefree, so fully herself as in these moments, these spaces where nothing was demanded of her but that she *be*. She felt herself merge with this giant, raving mass.

Limbs thrown every which way, faces set to dance mode, they shocked.

CHAPTER SEVEN

JULY 2018

Saturday 3.00 p.m.

Yaz dragged her feet as she and Ayesha entered the hallway, trying to hold on to their moment outside in the sunshine for as long as possible before they joined the others. Ayesha also hesitated. She looked down at her phone once more and noticed the single bar still showing in the corner of the screen. She hurriedly thumbed a message.

> Hey, are you on your way?

And pressed send.

Ayesha headed towards the kitchen, but Yaz pulled her to the left.

'Yaz, what are you—?'

'Shh, let's just have a quick look.'

Yaz pushed open a heavy door and they stepped into another unexplored room. The parquet floor glistened under their bare feet. On the walls were shelves reaching to the ceiling and the contents were stylishly backlit. Hundreds of books lined them, interspersed with valuable-looking vases and precious acquisitions from all corners of the world. An antique desk was placed in one corner with a rococo lamp and chair. In another corner two large armchairs with matching footstools and a heavy, standalone lamp arching perfectly over them, faced each other with a thick rug and stone fireplace between them.

Ayesha took in the museum-cum-library, marvelling at the sheer size of it. The money required to buy that number of books, let alone the antiques from around the globe, was unfathomable. She had spent hours and hours of her life dreaming about rooms like this. Cowering under the blankets of yet another strange foster bed, she would escape to her very own version of MTV Cribs – her favourite programme – with endless books and bedrooms for all her foster siblings to finally settle in, a home of her very own bought with money from her successful career that no one could take from her or move her on from. And here it was, in real life, in front of her. She felt a strong urge to move into one of the armchairs, settle down with her small bag of belongings and live her best life. At the same time there was an equally strong impulse to get the hell out of there before she broke something valuable and irreplaceable. And also something else. This dream room wasn't engendering the feelings Ayesha imagined it would. She stood looking at the tasteful decor, the books that promised infinite alternative worlds, and felt anxious, threatened even, a desire to run – *blurt*, as she and Yaz would say. Ayesha shook it off. Decades of living in a bedsit would do that to you – cultivate an agoraphobia of any space bigger than her own tiny flat. She tried to remind herself: She'd been invited. She belonged here.

'Too bad Frankie already bagsied this room,' Ayesha said with awe, 'this is next level.'

'Bitch, I could fully live on the rug alone and be content with my lot,' murmured Yaz.

'Bitch, same.'

And yet, they found themselves backing out of the room. In the hallway once again, the two friends looked at each other. Then Yaz glanced across to another door, a sparkle of mischief and adventure in her dark eyes. She headed over and cracked it open. They both peered in. A room at least twice the size of the one they'd just left stretched out before them. Decadent rugs covered the floor and the plushest sofa Ayesha had ever seen was placed at the centre of the room in a U-shape, facing an immense marble fireplace with a fire blazing despite the summer heat. A selection of iron pokers leaned either side and an ornate wooden-handled hunting rifle was secured above the mantelpiece.

'Okay, she can have her poky library. This vibe is mine.' Yaz took a running leap onto the sofa and sunk satisfyingly deep into its cushions with a muffled thunk. Ayesha did the same and they lay there for a glorious few minutes, relishing the complete decadence of it all.

'Why is the fire lit in the middle of a heatwave?' Yaz suddenly blurted out, disrupting Ayesha's reverie.

'I dunno,' Ayesha shrugged. 'It's welcoming, isn't it? Homely ...'

'Sure, just like Satan's lounge,' Yaz quipped. 'And where's the Wi-Fi? There's got be a router somewhere here.' But Ayesha could hear she was fighting the drowsiness that was overtaking her too, and they said no more. The heat of the fire loosening their limbs further, they listened to the crackling wood and watched the dancing light on the ceiling. A fragrant smoke wafted over them and Ayesha followed the trail to two incense sticks glowing on the window ledge. Ayesha's eyes began to droop. She let herself go with it.

'There you are! We thought you'd made a run for it.' A tinkle of laughter as the voice interrupting their perfect moment enjoyed her own little joke. Ayesha's eyes snapped open again. She and Yaz looked reluctantly in its direction. Clemmie's bejewelled silhouette framed the doorway. 'Will you join us for the first ceremony? The goddesses are waiting,' she sang lightly. But it wasn't really a question.

Yaz looked over at Ayesha grudgingly. Clemmie waited pointedly in the doorway. Ayesha smiled, but with confusion. Jessica still hadn't arrived. They were a goddess short.

'Already?' Ayesha ventured. 'Don't we need to wait for Jessica?'

Clemmie's smile tightened further.

'It's far from ideal,' she replied tensely. 'But as you've seen from the schedule, we have a lot to fit in. The timings are very important, as important as the numbers and the guest list, which was curated very carefully, but we have no choice but to proceed without her for now,' Clemmie concluded and continued to stand expectantly in the doorway.

'Sure,' Ayesha said, forcing herself up and out of the deep comfort of the plentiful cushions, fighting the heat and drowsiness. Yaz sighed and extracted herself from the sofa more slowly. They followed Clemmie into the kitchen.

India and Frankie were sipping more champagne from frosted flutes and leaning towards each other in mischievous cahoots. Clemmie joined Joni who was at the Aga, dipping a ladle into the pot she had been nursing and pouring thick brown liquid into delicate Wedgewood teacups.

'Er, what exactly is that?'

Ayesha spun around to glare at Yaz whose face was screwed up in disgust.

'A unique cacao concoction created specially for this auspicious celebration,' Clemmie replied.

'So basically posh hot chocolate. At three in the afternoon. In forty degree heat,' Yaz returned.

Frankie smirked. Clemmie looked sharply at them both.

Ayesha looked back at Clemmie, a desperate laugh escaping her.

Clemmie paused for a moment, her face hard to read. Then she took a breath.

'Sure,' she replied. 'Posh hot chocolate if you will. With a bit of a kick to help things along.' A flash of dangerous excitement sparkled in Clemmie's eyes. She glanced at India who sparkled back. Yaz frowned.

'What sort of kick exactly?' Frankie asked.

Clemmie turned to address them all.

'All the ingredients are one hundred percent natural and organic, ethically sourced, dairy and gluten free.' Ayesha saw India nod with approval. Clemmie grew an inch. 'You will experience a gentle high, but don't be alarmed,' she explained. 'This is also Mother Nature's uncontaminated gift.'

'Basically, it's all about to get a bit trippy in honour of India's big day,' Joni translated gleefully as she carried on filling the fragile cups with the mysterious brown gunk.

'Something like that,' Clemmie allowed.

'In the spirit of consent, how about you let us in on what we're about to experience so we can make an informed choice?' Frankie insisted loudly. Joni's face drained of joy in an instant. She froze with ladle and cup in hand. Clemmie looked calmly at Frankie.

'I'd be happy to give you a list of ingredients and where they were sourced – even the time of day they were harvested, so precise is my practice,' she returned.

'Clemmie interned with revered shamans on her extended stay in Peru. She's also a certified Ayurvedic practitioner and ceremony birther,' India championed confidently. 'Our minds and bodies are in safe hands.' She took a few steps to the mantelpiece at the end of the dining area and picked up a heavy frame holding a picture of Clemmie alongside a small, ancient-looking South American man dressed in traditional attire. Clemmie's face was painted in dark red stripes and she looked solemnly into the camera. India handed the picture to Frankie, who considered it.

'Well, this is certainly a different kind of collective experience we're about to have,' Frankie said. 'But one of many firsts for the collective this year.'

India retrieved the picture, held up her champagne flute and Frankie clinked it. They downed their drinks.

'Sounds great!' Ayesha enthused, 'Thanks so much, Clemmie, Joni. It smells delicious. Doesn't it, Yaz?'

She looked desperately at her friend, who looked back at her. Yaz shook her head gently, an expression of bemusement on her face. Ayesha continued to plead silently.

'Sure. Sounds delicious,' Yaz eventually conceded. 'Let's get this party started. In fact, Joni, let me help you,' she added with forced enthusiasm, then made her way over to the Aga. Yaz took a cup from Joni and solemnly walked over to India. She handed the concoction to the Queen Goddess first, who accepted it graciously and hungrily from Yaz's hands. Ayesha's shoulders lowered several inches as the activity in the kitchen started up again.

Yaz gamely presented each woman with a cup. Ayesha held hers tentatively, certain the thin china would crack and shatter in her clumsy hands.

Clemmie watched the women carefully, none of them daring to take a sip until they were instructed to do so. She looked towards the doorway several times and then at the heirloom clock hanging on the wall, her lips pursed. Ayesha also continued to wonder when Jessica might arrive. One delicate cup remained beside the Aga unfilled. They waited uncertainly for a moment, cups in hands, until Clemmie sighed and looked at them decisively.

'We will make our way outside for the first circle,' she announced. 'A gentle reminder that photos and social posts are not permitted in our sacred spaces.'

Yaz darted a look at Ayesha, Joni at Frankie. India nodded solemnly.

In the centre of the dining area stood a long, mahogany table with space for at least twenty guests. Along one side of it, large French windows opened onto the back garden.

Clemmie led the women, teacups in hands, through the doors and out onto the patio. The ancient, sun-warmed stone under Ayesha's bare feet gave way to the cool softness of the carefully clipped grass. She followed as Clemmie made her way to the far end of the lawn and waited for the five other women to position themselves. They stood in a circle, India to Clemmie's right.

Clemmie held the silence, commanding with her presence alone the attention of the circle of women. After some time, she turned her head to look at India. India returned the gaze and the two women, draped in their rich fabrics, beamed at each other.

Ayesha watched with a mix of pride and admiration, envy even, at the effortless, regal grace they both possessed. They let the moment linger between them. Yaz stood to India's right. To her right was Joni, then Ayesha, then Frankie. She saw Yaz begin to fidget as the moment endured and Ayesha willed her to hold it down, but soon she too was desperate to move, sit down, get out of the heat of the sun. The teacup was burning Ayesha's hands and she surreptitiously adjusted her hold so she was touching only the handle. Clemmie finally turned her gaze back to the circle. She smiled at the women and raised her cup.

'We have been called to gather here in celebration of a most precious soul. A woman who is the glory of womanhood, the Yin, the Shakti, the Parvati, the Hera. As she takes the sacred step to unite with her twin soul, we pledge our allegiance, our dedication and support, our undying loyalty to her and her journey. We drink.'

Clemmie's raised teacup was brought to her lips and she took three long sips. The other women followed suit, raising their teacups to their mouths and drinking the thick hot liquid. It was not the hydrating refreshment that Ayesha was hoping for. It burnt her tongue and then slipped slowly down her throat, coating it in a sticky hot layer before pooling in her stomach. She glanced at Yaz, silently conceding that she had been right. Hot chocolate in the heat of a scorching summer was not the one.

Clemmie placed the cup on the grass at her feet and joined hands with the women either side of her. The rest followed, finding each other's hands and grasping them. Clemmie looked around the circle and then closed her eyes. The women closed their eyes also.

Another silence ensued. Ayesha listened to the birdsong

made lazy by the heat, then Clemmie's voice rang out clear over it.

'I encourage you to look through your third eye and visualize your higher self. Embody her, feel her power, her fertility, her potency.' She paused as she allowed time for the women to do this. The sun beat down on them. Ayesha tried to remember where her third eye was meant to be. Perhaps somewhere in the vicinity of her forehead that was stinging with the heat of the summer rays.

'And now from your feet, connected directly to Mother Earth, draw up this power too. This potency. This life-giving fertility,' Clemmie urged. Ayesha sighed. She tried to focus on her feet, the tops of which were also stinging now.

'Let the two sources meet at your centre. Take three deep breaths now.'

Ayesha inhaled deeply then exhaled. She inhaled a second time, and released it. On the third she felt a tingling sensation begin to rise from her feet, ascending up through her body until it reached her cranium, a prickling feeling of lightness, elation. She opened one eye and looked over at Yaz whose eyebrows were already raised, and then had to look away as giggles threatened to bubble up inside her.

'Take this power, this potency, and send it to our sister goddess. Bless her with all your being. Feel the power of the circle enhance the blessing six-fold. This is a sacred space. An unbroken space. The goddess circle.'

The tingling in Ayesha's body gently intensified. She felt her eyes begin to roll slightly under her eyelids and tried to go with it. But the giggles threatened to surface again, and she couldn't help but think of Yaz's face, the surprise, the amusement, as her best mate contemplated this strange new high. She heard the faintest of snorts and it was enough. Ayesha burst into giggles at the same time as Yaz. It was awful. So awful she didn't dare open her eyes. Then another laugh bubbled up and she felt the woman to her left shaking. She opened one eye and saw Joni's shoulders quivering, tears streaming down her face as she laughed. One look at Frankie and she too began to chuckle. Ayesha saw a cold smile spread over India's perennially serene face as she seemed to look directly at Ayesha. Clemmie opened her eyes in surprise. Ayesha tried one more time to stop herself from laughing and failed, as another stream of hysterics escaped from her. Yaz wiped a tear away and tried desperately not to look Ayesha in the eye. It only made it worse. Clemmie took a deep breath, composed herself, then she began to sing. Loudly, insistently.

'May the circle
Stay unbroken
Today
Pledge allegiance
To the circle
Always'

She sang the words again. The third time around India joined her. The giggles subsided. A few sighs as the women gathered themselves. Ayesha threw herself into the song, earnestly attempting to make up for her outburst that had set everyone off. It was a simple, eerie melody that wound down the words in semitones. Soon they had all picked it up and the women's voices joined together. They sang and sang, over and over, the short refrain. The voices built in volume and passion, the birdsong halted in surprise. The strength of the united voices added to the high, and as Ayesha's eyes rolled faster, she felt the tingling intensify in her hands – the hands holding those of the women beside her – and they sang and sang.

And they kept singing. Ayesha began to wonder how long it would last. Her voice began to struggle out of her burnt throat which had fast become dry and parched. The hands of the women she was holding became unbearably clammy and she had to concentrate on keeping hold of them. The sun blazed down and she felt herself begin to sway. She didn't dare open her eyes, she willed herself to keep singing, to cling on to the high she'd felt just moments before, to keep the wave of panic that was slowly building inside her from taking over. Any moment now she would have to let go. Any moment now she might faint. But she kept going, as the song looped over and over on itself.

'May the circle
Stay unbroken
Today
Pledge allegiance
To the circle
Always'

The panic suddenly unleashed itself and Ayesha took a breath ready to scream. At that moment her hands were freed by the women on either side of her and the scream was swallowed just in time. She opened her eyes in surprise. The singing had stopped.

A breeze, barely tangible, brushed her skin and the relief was intense. After a pause, the birds attempted a tentative chirp again. Ayesha gathered herself and when she felt steady enough, she raised her head to look at the other women in the circle. They all seemed to have a dazed look on their faces, but it was unclear whether they had experienced anything similar. Spots of pink and purple clouded Ayesha's vision and she had to look down, blink several times to clear it.

'Very good.' Ayesha looked up to see Clemmie regard the circle with approval. She looked surreptitiously over to India, but she was only just opening her eyes. India inhaled deeply and let it out in a loud sigh, her eyes gleaming now, her body energized, her being empowered by the ceremony, the song, all for her.

India met Clemmie's gaze once again and they shared another moment.

'Time for a makeover methinks,' India said. Clemmie nodded once. She took India's hand in hers, glanced at the others, and together they led them all back into the house.

CHAPTER EIGHT

DECEMBER 2017

'It's a big one. Our biggest yet. So I'll be joining you,' Frankie announced as they sat in yet another backstage green room in yet another TV studio.

Ayesha looked at her with surprise. Frankie was very selective about her own media appearances, preferring the younger women take on most of the requests. But a decision had been made because this was a big step up, a live TV debate in a prime-time slot, the biggest exposure for the group so far. So, the whole gang was involved in one way or another – Frankie, Ayesha and Jessica in front of the camera, Joni rushing around behind the scenes like a protective Doberman.

Ayesha considered Frankie with awe. She had made this all happen. Ayesha thought of the years she'd spent hustling to get a decent gig at a comedy night and it all seemed so silly now. Here was someone who had committed decades of her life to fighting for women to be heard, for the justice system to be overhauled and for violence to end. And now Ayesha got to stand by her side on live TV and help change the world. Joni stood quietly nearby, mirroring Ayesha's reverence.

'How about I sit this one out then?' Jessica said. They turned towards her with surprise. She looked weary and fed up and not particularly chuffed at the change of plan.

'We need all hands on deck for this,' Frankie insisted.

Jessica stared at Frankie.

'But I don't want to do it,' she said simply.

Ayesha tried to suppress her shock at her words, but now, looking at Jessica's defiant face, Ayesha realized how tired she was and how much she too wanted to get off the ride, just for a bit, so she could catch her breath and remember why they were doing all this. It had been weeks and weeks, months of relentless events and appearances. They were all wired, weary and had been given no time to recover or even debrief. It was a never-ending schedule that Frankie was in charge of, that Frankie seemed to have endless energy for, and Ayesha was desperate not to let her down.

But Jessica had started to question what they were doing and why, at first quietly to Ayesha, who had no extra capacity to formulate an answer that was anything beyond the practised responses to the questions they got asked over and over in different guises. Then she started to challenge it more openly, asking direct questions to Joni and then Frankie about the group, its purpose and how it would lead to her getting justice.

Ayesha had begun to form her own questions, mostly about how she was going to sustain this all financially. She'd only managed to make a handful of paid gigs in the last few weeks and had slept through the last one, despite setting an alarm. Cash flow was becoming a problem, but no one else seemed to be concerned about this. She waited for someone to mention how they were funding this new lifestyle, but it didn't seem to concern anyone but her. And there was absolutely no way Ayesha would be the first to bring it up.

Joni stood just behind and to the side of Frankie. She bristled at Jessica's response but remained quiet.

Frankie let the words hang in the air for a moment. It somehow made them seem silly, childish. Then she continued.

'I'm going to need everyone to be very much on board and on message today,' she said sternly. 'United in that message. Is that clear?'

It wasn't a question.

'Look, it's my job to keep an eye on the bigger picture,' Frankie continued. 'We're part of a global movement that's effecting real change. That means changes in policy, in law, in systems. I know that's hard to fathom sometimes, but we're closer than you realize. Closer than we've ever been before to really changing things. The fact that our little collective has been afforded a prime-time slot is no accident. We need to play this by the book. My book.'

Frankie's pep talk was sterner, more loaded than ever. Ayesha nodded. Jessica looked down. Joni watched them closely, scrutinizing their allegiance then, seemingly satisfied, headed out first, disappearing to the other side of the cameras. Frankie looked once at Ayesha, then at Jessica and walked out of the room. Jessica made no move to go, so Ayesha stood up. She turned to her.

'Come on,' she said. 'Let's get this one in the can too.'

Jessica rolled her eyes, sighed.

'Look, you don't even need to say anything,' Ayesha tried again. 'We've got *the* Frankie Roberts on our team!'

Jessica looked hard at Ayesha.

'There would be no Frankie Roberts without us,' she said, and walked out into the lights.

The three women made their way onto the set and sat in their allocated seats to the left of the presenter. Opposite them were three men, already seated, with Julian, the programme's seasoned host, at the centre of the set. He nodded to them as they settled, a make-up artist giving him a final blot. They were given the countdown, the theme music played, and the show began.

'Welcome.' Julian began, solemnly. 'Women's rights, the #MeToo movement and global disclosures. A day of reckoning for mankind? Or the beginning of the end for men and their kind?'

More music and the lights homed in on the guests.

'Frankie Roberts, let's start with you.' Julian turned to face the women. 'You are, and have been for several years now, outspoken in your condemnation of violence against women. And in the last few months there has been a surge in disclosures – most of them via social media – and a fresh demand for women's rights to be a priority. Do you welcome this new focus on the very things you've been speaking about for so long?'

Frankie took a breath, a determined hardness in her eyes that Ayesha had witnessed so many times before, a zone she entered when it was time to deliver the message, raise the issue, speak truth to power.

'Well firstly, Julian,' she began confidently, 'I think that men are as much victims of this system we find ourselves trapped in as women. And male suicide rates attest to that. But yes, I am unapologetic in my focus on the deadly repercussions this system has for women and in my opinion this new movement, if we can even call it that, hasn't gone nearly far enough.'

Julian turned to his left.

'Trent, it hasn't gone far enough apparently. Could you comment on that?'

Ayesha looked across the set at the men, taking them in properly for the first time. She tried to remember what they had been told about them. Frankie had said that they were hoping for an MP, maybe a lawyer who would defend the justice system, but nothing had been confirmed with them, even by the time they were making their way to the studio.

The man named Trent smirked, taking his time to formulate a response. He was better turned out than his two companions who both sported long beards and, in one case, a leather waistcoat over a T-shirt topped off with a fedora, and in the other, sunglasses indoors. Trent, on the other hand, was pristine, his skin scrubbed pink, freshly barbered and shaved, in a crisp navy blue suit. His blue eyes were set like hard marbles in his gammon-hued face. Ayesha had seen him before, but she couldn't pinpoint where. He started lightly, almost reasonably, as his colleagues smiled furiously either side.

'Of course it hasn't. It will never be enough. And that's because it's not really about equality at all. We've seen our rights stripped away to nothing. Jobs, parental rights and money being taken from hardworking, honest men and I think we all know that that's what's really driving up the death rates. Those are the facts, not the feelings.'

And suddenly Ayesha knew who he was. An outspoken, men's rights activist with a following that seemed to be increasing with every #MeToo revelation. His media presence had also increased, as he was invited to be the counterpoint to all the PC wokeness that had suddenly erupted across the globe and was apparently destroying men's lives.

For balance.

Ayesha felt the other two women stiffen as they realized at the same time. It was a set-up. Live on TV. They were suddenly acutely aware of each other and, in the middle, Ayesha sat a little taller, trying to maintain a united front.

Julian turned to Ayesha.

'Ayesha. You're a relatively new recruit to this ... movement, thanks to a video that went viral of you speaking out about your experiences in the comedy industry and beyond. What do you think are the biggest obstacles facing women today?'

Ayesha remembered to take a deep breath from her belly before responding with the script she'd been practising the whole week.

'Well, we have new challenges now that women from other eras didn't have to contend with,' she replied. 'Not only are we vulnerable in everyday life – be it at home or at work or just walking down the street – but there's a whole new online world which can be very hard to navigate. You see—'

Julian raised his hand. Ayesha froze mid-sentence, conceding automatically to the power this national treasure of a limb commanded.

'I'll just cut you off there to go to a question from the audience. Yes, yellow jumper in the front.' Julian pointed a knighted finger into the darkness beyond.

A disembodied voice spoke into a microphone that had hurriedly been placed in front of them.

'Yes, hello. I saw that video you did online. You got thousands of views and now you're on the telly. You say women are vulnerable online, but aren't you benefitting from social media yourself? Hasn't it in fact launched your career and been the making of you? That's for the lady in the middle.'

The audience broke into applause.

Ayesha strained to see beyond the bright studio lights. But just like that night at her now-infamous gig, her adversary remained anonymous while she was very much caught in the spotlight.

Julian allowed himself a moment of amusement, and then composed himself. One of the beards smirked too.

'A fair observation, Ms Jones?' Julian said as he tilted his head towards Ayesha.

Ayesha felt the sweat begin to prickle on her skin in the heat of the lights and hoped the layers of make-up they'd applied would hold out a bit longer. She braced herself and recalled what they'd rehearsed.

'Well,' she began carefully, 'I think that when more traditional ways of getting your message across – reporting injustice, inequality, or even crime – don't work, people are resourceful. They find a way to be heard and to speak out to effect change. Women – especially women of colour – are extremely vulnerable online and tend to be exposed to extreme trolling. But it's also one of the few avenues we can use to really express ourselves and find our community—'

Julian directed his lopsided smile at the audience.

'I thought a troll was a little doll,' he admitted drolly.

The audience tittered. Julian turned to his left. 'Clive. Are you a troll?'

The man with the sunglasses widened his smile, leaned forward and jabbed the table with his finger.

'Well, Julian, if defending the rights of men to be men, if speaking out against this epidemic of liberal, woke censorship, if taking down those who are hell-bent on taking away my freedom is trolling, then yes – I am a troll.'

The audience burst into applause. It was like a punch to the gut. Ayesha tried desperately to keep her back straight, her chin up, give away nothing of the turmoil inside. She felt Frankie and Jessica either side of her sitting rigidly, all three stranded in the glare of the lights, trapped in a showdown they hadn't agreed to. Ayesha made out a dark ripple in the audience as several hands shot up.

Julian spun round once more, keen to keep the momentum going. He scanned the raised hands, but then Frankie leaned forward.

'Let's break down what Clive has just said,' she demanded, 'because there's a lot to unpack here and I want to check there's actual meaning behind these ... soundbites. I'm not quite sure what the phrase *the right for men to be men* actually means. What rights is it exactly you're fighting for, and is it the very men in the highest positions of power that you're petitioning? Secondly, you used the word *epidemic* to describe *liberal censorship*. What is your understanding of an epidemic? And isn't *liberal censorship* somewhat of an oxymoron—'

Julian's treasure of a hand rose again.

'That's quite a lot to unpack there too, Ms Roberts. Clive, I'll let you respond to that.' He swung back to the boys.

But it was Trent who leaned in; this time calculated outrage tinged his pink face.

'Look, you can attack my brother's choice of words all you like, but we make no apologies for telling it like it is, simply and clearly so everyone can understand. We stand for family, not feminists. We stand for veterans not vaginas. And we defend the workplace, not the womb!'

It was the man to his right, in the fedora, who started the applause this time, pounding his hands together with force. The audience wasn't far behind. Trent sat back, sated. Ayesha looked closely at the two men either side of Trent. She didn't recognize them, and yet they were all too familiar. The main act's hype men. His angry stooges. And then it occurred to her that maybe that's exactly how people saw her.

Julian looked knowingly into the camera.

'Yes, quite,' he remarked.

'But what does that mean?' Frankie asked with frustration.

But Julian's hand shot out again, silencing Frankie.

'Let's get another question from the audience.'

'I'm just confused to be honest,' came another phantom voice. 'Who is the victim here? Men or women? Can someone, anyone, on the panel, just give us a straight answer.'

A thunderous round of applause. Trent, Clive and Frankie all leaned towards their microphones at the same time, but Julian was quicker.

'Ayesha. Women are the victims. Yes or no?' He pointed a finger straight at her.

Ayesha gaped. Tried to recall the training. *You can turn any question to your advantage,* Frankie had taught them. *Just veer it back to the key message ... Always come back to the key message.* But Julian had already moved on.

'Jessica. We haven't heard from you yet.' He shifted his pointing finger a degree. 'Do you share your colleagues' opinion that time is quite literally up for men?'

Ayesha felt her friend jump slightly at the mention of her name. There seemed to be a long pause, which was probably only a few milliseconds, and Ayesha wondered if Jessica would answer at all.

Jessica sat up and cleared her throat.

'No, Julian. Actually, I don't,' she began, her voice slightly wavering before she caught it and put it back into check. 'I completely understand just how confused the audience member feels because I feel the same. And quite frankly I think this explosion of accusations is complicating things to the point where serious cases like mine are not given the attention they deserve.' Her voice solidified, sharpened. 'When I was a journalist working for a supposedly liberal paper, I was very seriously assaulted by someone high up there and I cannot keep quiet anymore. It's time the media stopped protecting this man and took my allegations seriously and I'm ready to speak out—'

Frankie jumped in.

'It is very important that we look at the criminal justice system first to see why so many women are being failed, and so there is a safe and contained way for women to report what happened to them,' she said loudly.

Jessica froze.

Ayesha's heart was pounding. It was not what they had practiced. Not even close. She felt the bristling of both women on either side of her while all three of them attempted to maintain a calm exterior. Julian homed in on Jessica again.

'This is a very serious allegation, Jessica,' he said gravely. 'Are you sure you want to proceed?'

Ayesha could feel Jessica trembling next to her, but her jaw was set, her chin high.

'Yes, I am. And I won't be silenced anymore. Not for political reasons or—'

'Everyone has a right to speak out about any abuse of power.' Frankie cut in. 'It is incredibly important it is done in a way that doesn't jeopardize any small chance someone has at proper justice—'

Jessica spun around to face Frankie. Ayesha froze between them.

'Why won't you let me speak?' she demanded.

'Not now,' Frankie growled back.

'Who are you trying to protect?' Jessica's voice was shrill, loaded. 'Hmm? Why? What's really going on?'

Frankie looked back at Jessica with shock. She opened her mouth to formulate an answer.

'Which man's life are you going to ruin now, eh? Who's in the firing line this time?' Trent suddenly yelled from across the room, his pink face had turned lobster red with rage, his comrades seethed quietly either side.

Jessica turned away from Frankie.

'I just want the chance to finally tell people what—'

'We've got ten seconds,' Julian asserted.

'It's disgusting that this programme is using taxpayers' money to give a platform to this defamation!' Trent exploded.

'It's about protecting vulnerable women who are—' Frankie shouted over the others.

'Really? Is it really about vulnerable women?' Jessica turned back to Frankie. 'Or is it actually about—'

'Facts not feelings! Family not feminists! Veterans not—'

'And that's the show for this week.' Julian cut through it all. 'Quite a charged one I think you'll agree, but that's what we do here. We bring current, real-world issues to you live and raw. Very raw. Until next week.'

It was over. For a moment, all the panellists glared at each other, breathing angrily, trying to contain the intensity of feeling that was like a six-way standoff. Ayesha was reeling. Everything felt far away and dreamlike. She had no idea what had happened or why it had spiralled into such an awful confrontation. She was desperate to get out from between Frankie and Jessica. The crew began to bustle about around them. Julian exited swiftly. They all got up slowly, dazed. In the buzz of activity Ayesha was nudged further and further away from Jessica. She looked back at her, her face set defiantly, appearing very alone among this flurry of activity. It dawned on Ayesha that Jessica had disclosed for the first time significant details about what had happened to her on live TV. The carefully worded blogs and articles hadn't revealed much about what she'd actually been through. But now Ayesha knew key information about her perpetrator, about the circumstances, about the timeline, along with everyone else watching the show. Jessica looked up and caught Ayesha's eye. Before Ayesha could think of what to say, Frankie was by her side.

'Drink?' Frankie suggested bitterly, without looking at Jessica.

Ayesha nodded.

She didn't quite see where Jessica went; she had no idea where Joni was. Ayesha looked around trying to spot them in the busy studio, hoping to regroup despite the tension of the last few minutes. But Frankie was leading her out through a corridor, seemingly unconcerned about whether the others were following. The click of a backstage door, the blast of cold night air quickly cooling the sweat from the heat of the studio lights, and she found herself out in the street beside Frankie.

Joni was calling Frankie's phone but she ignored it. She ignored everyone. Yaz messaged Ayesha once. Ayesha followed Frankie's lead and didn't message back.

The two women walked the streets of Soho till they came to a pub. An old Victorian watering hole that was a labyrinth of cosy nooks and shadowy alcoves. Frankie got in a couple of pints. Ayesha watched her carefully, looking for the cue as to how to respond to what had just happened. She had assumed they would all somehow end up at the pub together, but it was suddenly clear that for some reason, the others weren't invited. Frankie looked shaken, defeated almost, but there was anger there too. She was livid. Ayesha held on to that, hoping it was enough to pull them all through this.

'Cheers.' Frankie said grimly, as she raised the pint glass and took several gulps.

This was the first time, Ayesha realized, that she had found herself alone with Frankie. She felt a sudden urge to prove herself worthy of this moment. She fought against the shock that had literally struck her dumb since Jessica's outburst, struggled desperately to think of something to say.

'Well, just when I thought I'd had my toughest gig ...' she tried weakly.

Frankie managed a grimace and then deflated again. She

chewed the inside of her mouth for a while, an angry glint in her eye.

Ayesha tried again.

'I'm sure you've faced much worse over the years,' she said lightly. 'You probably take this kind of thing in your stride. All part of the—'

'We were ambushed. We were fucking ambushed. On live TV,' Frankie blurted out. 'And what was she thinking? Where did that all come from? It was crazy talk. She's so bloody naive. Not only did she fuck it up for us, but she could have cost herself any chance of getting justice.' Frankie stopped as abruptly as she'd started, chewing away again angrily at the insides of her mouth. Her phone buzzed again. She switched it off, let it drop with a clatter on the table.

'Who, Jessica? I mean, yeah, that was mad. Where the fuck did that all come from?' Ayesha said with more conviction, suddenly keen to distance herself from her outburst.

She still didn't understand why Frankie had chosen her to escape with, why they were ignoring Joni, but as Frankie's chosen confidante for this situation, it felt very important that Ayesha get this right.

Frankie shook her head, still seething, still chewing. Ayesha shook her head too as her mind raced to fill the silence once more. No more jokes. This was not the time for jokes. Outrage, that was what Frankie felt, and what Ayesha should be feeling too. But she had nothing. Felt nothing. She racked her brain for the right thing to say, but years of conditioning had trained her to keep very quiet in moments of conflict – especially around angry people. And her mind had gone blank, her mouth remained shut, however hard she tried.

She watched Frankie carefully. Frankie leaned away, turned her head to the side in private contemplation. Ayesha panicked, suddenly scared she was losing her.

'Do you ... reckon she was in on it?' she blurted out.

Frankie looked up. She waited for Ayesha to continue.

'I mean, I'm just spitballing,' Ayesha said, improvising desperately, 'and you know her better than I do but ... is there a chance she planned it? Maybe even got offered some kind of deal to—'

Frankie slapped the table hard. The drinks jumped, as did Ayesha.

'I mean, fuck that. Fuck it. Not again, for fuck's sake. I can't go through this all again.' Frankie's voice quivered with emotion, her face red with pain and rage.

Ayesha tried to keep up.

'I ... I don't—'

'Do you know the time I've put into getting these guys onside?' Frankie demanded straight into Ayesha's face. 'The fucking hours of schmoozing with the right journalist, the right OBE, the right MP? Just to get us some airtime. The amount of foolish young women who I bring in and train up and after five minutes they think they know how to play the fucking game?' Frankie sat back, shaking her head. 'She has no idea. They're playing her, and she can't see it. She used us. She used us to get five minutes in the limelight to push her own agenda and now she's burnt all her bridges.' Frankie folded her arms and sat breathing heavily, angrily.

Ayesha's heart sank. She hadn't really meant what she'd said. It was more to fill in that excruciating silence. And now, thanks to her, Jessica was enemy number one. She suddenly felt awful, wished desperately she could take it back.

'It was just a theory,' she tried, 'But come to think of it, it's a bit far-fetched.'

Frankie stopped her chewing and glared at Ayesha. Ayesha raced to explain.

'I mean ... sure, she can be a bit self-involved, but I don't think she's that calculating to be honest. Or that clever,' she added, trying to get the right balance between defending Jessica and appeasing Frankie at the same time.

Frankie looked away again.

'Fuck it. That's it,' she said, stabbing the table with her finger. A full stop.

'What do you mean?' Ayesha asked.

'We're not doing any more of those,' Frankie decided.

'Okay.' Ayesha nodded, relieved that Frankie seemed to be veering away from condemning Jessica.

'Every time we agree to one of those, we're being co-opted back into the game,' Frankie explained. 'And the game's rigged. It will always be rigged. Just like the system ...'

Ayesha kept nodding, trying to follow.

'So, we step out of the ring. We don't play a game that's rigged.'

'No way,' Ayesha replied.

Frankie leaned forward over the sticky pub table.

'We should never have been waiting to be invited in anyway,' she said conspiratorially, quietly. 'The whole point is that we're dealing with an epidemic. It touches everyone's lives and that means we automatically have a huge audience hungry for content. So we provide it. But on our terms.'

'Yes! Brilliant,' Ayesha gushed, relieved to see Frankie galvanized again, finding a way to keep it all going. 'Our own content. Fucking brilliant.' She took a messy gulp of beer, banged the glass down on the table a bit too hard.

Frankie sat back. 'Those mainstream appearances have served their purpose. They've made people aware of who we are and now we can branch out on our own.'

Her gaze had been on Ayesha throughout, but in a vague way as she reached for something, searched, formulated. Now Frankie really focused on her.

'And we haven't made nearly enough of your potential.'

Ayesha blinked with surprise.

'There just hasn't been space to make use of your gift, Ayesha. You're funny. You're really fucking funny. And if this movement needs anything, it's a sense of humour.'

Ayesha beamed. Frankie's approval felt like the sun itself, and she let herself bask in it, breathe it in. She was close to tears. It felt like ages since she'd cracked a joke, or even laughed. She realized how much she missed it, and how relieved she was to get a chance to do it again. Permission, almost.

Frankie leaned forward again, her eyes ablaze now.

127

'I think we work really well together,' she enthused. 'We're different, you and me. We play off each other. It works.'

Ayesha nodded enthusiastically, felt it to be true. Frankie and Ayesha. What a duo. A perfect complement of person-alities. The possibilities suddenly seemed endless. And thoughts of Jessica and the others faded swiftly.

'And I know exactly who should join us,' Frankie contin-ued. Ayesha blinked again, trying to keep up with Frankie's train of thought. The image of them as the ultimate duo, a picture of the two of them framed and placed at the centre of Frankie's wall of photos splintered into something hazy, unclear.

'What time is it?' Frankie asked, glancing down at Ayesha's phone. She tapped the screen. Ten to ten. Frankie did a quick calculation in her head, downed the rest of her pint and stood up.

'Come on.'

They caught the tube eastwards and jumped out at Old Street, walking further east into a maze of converted warehouses and reclaimed industrial buildings. Everyone they passed was young and beautiful and creative and edgy. This was not the city Ayesha had grown up in. These were not the people she recognized as sharing the same classroom, estate or corner shop. The same grief and horror in the last year ... These were the ones she had glimpsed so many times from the top of the bus and longed to be amongst. But walking beside Frankie, Ayesha smirked condescendingly at her old self. So desperate, so naive. She glanced over at Frankie. *They* were the real deal. *They* were really doing something. Shaking things up – not just for the sake of it, but to really change things for the better. A duo.

She watched Frankie move effortlessly, confidently through them, almost as if walking directly at them, forcing them to change course. Ayesha followed in her slipstream. Frankie glanced back at her and grinned mischievously. Then they turned into a car park that was filled with pop-up stalls – some selling food, some drink, some selling art, some blaring out music – all with an orbit of these trendy twenty-somethings who had reclaimed and upcycled this corner of her metropolis. Frankie circumnavigated it all and headed through the entrance to one of the buildings overlooking the car park and up the stairs. Ayesha followed.

The old brick walls were painted white and the industrial details on the stairs, the windows, the ceiling had been preserved. More beautiful, cool people passed them on the stairwell that wound in tight squares up through the converted warehouse floors. When they got to level 4, Frankie glanced over her shoulder at Ayesha and led her through to a corridor with several doorways leading off it. They were all open and people were wandering in and out of each one. Ayesha peered into the first one and saw a room full of bright, modern artwork. Some pieces covered the wall, more leaned against it in rows. In one corner, a desk with a pot full of paints, spray cans, and a neat pile of colourful business cards. A similar set-up in the next room, and the next. At the end of the corridor they turned right, and the space opened up into a vast central area. It was much darker here and the music was louder. Dry ice filled the air and coiled down Ayesha's throat. There were groups gathered in the corners talking animatedly, but a much bigger crowd was gathered around something in the centre of the room. The two women weaved their way through the circle of people and came to the edge of the centre of the crowd, facing into the middle. A naked woman stood in an ever-changing spectrum of colourful lights. Across her body were clusters of words written in something red and dripping. She twisted and squirmed, gyrated slowly to the rhythm of what Ayesha realized now wasn't music, but recorded voices amplified around the space. They all watched, mesmerized, as she writhed, the lights catching different words which appeared to be carved into her skin. It took a while for Ayesha to tune into the voices playing overhead. They were snippets of accounts of some kind and it slowly dawned on her it was a montage of different accounts of being raped. The phrases written on the woman's body were a transcript of the recordings.

Ayesha felt her throat constrict. She dragged her gaze away from the naked, bloody woman and looked around at the audience. The smoky lights trained on her bled into the surrounding darkness and revealed the first couple of layers of faces. They all seemed captivated. Transfixed. Locked in somehow. The piece built in intensity, the voices and descriptions becoming more desperate, her twisting and writhing more extreme, contorting herself into painful positions. Drops of red liquid fell from her. The appalling words landed on Ayesha like a physical violence. A detail of one account, a phrase of another; individual words all came together to form something so like her own unspoken story it catapulted her into another place and time where unthinkable and unspeakable things were being done. She looked around wildly, trying to anchor herself to something in the present, but the glee of the intoxicated crowd, the fervour of the performer made it even more appalling. Ayesha needed it all to stop, felt impossibly trapped there at the edge of the circle, next to Frankie who was watching with intense exhilaration. She tried to block out the desperate voices, concentrate on something concrete, but the ever-morphing lights made everything a sea of impermanence and she could hold on to nothing. It was horrific. And yet they continued to watch, enthralled.

And then the lights snapped off. Silence. Then applause. Loud, passionate applause for the horror show that had left Ayesha reeling. As her eyes adjusted to the sudden darkness, she could just make out someone walking to the centre, covering the performer in something and guiding her off-stage. When the lights came on, much brighter now, she had disappeared.

Frankie turned to Ayesha.

'That's India.' she said.

Ayesha followed Frankie through the blinking crowd, who were just beginning to emerge from India's powerful trance. She took big gulps of smoky air, trying to gather herself again, the remnants of that acute anxiety still lingering in her body, still locked in her throat. Through a small door at the far end of the spacious room, the two women stepped into a tiny space, not much bigger than a broom cupboard. It was stocked with a range of art resources – from paints, pencils, brushes, to canvasses, easels and tools. It smelled strongly of white spirit and oil paint. It also appeared to be serving as a dressing room. A chair had been placed at the back of the room, facing a makeshift table made out of a horizontal easel with a mirror perched on it. India sat on the chair, a silk kimono shrugged off her shoulders and pooled at her naked waist while the most beautiful man Ayesha had ever set eyes on carefully and methodically wiped the red lettering from her body.

'So this is where the cool kids hang out.' Frankie's signature grin was firmly set in India's direction. India turned, gracefully, and the man paused mid-wipe and looked up also. His dark eyes matched his thick black hair, a perfect beard and moustache framing his impossibly symmetrical face, his colouring very similar to Ayesha's. His gaze settled on her for a moment and she couldn't help but smile shyly. He did not smile back, but allowed his eyes to move to Frankie, then back to India where they remained.

'Daughters of Hera. How very blessed this room is. You made it,' India beamed back.

'Course we did. We wouldn't let a little gig on a live TV show get in the way of the important stuff,' Frankie replied warmly.

The two women beamed at each other. India turned to Ayesha.

'Ayesha. I've heard so much about you. Welcome,' she said.

Ayesha's heart swelled. India knew who she was. Ayesha wasn't actually sure who India was, but it was clear that she was Someone, and that not knowing her was an oversight.

'Thank you! Thanks so much. That was really, wow, super powerful. Like nothing I've ever . . . No really it was . . . amazing,' Ayesha gushed.

'Essential yet messy work,' India replied. 'Messy in more ways than one, but it is what I was called to perform. As were you. We are performer–sisters, no?'

'No, sure. Yes, totally,' Ayesha blurted.

The gorgeous man continued wiping India's body tenderly. India turned her gaze slowly on him and their eyes met. He paused. They shared a moment then India turned back to the two women.

'This is my partner in creative crime, my equal, my fiancé, Hassan.'

Hassan bowed his head at Ayesha who waved uncertainly. He was younger than India, younger than Ayesha, and yet it was the most perfect match she had ever seen. This couple, sitting in an art cupboard, he wiping her naked body of fake blood with such care, her silk kimono draped around her haunches, also stained with red, probably ruined, but all in the name of such important, powerful art. And once again, for the umpteenth time that month, Ayesha wondered what her life had become. A surge of gratitude at just being there, witnessing this, them, overwhelmed her for a moment. And they all stood in this tableau as the man continued with his careful work and India allowed herself to be watched and wiped.

When some moments had passed, India broke the silence.

'If I know you well, Ms Frankie Roberts, then there's more to this visit than just an appreciation of my performance art piece,' she said, gently probing. 'What are you cooking up in that cauldron of yours this time?'

Frankie laughed and returned the mischievous look.

'You know me too well, Ms Baxter-Wright,' she conceded. 'The cauldron is indeed bubbling with ideas and schemes and collaborations and we three feature heavily.'

They glanced at Ayesha, including her in the clan, and she felt herself blush.

'Of course,' India replied. 'It was only a matter of time.'

Hassan finished wiping the last remnants of red from her leg. India swivelled around in her chair, still naked apart from the ruined kimono. She crossed her legs and opened her arms.

'Pray, tell.'

CHAPTER NINE

JULY 2018

Saturday 4.00 p.m.

Ayesha was parched. She followed the group back into the dining area and tried to manoeuvre around the others to get to the kitchen sink. A mug was shoved into her hand. It was blessedly cool. She gulped hungrily only to feel bubbles fizzing up into her nose moments later. She looked up to see Frankie's grinning face.

'Cheers,' she said, holding yet another bottle of champagne and clinked glasses with Ayesha. Disoriented by the tingling that was travelling up and around her scalp, and confused by the relief of the cold drink in her hand, Ayesha couldn't quite figure out if the champagne was quenching her thirst or making it worse. She looked longingly at the large sink at the other end of the room and the bodies in between, and resignedly took another sip. The liquid tickled and cooled her throat. Frankie watched with approval.

Frankie, the living legend. The one who had introduced Ayesha to the others, brought her in, taken her under her activist wing and helped her find her inner change maker. Frankie who had been consistently shouting the same message for decades, before it was Hollywood to do so. Ayesha watched her grinning friend swigging her bubbles and topping herself up. She tried to think clearly, look at her with fresh eyes. What made Frankie Roberts Frankie Roberts? It was that consistency, the doggedness that kept her on message year after year, despite the fickleness of the rest of the world. A sadness came over Ayesha then, at the realization that she wasn't like Frankie. Sure, she'd had a moment, an outburst of frustration that someone had recorded, something that was thankfully articulate enough to make some sort of sense, some sort of impression, but there was no consistency. Ayesha was a chameleon, changing colour whenever needed, modifying accent and outfit, allegiances and expressions, to fit in, to survive, to belong. There was no consistency without Frankie to keep her on track. But just as this thought ebbed, a new realization dawned on Ayesha. Because that consistency of Frankie's was also rigid. And it stiffened her being and body, making her awkward, taut, slow to laughter. And so Frankie drank. Pints and wine and bubbles. When she wasn't on stage or on camera or just *on*, Frankie had a glass of something in her hand and always made sure you had one too. And Ayesha obliged, often not really up for drinking, but because Frankie insisted, and with Frankie incapable of small talk, the awkward quiet proved too much even for a seasoned silence-filler like Ayesha. And so she clinked glasses and drank. It didn't so much relax Frankie as soften the edges a little, but that would do.

Joni sidled up and playfully took Frankie's glass out of her hands. She took a sip and returned it to her, smacking her lips ironically.

'A good year,' she said, a glint in her eye, which was firmly locked onto Frankie.

'Is that right?' Frankie retorted sardonically.

'Yep.' Joni grinned.

'And what year would that be?' Frankie tilted her head playfully.

Joni held her gaze, her mind working hard.

'The good one,' she replied, finally.

They laughed. It was always easier when Joni was around. Her natural warmth and effortless way cancelled out Frankie's stilted demeanour somehow. Ayesha realized what a difference it made to her to have Joni here and a wave of affection for this cheeky Essex gal washed over her and added to the blissful high that had swiftly returned. She wanted to say something, but the moment passed, and she was left looking from Joni's mischievous expression to Frankie's amused grin and back again, a wide smile on her own face too. The fizzing in her head increased and she blinked slowly as a wave of love washed over her and out towards the two women.

Frankie eventually looked away. Ayesha caught a moment

of dejection pass over Joni's face before she quickly gathered herself again. Frankie was looking over the heads of the other women.

'What's the hold up? I thought we were having a make-over?' she called to the room.

A makeover. That sounded a bit more like it. Ayesha perked up at the thought of something more familiar. The distress she had felt during that strange ritual dissipated as she pictured them all applying lipstick, spraying Frankie's hair with glitter, doing Yaz's nails. She was quite good at all that grooming. Maybe it was the Middle Eastern in her, but Ayesha had a knack for always being nicely turned out. Come to think of it, she'd been eyeing Joni's eyebrows for some time, and was keen to give them a shape.

Ayesha looked instinctively for Yaz and saw her in the corner of the dining room, India talking to her in secretive tones, gesturing to her dress and then playfully holding a piece of the fabric against Yaz's leg. Yaz stood still, an amused look on her face, observing India coolly. Their faces suddenly twisted and contorted, and for a moment Ayesha was sure she saw them look at her and laugh. It sent a jolt of panic through her, but when she looked again, India held her dress as before, Yaz retained her distance. Ayesha shook her head, trying to clear it and reached out for something solid to hold on to.

Clemmie glided over to Frankie.

'We thought we'd wait a little longer to see if our seventh and final sister soul would arrive.' All three women looked confused for a moment, and then they remembered: Jessica.

'She's already missed one ceremony, which is not ideal. We really do need the seven for optimum potency,' Clemmie explained. There was an apologetic but at the same time condescending tone to her voice. *You really should have figured it out*, it said, *it's quite a chore to have to explain the basics to you.*

Ayesha felt them all tense up. Jessica. With everything that had happened between them, why had India chosen to invite her? Was it some kind of power move? Or maybe, like Ayesha, she too had kept in touch privately. She thought back to those precious late-night conversations and wondered if India had needed them too. Ayesha looked over at her and couldn't quite imagine that level of vulnerability, the rawness that was only ever revealed in those calls that had become so important to Ayesha.

'Yeah, what is the deal with that?' Frankie put her glass down with a little too much force. Joni stiffened, looked from the glass to Frankie and back again. 'I had no idea you and Jessica were so close.'

India paused her conversation with Yaz and turned to the group slowly. She looked directly at Frankie.

'What's the question, Frankie?' she asked calmly.

'The question is simply, why have you invited Jessica?' Frankie responded, just as calmly.

India smiled, took her time.

'Why wouldn't I invite Jessica?'

'How's that choice working out for you?' Frankie countered.

'Are you troubled about how it will work out?' India replied.

'Did you take enough trouble over making that decision?'

'What do you mean?'

'Was it just numbers you considered? Or did you consider dynamics too? Loyalty? Integrity? Family even?'

Ayesha's head moved from one to the other as this bizarre tennis match of questions played out. Their voices remained composed, dangerously so, the quiet quizzing worse somehow than outright yells and accusations. Ayesha's head swam once more. The edges of Frankie's and India's faces jarred suddenly and then took on a monstrous aspect, snarling and hissing at each other. Ayesha gasped, and then they swiftly returned to normal. She fought desperately to keep their features in place.

India smiled wider.

'To clarify, I am free to invite whoever I want.'

'Of course you are. I just wouldn't want such a significant moment of yours to be compromised in the same way mine was. I hope we can all learn from my mistakes,' Frankie said steadily.

Joni put a hand on Frankie's arm. She did not respond.

Ayesha's eyes rolled. She tried to stay focused, desperately hoping a kindness would be uttered about Jessica that would dissipate the tension and level her out a bit. The fizzing intensified and the jolt she'd felt earlier was close, threatening to morph this scene into a devilish tableau at any moment. She breathed deeply and kept her eyes on India, willing her to stay as India and not the gruesome gargoyle she had momentarily turned into seconds ago.

India softened half a degree. She tilted her head.

'In a funny way I'm almost grateful to Jessica. Her actions led to you and I reconnecting and rebirthing the collective in its new form. She made space for me.' She twinkled.

Ayesha marvelled at India. How she somehow seemed above all misunderstandings, controversies and politics. She was there to lead, to be followed, literally. Just like Frankie. Ayesha longed to learn how to be like that. She thought of India's socials. Her online followers. They were in their tens of thousands. How did someone know so many people? It seemed somehow connected with her ability to assume a position slightly above the rest of them. It allowed her to always be cool with everyone because she'd never stoop to falling out with anyone.

Ayesha's mind flashed back over the people who had left her over the years, her parents, key workers, agent, and she felt a sinking in her stomach, a familiar shame, the pleasant fizzing in her head dissipating rapidly.

And then a flash of red and Jessica's cool, pale face filled her mind. She felt a stab of sadness and guilt as she realized how much she missed Jessica. The hours of being in her company had become familiar, almost pleasant. She could see her slowly disappearing from her life. And it was her fault. She had burnt that bridge. And she had planted the seed that had ostracized Jessica from the group. She was the opposite of India.

A forced lightness came into Frankie's voice whenever the night of the live TV debate was referred to. Just like Ayesha's rant, it had gone viral. The weeks that followed had been a relentless wave of requests for comment, thousands of mentions that were impossible to keep up with, demands for a rematch and a range of hashtags including #SaveOurMen and #Justice4Jessica. Jessica was still officially part of the gang, but she was tolerated at best. India was on board now. Things were moving even faster, and Jessica seemed to be fading from the group.

Ayesha looked back at Frankie. Her face remained stern, her chin raised, but there was also a respect there, a small acquiescence, a concession made for India's justification. Joni also watched her carefully. Ayesha felt that involuntary part of her take over and before she knew it, she was saying something. Loudly.

'Well, I don't know about you lot but I am dying to get into some neon polyester, throw on a pink sash and plastic crown and sing Spice Girls!' she announced.

They all spun around to look at her. Yaz almost spat out her drink.

'Oh God, no, it's not that kind of ... of ...' Clemmie couldn't even finish her thought, so overwhelmed was she at the numerous offences Ayesha had managed to cram into one short phrase. Revulsion and shock twisted her delicate features.

'I'm joking. Of course not. It's not that kind of hen do. Obviously,' Ayesha replied quickly. She looked appeasingly at India who regarded her coolly.

Clemmie bristled at the phrase *hen do*. Ayesha shrunk. The melting mass of pink congealing in her car boot flashed before her mind's eye again. She shook her head, trying to eliminate the disturbing image.

The high that had been dissipating rapidly took another dip, swiftly followed by a wave of anxiety as she realized she'd got it wrong, again.

'The makeover we have in mind is quite different to what you just described,' Clemmie explained patiently.

Ayesha nodded, chastened, and sighed deeply.

'It was just a joke,' she tried weakly.

'A what?' Clemmie asked confused.

'A joke. Just something to lighten the … fill in the …' Ayesha gave up.

Joni suddenly grabbed Frankie's glass and drained it.

'Right. Come on then. Let's pimp this party out, India-style,' she announced.

Joni took Frankie's and Ayesha's hands in each of hers and led them over to India and Yaz. Clemmie pushed through them to stand in front of India. She cleared her throat and reassumed control of the moment.

'It is time for your second transformation,' she said mysteriously. India smiled.

'Yes. Of course,' she replied. With a final glance at Yaz, India stepped through the group and headed out of the room.

Clemmie watched her go and then turned to the remaining women.

'Follow me,' she said.

Back through the dining room, the kitchen and into the hallway. To the right of the kitchen entrance, leading behind the library, was a corridor and the women filed along it. Yaz was in front of Ayesha and she looked back at her as they headed along the narrow space in single file, her eyebrows raised, a slightly amused look on her face. Ayesha knew this was her way of checking in. They'd been separated for a while now. A lot of weird stuff had gone down. She put her hands on Yaz's shoulders and they congaed along the corridor. It didn't take much. Ayesha felt the warmth of her friend's shoulders under her hands and revelled in it. The looming dark cloud lifted swiftly in the presence of Yaz's bright rays.

The roof was lower here, everything cosier and earthier somehow. This felt manageable to Ayesha, and with her hands firmly anchored to her friend, the dimensions of this space containing them comfortably, the buzz returned and a quiet giggle escaped from her lips. The corridor came to an abrupt end at a room that appeared to be part of an exten-sion to the main building. Ayesha tried to keep her bearings. Failed. Clemmie raised a simple wooden latch and the door opened. She took two steps down into the room beyond. They filed in. Gasps and excited chatter reached Ayesha before she saw for herself. The room was a modest size compared to the others, although it was hard to tell exactly because it was packed with stuff. Dark blue wallpaper covered the four walls with a pattern of bright peacock feathers repeating across it. Most of the space in the room was taken up with open racks of outfits draped on hangers, piled onto high shelves and spread onto chairs and stools. Saris, feathered headdresses, animal masks, ornate jewellery, body paint and so much more. The women were already elbow-deep in the racks and stacks of material, exploring, considering, experimenting, matching. Clemmie sat herself in one of the plush rococo chairs that was free of accessories and watched contentedly as the others chose their attire. Ayesha looked for India, but she wasn't there.

Yaz was more tentative than the others. Ayesha watched her glance at the bright colours the other women were considering and then slowly pick her way through, searching for something subtler. But there was something here for everyone. Soon she was pulling out a full-length fitted leather coat in charcoal grey and rich dark teal leather trousers. Ayesha turned to the rack closest to her and started to pull out a silk kimono, then a brightly coloured South American floor-length dress, a royal blue sari with gold thread detailing and tiny mirrors sewn into it. She settled on the South American one – generous lengths of deep green with large bright flowers hand-woven into it. Joni considered an ornate golden ancient Egyptian headpiece, then chose a bright red Ziggy Stardust wig and experimented with what looked like a badger's tail. Frankie was painting her skin blue.

This rush of content and colours pushed her to a new high and Ayesha waded through it as if in a technicolour dream. She lost all sense of time in that room. Every drawer opened revealed more treasures, every hanger a new possible iteration of her inner goddess. Once the main outfit was chosen, there were the accessories, the jewels, the headpieces, anklets, toe rings, nose rings, the make-up, the multi-hued glitter and body paint, the hair, the masks, the tails, the furs.

Clemmie added a peacock feather to her headdress, smeared golden sparkle onto her cheekbones, pressed a bhindi into her third eye, and made suggestions, adjustments, additions, revisions to each woman's outfit until they were all finally bedecked in a mesmerizing array of fabrics and colours. To Ayesha's surprise, Clemmie then held up her phone, turned the camera on herself and with the others in the background, pressed the round white button.

It was an eclectic clan. As Ayesha looked around, there was a moment of panic as the clashing costumes created a nightmarish tableau. They were very suddenly all horrific creatures, herself included – outcasts from every corner of the globe, every genre and era thrown together in this purgatory room. Ayesha gripped onto the arm of a chair and took a deep cleansing breath. She looked again, forcing the women back into their original shapes. Taken individually, each woman looked remarkable, the Narnia-cum-superhero version of themselves, and they beamed back at her and she in turn smiled. For a while they all stood there grinning at each other, their blinking slowed. All apart from Clemmie who remained staring at her phone, her face a serene smile, her fingers working quickly, frantically. Typing then scrolling hungrily. Ayesha remembered vaguely that they weren't allowed phones in sacred spaces. And she still hadn't been given the Wi-Fi code ...

Then a voice cut through.

'What a glorious sight to behold. The deities have truly landed on Earth.'

In one deft motion Clemmie spun around and pocketed her phone, the serene smile never wavering.

They turned to see India standing in the doorway, a couple of steps above them. She had changed outfits. A bespoke poncho draped decadently over her shoulders with pink, purple and turquoise hand-sewn patterning and a low-cut neckline. Her legs were bare, with suede moccasin boots on her feet. On her head was an enormous Native American headpiece with feathers dyed the same colours as her poncho. Handmade golden earrings swung so low they grazed her shoulders. Her hair had been worked into long, dark plaits with a severe mid-parting and freshly applied pink, turquoise and purple war paint adorned her face. She was a vision. Once again, Clemmie led the applause, loudly and assertively, insistently even. Joni joined in enthusiastically, willing Frankie to do the same. Ayesha clapped uncertainly, Yaz refused to clap. India beamed down at her goddesses, seemingly oblivious to controversy, absorbing the acclaim like a hoover.

Again, the applause seemed to last an uncomfortably long time. Long enough for Ayesha to take in India's costume in painful detail. It wasn't okay. And it didn't get any better the more she looked. She felt Yaz's disapproval and knew how much it was costing her not to say anything, because it was costing her the same. Once again, Ayesha felt that excruciating pull between wanting so much for it all to be all right, for them all to get along, and the growing responsibility she felt to call this shit out. In the end, she didn't have to.

'Why aren't you clapping, Yaz?'

The singsong tinkle in Clemmie's voice was unmistakably dangerous. India turned to Yaz too. They all did. The clapping subsided.

Yaz remained calm.

'What am I meant to be clapping?' Yaz kept her tone calm, flat, somehow exposing Clemmie's artifice.

Clemmie did a half laugh of mock surprise. She turned to India, made a gesture that took in India's whole look.

'How could you not want to celebrate this vision?' she gushed incredulously.

'Because it's problematic,' Yaz replied flatly.

Every muscle in Ayesha's body was taut. She couldn't stand conflict, especially not between the people she loved. Her mind raced to think of the thing that would make this all okay. A joke maybe?

India raised a bejewelled hand in placation.

'She's right,' she declared, looking at Yaz closely. 'This ensemble is potentially problematic, but my motives are pure. I see it as a way of celebrating all women everywhere. Donning their traditional dress – with my own playful spin which expresses my sexuality freely with no need for performed modesty – is a way of bringing all women into our space, our circle. I have had the extreme privilege of travelling the world extensively, and I don't know if you know this, but I do workshops with disenfranchised women in developing countries. For free sometimes. And then there's my connection to Hassan. Our future children will be Of Colour,' she cupped her stomach with both hands, the wooden bracelets on her arms tonking against each other. 'That is something I want to embrace with my eyes and arms wide open.'

Ayesha watched Yaz carefully. Yaz was listening to India with a frown of confusion and growing alarm. She waited for further clarity, but India seemed to have come to the end of her speech. Satisfied she'd clarified the situation, India sighed in conclusion. Yaz seemed to have been stunned into silence.

Clemmie waited a while longer, letting India's words really land, then stepped up onto the threshold and gave India a long embrace, carefully preserving both their looks. Joni turned around and looked at the other women. Then she grabbed a jar of something and smeared a line of gold down Frankie's blue forehead. Yaz looked at Ayesha who smiled weakly back. Eventually, Yaz turned away, shaking her head, and picked up a pot of something black. Ayesha felt a rush of relief, then elation. She needed to hug someone, but it was clear that Yaz was not to be approached right now. Impulsively, Ayesha surged forward and embraced Clemmie and India who were still embracing each other, trying at the same time to respect their personal space and also convey her deep gratitude. India stiffened, allowed herself to be hugged momentarily, and then held Ayesha at arm's length.

'Our very own Frida,' she exclaimed, her hazel eyes gleaming, but coldly. Ayesha looked down at her floral dress, then back up at India. She saw herself through India's eyes. Frida. Yes. Of course.

She realized that this was the closest she had been to India all day and began to formulate an apology, an explanation for her behaviour the last time they had been together.

But Clemmie was also scrutinizing Ayesha's look carefully.

'We just need to sort out that deliciously unruly hair of yours,' she mused, leading Ayesha to a chair and pushing her into it. Clemmie produced a brush from somewhere and before Ayesha knew what was happening, the brush was clawing its way through her thick curls. She fought a wave of horror as she realized too late that there was no saving them. Once they were touched by a brush, they turned into a mess of frizz and static that could only be undone with a very specific ritual of washing, conditioning and sculpting and a complex variety of products, none of which she had brought with her.

'Oh wow! You're really going for it,' she managed through gritted teeth. It was the same sensation as scraping nails down a chalkboard. She felt slightly nauseous. India looked on, fascinated.

'It's so thick and knotted. You really ought to take better care of it,' Clemmie's voice lectured from behind her over the rasping of the brush. Ayesha opened her mouth to protest.

'Don't worry, I have coconut oil.' Clemmie continued.

The brushing stopped abruptly. Ayesha was grateful not to have a mirror in her eyeline. She tried not to focus on the static electricity that crackled around her scalp and in her ears. It was unbearable.

India continued to watch her carefully. She brought a

perfectly manicured hand up and touched Ayesha's hair. Ayesha tried not to recoil.

'You look so different. Wilder,' India said as she scrunched and stroked. 'You really should wear your hair more natural, Ayesha. Reclaim it.'

'I do. It is natural. Just not—'

Two hands banged against the top of her head and then ran down the sides, slathering on way too much oil as they went. Ayesha felt traces of it grease her earlobes.

'It's completely natural and organic. All the way from Sri Lanka. So much better than those hideous products full of chemicals,' Clemmie sang as she worked. 'You could literally cook with it, it's so pure.' Ayesha's hair morphed from a charged mass of frizz to limp, greasy clumps hanging down the back of her neck.

'Now,' Clemmie said behind her, with chilling resolve.

A sharp point scraped a line from the front of Ayesha's hairline back down the middle of her head. She tried to stop her teeth from grinding, turned her grimace into a smile for India who was following closely. They were bonding. This was good. Clemmie was giving her a makeover and that's what you did with your besties. Just like the two of them, Ayesha was being given the privilege of another transformation. And it was a wonderful thing. Really wonderful. Clemmie ran the comb through both sides of the oily parting and began to plait Ayesha's hair aggressively. Ayesha tried to look to the side, desperate to see if Yaz was witnessing this, whether she might know what to do, perhaps intervene while there was still some hair left on her head, but Clemmie kept her in a vice-like grip that forced her to face forward.

India looked on silently, serenely.

'You look amazing,' Ayesha said to India, indicating her outfit and desperately trying to pretend this was all okay.

India beamed.

'As will you, once Clemmie has finished with you.'

Clemmie tugged and pulled, scraped and slathered. Ayesha kept talking.

'Thank you so much for inviting me, both of you. Honestly. It's amazing. I didn't think you thought of me as such a close friend ...'

There was a moment's hesitation from Clemmie, barely noticeable. India kept her gaze firmly on Ayesha.

'Of course, I do. This gang of ours, this kick-ass sisterhood of activists, change makers, is everything. It's incredibly important we remain close. Loyal, honest with each other,' she said intensely.

'Yep. Yes,' Ayesha agreed with relief. 'And Yaz?'

India looked over Ayesha's shoulder at Yaz, contemplated her for a moment.

'A sister of yours is a sister of mine,' she said.

Ayesha smiled back, paused, then added,

'You know we're not actually sisters?'

India looked at Clemmie and they both burst out laughing.

'Yes, I know,' India said between the laughter. 'Just because you're both Asian doesn't mean you're related. I'm not that ignorant, Ayesha.'

Ayesha was mortified.

'Of course you're not! I'd never – I just wasn't sure cos you said . . . Ouch! Ha ha! Easy there, Clemmie.'

'Almost done.' Clemmie was now twisting the plaits painfully and scraping small, sharp metal objects across Ayesha's scalp. This might have been the most pain she'd ever been in. India's gaze remained coolly focused on her. Ayesha's mind raced to think of more things to say.

'Great! So I know this is random, but what would you be if you could be any animal on the whole planet?' Ayesha asked lightly, blinking back the tears in her eyes.

India looked at her with surprise, then amusement. She tilted her head, contemplating.

'Hmm . . . I once volunteered in a pangolin sanctuary in Uganda. Fascinating creatures. Seemingly tough, impenetrable, but actually very vulnerable. Rare. Under threat,' she replied thoughtfully.

They contemplated India's tasteful choice. Ayesha tried to nod and failed as Clemmie kept her head clamped tight. She waited to be asked about her favourite animal. No one did. So after a lengthy pain-filled silence she offered her unsolicited choice.

'I always thought it would be cool to be a duck.'

India turned her focus back onto Ayesha, with surprise.

'Yep,' Ayesha continued. 'Cos then you can fly and walk and swim – you've basically got the best of all worlds. And you don't mind when it rains.' Ayesha shrugged to conclude her witty explanation.

She waited for India to laugh. She didn't. Instead, she looked at Ayesha with what appeared to be pity. She tilted her head at her and sighed.

'Ducks have one of the highest rates of rape in the animal world, Ayesha,' India said.

Ayesha's face dropped.

'Oh really? Oh shit, I had no – I don't remember that from Blue Planet – my bad—'

Ayesha suddenly wanted to focus on nothing but the sweet pain of her throbbing scalp. It was less excruciating.

'Done.' Clemmie said with a painful pat on Ayesha's head that embedded the hairpins deeper into her cranium. Ayesha winced and then turned it into an awkward celebration.

Clemmie produced a tasteful vintage hand mirror and held it out. Ayesha looked at herself. The parting wasn't quite central. Patches of coconut oil were smeared at the edges of her forehead. The plaits were uneven and had been pinned lumpily to the top of her head. On top of the plaits a crown of red flowers had been fixed, slightly askew.

India leaned into the frame next to Ayesha, her perfect parting, the smooth, slick plaits a painful contrast to her own.

'Twins,' she beamed.

Ayesha tried to smile. The mirror moved an inch and suddenly Yaz's face appeared in the reflection behind them. She stood watching. Silently appalled.

CHAPTER TEN

JANUARY 2018

'Welcome to *Agitated*. A brand-new podcast that's feminist, funny, and fucking furious. I'm your host Ayesha Jones – comedian and activist. To my right is sister survivor Jessica Scott, to my left is artist and activist India Baxter-Wright and to my extreme left we have veteran agitator and patriarchy dismantler Frankie Roberts.'

They were in a studio in a mansion in St John's Wood. India had made a few calls and an old flame from boarding school, whose dad was a famous rocker and whose mum was a duchess, had offered up his bespoke home studio for their first pilot recording. Joni was in the operations booth watching as the four women navigated the tight half-hour script: Ayesha facilitating the conversation, India adding her charm and eloquence, Frankie bringing the force, the anger, the call to arms, and Jessica being allowed a few brief and contained soundbites.

It was a change that no one seemed to be fully acknowledging. India had slipped into the gang seamlessly, as if she'd been there from the beginning, as if it had never been any different. Ayesha tried to read Jessica, to determine whether she was upset at being so swiftly demoted, or relieved. But Jessica's neutral expression gave nothing away, and they never had a moment alone together these days. Now that Frankie had decided that media appearances were out, there was no green room downtime. Ayesha was surprised to note that she actually missed those moments of loaded silences that had only recently become comfortable moments of shared quiet. The pace had ramped up another notch, if that was possible, and Ayesha found she had no time to really fathom any of it. She just kept on keeping on.

Joni edited throughout the night, clipping Jessica's segments even further. Frankie made a few calls, pulled in some favours and it went out the following week – self-released, independent and uncensored. India managed to come to some kind of arrangement with her old flame which seemed to consist of her telling him what was going to happen and him agreeing to it. Ayesha was kept busy writing the scripts that formed the framework for each episode. They recorded five more and staggered the launches of each one – every two weeks seemed to be the sweet spot.

India and Frankie tweeted heavily, and by the time the fifth one went out, the numbers were already impressive. Ayesha watched as, for the second time in her life, the likes and shares multiplied exponentially. Frankie had been right, she thought, there was an audience hungry for this show, in desperate need of this conversation, craving the language with which to make sense of their experience. And *Agitated* delivered, as did India's contacts, and her many, many followers.

In their increasingly sporadic hangouts, Ayesha had played a segment she thought was particularly kick-ass to Yaz, who had listened carefully, nodded.

'Your comebacks are sharp,' she said. 'You always were a heavyweight improviser.'

Ayesha beamed, relieved that her friend approved.

'That level of skill should be paid for. Paid well.' Yaz had turned to Ayesha and looked at her pointedly. 'It's a lot of hours you're putting in. You clocking it all? Invoicing it?'

Ayesha swallowed. She tried hard not to think about the messy pile of official-looking envelopes on her small dining table that had recently started bearing scary-looking words stamped in red. She had stopped opening them weeks ago, knowing she didn't have the means to do anything about the demands they contained.

She felt impossibly stuck between that very real pile of final notices, Yaz's conviction that she should be getting paid for this gig and the complete lack of the mention of it in the group. This work was sacred, and besmirching it with money-talk seemed wrong. But there was no way Yaz would understand.

She forced a weak nod.

'Course!' she replied, a bit too loudly.

Yaz nodded back, watching her closely.

'Good.'

'So the inevitable has happened,' Frankie told the group one day in a meeting at her house. 'A few producers have got in touch. A couple of broadcasters too.' The women reacted with excitement, though Jessica remained mute. Ayesha hoped anxiously that this might finally lead to a pay cheque.

'I've said no to all of them. We're not falling into that trap again,' she said sternly. 'We've got a great team here. Everyone's playing to their strengths and it means we have full control over what we say and how we say it. As far as I'm concerned, if it ain't broke, don't fix it.'

Ayesha slumped with despair.

Frankie turned to Joni, who took a step forward and addressed the group.

'Listening numbers have been increasing nicely. So phase two is taking the show to a live audience. We've got four wicked women who are brilliant in front of a crowd so we're taking *Agitated* to the people. We've secured a mid-sized venue in South-East London – an up-and-coming, trendy, young arty crowd – and tickets are going on sale tomorrow. Frankie and India have kindly agreed to share the link with their followers, and if we all do the same, we shouldn't have any problem filling it.'

Ayesha was trying to keep up. Several decisions had been made that seemed to be important ones and she appeared to be the last to know. She glanced over at Jessica and thought she glimpsed a slight frown, but couldn't be sure. Ayesha had a lot of questions, but Joni's words seemed to have ended the conversation and everyone was dispersing. A spark of frustration flashed momentarily in her. She rubbed her forehead with exhaustion. She was always on the back foot, always playing catch-up – with these women, their decisions, the next step, what was required of her, the bills, the rent … It had been months of feeling less and less in control of her life and time, and she needed to talk it through with someone. Ayesha began to move towards Jessica, hoping to grab a moment with her, but Jessica quickly followed the others as they headed out.

As she watched her one potential confidante slip away, Ayesha felt repentant all of a sudden, desperate to be brought in again, to pretend like she'd been in on it all along, part of the decisions the others had made. This group was a net that had caught her while she was freefalling, she had even been a part of the weave of it, extending it and catching others in its network. But things were changing and she wasn't so sure of her footing anymore. Just like that, she felt like she was on the periphery, the cold of the edge so different to the warmth of the heart, and yet so familiar to her. She shook it off. Didn't this mean a gig? An actual live gig? Maybe even payment? Wasn't this what she'd been hungry for? What was she going to push back against, the very thing she had longed for?

'*Boom!*' she shouted enthusiastically to an almost empty room.

* * *

The following week, Ayesha peeped out from the wings as the crowd slowly filled the venue. Young women mostly, excited, energized and chatty. She couldn't help but remember how different the atmosphere had been just a few short months ago, that night her gig went viral. How different the world seemed now, how galvanized they all felt to gather, to discuss, to listen and to fight. A tipping point and, somehow, she had ended up at the front of it, hosting, holding this space that seemed to fill itself. The hundreds of public disclosures pulling them all out of the dark, into public spaces, to connect and to speak it out loud. It never occurred to Ayesha to share her own story. That wasn't what her role was. She was the funny one, the facilitator, the filler of silences, and the stage was her safe space.

'Pretty damn beautiful, huh?'

Ayesha turned to see Frankie standing behind her, looking out at the crowd too.

Ayesha smiled.

'It is,' she managed, her chest filling with emotion.

'Hmm.' India's rich tone reached them from the side of the stage as she stepped up to join them. 'And so, we three meet again.'

Ayesha looked around for their fourth, but Jessica wasn't there.

'Is Jessica ready? We've not got long—' she began.

Frankie and India exchanged a look.

'Jessica's sitting this one out,' India said assertively. 'It's safer, and for the best.'

Ayesha felt the jarring in her body. Yet another decision she hadn't been privy to. For a moment she remained confused, wrong-footed, but she quickly understood. They couldn't risk giving Jessica a platform on a live show. It was one thing to include her in the recordings where they could control exactly what she said in the edit, quite another to risk her going rogue in front of a live audience again.

Ayesha nodded, tried to smile. She wondered how much her own words about Jessica had contributed to that decision.

She glanced once more behind the two women for a Jessica that wasn't there, then turned back out to the eager crowd.

It had been months since she'd done a proper live gig and she was so hungry for it. The buzz of the audience, the smell of the venue, the warmth of the lights, the exhilarating trajectory of the last few months was all the fuel she needed. She let Jessica's face slip away, squared her shoulders and switched it on. There was a show to do.

The lights went down, Joni cued in the theme music, and Ayesha walked onto the stage.

The audience was already on side. She could feel the warmth emanating from them and every joke in her opening landed perfectly. Compared to the stand-up gigs of yore, this was a walk in the park. They cheered loudly as she introduced India and Frankie, established celebrities in these women's world. It was, Ayesha realized, an audience made up almost entirely of their followers. The back-and-forth between the three of them worked well, the mix of personalities offering something for everyone, and they got a standing ovation at the end. Ayesha stood with the other two women at the front of the stage taking in the applause. Somewhere out there was Joni too, quietly beaming.

Ayesha had looked out at the crowd and saw, above all else, relief. People were desperate to make sense of what was happening and what had happened to them, and were lonely, very lonely, until that moment in that room.

India pulled out her phone from the layers of her beautiful dress and took a selfie of the three of them with the crowd cheering in the background.

As the crowd dispersed, she saw groups of people discussing the content intensely, individuals tentatively turning to someone near them, reaching out, knowing they were safe, like-minded. Her tech chores done, Joni joined them on stage as they all watched this new community begin to take shape before their eyes, a community they were creating. They didn't speak, just watched, Frankie grinning, Joni's chin trembling with emotion, India quietly satisfied.

Her picture, filtered and uploaded in an instant, summed up the moment perfectly. Ayesha felt a fresh surge of joy when she saw it. As if the night couldn't get any better, she was now officially on India's Instagram. There was Frankie looking awkward and determined, India sensual and inspiring, the crowd behind them leaning in, desperate to be included, and Ayesha herself, at the centre, elated, ecstatic and so incredibly grateful. She couldn't remember ever being this happy.

* * *

'Cheers.'

Ayesha, Frankie, India and Joni raised their glasses in the air. They clinked them together clumsily.

They were in the pub after another successful show, standing by the bar. They took a collective sip, hungrily, wearily.

Ayesha blinked the dryness from her eyes, eyes that had spent too long staring at screens, looking out through dry ice at the crowd, squinting in the light. It was a lot of work. The group now met at the weekends too and spent almost two full days discussing content. Then it was up to Ayesha to mould that into some kind of script and get it to Frankie and India in time. They would add their flourishes, phrases and idiosyncrasies to it and then it would come together on the night. If there was a dip, a blip or a lull, Ayesha jumped in and cracked a joke that got everyone on side again. The vibe was saved, the show would go on.

The listeners continued to grow, the venues continued to fill, the shows selling out easily, if not effortlessly.

'To *Agitated*!' Joni said drunkenly, sloshing her pint into the air once more. She took a messy sip and Ayesha laughed.

India watched Joni with fascination, but not quite amusement. Frankie watched her girlfriend too.

'It's been a big month,' she said.

Ayesha laughed loudly.

'Congratulations.' A familiar voice made them turn in the direction of the entrance. Jessica stood nearby, her face set in a neutral mask once again. Ayesha saw Frankie bristle slightly. India's face mirrored Jessica's.

'Jessica!' Ayesha gushed and took a step towards her. 'It's been ages ... Well not that long really ... But it feels that way. How have you ... What's been ... How's things?' she tried desperately.

Jessica kept her eyes on Frankie.

'I just came to say hello. See what the gang's up to. Congratulate you on ... I watched the show. It was ... good,' Jessica managed.

Ayesha watched her face closely. She saw a quiver of emotion pass over it for a millisecond before it was tucked swiftly back behind the mask. Jessica turned to look at India. India kept her gaze steady.

'Thank you. It's been fun,' India replied.

Jessica and India stood looking at each other for some moments. Ayesha could think of nothing more to say.

'Oh shit,' interrupted Joni who had just clocked Jessica. 'It's you.'

Joni looked at Frankie who shot her a warning look.

Joni put her hand over her mouth, tried again.

'Mate. Come here,' she said as she swung a drunken hand around an alarmed Jessica. Ayesha couldn't recall seeing anyone hug or touch Jessica before. Joni swung her other arm over Ayesha, spilling some of her drink on Ayesha's shoulder.

'It's fine,' Joni said reassuringly to Jessica. 'It's all fine. It doesn't matter. All is forgiven. Forget it. You gotta forgive your family, innit? Thass what we are ... family ...'

She pulled them in tighter.

'Let's just keep to the plan, yeah?' she almost whispered. 'If we all just stick to the plan, everyone wins!'

Mercifully, Joni let go of them both.

'What are you drinking?' she asked Jessica.

'I'm not ... I'm not staying. I'm just passing through,' Jessica clarified.

'Don't be silly,' Joni insisted. 'Have a drink for fuck's sake.'

'JJ,' Frankie said sternly. 'You heard her. She doesn't want one.'

Joni seemed to sober up immediately. A look of hurt flashed across her face. She held her hands up in surrender and turned away.

Frankie turned to Jessica.

'Thanks for popping by, Jessica.'

Jessica barely flinched. She nodded dumbly, cast a look at Ayesha, then India and turned, walking out of the pub.

India's eyes were bright with intrigue. She watched Jessica go and then turned to the others.

'Hmm, such a tortured soul. Her energy is so dense,' she said lightly.

'She's been through a lot,' Ayesha managed, her heart heavy.

India smiled briefly and turned away. She leaned against the bar and angling her phone so that it took in the old man sitting behind her and his pint, she took a few experimental selfies.

Joni had retreated to the far end of the room, her back turned to them, wiping angrily at her eyes.

165

Frankie turned around to lean on the bar, looking out to the rest of the pub, seemingly oblivious to her girlfriend's despair, if not slightly annoyed. She sighed.

'There's a little trip I need to make next week,' she said to Ayesha. 'One of those honorary degree thingies. Couple of speeches, workshops. They come up every now and then. Fancy coming?'

Ayesha turned her gaze away from the door Jessica had just left through. She looked at Frankie with surprise.

'Is Joni not up to it?'

Frankie shrugged.

'She's not feeling a hundred percent at the mo and I could do with an ally. What do you reckon?'

Ayesha shrugged.

'Sure. Where is it?'

Frankie kept her gaze on the room.

'Edinburgh.'

As they stepped off the train at Waverley station, Ayesha spotted the young woman first, holding a sign that said FRANKIE ROBERTS in bold lettering.

From the moment they had met at Kings Cross, Ayesha had done all she could to prove herself worthy of this trip. She already had a flat white ready for Frankie and, as a back-up, had located the nearest and nicest alcohol-selling establishment, even though it wasn't quite 11 a.m. On the long train ride north, Ayesha thanked Frankie over and over, until she saw her face do that thing that it did when

Joni was annoying her, so she stopped. Ayesha allowed herself a moment to take in the fact that she was in first class, heading to an important event at the University of Edinburgh with Frankie Roberts. Because this was her life now, apparently. As the inspector checked their tickets, she wondered what he saw when he looked at them both. Not just your average business people doing the long commute to some dull meeting where they would just make more money for The Man, but two kick-ass women travelling across the UK to start difficult conversations, speak truth to power and be change makers. Ayesha allowed herself to think of the young people they would meet, people who might have never had the chance to talk about this stuff, find allies, break the silence. A lump of emotion swelled in her throat and she wiped a quiet tear away, hoping Frankie hadn't seen. She had cancelled her last paid gig to be here. But in this moment, it was crystal clear to Ayesha that it was totally worth it.

The young woman holding the sign beamed at them and waved enthusiastically as they made their way over to her, pulling their cases behind them.

'It's an honour,' she said in her warm Scottish lilt, pumping Frankie's hand. 'I'm Hannah. We've been emailing. It's so good to have you here in person! I can't tell you what this means. Let's get you to the hotel and then we can talk through the itinerary.'

Hannah led them out of the station. The chilly spring air hit Ayesha as she was ushered into a taxi. It had a bite to it that even the coldest, most disappointing Scottish summer's day did not have. As they drove through Edinburgh, Ayesha watched streets and landmarks pass by that were almost as familiar to her as her own city's. She'd been here many summers, often having started saving from December to make it through the famous Fringe festival that spanned the whole of August. A festival that encompassed, encroached on and consumed the entire city. A city that became overrun by zany, loud, eccentric actors, acrobats, comedians and clowns who swarmed across the border armed with flyers, posters and props, battling daily to get another precious bum on an increasingly costly seat. The competition was fierce; on any given day there were over two thousand shows being performed. Every conceivable space was turned into a venue – schools, churches, buses, beds. Every house, flat, room was crammed full of performers, producers, directors, reviewers and their mates. Ayesha had shared beds, sofas and floors – even a tent, one desperate year, with a giant black opera singer from Chicago who played an adult baby in *Jerry Springer: The Opera*. When she lost her voice halfway through the month, he had given her a miraculous yellow concoction that burned her throat and restored her vocal chords instantly.

Ayesha could think of no other city that could hold this carnivalesque extravaganza with such grace. The imposing Edinburgh Castle watched over it all with a stoic, rugged strength that emanated from the very stone it was built with and showered the city with a nightly display of fireworks, in case the whole affair wasn't camp enough.

Night after night, summer after summer, Ayesha had rushed from one venue to another, performing her set wherever there was an opening, taking part in live comedy panel shows, improv nights and themed bingo events. But every year it became less feasible. Rent for even a shared room in August was now as expensive as accommodation in the trendiest parts of London. Venues had started charging performers the equivalent of a down-payment on a house, and now you needed an extra grand to hire a professional PR team, because handing out flyers on the Royal Mile didn't cut it anymore. Ayesha realized with sadness that this year, she wouldn't make it to the festival.

Frankie and Hannah talked intensely about the schedule as Ayesha looked out at the streets that were so much quieter now, less colourful without the endless ads for endless shows. She saw a smattering of locals seemingly immune to the brisk Caledonian spring going about their daily business, and she wondered where the thousands of others who came here every summer had been scattered to. Ayesha had made a list of the city's best comedy venues with Yaz and hoped to coax Frankie out for a night of fun, but her fave seedy burlesque venue seemed to have turned back into a lecture room, the adult puppet show was a book shop once again. The circus had left town and the emcee had turned back into a coffee barista. Ayesha hardly recognized any of it.

They were here for a very different purpose, though, a very different audience and a much more sobering show. She tried to remember how lucky she was to have been chosen.

Soon they were dumping their bags in the hotel, getting back into the taxi and heading straight to the university campus where there were even more people waiting to greet them for an intimate seminar that Ayesha assisted Frankie with, followed by discussions and introductions, dinner, and then they both headed straight back to the hotel and collapsed into their respective beds in their respective rooms.

Ayesha woke the next morning to the phone ringing on the bedside table. An early morning call to inform her Hannah was waiting in the lobby. She dragged herself up and out and met a grumpy, sleep-ruffled Frankie by the lift. Something in Frankie's demeanour stopped Ayesha's morning greeting from leaving her lips. It was clear she was not to be disturbed quite yet. They descended in silence and when the lift doors opened again, there was Hannah, fresh and eager and holding two takeaway coffees. They drove back to the campus in yet another cab, Frankie coming to life with every sip of caffeine. This time Ayesha took her place in the audience alongside the students as Frankie stepped onto the stage to receive her honorary degree. She was fully awake now. Galvanized and ready.

Frankie took her place at the podium and paused before starting with some tough statistics.

'One in every four women here will be or will have already been sexually assaulted. That's one in four. And that's a very conservative statistic. That's based on cases that actually get reported. And we know that there are many, many more that never see the light of day. Look around you. At your friends, your flatmates, your peers, your family. Think of the seminar groups you attend. The house you live in. How many of you sitting in that room will have experienced one of the worst things that can happen to someone in their lifetime? And what is it like to have to live with that day in day out?'

Ayesha watched as the young faces looked around furtively, took in this statistic made real, began to wonder – or else knew all too well – who it was that was silently carrying the weight of this secret with them daily. Frankie elaborated on the many ways in which it affected every aspect of someone's life and backed it all up with statistics: the chances of getting lower grades, of failing, of your career stalling, your inability to trust others and yourself, build relationships, the isolation that came with it, the depression, the very real physical health problems brought on by such trauma and the devastatingly low number of police cases that ever ended in a conviction. And then the moment Ayesha loved the most, when she turned all those numbers on their head, reached beyond them to remind them all that each statistic was a person with resources and potential that could surpass any limitations or traumatizing experience. The ability to heal smashed those percentages to pieces and made light work of those charts. The miraculous human drive to surpass the terror and oppression handed to each generation was witnessed in

every movement in human history. And this was no different. It was okay to be angry. And it was okay to shout. And
it was okay to speak the unspeakable. The world was finally
listening.

Ayesha still felt goosebumps even though she'd heard
a version of this speech several times before. She looked
around with tears in her eyes and saw them mirrored in
each young face in the audience. She also felt a deep gratitude. Many of them, Ayesha knew from the statistics Frankie
had made them memorize, would have already experienced
abuse, assault, unspeakable things – most likely at the hands
of someone they knew well. Maybe college was the first safe
place they'd known; maybe this was the very place it had
happened. Frankie saw them all, spoke on their behalf, made
the unspeakable spoken. Ayesha looked around at the eager
faces, trying to pinpoint who was spending every ounce of
their energy trying to keep the smile from wavering, trying to
keep the world from disintegrating, trying to appear normal
and carry the horror of their experience all at the same time.
Just like she did.

At the reception afterwards, Frankie was surrounded by
eager disciples, desperate to take this once-in-a-lifetime
opportunity to speak with their idol.

Ayesha stood back and relished her special status. She'd
hardly managed to speak to Frankie on this trip as she was
either busy rushing from one event to another, or exhausted
and in need of some quiet time. But Ayesha didn't mind.

Hannah and her team had taken good care of them both, and it wasn't long before she, too, had her own little gathering of people keen to talk with her.

'We saw your video. The way you took that guy down? The best,' enthused one young woman.

Ayesha laughed along, adding her own colour to the well-known anecdote, letting them in on lesser-known details about that now infamous night. At one point she noticed another figure hovering a few feet away from the group that had gathered around her. She had short cropped hair, similar in length to Yaz's, brown skin and wore a baggy tracksuit a couple of sizes too big. She stood uncertainly behind the others. There, but not there. She didn't speak but let the others stumble over each other, gushing at Ayesha as she watched them sideways, glancing nervously and then down again. Ayesha made eye contact. Smiled. The girl's eyes darted away, alarmed, but she stayed where she was, still hovering.

As the group finally began to dissipate, mostly drifting towards Frankie, Ayesha turned to the young woman.

'So, so far I've had a haggis burger, neeps and tatties and a deep-fried pizza. What classic Scottish delicacy have I missed?'

The young woman frowned, seemingly unconvinced by Ayesha's clichéd take on Scotland. Her eyes darted up again and this time settled longer on Ayesha. There was an almost smile. Ayesha gave her a moment. Something told her she was gearing herself up. Eventually . . .

'Maybe . . . some lorne?'

'Lorne? Sounds exotic,' Ayesha enthused. 'Can I put it in a sandwich and wash it down with some Iron Bru?'

The young woman smiled at the floor and shook her head.

'Sure,' she shrugged.

'You a student here?' Ayesha asked.

She shook her head again. Looked up.

'I came from out of town. Small place.'

'Ah, so you're just visiting?'

The young woman shrugged again.

'I heard about you guys coming ...' She hesitated, uncertain how to continue. Ayesha jumped in.

'Do you follow Frankie's work? She's pretty impressive, huh? I could introduce you if you—'

'I saw the video,' the young woman suddenly blurted out. 'Your video. You were so ... Sometimes I feel like that. But I don't know how to ... How do you ...? When so much has happened, how do you stop ... ?' She struggled with the words, with the intensity of emotion she'd been holding in for so long.

'Stop what?' Ayesha encouraged, gently.

'Stop feeling so ... angry all the time. I'm so angry. I don't know how ... I just want to ... And then you're so funny and you can laugh too, and I want so much ... so much to be able to ...'

She looked up at Ayesha again, this time a fierce pain in her eyes. They were burning bright with years of things unsaid, unscreamed. At the same time, she seemed to look straight through Ayesha, straight to the core of her, and recognize something there.

Ayesha thought for a moment. Took a step closer to her.

'But you're doing it,' she said, gently. 'You came all this way. You found us. And there's so many more people here you can find. Who could find you, if you let them.' Ayesha paused, trying to find the best words, watching the girl closely as she took one more step towards her, careful to still give her some space. 'I think it helps when you can share it. Even a small bit. Even with just a couple of people who are cool. Who are safe enough ... It's also much easier to have a laugh when there's someone else around.'

Ayesha saw the girl's fierce determination to hold it together begin to waver. She looked at Ayesha, sideways at first, and then straightened up slightly. There was another almost smile. And then Ayesha saw tears threatening to burst.

'Ayesha. Frankie's ready. We'll head over for the photo shoot.' Hannah was at her elbow and the young woman turned away, wiping an eye surreptitiously.

'Sure, I'll be there in just a sec.' Ayesha turned away from Hannah, but Hannah stayed put. The young woman refused to turn back towards her, her back a fortress now. Ayesha hardened, turning to Hannah once more with an urgency, an assertiveness even, that she didn't know she had.

'I'm going to need you to give me a minute,' she insisted sternly.

Hannah paused for a moment longer, before nodding

and heading back to Frankie. Ayesha turned back to the woman.

'What's your name?' Ayesha tried. The young woman remained silent, closed. Ayesha waited patiently, quietly. Eventually she noticed her shoulders relax a fraction and she began to turn slowly towards Ayesha once more.

'We're on a tight one today, Ayesha.' Frankie's stern voice cut through.

Ayesha kept her eyes on the young woman as she hardened into a fortress once more.

Ayesha looked at Frankie pleadingly, looking back at the girl, hoping Frankie would understand, but Frankie was already eyeing the exit impatiently. In fact, she seemed not to notice the girl at all, her eyes and mind on the academics she had just been talking to. And then two more volunteers descended to lead them both to the next important thing on the schedule.

As she left, Ayesha looked around one more time at her, standing alone in the crowded hall. Just before she turned away, Ayesha saw a student approach her with a clipboard and a pen. She held them out to the young woman who looked up slowly, and then the door closed on the reception hall.

They arrived late back at London City Airport. Frankie had made the executive decision to get a flight back 'on expenses'. Ayesha wondered whose expenses. But silently. Not much had been said on the return journey. Frankie was galvanized by the speeches, the brushes with academia, the elite audience and star treatment. She typed up notes, dozed, scribbled thoughts in a Moleskine notebook, drank. Ayesha was drained, exhausted and raw. Nevertheless, she tried to engage Frankie a bit, hoping there'd be a chance to talk through her experience with the young woman. Ayesha hoped desperately the girl had taken the pen, written her name down, wished she'd lingered a moment longer to see it happen. But Frankie didn't bite. Ayesha sat quietly on the plane trying to make sense of the sadness, the disappointment even, that she was feeling, and realized that it was directed at Frankie. She couldn't help but see her differently now. This trip had revealed something about her that Ayesha was finding hard to integrate with the hero she knew Frankie was. At the same time, Ayesha had the sense that she had failed Frankie somehow. That she had been chosen for this important trip, had been brought to Edinburgh and back for free, and now Frankie seemed irritated, aloof, closed off from her. She suddenly thought of Joni, those puppy-like glances at Frankie, the eagerness to impress, to stay in her good books, coax a smile of approval from her, a kind word. The only moment Frankie spoke to Ayesha was somewhere in the middle of the flight when she was typing something up on her laptop. She suddenly turned to her with determination and took off her reading glasses. Ayesha sat up, keen to talk.

'What's the correct way of referring to a black person these days? Do you capitalize the B, or not?'

Ayesha looked blankly at Frankie. Frankie's open expression began to default back to its closed, frustrated previous one.

'Capital. Definitely,' Ayesha quickly blurted out.

Frankie nodded with approval, went back to typing.

Ayesha sank back into her seat with relief and stared at the seat back in front of her. It occurred to her then that they'd never made it to a comedy club.

Joni was waiting for them in arrivals. She hugged them both and looked searchingly at Frankie.

'You look exhausted.'

'I'm fine,' Frankie protested weakly.

Joni turned to Ayesha.

'I bet she hasn't been eating properly. Or sleeping.' She turned back to Frankie. 'You're no good to anyone if you don't look after yourself properly.'

Frankie's brow furrowed. She leaned away from Joni's scrutiny with irritation.

'Right, you,' Joni insisted. 'You're taking a day off.'

Frankie opened her mouth to protest, but Joni had already started walking away.

Ayesha was relieved to hand over to Joni. She led them out of the terminal to the car, chatting incessantly, thawing Frankie's frigid aura.

'We could have got a cab, JJ,' Frankie eventually managed.

'I'm sure you've had your fill of cabs,' Joni retorted. *'Okay you wee scoundrels, first stop – Ayesha's place.'*

178

It wasn't a bad Scottish accent. Ayesha settled into the back seat as the couple caught up in front, Joni fussing over Frankie and filling the car with warm chatter. The milder temperature made a difference, the muted London night was a relief after the bite of northern chill. But as her eyes started to close, that young woman's fierce, pain-filled gaze filled her thoughts. She looked away from the window, searching for a distraction. Next to her on the seat lay a newspaper. She blinked as she recognized the face staring defiantly back at her from the front page.

Jessica.

CHAPTER ELEVEN

JULY 2018

Saturday 7.00 p.m.

India gazed at Ayesha intensely through the mirror, surveying Clemmie's handiwork with satisfaction. Clemmie handed India the mirror and slipped out of the door.

'Yes,' India said simply.

Ayesha felt a surge of relief at the Queen Goddess's approval. She had seemed distant, colder than usual towards Ayesha. Ayesha could think of several things she had done to deserve this and several things she was willing to do to make up for it. Maybe this was her penance. Maybe being absolved of your sins and transforming into divinity took some pain, some sacrifice. Maybe this was all worth it.

Maybe.

Ayesha kept her eyes firmly on India's reflection. She couldn't bear to look at her own greasy one right next to it or worse, at Yaz's appalled expression behind her. But the mirror swung a few degrees around again and there they were – India and Ayesha, with a grim looking Yaz behind them.

'India, I'm—'

Ayesha began, once again, to formulate an apology and an explanation, even as her very cranium rang with pain.

'Take no notice,' India suddenly said quietly, sternly. 'She's got no right to judge us just because we're having a bit of fun together.'

Ayesha's heart jumped. India was looking at herself admiringly, but she glanced at Ayesha momentarily and then at Yaz behind them.

'You're allowed to have other friends too, Ayesha. Remember that.' India had lowered her voice to a murmur. 'And be careful,' she suddenly locked eyes with Ayesha. 'This level of jealousy is incredibly toxic – for everyone involved.'

'Jealousy?' Ayesha managed.

'Yes,' India confirmed quietly. 'Consumed with jealousy. Of our special connection, our sisterhood, of our collective, of Jessica. It's all she talks about. It's like she's obsessed.'

Ayesha was shocked. This didn't sound like Yaz at all. She tried to look at her in the reflection once more, but India had tilted the mirror so that only the two of them filled the frame now.

Her stare melted into a smile and she leaned even closer to Ayesha. 'Make space, Ayesha, always have some space between you. For your own safety.' She lowered the mirror and laughed briefly, dispelling the intensity of the moment, and making it seem, for all who might be watching, like they'd just shared a private joke.

Ayesha remained speechless. Yaz's disapproving comments, her cold reception of Ayesha's involvement in the group, the collective, her suspicion and obsession with Ayesha getting paid suddenly seemed more sinister than it had done before. Maybe it wasn't just Ayesha's interests she'd had at heart. But when had India had the opportunity to talk with Yaz properly? How did she know Yaz was obsessed?

Ayesha's head throbbed painfully. She felt suddenly very sober.

With a rustle of fabric, Clemmie appeared in the doorway holding an ornate golden circular tray. Carefully arranged on it were seven small brown cubes.

'Please take one each,' she instructed the women as she circulated the tray among them.

'What's this?' Frankie asked.

'Round two?' Joni suggested.

'It looks like hash brownie finger food,' Yaz observed.

A tinkle of laughter escaped from India. She suddenly beamed at Yaz. Ayesha frowned in confusion.

'Something like that,' Clemmie quipped, almost gamely, but mostly condescendingly. 'Frankie, would you like a list of the ingredients before we partake?'

Frankie the Avatar raised a placatory blue hand.

'I put my goddess self in your capable hands. And trust you'll get us perfectly sloshed.'

Joni giggled. Clemmie produced a high-pitched sound that was almost a laugh.

'By *sloshed* you of course mean that I have spent weeks gathering just the right ingredients and meticulously fusing them into this complex composition so that it will perfectly facilitate our transformation,' she said a little too forcefully.

There was a surprised silence. Frankie recovered.

'Yep. Exactly that,' she agreed. 'Also, I'm bloody starving. These better be filling,' she added, picking up a piece between thumb and forefinger and looking at it with disappointment.

Ayesha's stomach suddenly rumbled very loudly. She realized how hungry she was too. The bubbles and the cacao drink were having a strange effect on her empty stomach. She remembered, with longing this time, the cake in the boot of her car and wondered how hungry she would need to get before she would resort to eating that mess of sugar, sparkles and plastic. Surely Clemmie had made provisions?

'Hunger is a craving,' Clemmie pronounced in her condescending voice. 'Any spiritual experience worth its name will include an element of abstinence and purification. We will be abstaining from food for the duration in order to purify and prepare for the journey we have already begun.'

'You best be joking,' Yaz said dangerously. 'You're not gonna offer us any food?'

Clemmie turned to Yaz slowly, purposefully. She raised the tray a little higher.

'This is my offering,' she said simply.

Ayesha watched Yaz's face drop. Yaz's metabolism was

swift and efficient. There was no space between full and empty. When Yaz needed to eat, she needed to eat then and there. Of all the things Ayesha had put her through, of all the offences she'd experienced since they'd arrived, this was by far the worst.

Ayesha thought regretfully of the many service stations they'd passed on the drive up that had promised snacks, fast food, baked goods. They had stopped at none.

But as Ayesha watched her, Yaz's face took on a new resolve. She calmed, nodded briefly.

'Sure,' she replied simply.

Ayesha tried to hide her smile. She knew that Yaz had decided she would eat. Whatever the rules were, this was a step too far, and however much Yaz had been brought up to respect people – especially in their own home – you simply never, ever let anyone go hungry under your roof. Yaz would find food. Or else she would leave and find food elsewhere.

They all took a square from the tray. Ayesha held hers between thumb and finger and surveyed it with trepidation. She recalled the moments where the others had all suddenly metamorphosed into demonic creatures before her. She glanced around at their heavily decorated personas and panic began to build in her again. She was struggling to recognize them as it was, struggling to know who to trust and what was true; she needed no extra help from any more of Clemmie's concoctions. Ayesha turned back to the tray Clemmie held. One solitary cube remained just off-centre. Clemmie stared at it, anger beginning to tighten her features. She swivelled round before Ayesha could place her square back on the tray.

'Now, where *is* Jessica? She can't miss out on the transformation too. It won't work.' Clemmie huffed impatiently, the singsong cadence of her voice forced now, tinged with rage.

'It really is just rude to keep us waiting. I don't quite think she gets how lucky she is to have been invited. And the numbers. The numbers are so very ...'

Clemmie's face began to pinken. Yaz tried to hide a smirk. Joni scratched her head awkwardly.

'Did she reply to the emails?' Ayesha asked hopefully.

'Yes, she did,' Clemmie confirmed. 'Well, she sent a thank you a couple of weeks ago. Short and simple, but grateful at least. At the very least,' she repeated. 'And then a few days ago she sent a rather formal one accepting our invitation and confirming her attendance. It was a bit over the top, but then that's Jessica Scott for you.'

Clemmie looked at India knowingly. India rolled her eyes.

'She's always been a bit socially awkward,' Frankie remarked bitterly, her newly painted face hiding the full extent of her resentment. 'And a woman of few words ... Until she's got the whole nation watching, of course.'

Frankie looked at Joni. Joni looked back from under the bright red wig and smiled appeasingly.

'It's quite impressive really,' India mused. 'She certainly knows how to play the game.'

Ayesha felt increasingly uncomfortable at this cold evaluation of Jessica. She wished it would stop.

'Do you think, maybe, she feels a bit ... worried about joining us? It's been a bit tense lately,' she ventured.

India turned to Ayesha.

'That's why I invited her. Unity. Forgiveness. Inclusion. That's what I'm about, Ayesha. That's what my spaces are about,' she explained patiently. 'She does herself no favours, and yet, I can't help but think she's ... salvageable.'

Clemmie put a hand on India's shoulder.

'You're generous to a fault. To a fault,' she said with emotion.

India bowed her head humbly, then looked back up with a new resolve.

'You're right,' she said lightly. 'It is a fault of mine. I have no problem admitting that. And it's time to be a little more firm in my personal boundaries. Selfish, even.'

She shrugged nonchalantly, stood a little straighter.

'I gave her a chance, despite everything, and she's thrown it back in my face. She's dead to me.'

Ayesha blinked, not sure if she had heard right. India's delivery had been so silky, almost throwaway, that she couldn't possibly have just cancelled Jessica.

'Wow,' Yaz exclaimed. 'That's a strong statement right there. You full-on just switched on your girl. Proclaimed her deceased.'

'Boundaries,' India crooned. 'It's actually very healthy. For everyone involved.'

Clemmie nodded solemnly.

'In fact, that's something I admire in you, Yasmin,' India continued. Yaz looked at India with surprise, unsure what to make of this unexpected compliment, and the use of her full name. 'It also means, energetically speaking, space is made for others to come closer.'

'Is that right,' Yaz asked steadily.

'That's right,' India beamed.

Ayesha raised her eyebrows, even though it meant the grips dug further into her skull. She remembered the moment when Yaz and India had transformed into gossiping monsters in the dining room. They had both looked at her and she was sure she saw them sneer before turning back to each other in cahoots. Her stomach sank. Was something going on between them that Ayesha hadn't quite clocked? What had they spoken about in the dining room earlier? What did they have to talk about anyway? Was that what India was referring to? Is that when Yaz had revealed her jealousy and resentment?

Yaz looked around the room and found Ayesha. Her eyes said, *Are you getting this?*

Ayesha calmed herself down, rubbed her eyes wearily. Before her stood her best friend, the same Yaz she knew so well, who she had dragged here for her own benefit, who stood here hungry and a bit freaked out. And beside her was the lovely India. India who had been so benevolent and forgiving, who was making such an effort with Yaz, despite Yaz challenging her at every turn. Surely India's warning about Yaz must have been a misunderstanding? Ayesha couldn't help but remember India's kind words as they had helped her with her transformation: *a sister of yours is a sister of mine.* Ayesha clung on to this, tried to forget the rest.

Yaz watched Ayesha carefully and then sighed.

'You know what, if it means I get an extra bite of that space cake then she's dead to me too,' she said dryly and reached out for the remaining cube of cake. India beat her to it. She grabbed it, playfully bit into half of it and then fed the rest to a surprised Yaz who paused before opening her mouth warily to accept the offering. She chewed on it thoughtfully. India glanced at Ayesha, a mischievous twinkle in her eye. Yaz raised her own hand which still held the original square she had taken from the tray and looked at it as she chewed. Ayesha panicked suddenly.

'You know, I think with edibles it's quite easy to lose control of how much you're actually taking, so maybe—'

'Are you telling Yasmin what to do?' India snapped, turning on Ayesha with sudden coldness.

'No! No, of course not,' she replied, mortified.

'Because I'm sure she's capable of making her own decisions, Ayesha.' India's voice had returned to its usual amused tone, but there was still a bite lurking just beneath it.

Ayesha didn't know what to say. She hadn't meant to be bossy. She looked at Yaz who looked back at her, eyebrows raised.

'Go for it,' India urged.

Without breaking eye contact, Yaz popped the remaining square into her mouth.

Ayesha tried to look encouraging. India was still watching her.

Joni turned to Frankie and fed her a square. Frankie did the same in return.

Clemmie was now feeding India. Before she had time to think too much about what she was doing, Ayesha popped the squishy brown square she was holding into her own mouth. It was stringier than she expected, less homemade and comforting, more . . . organic-tasting. More bitter than sweet, similar to the cacao drink. It coagulated in Ayesha's mouth. She chewed laboriously, desperate now for some liquid to wash it down. Water. Some blessed water. She looked around at the others who were also struggling, and for a moment Ayesha saw another bizarre tableau – this room full of grown women, dressed as otherworldly beings, gurning and chomping furiously on some cake. She tried not to laugh, failed, and then choked on the food filling her mouth. She choked again and a fountain of brown liquid exploded out of her. It rained down on the decadent, richly coloured fabrics and priceless décor, adorning them with dark brown stains. Ayesha, mortified, tried to gasp, the mixture stuck in her windpipe and she coughed even more violently. This time blobs of half-chewed vegan brownie reached Clemmie who turned just in time to have it shower both the back of her hair and the front of her outfit, but managed to shield India who mercifully stood behind her. Ayesha swallowed the rest of it down urgently and tried to control her breathing. There was a stunned silence as Clemmie stood open-mouthed, surveying with horror the damage to her costumes, her property, her hair, her person.

Ayesha wanted desperately to apologize, more than

anything, but all she could do was swallow and swallow again, fighting to keep the rest of the brownie down and at the same time get some air into her lungs so she could speak.

'Breathe, sis, breathe.' Yaz walloped her on the back twice and Ayesha finally gasped. She bent down and put her hands on her knees, trying to stop the room from spinning.

Yaz leaned over too, breathing with her friend. When she was sure Ayesha was okay, she sighed with relief. But the sigh turned into a giggle, and then a guffaw. Ayesha winced. *Not now, please not now.* But once Yaz started laughing, Ayesha could only fight it for so long. It was all so awful, so serious, that the absolute worst thing she could do right now would be to laugh. She struggled desperately against the giggles that had already ruined one ceremony. Tears streamed down her face as she tried to stop herself. She shook her head helplessly.

'I'm so sorry,' she managed, before both she and Yaz doubled over, wheezing and snorting with laughter, as a final string of brown saliva escaped Ayesha's mouth and landed on a satin shoe.

'Is this your idea of a joke, Ayesha?' Clemmie said finally. Her voice trembling now.

Ayesha shook her head, looked up, and sobered immediately. Clemmie had tears in her eyes.

'Because it's absolutely disgusting,' she concluded.

'No, no. Clemmie. Oh god. I'm so sorry. I'm so, so sorry,' Ayesha grovelled. 'I'll pay for it all to get cleaned. Properly. I—'

Yaz had recovered too now, and it was suddenly not very funny at all. There was a blob of brown hanging from Clemmie's tousled blonde hair that Ayesha wanted desperately to reach out and wipe away, but she didn't dare touch her.

Joni, however, was on it. She descended bearing a wad of tissues and began to wipe and dab at Clemmie.

'Ah, what's a bit of gob among friends,' she quipped merrily. 'Call it an extra blessing from your goddess friend here. It probably makes you the most blessed of the lot of us!' She winked at Ayesha and held out more tissues. Ayesha grabbed a wad and joined in the wiping.

'Ha! It's true! Didn't your grandma do that thing where she would spit on a tissue and clean your face with it?' Ayesha asked hopefully.

Clemmie said nothing, but she stood, allowing them to wipe her.

'That's enough, Joni,' Frankie said after a while. But Joni carried on wiping. Ayesha looked at her and saw a grim, desperate look on her face as she scrubbed at every possible stain she could find.

'Just ... a bit more ... and we'll be right as rain ... right as ...'

Frankie's hand descended onto Joni's and stopped it. Joni looked up and seemed to wake from a trance. She nodded and scrunched up the remaining tissue in her hands.

'That's probably enough for now,' she said quietly.

Clemmie continued to seethe.

191

'Look, man. It was an accident. She legit couldn't breathe for a minute,' Yaz reasoned.

India stepped forward and gave a carefree wave of her hand.

'It's just stuff, Clemmie. Just heaps of stuff. That's all. Most people make do with much less,' she explained patiently. Clemmie turned to India, a look of shame beginning to form on her face.

'Hassan travelled an entire continent with only the clothes he was wearing,' India said. 'And they were less than immaculate by the time he arrived here.'

They were all chastened, standing in their mismatched, ostentatious outfits in this room full of things.

'In Ayesha and Hassan's part of the world, it is actually quite common to spit on your nearest and dearest in order to ward off the devil,' she informed them. 'I'm sure Ayesha was just embodying fully her Middle Eastern deity and that there was no malice intended.'

'Yes! Yes, it's true,' Ayesha said enthusiastically, although she didn't have a clue what India was talking about. 'No! of course not. No malice at all. Oh God, no.' She threw a grateful look at India who nodded generously once.

'Goddess.' Clemmie said.

Ayesha looked up.

'Sorry?'

'Goddess. Not God,' she explained.

'Yes, of course. Sorry. Again,' Ayesha said, her heart pounding.

India looked at Clemmie head on. She carefully selected a clean section of hair and picked up a lock between two fingers.

'If I'm being brutally truthful, it wasn't your best look anyway,' she said bluntly. 'It didn't quite work with your natural tone and ... my colour scheme.' India took in her own outfit.

'Oh,' Clemmie exclaimed, suddenly chastened.

'Maybe it's a blessing ... in disguise, then?' Joni offered.

This time it was Frankie who snorted first, then Joni, who began laughing hysterically at her own joke. Even India beamed, which made Clemmie smile and shake her head at her own ignorance.

Ayesha turned to Yaz who looked uncertainly at the others who were now laughing Ayesha's awful mishap away.

India sighed loudly, putting an end to the merriment.

'Let's push on,' she instructed.

Clemmie hesitated.

'It's just, as I said before, the numbers are very important,' she insisted nervously. India stared at Clemmie, then said levelly,

'Okay. Let's just sit here in this room then, all dressed up, with bits of shit on us and wait.'

'Well, no, I don't expect—'

'No, no, you're right. The numbers. They're much more important than anything else,' India insisted calmly.

Clemmie watched India carefully. For a moment, she seemed to consider protesting again then, quite suddenly, she turned to the other women, took a breath, assuming her ritual birthing persona once again.

'Our transformations are complete. With the rising of the moon our human form has been cast aside and our higher selves have been revealed. Goddesses, every one.'

There was relieved nodding.

'Hear, hear,' Joni added gamely.

'And what a queen we have to rule us.' Clemmie turned back to India. 'The embodiment of Mother Nature herself,' she exclaimed, taking in the feathers, the suede, the metals of the earth, the earth itself smeared beautifully across India's delicate features. Yaz shook her head quietly. Ayesha smiled desperately.

'And so we pay homage,' Clemmie continued. 'We turn to the gifts of the earth and lay them at her feet. Now that our metamorphosis has been fulfilled, we head to the forest to forage and to revel, to venerate and celebrate, to reconnect and remember. Run. Fly. Dance. Go!'

'You heard her sistas! To the woods,' Joni affirmed.

She grabbed Frankie and Yaz's hands and rushed through the doorway. Yaz took one more look at Ayesha, trying to understand what was happening now, but was soon led out of the room with a blue-painted Frankie and a crimson-headed Joni. Ayesha looked at Clemmie and India expectantly. She almost held out her hands just like Joni had done but stopped herself just in time.

'What are we meant to be . . . ?' she began.

But Clemmie and India stood staring at her pointedly.

India nodded once and Ayesha understood this to be encouragement to join the others. Ayesha had contributed quite enough here. She nodded back, lifted her heavy skirt and headed out.

The newly transformed goddesses fled from the room, along the corridor and back into the kitchen. Ayesha watched as Yaz broke free from the other two, just long enough to open a couple of cupboards and then resort to taking a deep swig from a bottle before deciding to take it with her. Joni grabbed her hand once again and pulled her out of the French doors into the twilit dusk. Ayesha looked around for something to swig or eat too, but only the cups of congealing brown liquid remained. So she followed her friend out of the door, hoping to grab the bottle from her.

The last fragments of daylight still lingered beyond the trees, but behind the mansion the night sky loomed, and there was the moon, less than half full, but with one bright star beside it. They rushed over the still-warm stone of the patio, across the soft lawn where they had gathered in a circle hours earlier, and beyond into the wilder grass of the field. The long reeds brushed Ayesha's shins as she chased the women towards the wood beyond the meadow, her scalp still throbbing with pain. Yaz, in her long leather coat, her cropped hair slicked back, two dark lines painted under her left eye, looked back at her friend. She sipped the contents of the bottle with a mischievous grin as Joni pulled her into a run. She was a few feet ahead, but Ayesha could see in the last traces of light that Yaz's pupils were dilated. A bubble of laughter and relief rose up and out of Ayesha as she tried to catch up with her. Yaz turned around and let herself be pulled on. Ayesha accelerated and then gasped. A sudden sharp pain shot up her leg and she hopped onto her other foot. Another sharp pain in the other foot made her slow down. It took her a moment to focus her mind and then she realized that the idyllic looking meadow was hiding a mine-field of sharp thistles. She stopped, unsure of where to place her bare feet next. She turned back to the house, but it was as far back as it was to the other end of the field, and the dark sky loomed ominously towards her. The women ran on. A surge of panic at being left behind forced Ayesha forward. Every few steps the shock of a barbed prick made her want to stop dead, but the fear of the encroaching darkness and the increasingly distant voices pushed her on, until finally she too made it into the woods.

As they made their way into the denser inner layers, Ayesha felt the chill of the air where the season's hot rays had not reached. At first it was a welcome sensation, but her bare feet soon began to absorb the cold of the ground and it seeped into her body. She caught up with the others and paused for a moment, relieved to be back in the fold, the chill sobering her up a bit.

The women skipped around the trees, picking up treasures from the floor, the bushes, the branches, experimenting with adorning themselves in crowns of leaves, rubbing earth into their skin. They hadn't been instructed to do any of this, and yet here they all were. Ayesha watched Frankie, of all people, whisper a secret into a pine cone and had a moment of acute clarity: they were really fucking high now. Joni had a handful of damp, dark earth she was completely engrossed in and even Yaz was flirting with a handsome-looking tree. Ayesha giggled as she watched her friend playfully bat away a branch, run the leaves over her face, caress the bark experimentally. And then she felt a rush as she joined them. It was true: the world was positively ringing with life and colour. Ayesha looked from one woman to the other, then at the trees around them, their edges fizzing. She turned away and glimpsed the darkening blue of the water beyond the trees – what was that? – and to the left, a rudimentary track leading through the trees and beyond to the far edge of the land. At the end of it she could just make out the crisscross of rusty metal in the semi-darkness that may have been the gate she and Yaz had driven up to when they first arrived. But the dusk was closing in and Ayesha couldn't be sure.

A flash of red in the corner of her eye. A toss of auburn hair? Ayesha turned, trying to locate it, but only Yaz, Frankie and Joni were there. She spun around once, trying to catch sight of it again, but the forest turned of its own accord now, the humans and the trees swaying as one.

A flute reverberated suddenly around the trees, and the women looked up, like woodland creatures alert to the tread of a predator. The melody wove around the forest, bright and clear and loud, and then a drumbeat started up, tribal and ancient and vital. It insisted they dance. Ayesha looked around to find the source of the music and saw Clemmie standing next to state-of-the-art portable speakers that were placed on a tree stump nearby, her phone beside them. She had changed into a forest-green dress with silver fringing. Her hair was sprayed green and silver and two majestic horns seemed to grow directly from her head. She held a long silver staff and her eyes were now a luminous emerald green. She beat the staff into the ground in response to the drums.

Joni moved first. She sprung into the air, her elbow following soon after, and continued to jump up and down, not quite in time with the beat. She pulled Frankie into an awkward dance and they threw angular, mistimed shapes into the cool forest air.

India appeared, a golden Grecian nymph now, her skin shimmering with a thousand sparkles in the dark forest, and she stepped in to join them, her arms wide, circling around slowly, relishing her own outfit and the way it spiralled around her body when she turned. Ayesha found herself being once again lifted into a high by the beat, only to be brought down as quickly by the irregular movements of the women. Something about their timing reminded her of the balloon bashing its rhythm just off the beat and it was ruining her high. But then Yaz was in her face, her eyes dark and bright, her South London screwface set to dance. They raved. Staring into each other's eyes, they blocked out the rest and found their own groove. The beat rose and so did they; on a new high, they expanded their movements, luxuriated in each other's transformed appearance, and synced their steps. As the music intensified there were whoops and screams. Someone ululated. Then a hand found Ayesha's hand and another found Yaz's. The two friends turned and were separated from each other as they all formed a circle once again, stomping, gyrating, whooping. Ayesha held on tight. To her left was India and to her right, Clemmie. She squeezed them both and they squeezed back and all was forgiven and the beat built and built. Clemmie looked meaningfully at each woman and then closed her eyes. They followed suit. The honour, the elation, the gratitude filled Ayesha up. She cried tears of joy at being chosen, being placed between these two incredible women, at the layers of exquisite fabric embracing her, the cool earth below her and that sick beat blasting into her thorax.

The group. The collective. The circle. Unbroken. But some-one was missing. The circle wasn't complete. Jessica's scornful face flashed across Ayesha's closed eyes and she gasped. Her stomach sank. She tried to shake it off. To remember. She belonged. She belonged here.

But deep inside her, that sense of dread began to build again. The hands and the heat and that incessant beat took on a nightmarish tinge. The woods and the track and the water beyond. The water. She suddenly felt so thirsty. She wanted water so badly. She wanted to break free of these clammy, incessant hands and run. Run to the water and gulp it down, scoop it up to her face. But she was locked in somehow. She couldn't move, couldn't leave. It was such an honour to be here, but it meant you had to stay. Stay and be silent. Stay and accept the aggressions. Stay, even if it meant choosing between your oldest friend and your newest ones, between speaking out and holding your tongue, stuffing it down, paying the price. Stay and hold hands. Stay and be chosen. Stay. And belong.

May the circle
Stay unbroken

She felt the pleasant tingling morph into a strange buzzing that started at the top of her head and the bottom of her feet – both similar and different to the feeling in that first circle, out in the heat of the sun. It intensified and then started travelling from both the top and the bottom, out through her hands, as if she were being drained. She breathed deeply and tried to hum a gentle tune under her breath to comfort and calm herself. She stomped her feet lightly to try to rid herself of this unpleasant sensation, she tried to ground herself, to override that sense of being sapped of vital energy. It wasn't working; her very life force seemed to be pouring out of her core and through her hands into the two other women, and now she felt faint, and again the scream began to build. She swallowed, she breathed deeply through her nose, but it was no good, she couldn't stop it this time. A sharp intake of breath and then she was screaming with all her might.

The scream rang out, deafening her own ears, but barely piercing the loud music. And then a high-pitched sound hit her from the right, and then from the left, and then the whole circle was screaming.

CHAPTER TWELVE

APRIL 2018

Ayesha watched as Frankie and Joni drove away. She turned to her own front door and lugged her suitcase inside, thinking about what she'd seen. There had, in fact, been two papers on the seat. Both with Jessica's face on the front. Both national tabloids. Both in-depth interviews. Joni had summarized the content as she drove them home. Jessica had all but given away her perpetrator's name – someone high up in a rival broadsheet newspaper and the tabloids were dining out on it, making political connections and suggesting it was part of a much larger network of serial predators masquerading as liberal, woke men.

There were TV interviews too. Suddenly Jessica seemed to be everywhere. Ayesha was beyond exhausted, but she sat up in bed, wired and glued to the little screen of her phone, watching Jessica repeat variations of the same story, carefully prepared and obviously consulted on for maximum effect with minimum legal repercussions.

She looked determined, her jaw set in that defiant way Ayesha had come to know so well. She drove the interviews as if she were in charge, Frankie's training showing clearly in her technique. But there were moments when a question was phrased slightly differently – where the delivery was gentler than expected – when the mask would slip and Ayesha saw again the woman she had first met: cold, clipped, but also hurting, raw. Seething with pain and confusion. The moment that stood out the most was when they'd asked her about her connection to Frankie Roberts' collective. Ayesha thought for a moment she might break down, and then watched in close-up as Jessica gathered her features once more into that stoic mask.

It was the same look on the face of the young woman in Edinburgh.

But it wasn't just that expression of raw pain they shared. Ayesha suddenly realized they had also both looked at *her* in that way that seemed to see into her very core. Pierced the funny front she had honed for decades. Saw beyond the jokes and the small talk to the silence. The dark. Not invasive or intrusive, but knowing. It takes one to know one. To see the cost of living with it every day, of staying upbeat, playing at normal when you've experienced the darkest of humanity. The worst thing. The thing that changes you forever and pushes you to the margins, the periphery, where you watch the rest of the world laugh and connect, move forward and

202

thrive, knowing that you're broken now and not sure you can be fixed, or ever join in again.

The girl's words came back to Ayesha once again. The effort it had taken to turn up, make eye contact, speak. And suddenly the exhaustion of the last few days, weeks even, maybe years, overwhelmed her. And she wept. For them all.

She let the sobs come and come. It was too much to carry. Too much to see, to know.

And then, hand shaking, she picked up her phone again and called the only person who would really understand.

That was how it started.

'Did Frankie put you up to this?' Jessica's voice was even more hostile than usual, but Ayesha was surprised to feel a rush of affection for this relentlessly defensive woman.

'No, Jessica. No one put me up to this. I just needed to . . . It's not been the same. Without you. It's been really . . . hard.' Ayesha tried to keep a fresh wave of sobs at bay.

'I'm surprised you even remember who I am. I've pretty much been erased from the group, or *the collective* as Frankie seems to be calling it now.' Jessica snorted derisively. 'Collective. I'm sure you all came up with that name *collectively* . . .'

Ayesha frowned, rubbed at her temples. She hadn't even thought about it. Couldn't remember when they had started using the term, who had started using it first.

'Let's be honest, India Baxter-Wright has taken my place,'

Jessica continued. 'Jumped in my still-warm grave ... An interesting choice on Frankie's part. Clever really. She's very well-connected.'

'I suppose,' Ayesha tried. 'But she hasn't taken your place, Jessica, no one could. You're still an important part of the ... It's just ... I don't know. I think ... I don't know what I think anymore. It's been ... We just got back from a trip and it was so ... hard. I'm so tired, and there was this girl ... She was in so much pain. I didn't know who else to ... Who else would understand.'

There was a long silence. Ayesha fought the desperate urge to fill it.

'You sound exhausted, Ayesha.' There was a hint of softness in her voice. A sigh, as she let one of the hundreds of barriers down. It was enough for Ayesha. She sighed too. A deep, painful breath of exhaustion and despair and relief. Jessica gave this space. Ayesha did too.

'Well, you haven't cracked a joke in at least three minutes. And you haven't tried to get any information out of me so far, so if you are a spy, you're a shit one,' Jessica said.

Ayesha snorted. A kind of half laugh, half sob.

That first night Jessica let Ayesha talk. She had told her story many times now, had owned it. But this was the first time that Ayesha had tried to find the words. She faltered often, stopped, started again, had to miss things out, have them implied, but knowing all the time that she was talking to someone who understood.

Many of the homes had been safe, in the most rudimentary

of ways at least. Some had even been nurturing. But she never stayed long. Sometimes Mum would get better for a while and Ayesha would hope this time she might be able to keep her that way, but soon enough she would wake to find her talking funny again, saying things that weren't true, that didn't make sense, and soon others started to notice too and Ayesha would be packed off once more, never knowing for sure where she would be taken next, who she would be taken to, who would take her there.

There were several of them over the years. All as horrifying as each other, as life-shattering, as unspeakable. And there had been nowhere to go. No one to tell. She remembered how desperately she had wanted her mum. She would have given anything just to be with her mum, feel her beside her, smell her, hear her voice ... But it was a mum that didn't really exist. And a home that had never truly been. Just a series of placements. And perpetrators.

But did they really exist? Had it really happened if no one else had witnessed it? If it had never been spoken aloud? Ayesha knew it had changed her forever, but it had never been named and that caused a whole new schism in her that made her feel terrifyingly similar to her mum. So she spoke it now, clumsily, quietly, imperfectly. But she spoke it. And Jessica listened. Bore witness. And believed her.

Over the coming weeks the calls became regular; every few days either Ayesha or Jessica would ring, always late at night, when the rest of the world was enjoying an untroubled sleep. They spoke of fears and nightmares and laughed at the strange ways it had warped their view of the world, made them mistrust the silliest things.

It was never directly said, but it was implied often, that campaigning against this and living this were two very different things.

CHAPTER THIRTEEN

JULY 2018

Saturday 8.00 p.m.

The screams overlapped each other, building in piercing layers of sound. Ayesha opened her eyes in shock. She looked to her left and saw India take a deep lungful of air and release it in another high-pitched shriek. But her face didn't mirror Ayesha's terror. India looked elated, energized, rejuvenated by this thrilling release. It chilled Ayesha to the core and froze her own voice in her throat.

At that same moment a loud electronic ping overrode the music, amplified through the speakers. The screaming stopped. India's eyes opened with surprise. The women turned in confusion to the tree stump where the speakers were placed and saw the screen of Clemmie's phone light up. Clemmie frowned and dropped the hands she was holding.

Ayesha felt a wave of relief as the blood seemed to return

to her body once again. She tried to breathe deeply, tried to make sense of what had just happened, that terrifying feeling of being drained of her own vitality. It now seemed a bit extreme, an overreaction, but the weakness in her legs and the uncontrollable shaking of her hands felt real enough.

The music had dipped in volume momentarily when the alert had come through, and Ayesha had caught the words 'I didn't think we had reception anywhere near . . .' as Clemmie walked over to the phone and picked it up. She read the message and her frown deepened. They all looked around, awoken from their screaming frenzy, and tried to make sense of the disruption. As the echo of the alerts faded, the music returned to its regular volume again. But Clemmie stood with her phone in her hand, chewing the inside of her lip. India sighed heavily.

Clemmie tapped her phone and the music stopped. She turned her head, looking around, searching for something, someone beyond the clearing, into the trees.

'Come on, DJ! Sort it out!' Yaz protested. She carried on raving to her own imaginary music, whooping and throwing shapes. India looked over to Yaz, a smile of approval spreading over her face, and began once again to twirl.

Ayesha felt for her phone. Her dress had no pockets. She vaguely remembered leaving it somewhere back in the vast house.

'What's up?' Joni asked.

Clemmie blinked, her gaze returning to the group.

'It's Jessica,' she said.

Ayesha felt a surge of hope. She stepped forward eagerly.

'Is Jessica here? Should someone go back to the house to meet her?' The thought of getting out of this wood, away from this bizarre atmosphere, finding the one person who would understand her strange panic attack was very appealing.

'Where is she?' Frankie demanded.

Yaz and India stopped their dancing.

'What's going on?' India asked, glaring at Clemmie.

'It seems our seventh goddess will not be joining us after all.' Clemmie showed India the message on her phone. India raised an eyebrow. Looked around.

'Good of her to let us know so far in advance,' she said sarcastically.

'It's just ... she seemed so determined to come,' Clemmie continued. 'And ... the thing is I saw ...'

India tilted her head.

'What did you see?' she asked.

Clemmie looked at India.

'I'm not even sure.' She shrugged.

'I don't understand. Is she here or not?' Yaz demanded.

'I'm not sure I care much,' India replied shortly.

'Me neither,' Frankie chimed in.

Yaz huffed impatiently.

'Just play the music, fam,' she protested, 'Blast it out. If she's not coming, why are we ruining the high? Come on. This vibe is getting stale.'

Ayesha cringed, looked nervously at the others. Yaz seemed hell-bent on losing herself in the music and the high.

Nothing else seemed to matter to her more than keeping the rave going now. Then Ayesha felt a surge of guilt as she understood that this might be the only moment Yaz had actually enjoyed so far. No goddess-speak, no forced applause, no debate about appropriated fashion statements, just beats and drugs and shapes – three things she could handle.

But she worried that Yaz's demands might offend, that her comments might come across as judgemental, offensive even, that they both might just be a bit *too much.*

India turned around, looked closely at Yaz.

'She's right. This weekend is not about her, so let's not make it about her. I want to dance. Let's dance.'

'Hear, hear.' Frankie responded.

There was an awkward moment. No one quite knew what to do next. Clemmie looked flustered. Joni glanced at each of them nervously.

'The thing is,' Clemmie explained. 'The balance isn't right. Something is off. We're all feeling it I'm sure—'

'If this is about the fucking numbers again, I swear—' India spat at Clemmie.

Yaz turned to India, a newfound respect for her spreading across her face.

India stared at Clemmie expectantly. Clemmie eventually looked away, back in the direction of the house and then down to her phone. Ayesha began to edge towards Clemmie, hoping she might take a glimpse at her phone, read the message for herself.

'I wonder if I could just—'

But Clemmie tapped the screen and the music started up again. Yaz whooped and raised her gun fingers in the air. India twirled and tried out some ululating. Ayesha stood, unsure. She couldn't shake off that moment of terror, that strange sensation of being drained somehow. And now Jessica? She looked over at Yaz who had wandered closer to India and was dancing with her now. Ayesha sighed. She was desperate to see Jessica, or at least speak to her, felt that somehow she would be able help her feel sane, normal again. But it was clear that she must stay here, dance.

Joni was trying to get Frankie to dance, but Frankie continued to look around her, Clemmie too. Eventually everyone seemed to concede that the rave in the woods was done.

India stopped twirling. She looked at Clemmie who once again stopped the music before taking a breath and composing herself.

'Okay. Let us move on to the next phase in our journey. Gather your offerings carefully,' she instructed. 'Time to bring them to the altar.'

The women collected the treasures they had found and headed back towards the house. Ayesha hastily picked up some pine cones and a twisted-looking twig. She took one more look behind her. She remembered the flash of red she had seen earlier and searched desperately in the darkness between the trees for a trace of it. But there was nothing. She turned reluctantly to see Yaz beckoning her out of the forest. Ayesha followed, unwilling to fully accept that Jessica wasn't coming.

211

They made their way back to open ground. Ayesha picked her way more carefully through the thistle-riddled field and landed on the lawn mostly unscathed. They were all carrying gifts from the forest: a perfectly symmetrical leaf, a curl of bark, berries, a feather. Clemmie led them through the house and into the vast living room. Ayesha saw her phone on the window ledge in the hallway where she had left it on the way back from shoving the balloon into the car boot. The screen was dark, revealing nothing. She held back and when the others had all gone through, she picked it up. There were no messages, and in the top left corner the words confirmed, NO SERVICE.

Ayesha opened the front door and stepped out into the driveway. The sky was clear and dark now, but the heat of the day still lingered in the air. She moved around, holding her phone up, looking for the spot where she had made the call to Hen Men earlier.

She glimpsed the precious bar appear again where there had been none and froze. She waited, but no message came through. Disappointed, Ayesha tried again.

> Hey, I heard you might be having second thoughts?
> Hope I got it wrong. Please come x

She pressed send and waved the phone about a bit hoping it would do the trick. Ayesha sighed and gave herself a moment in the dark outside on her own, the thought of Jessica somehow making her feel less alone out here, even if she really wasn't coming.

A buzz and then a beep and then a glowing screen made her heart leap. Ayesha looked hopefully at the message.

You've made your choice. Now leave me alone.

Ayesha's stomach sank. What choice? When? Why was Jessica upset with her? Hands shaking, Ayesha pressed the dial button immediately, but a series of repetitive beeps informed her that she had lost the signal again.

'No! Please!' Ayesha tried again and again to get through to Jessica, but failed.

'You okay mate?'

Ayesha spun around to find none other than Jessica herself stepping out of the imposing entrance of the mansion.

She screamed and dropped her phone. But when she looked up again, a concerned looking Joni in her flame-red Ziggy Stardust wig stood before her instead. Ayesha blinked several times, shocked at her own mind's ability to play tricks on her.

She retrieved her phone and shakily stopped the call. She took a deep breath and shook her head, trying to keep her vision steady and calm herself.

'Yep, all good. Just breaking the rules and checking my messages,' Ayesha admitted.

Joni took a few steps into the night. She gazed out into the darkness.

'I won't tell if you don't. Besides, I think I saw Clemmie doing the same thing.'

Ayesha's eyes widened.

'The mistress of ceremonies?'

'Yup,' Joni confirmed. 'The Duchess of Edibles herself.'

Ayesha giggled.

'I think she's addicted to the old 'gram,' Joni added. 'She's been checking it every few minutes and hoarding the Wi-Fi for some reason.'

Ayesha's eyes widened.

'Don't you think she's just checking if Jessica's coming?'

Joni shrugged.

'Maybe,' she replied. 'But she's not coming, so ... just need to crack on now, make it extra special for India. Good vibes only.'

Ayesha looked at Joni gratefully.

'Thank you,' she said.

Joni turned to her.

'For what?'

'For helping me clean up the mess earlier.'

Joni shrugged.

'Just a shame you wasted our only food for the weekend,' she retorted.

Ayesha was reminded of the empty feeling in her stomach.

'What's with the Wi-Fi and food hoarding? I don't get it,' she said.

Joni shook her head.

'I don't pretend to understand the rules, I just try not to break 'em,' she replied.

Ayesha grimaced.

'Yeah ... I'm not doing very well on that front,' she said meekly.

Joni looked down at her feet.

'We all mess up at some point,' she said simply.

'I seem to put my foot in it more often than others,' Ayesha confided.

Joni smiled, kept her eyes on her feet.

'Nah, you're all right.'

They stood quietly for a moment, then Joni noticed Ayesha watching her. She snapped out of her intense reverie.

'What?' she asked self-consciously.

'Nothing. I just ... I'm really glad you're here,' Ayesha replied.

Joni looked back at her gratefully.

'This is proper family, innit?' Joni's face was tinged with sadness. 'That's the beautiful thing about people like Frankie. They bring people like us in.' Ayesha saw a vulnerability in Joni that she hadn't seen before.

'Yeah, I suppose,' she replied.

'You got family?' Joni asked. It was a very direct question, but one Ayesha understood to come from someone who knew what it was like not to have family.

'Not really,' She shrugged, 'I grew up in foster homes mostly.'

Joni nodded knowingly.

'Some weren't too bad,' Ayesha continued, well-practiced at what to omit and what to include when summarizing her past. 'I've got my foster mum to thank for the car.' They both looked at her battered old Peugeot sitting humbly in the drive nearby. 'It was a hand-me-down when she upgraded. She wanted to help set me up as a grown, independent woman. A Care Leaver.' She smiled at the memory of that younger Ayesha, stepping out into the world as a woman in her own right. Her smile waned as she thought of those who weren't there to witness that moment, and so many moments before that.

'I get my looks from my mum. She's Iranian,' Ayesha explained. 'She was sectioned for the first time when I was seven. "Unfit to look after a minor".' She spoke in a mock-official voice that was meant to mimic the social worker who had used the phrase at the time, confusing the distraught seven-year-old Ayesha even further.

'What about your dad?' Joni asked.

Ayesha smiled wryly. 'That's where I get my comedy chops from. My parents weren't really ever properly together. But my dad did come to visit when it happened. He'd bought some stickers from the pound shop down the road. Handed them to me wrapped in a plastic bag. Then he sat me down and explained how his "life on the road" as a stand-up comedian was no place for a little girl. It broke his heart, he said, that he couldn't take me with him. But people had their calling, and the road kept calling.'

Ayesha recalled how he'd looked out into the middle distance, lost in the glammed-up movie version of his own mediocre life as the social worker took her away. She sometimes looked him up. He didn't seem to have got very far down the road career-wise. Maybe something else she had inherited from him.

Joni looked at her intensely, waves of emotion passing over her face. It was a bit too much for Ayesha, who didn't dwell too long on those memories. Or feel them too hard.

'Thing is, I'm not sure he's actually that funny. But as a dad he's a fucking joke.' It was a line she'd used before, whenever she needed to segue from just how gravely dysfunctional her childhood was to just how fine she was now.

Joni didn't laugh, but she softened, sighed, then turned away before it got too much, for either of them.

They looked out into the darkness.

'I was out by fifteen myself,' Joni said after a while. 'Couldn't wait to escape. Moved from one place to another. Worked and lived in pubs and bars. Got in with the wrong people. Got myself out. Got into some bad relationships. Got out again. Kept moving, ducking, diving . . .' She had an amused sparkle in her eye, but Ayesha could see the effort it took to keep this story light.

'Thing is, that's cute when you're in your twenties. Not so smart when you get older. But then Frankie found me. Just in time really. I was in a bad way. Just escaped another bad situation and was a bit battered and bruised. Literally. Frankie took me in. First place I really felt safe to be honest.' Joni glanced at Ayesha. A moment of understanding passed between them both.

Ayesha thought of how hard Joni worked to make every-one feel welcome. How hard she worked to keep the collective going. The family. How she tirelessly found ways to compensate for Frankie's aloofness, her awkwardness. She felt a rush of affection for this endlessly loyal woman. Saw so much of herself in her.

Joni looked to the floor again and shook her head sadly.

Ayesha reached out a hand.

'Ah, fuck it,' Joni said, trying to shake it off.

'Are you okay?' Ayesha asked.

'It's all good. I'll drink it off.' She grinned at Ayesha. 'How's the high treating ya?'

Ayesha frowned. 'It's ... er, intense. Kind of lovely and gentle, then full-on freaky.'

'Yep.' Joni nodded. 'Apparently Clemmie did some course in Peru with some kind of shaman. She's a whizz at whipping up natural highs. I had very little to do with it. I just stirred when she told me to.'

'Great. So no one knows exactly what went in it?' Ayesha asked.

'Not apart from the head chef herself.'

'So many secrets!' Ayesha exclaimed.

Joni gave an uncertain smirk.

'Speaking of, I've actually got one of my own,' Ayesha continued on a whim.

Joni looked up.

'Since we're sharing ...' Ayesha steeled herself. 'I brought some ... accessories with me. In the car. They're really inappropriate.'

Joni's eyebrows were raised.

'Like what? Drugs?' she asked.

Ayesha shook her head.

'Much worse. Willy wands, pink feather boas ... There's a cake,' Ayesha looked over her shoulder dramatically, leaned in. 'And it's not even organic.'

Joni's eyes widened.

'I should have known you two would be starting a rave in the car park.'

They spun round to find Frankie grinning at them from the doorway. Joni glanced once at Ayesha, then back to Frankie.

Ayesha wondered guiltily if Frankie had heard her confession. She took in her aqua-tinted skin. It did indeed transform her into something and someone completely different – until she spoke, and then the original Frankie reasserted herself. It was a strange effect that played tricks with Ayesha's already wavy mind. She wasn't sure she liked it.

'Just swapping life stories. The usual small talk,' Joni quipped.

'Ah, it's that part of the trip already, is it?' Frankie retorted.

She stepped out to join them contemplating the dark country night, still just within the glow of the heat-filled mansion.

'I'd add mine to the mix, but I've got a few extra years on you both and we'd need to fill our glasses first,' she added drolly.

Joni laughed, pushed Frankie playfully, possibly a bit too hard. Frankie looked almost alarmed.

'So, what are the odds Jessica's gonna fuck this one up too?' Frankie asked.

219

Ayesha's heart sank. Joni also cringed.

'Ah, sounds like she's giving it a miss, so might as well crack on,' Joni repeated.

'It's just mind-boggling to me how someone could be so utterly self-serving,' Frankie continued. She looked at them both expectantly, waiting for someone to agree, but this time they both remained quiet.

Frankie shook her head, formulating her next dissection of Jessica's character, but then she swayed uncertainly and reached out for something to steady herself on. The other two grabbed her as her legs gave way. It seemed that Ayesha wasn't the only one struggling to stay level.

'Woah there,' Joni exclaimed, 'I think all this fresh air is messing with you. Time to head back into the overheated, smoky indoors. You'll feel much better there.'

'I'm fine.' Frankie recovered and tried to straighten up, 'I reckon a glass of that expensive whisky in the library'll sort me out.'

'Coming right up.' Joni gave Ayesha a knowing look as she led Frankie back into the house.

Ayesha watched them disappear through the doorway. She felt her own light-headedness more acutely now she was alone and reached out with one hand to lean on a car parked nearby. She blinked slowly, remembered the trees and the people fizzing in the forest, thought of Frankie swaying uncertainly, Yaz's dark eyes dilated, everyone screaming and gurning and coveting twigs like they were treasure. They were high. They were all high as kites. Whatever ingredients

Clemmie had used were strong. She looked out into the darkness, trying to get her head straight and willing her friend to come out from the thick black country night. The darkness moved and morphed before her eyes. Black swallowed purple swallowed indigo in an endless cycle. It wasn't necessarily unpleasant, but it was disorientating. She almost forgot why she was staring out at the night, was unsure of how long she'd been standing there. She took a breath, tried to get her bearings, make sense of the last few hours, and thought of Jessica once again. She decided to try one more time. But as she raised her phone to her face, the screen shone brightly with a new message.

Stop calling. You're dead to me.

'Yeesh. Come, man. There's another … thing happening.'

Ayesha turned to find Yaz standing in the doorway, looking from her out into the darkness and back again. Heart pounding, Ayesha looked back at her phone, unable to speak.

'Yeesh, man. Come,' Yaz insisted urgently.

Ayesha nodded and headed inside, dumbstruck.

She took one more look out into the dark and shut the door behind her, leaving her phone on the windowsill.

CHAPTER FOURTEEN

MAY 2018

'Did I wake you up?'

'No. I'm sitting on the window ledge, looking at the rooftops. Don't worry. I'm not going to jump.'

'That's not funny, Jessica.'

'Okay. Fine. I'll leave the jokes to you.'

Ayesha could hear the sounds of the city street echoing faintly in the background. Jessica sighed then said,

'I'm thinking of taking up smoking.'

'Okay. Why?'

'I just feel that if I'm going to get into bed with the uber-capitalists, I might as well go full global destruction.'

'Sounds more like self-destruction.'

'Sure. But I'll take a few acres of rainforest down with me.'

'You're not getting into bed with the uber-capitalists, Jessica.'

'Oh, but I am. Let's be honest. Let us please agree to be brutally,

unwaveringly honest with each other, Ayesha. I need just one person I can actually trust.'

'Okay.'

Ayesha thought of the countless media appearances Jessica was making now, almost on a daily basis, her delicate features seemingly everywhere in close-up. She had more opportunities now than she had had as part of the collective, but it was a very specific type of exposure. The clip that had been replayed, reshared and focused on was the moment Jessica had disclosed that her perpetrator was 'high up in a supposedly liberal paper.' And now the tabloids, the openly right-wing broadsheets and the conservative media broadcasters had turned it into a campaign, seemingly to expose those bad apples on the left for the good of womankind, and Jessica was their coat of arms.

'At least it's a choice. I know what I'm getting into. I think. Not that I had hundreds of options to choose from. It would, of course, have been nice to be able to just report this shit and have it dealt with through the official lines. But that's not how it works.'

'No.'

A pause. Ayesha could tell there was more that needed to be said. She stayed quiet, noticed for the first time that this was why their calls often lasted an hour or two. It was the only time Ayesha could bear long bouts of silence between the words, relished them even. Several cars drove by. A beep. The city settled. Jessica continued.

'I'm scared I'm losing myself.'

'What do you mean?'

'I'm surrounded by these ... these intensely privileged, powerful people who keep telling me how awful what happened to me

was. How brave I am. What a service I'm doing for the country by speaking out about it. And I know they're just using me to bring this guy down. They don't even really hide it very well. They're falling over themselves to give me everything I could possibly want so I give them the key to his downfall. I'm just a chip in their game. A really cheap one too. So who's going to hell? Him, them or me?'

'You're not going to hell, Jessica. Don't talk like that. And they came to you, remember?'

'Sure. I've just suddenly become the face of the right in this country and I don't think that's something I consented to. To be perfectly honest, I don't know what I stand for. I don't know what I ever stood for. I just wanted someone to know what happened. To care. To be outraged. But at what cost?'

Ayesha arrived half an hour late, flustered and wired, several hastily written last-minute lines overlapping in her head. Extra copies of the script were stuffed in her rucksack as she burst into the small backstage area in the central London venue they'd booked for the next live recording of *Agitated*.

The others were already there, crowded around one of the chairs facing the mirror which was lit brightly with a border of bulbs, one flickering slightly.

India sat in the chair adjusting her hair. She looked stunning tonight. Joni and Frankie stood behind her and Hassan sat nearby, his beautiful face stopping Ayesha in her tracks for a moment. She recovered quickly.

'Sorry guys. Hi! India, you look amazing,' she gushed.

India beamed. 'Thank you, sweetness. We have a special guest in tonight so an extra effort has been made.'

'Really? Shit. Who? I'm a mess.' Ayesha suddenly became painfully aware of her own hastily chosen attire, her frazzled face, her untamed hair dragged up into a frizzy pineapple.

'Lynne Lexx. Agent. We've been courting for a while. She's finally bitten,' India divulged.

'An agent? Awesome! Okay let's smash this. Get you hooked up.'

Ayesha passed around the latest version of the script.

'No major changes. Mostly just a few extra bits to my chat. Current affairs stuff. Keeping it fresh,' she explained to the others.

The women perused the pages. Hassan got up and kissed India indulgently on the lips.

'I will see you after,' he said, and with a nod to the rest of them, he headed out.

They contemplated him quietly as he went, a silent salute to his beauty. India watched the other women watch him, a look of serene satisfaction on her face. Joni turned to India.

'I'm just going to say what everyone's thinking,' she said, emotion threatening to spill over. 'You two are perfect for each other.'

India put out her hand and Joni held it with gratitude.

'We are truly blessed to have found each other,' India replied. 'And to have you to witness it.' She paused; there was more. India had a way of commanding any space she was in.

The others held their breath and waited for her to be ready. She inhaled indulgently and began again.

'I look around this room and see my sisters, in the truest sense of the word. What we are birthing is magical and essential and ever evolving, just like the birth of Hassan's love for me. That's why I'm sharing this with you first. He came to me over land and water. A long, treacherous journey that many did not make. But he was destined to survive, to find me, his soulmate. I myself have researched my ancestors and found gypsy blood on my mother's side. We were travellers too. And that is why I know the truth of his experience, his journey here, that is why we are connected through our bloodlines.'

'That makes so much sense,' Ayesha gushed.

'I opened my home to him. As a privileged white woman – albeit with Traveller bloodlines, which is why I tan so easily – it was my duty to do so. He moved onto my couch. And then he moved into my bed. And now I have invited him to share this life with me. I have asked him to marry me, and I want you all there with me.'

They gasped. Joni's eyes filled with tears as she nodded enthusiastically. Frankie was the first to hug India.

'Our first marriage in the collective. That's pretty damn beautiful,' she said.

Joni managed a croaky, 'Congratulations, man, that's fucking awesome. The family's just getting bigger, better ...'

Ayesha waited for a moment to step in too. She hugged India who received it graciously, turning her head away in order to preserve her face.

'Amazing news,' Ayesha said carefully into India's shoulder.

Of course. Of course she would marry the most perfect man. There was a pang of something painful the moment India had announced it. A sudden sinking feeling that was quickly replaced with gratitude at being included in her joy. Because that was the way of things. The Indias got the breaks. The Ayeshas got to witness it.

And the Jessicas ... Where were they in all of this? This growing family? Did she get to share in the joy too? Have some wins of her own? Ayesha shook her head, reprimanded herself silently. This was India's moment, and she had been included in it. And it was wonderful.

'Have you got a date in mind?' Joni asked.

'Late summer,' India replied. 'It will be a wild, colourful, three-day festival-themed celebration on my parents' land. Bell tents and organic food stalls and wellies and spontaneous ceilidhs.'

'Amazing!' Ayesha said.

'And I will be relying on all my sisters to help make it happen. I have another sister-friend who is the most amazing spirit. She is an ideas doula. She helps birth such perfect ceremonies and rituals, and she will be joining the wedding team and bringing her invaluable gifts and contacts with her. I can't wait for you to meet her.'

'Mate, that's so soon!' Joni said excitedly.

India spun around to face her, a hint of defensiveness in her jaw now.

'Why wait?' she challenged. 'He said yes. We have the venue. Clemmie will take charge of the details. And those fuckers at the Home Office can't touch him once he's mine.'

There was a shocked silence. Ayesha was pretty certain it was the first time she'd heard India swear. Joni looked terrified. Frankie looked impressed.

'Fuck the fucking Home Office,' Frankie chanted with approval.

'Quite,' India agreed, recovering her composure quickly. 'There are bigger battles, bigger enemies to defeat. We must unite. I have decided that the concept of the whole occasion will be unity. Of race, of creed, of class, of cause. I want us all to come together. All of us. I want this event to bring us even closer. To build bridges. A chance to forgive and to forge new unions. And to rebirth old ones.'

They nodded solemnly, but Ayesha was pretty sure the others were as confused as she was about what this actually meant.

While the others looked over the new script, Ayesha took a moment to leave the suddenly airless dressing room and find a corner to gather herself before the show. As she made her way to the backstage door, she found Hassan hovering just outside, his serious, perfect face hard to read. Ayesha faltered. Hassan looked up, and she was caught in his beautiful gaze once again. There was a moment of surprise on both sides before they composed themselves. Hassan smiled with his eyes and nodded once.

'I just heard the good news,' Ayesha ventured. 'Congratulations.'

Hassan's eyes warmed further.

'Thank you,' he said in a gentle voice, 'I am very lucky.'

'You both are!' Ayesha gushed, before checking herself, 'I mean, you're a lovely couple. Perfect really. Just really ... perfect.' She nodded enthusiastically. Hassan broke into an amused smile.

'Thank you, Ayesha.' He said her name like it was supposed to be said. It flustered her even more. He suddenly seemed a lot more human with a big grin on his face. He seemed to be waiting expectantly for her to say more, but for once, Ayesha found herself out of words. She nodded a few more times and then walked backwards into the building, a look of disappointment replacing Hassan's smile as the door closed.

Joni was up front as usual, making sure everything was running on time. When the audience had settled, she cued up the intro music. A warm cheer from the seats and Ayesha bounded on. She was still flustered from the last-minute rewrites and India's announcement which had taken up any precious time she'd had backstage to put on make-up, tame her hair or eyebrows. But something about that gave her a fresh sense of freedom. She knew this crowd now. They knew her. They didn't care if she was a bit frizzy around the edges. This was India's night anyway. So she loosened up and played with her opening bit, relaxed into performance mode and commanded the space with well-honed ease. Laughter and bright-eyed excitement returned to her from the audience. She enjoyed them enjoying her.

But as soon as she introduced the other two, she noticed something was off.

India swept onto the stage, claiming the space and the spotlight but with an aggression that Ayesha hadn't seen before. This seemed to put Frankie off balance. Her grin was tighter than usual, her natural awkwardness magnified and her militant stance exaggerated to compensate for it. It wasn't a warm entrance. The banter didn't quite land. Ayesha had to work extra hard to keep the laughs coming and all three of them seemed to be deviating from the script more and more.

'So last week I changed my profile description to comedian-slash-activist,' Ayesha began, 'and I'm not gonna lie, it was a struggle to embrace that word. No, not comedian, thank you, I mean activist. Now these two legends have been using the word willy-nilly for—'

'Willy. Such an unfortunate choice of words,' India chipped in.

The audience laughed.

Ayesha paused for a millisecond and then continued.

'Yes, sorry. Not perhaps the best choice of phrase—'

'It just goes to show, at the end of the day, we are all slaves to the D.'

A louder laugh.

Ayesha let it run. Both those lines had been hers in the script and they sounded wrong in India's voice. She flashed a look at Frankie who remained stoic and unreadable, despite it being the second time they had found themselves in a live recording with a teammate deviating dangerously from the script. Ayesha was determined to get it back on track.

'Indeed we are, India. Indeed we are ... But that word activist. It's a loaded one, isn't it? I mean, I don't own a placard, or Doctor Martens boots, I have literally no piercings or tattoos—'

'I think the most controversial thing I've seen you do is wear leopard print with dogstooth.'

More laughter, longer this time.

'—with dogstooth. Yes, that was just what I was going to ...' Ayesha glanced one more time at Frankie, who stared back at her with an expectant look – a markedly different response to the outrage she had expressed when Jessica had thrown a spanner in their best-laid plans. Ayesha sighed, said goodbye to the lines she'd worked so hard on, tried a different tack.

'Okay, well, India, you're a veteran activist. What makes you so comfortable with the title?'

India took her pause, gathered herself.

'As a woman, sometimes merely taking up space feels like an act of anarchy. Speaking truth to power, prioritizing my pleasure, uplifting my sisters, taking what I need, what I want. All this is activism.'

'Truth. Truth,' Ayesha replied. 'But when did you actually decide—'

'My work is my activism,' India interjected. 'My medium is

art. I have written the unspeakable across my body in blood. And I won't stop there. The patriarchy makes us all victims, and none more so than men themselves. I have been blessed to be in a relationship with a beautiful man of colour. Our children will be children of colour. And the plight of his people, our people, his ancestors, our ancestors, chills me to the core. It is erased from our colonial education system. It is rewritten in the HIS-story books. And that's why my new project, *The Whites of Their Eyes*, will be an exploration of the plight of all people of colour.'

The audience applauded, loudly. India beamed. None of this had been scripted, but Ayesha let it run.

'Wow. You heard it here first, peeps. Stay tuned for more info on *The White* . . . ?'

'*The Whites of Their Eyes*.'

'Indeed.'

They made it to the end of the show. It felt like years had gone by. If Ayesha had felt frazzled before it had started, she was a hot, exhausted mess by the end of it. But it was done. Recorded. In the can for the next release date.

Ayesha realized that she was suddenly really fucking angry. At them all. They were behaving as if nothing had happened, but a line had been crossed, and weeks of hard work, getting the script as tight as possible, had gone out the window on a whim of India's that everyone seemed to be okay with. Jessica had literally been cancelled for the same thing, but today everyone seemed fine with it. India was delighted with her own performance, Frankie was calm and upbeat and did not suggest doing a runner to the nearest pub to discuss India's offences and to reinvent the team, and Joni remained low-key emotional and in awe of them all.

The audience crowded around the three hosts while Joni wrapped things up in the background.

Tonight, it was India who had the biggest entourage. Young white women keen to hear about her new project, eager for an introduction. Requests for support for their projects, charities, organisations. Ayesha seethed silently. She had clocked from the first live show just how white the audiences were, but that was something she was used to from the comedy circuit. Tonight it just added to her frustration. Hassan hovered at the edge, his face a perfect mask again. Ayesha was aware of him in her periphery as she dealt with the post-show bustle. She thought of chucking him a cable or a mic stand to pack up – anything to get him involved, but one look at India and she was sure that would be overstepping the mark. He was exactly where he should be.

As Ayesha's modest entourage dissipated, Joni handed her a bottle of cold beer with a pat on the shoulder and carried on packing up. Ayesha took a couple of steps away from the crowd and sat on a speaker, taking a long swig from the bottle, her very bones tired, her spirit fed-up. Another hand on her shoulder. She looked around.

'Ayesha. Pleased to meet you. I'm Lynne Lexx. Could we talk?'

CHAPTER FIFTEEN

JULY 2018

Saturday 9.00 p.m.

Ayesha stepped into the lounge. The fire still burned fiercely in the grand fireplace with the old rifle mounted firmly above it. She wondered vaguely who had been feeding it, keeping it burning all this time.

At the far end of the room was an ornate Persian rug with an arrangement of flowers, incense and semi-precious stones placed on it in a semicircle. In the centre was a crown fashioned out of twigs, berries, leaves and wildflowers. The offerings from the forest had been added too, along with small circles of string and thread, creating an altar of natural treasures illuminated by two red candles. The room was empty and stifling. Ayesha looked at her wonky twig, the partially crushed pine cones that were slightly damp, and decided they weren't acceptable additions to the tasteful hoard. She turned and quickly chucked them into the fire. They landed on the edge of the roaring flames, wedged just far enough away to remain conspicuous. Ayesha sighed and pulled a weighty poker from its holder, trying to cajole them further in.

She heard a creak and spun round to find Yaz sauntering in through the doorway, holding a bottle of champagne and taking a swig straight out of it. Yaz looked at Ayesha holding the poker aloft and took another swig. Ayesha lowered the weapon.

'Is it at least chilled?' she asked Yaz.

'To perfection.'

Ayesha reached out for the bottle. Yaz hesitated for a second. Ayesha glared at her, surprised that her friend would be so stingy. Yaz relented and handed it over, watching Ayesha carefully as she took an exaggerated glug from it.

'All right, take it easy,' Yaz protested and snatched the bottle back.

Something had changed. There was a hardness to Yaz now, a defensiveness that hadn't been there earlier. Ayesha's eyes narrowed.

'What's with the snatching and the hoarding?' Ayesha said.

Yaz turned to her.

'What's with the skinning teeth and brown-nosing?' she threw back.

It hit Ayesha hard. She couldn't think of a reply.

Standing face to face, she suddenly saw her friend in a whole new light, clearer than before. She wondered if, finally,

Yaz's true colours were beginning to show. The quality that had up until now appeared to be healthy self-confidence was turning into something meaner, more selfish. Perhaps this was what she called on to push her career forward, why *she* had managed to go from strength to strength in such a tough, ruthless, male-dominated industry and why Ayesha hadn't – because deep down Yaz was tough and ruthless too. And maybe this was what she had been plotting and scheming with India about in the kitchen. Maybe she had decided to use this weekend to further her own career, see what India's connections could do for her . . . Was that why she was flirting with India? Was she using her? Had she been using Ayesha to get to her? Ayesha shook her head in frustrated confusion, her thoughts overlapping like frantic waves crashing on an uncertain shore. Whatever it was, her friend's presence wasn't having the reassuring, anchoring effect it had had earlier, and Ayesha resented that. After all, she'd brought her here for support. She took another greedy gulp, just to make her point.

Yaz shook her head, went to say something more, but was cut short.

'Cheers,' said a voice behind them.

Ayesha and Yaz turned to see Frankie and Joni in the doorway, each holding a weighty looking crystal glass with a rich amber liquid in it.

'Looks like you found the whisky.' Ayesha grinned.

Frankie grinned back.

'Indeed we did,' she replied. They held their glasses up. Yaz gripped the champagne bottle by its neck and shoved it in the air before taking another swig. Ayesha snatched it off her and drank deeply too. Yaz used both hands to swipe it back.

'Easy!' Ayesha protested, looking at her friend with indignation. 'There's literally a whole fridge full of the stuff.'

'Sis, if you want me to get through this next … thing, I need to be a lot more mashed up than I am right now,' Yaz explained firmly, a little aggressively.

Ayesha noticed her eyes roll involuntarily and remembered the extra half of the brownie Yaz had taken. It seemed that Ayesha might not be the only one trying to keep the edges of the world straight.

Yaz talked tough. Always. But now Ayesha could see the desperation underneath it. It was suddenly clear to her that this whole situation was taking its toll on her friend. She felt a surge of guilt for judging her so harshly, for being so suspicious of her, and rubbed at her forehead in confusion. She felt even worse about her own funny turns in the circle and in the woods. She was so focused on holding down her own panic, not causing a scene, making sure Yaz wasn't being too … *Yaz*, that she hadn't really been aware of just how much Yaz was struggling. That she must have felt alone in all this, unable to turn to Ayesha for support. This wasn't her scene at all. She was here because Ayesha had begged her to come, and she was trying to get through this as best she could by getting very drunk and high. At the same time, Ayesha wished Yaz would broaden her mind a little, be open to a new scene, just like being in the collective had done for her. She looked at Frankie's lopsided grin, thought of India's radiance, and wanted so much for Yaz to love them too; she was the fiercest, wickedest person she knew and these women were just the same. A sisterhood of kick-ass women who had changed Ayesha's life. And she just wanted them all to get on.

'It is all a bit ... woo woo,' Frankie agreed. Yaz looked at her with suspicion, not sure this was the ally she was looking for. Frankie continued, 'I'm not convinced that dressing up, singing in a circle and offering some bark to a pagan spirit is the way to move society forward to be honest. Give me cold hard facts, statistics and politics and slippery patriarchal bullshit I can call out. We could be using this space to organize, plot, take action.'

'Yeah, but even you need a day off,' Joni countered. 'Maybe even a whole weekend?' Frankie turned to her girlfriend, was about to argue back, but Joni hadn't finished.

'Look, this is India,' she insisted. 'Our India, and she's been so generous with her contacts and time. She deserves this and so much more.' Joni looked at Ayesha who nodded warmly. Encouraged, Joni turned back to Frankie. 'She thinks the world of you. She's chosen our gang to be here with her on this special day, out of everyone she knows. We're family, man.' She was almost pleading.

Frankie softened, took another swig of the expensive nectar in her glass. 'India's special brand of magic has definitely furthered the cause,' she acquiesced. 'And the bar's well-stocked at least.' She drank again and glanced at Yaz who was still trying to figure out what she thought of this new allegiance.

'What about Jessica?' Yaz blurted out.

Ayesha cringed at the words. Frankie stiffened. Joni, in turn, deflated a little.

'What about her?' Frankie asked, trying to keep her voice neutral.

'What's the deal?' Yaz pushed. 'How come she bailed last minute? Where even is she?'

Frankie smiled stiffly.

'I had no idea you cared about her so much,' she said, swirling her drink around nonchalantly.

'I don't,' Yaz shrugged. 'I don't really know her. But I know she seems to take up a lot of everyone's head space and I don't get it.' Yaz turned to look directly at Ayesha.

'Yaz, man, it's complicated ...' Ayesha tried, desperate not to have to deal with the pain of listening to them dissect Jessica yet again.

'It's okay, Ayesha. Yaz is right,' Frankie said. 'That's exactly it, isn't it? She manages to take up space even when she's not actually here. Look, I've been in this game for a long time, Yaz, and unfortunately, I've seen it before. There are a lot of damaged people out there and they tend to deal with their trauma in different ways. Some turn on themselves, some go crazy with the injustice of it all, some retreat from the world altogether. I do all I can to draw them back in, to get them to channel that pain into something positive, to belong somewhere and to find like-minded people who want to speak up, fight and make things better. But there are some that take all that investment and use it solely for their own benefit, sabotaging things for the others as they do.' Frankie's face took on a grim, ironic bitterness. 'I can't tell you how many times I've had to start again, from scratch, get rid of the dead wood, gather a new collective together, hoping this time they'll appreciate what I've built for them.'

Frankie's voice wobbled towards the end – with sadness, but also with anger. Joni put a tentative hand on her back, but Frankie stiffened, so Joni returned it to her side.

The fire crackled, raged. They stood in the overheated room by the carpet of offerings, taking in Frankie's words. Joni tried again.

'Then we make this even more special,' she said resolutely. 'We double down and celebrate our sisters even more. Let's focus on that, eh?'

Frankie looked at Joni and nodded slowly, the bitterness dissipating.

'Sure,' she said. Joni looked relieved, held up her glass and mercifully Frankie clinked it. They both took a healthy sip, looking into each other's eyes.

Ayesha should have felt relief. Some kind of line had been drawn, but actually she was shaken and even less sure of things. At first it had been just the three of them – Jessica, Frankie and Ayesha. And then Jessica had been pushed out, replaced so easily and swiftly, and now there was India, Clemmie, and Yaz too. Ayesha wasn't quite sure who was in or out and who was making these decisions. And most importantly, where that left her and her many indiscretions. She tried not to think of Jessica somewhere out there, alone. But her pain-filled, haughty expression appeared in Ayesha's mind regardless. Jessica. Jessica who rejected and sabotaged when what she wanted was to stop hurting and come into the warm glow of the circle.

But then Ayesha frowned, shook her head slightly. It didn't fit. That wasn't really Jessica, just the story Frankie and the others had created to make sense of what she'd done. She couldn't imagine Jessica actually wanting to be a part of this. She had so much going on, was only just keeping her head above water as it was. But why would she accept the invitation, only to reject it and cut all ties? It didn't make sense. Ayesha suddenly realized she had a lot of questions.

'Why are *we* here?' Yaz suddenly demanded.

Ayesha lost her train of thought. She turned to her friend with surprise, as did the others.

'What do you mean?' Frankie asked.

'Well, you said it yourself. Out of everyone India knows, and apparently, she knows everyone, she's chosen us. I'm not being funny, but I don't get it.'

'We're family,' Joni insisted.

'I'm not,' Yaz countered.

'You're Ayesha's family. That makes you family.' Joni's voice had an edge to it.

'Are you sure?' Yaz pushed. 'You can't think of any other reason why we four in particular have been chosen?' Yaz pointed at each of them individually. 'You two? Me? Ayesha? It's nice and diverse, no? Looks good on the old socials ...'

'Yaz, man,' Ayesha begged.

Then Yaz turned to Frankie.

'Is that the real reason Jessica didn't make the cut? Didn't tick enough boxes for your *collective* either? Is that why you want me in the shows instead? Why you're so angry that India invited her—'

'Enough,' Joni growled, suddenly red with rage. She stepped in front of Frankie protectively. 'You don't talk to her like that. You don't say those things.' Joni's voice wavered with anger and emotion as she glared at Yaz, pointing a threatening finger in her face.

Yaz regarded Joni coolly. If she was surprised by this sudden outburst, she didn't show it. She simply watched her carefully and held her tongue.

Ayesha held her breath, her heart pounding. She looked from one woman to the other, and then saw Joni lower her finger, rub her forehead anxiously.

'I'm sorry,' she said mournfully. 'I'm sorry man. I didn't mean to ... I just ... You crossed a line, man. Frankie did so much to bring her in. She does so much ... And I can't stand it when ... I never meant to ... Honestly, I'd never ... I'm sorry ...'

She looked at Yaz pleadingly and then at Ayesha.

Ayesha watched Yaz, whose face gave nothing away.

Eventually Yaz sighed, softened a fraction.

'It's good,' she said to Joni. 'It's all good. We're all a bit ...' Yaz shook her head. Joni looked up at her gratefully.

'Come here, man,' she said suddenly emotional and grabbing a surprised Yaz in an intense embrace. Yaz patted her back reluctantly.

'I love you, man. You're wicked. You're fucking wicked. That's why you're here. Cos you and Ayesha are the best fucking thing to happen to this group in ages. That's why. No other reason,' Joni said with conviction.

'Okay, okay.' Yaz placated her.

Joni released Yaz and wiped at both eyes, frustrated at her inability to control her emotions. She glanced up at Frankie who had remained quiet throughout. Ayesha looked up too. Frankie watched Joni with a silent expression of approval, pride even, and Joni gave a sob of relief.

'Thank you for your patience, sisters,' said an assured voice from behind them.

They turned to see Clemmie filling the doorway. She had changed into an ornate, colourfully beaded collar with matching earrings and her body and hair were wrapped in bold African print, a complex series of twists and knots causing the material to stand dramatically out at an angle from her head. There was a general gasp, and then Clemmie stepped aside to reveal India standing behind her. She wore a dashiki of brightly coloured African design that ended mid-thigh. Her dark hair had been woven into tight cane-rows revealing strips of pale scalp beneath, the paleness contrasting dramatically with the colour of her face, covered in foundation several shades darker.

Ayesha automatically glanced at Yaz, who was frowning

at India before turning to Ayesha and blinking with confusion, like she was trying to make sense of what she was looking at and clear her head, sober herself up, despite her determined effort to get as drunk as possible up until then. Ayesha's stomach twisted in knots as she tried to square impossible circles in her already confused head. She smiled and shrugged, hoping that Yaz would also make light of it. It was no use. The confusion on Yaz's face was slowly being replaced by tired outrage.

'What now?' Yaz asked weakly. But her words were lost under the applause Clemmie had once again started, Joni ensuring that Frankie engaged with enthusiasm.

'Are you kidding m—' Yaz tried once again, but the next phase of the evening was in motion now and the exhaustion showed on Yaz's face as she realized no one was listening. There were too many fights to be fought, one confrontation after another, and not enough booze to compensate.

Clemmie led India to the altar and lifted the handmade crown. She placed it carefully on her head, over the braids. A bouquet of wildflowers was also presented to her. Joni clapped eagerly. Yaz stood shaking her head and trying to summon the energy to say something. Ayesha watched her closely, grateful now for how much alcohol Yaz had consumed already. She just wanted to have a good time. She didn't want to choose a side or be the one to have to speak out about how politically incorrect this all was. And she wanted the fun Yaz, the raver, the smoker, the shape-thrower, to just let loose with her. Couldn't they just let this one slide?

From a corner of the room, Clemmie carried over an ornate chair, ancient oriental carvings framing silk upholstery. She placed it in front of the altar and India positioned herself in it.

'Please join me,' Clemmie said and arranged herself on the carpet. The other women gathered in a circle with India's throne as the focus. Yaz didn't move, but she was standing closest to India and so the circle inadvertently found her. From her standing position she stared down at India's pale scalp visible between the cane row. Ayesha willed her friend to relax, for the bubbles and brownies to do their work and bring her up so she could sit down.

Clemmie began to carefully select pieces from the altar and the other offerings. She held up a clump of daisies and tied some string around them, then added a thick sliver of bark to the stems, creating a body of sorts. As she picked up two identical leaves and fashioned them into hands, she spoke again.

'To pay homage to our goddess of goddesses, we will now make her likeness out of the bounty of Mother Earth.'

The women hesitated for a moment. Ayesha grabbed a large pebble and gamely pressed berries on it for eyes, hoping to move things forward and keep everyone busy. The others began to create their mini-Indias too. All except Yaz, who remained standing staring at the top of India's head with disdain. If she noticed, India didn't let on. She seemed to be fine with Yaz standing beside her.

When Clemmie was done, she lay her creation at her feet. The others did the same. The small effigies varied in style, but also in quality. They all had a head of sorts, a body and some limbs, but Clemmie's was by far the most superior design. Ayesha's looked a bit like a potato head, but she was relieved that she had at least discarded her own wonky offerings in the fire earlier.

India surveyed each one with delight, seemingly unaware that Yaz hadn't made one.

'Goddess of goddesses,' Clemmie began. 'You have been crowned and throned. You have been immortalized and recreated. This is your time, your space. We are here to honour you, to encourage and serve you. Tell us your desire,' she urged India.

India closed her eyes and took a breath. Then she slowly opened them and smiled. She glanced over to Yaz and then away. She got up, put the bouquet on the chair and stepped over the effigies into the middle of the circle. With one swift movement, she shed her dashiki and lay down naked on the floor.

'I want you to massage me,' she demanded.

Clemmie was at her head. She nodded solemnly, seemingly nonplussed by the nakedness. She placed both her hands on India's temples and began to massage, careful to avoid the tightly braided cane row, working the dark make-up deeper into India's skin. Joni dutifully kneeled by one arm and began to massage it. One quick look from her and Frankie followed suit. Clemmie looked pointedly at Ayesha who was positioned near India's feet. Ayesha swallowed down any aversion she might have been feeling, smiled gamely and started with an ankle. Clemmie moved her gaze to Yaz who was still standing in her place at the edge of the circle, staring with disgust at the scene before her. Ayesha looked at Yaz too. They locked eyes.

Yaz glared at Ayesha, weariness and disappointment present in equal measure.

Ayesha glared back in desperation.

Yaz then looked from Ayesha to India to the women around her each holding a naked body part and working the skin. India's shins and forearms were a rich golden brown that almost matched the leather tan of her face. But towards her upper thighs and arms the skin became paler, uneven, stripy until her torso and genitals were almost as pale as her scalp. Ayesha tried not to look at the tuft of mousey brown pubic hair, or too closely at the foot she was touching. She kept her eyes locked on Yaz, imploring her silently to get involved.

There was a moment where Yaz seemed to seriously consider taking part for Ayesha's sake, but then she reeled back in revulsion. Ayesha watched as Yaz straightened up, gestured and opened her mouth to finally speak.

'Fuck this.'

There was a bang. And then another. A bright flash and a hiss. Three even louder bangs and the sumptuous silk chair that India had been sitting in moments before burst into flames. The women leaped up in horror. Another perilously bright ember landed with a fizzle on the far corner of the priceless rug and began to singe a hole through it. A scream. A scramble. Ayesha's voice stuck in her throat. Flames. Not flames. Anything but that. They had to get out. This time they would all get out. But she found herself unable to move. Yaz appeared by her side and they held on to each other. India pushed past them. Clemmie disappeared. Someone else pulled them away from the blaze and then headed towards the burning chair. With a huff and a thump, thump, thump, Joni attacked the fire with a heavy blanket. Ayesha watched the flames rage higher, but Joni persisted, red-faced, resolute, and finally the flames began to surrender. Another thump in syncopated rhythm to Joni's, and Ayesha turned to see Frankie attacking the carpet with a booted foot. The two women worked until the fire subsided, then stopped, exhausted and speechless.

For a moment they stood catching their breath, then a metallic click made them all look up. India stood, naked and determined, a heavy rifle in her hands. Ayesha looked from the charred chair to the fireplace, and realized that India had wrested the gun from above the mantelpiece. She watched with horror as India trained the gun on her, then Yaz, then continued moving the barrel across the room.

'Watch it!' Yaz exclaimed.

Then Clemmie stepped into the doorway.

She stood with another rifle cocked and aimed at the room. Her eyes scanned the group, the barrel of the gun moving with her gaze. Ayesha and Yaz gripped each other harder as the gun momentarily hovered in their direction once more. To their relief, Clemmie stepped forward but then past them both and joined India, both rifles now aimed towards the chair, and therefore Joni.

Joni looked back calmly, almost surrendering to her fate with a complete acceptance that chilled Ayesha to the bone.

They waited a moment longer, all frozen in this bizarre tableau, then India swung around and looked closely at the fireplace. She poked at a log in the fire with the barrel of the rifle. It spat an arch of golden embers at her that made them all flinch, then settled into a steady roar of heat.

Relief rippled around the group, but also confusion.

'You might want to put that down,' Joni said slowly to Clemmie who still had the gun trained on her. 'And rethink that fire.'

Clemmie lowered the rifle, shaking her head resolutely.

'There's nothing wrong with that fire, or that fireplace,' she replied. 'In all the decades, centuries our family has been here, there's never been an incident like this. It's literally designed to ensure it's almost impossible for that to happen.'

Ayesha studied the thick hearth that jutted out expansively into the room, the face of the fireplace and the mantel made of the same cold, dark stone that covered the outside of the house and seemed to defy the light and heat.

'Someone's been tampering with the fire. They've put something in with the wood. Or on the wood,' Clemmie concluded, joining India beside the flames.

'That's a bit of a jump,' Ayesha heard herself blurt out.

India and Clemmie spun around, their eyes wide with surprise.

'I mean, it just spat a bit,' she tried again, 'that's all. Y'know like when it's a bit damp ... I don't know. It just seems a bit harsh to suddenly jump to conclusions ...' Ayesha's voice faded as the two women glared at her.

'You seem to know a lot about fires, Ayesha,' Clemmie suggested lightly. 'Is there anything else you want to tell us?'

Ayesha felt Yaz grow an inch taller next to her.

'You wanna tell us why you're holding a gun first?' she said grimly. 'A fucking gun.' She spat the words out at Clemmie.

'To keep us safe,' Clemmie spat back. 'To keep my family's property and possessions safe. To keep my body and my person safe.'

'Where do you keep the firewood?' Frankie suddenly stepped between them both with a new determination. Clemmie turned to look at Frankie, keen to engage in this new possible thread.

'There's a sheltered spot to the side of the house,' Clemmie replied.

'Outside?' Frankie confirmed.

'Yes.'

Frankie looked at Clemmie, her eyes wide, her jaw clenching and unclenching. India joined them, looking excitedly from one to the other.

'That could be where they got to the wood,' India said resolutely. Clemmie and Frankie nodded enthusiastically.

'It's got to be,' Clemmie concurred. The more the three women looked at each other, the more determined their expressions, the surer they were of their theory. And then they seemed to come to the same conclusion at the same time.

'There's really only one person it could be,' Frankie stated firmly. 'It makes sense now. Accepting the invitation, cancelling last minute, only to have planned to sabotage the whole thing. Just like she did before.'

Clemmie nodded quickly as she pieced this all together. India thumped the floor aggressively with the butt of her rifle.

'There's no limit to what she would do to ruin my special day,' she added.

'The fuck are you talking about?' Yaz exclaimed, looking at the three women with alarm. 'She's not even here.'

Joni also began to protest, but Frankie was already stomping out of the room.

Clemmie swung around and followed Frankie out. Seconds later, lights flooded the grounds outside. Ayesha stood frozen, watching through the window as Clemmie aimed her rifle beyond the lights into the darkness.

'You've gone too far, Jessica,' she called into the night. 'You could have really hurt someone. If you're on my property, come out now.' She swung the barrel slowly along the dark horizon. India joined her, her dashiki hastily retrieved, her stance a perfect mirror of Clemmie's, her eyes wild, hungry, her jaw now rigid.

'Jessica, enough. You've fucked up my party. You've fucked up the house. Now come out before things get really serious,' she commanded.

The darkness of the country night remained impenetrable.

'Right. Enough of this. Let's smoke her out. I'm heading this way. You do a round of the house,' India instructed, and set off to the left before Clemmie could protest. Ayesha turned her head to see Frankie enter the room only to grab a poker from the fireside and march out once more to join them.

'I'll head the other way,' she heard her say.

The three women stomped in different directions while Ayesha, Yaz and Joni stood watching from the scorched lounge. The open front door had allowed some of the stifling heat to escape and Ayesha realized she felt relieved, despite the hunt for Jessica that was now in full swing. Relieved she wasn't massaging India's naked body, relieved she didn't have a gun pointed at her face, relieved she wasn't under suspicion, and relieved that she was still holding on to Yaz.

She was also very glad that no one had been hurt – either by the fire, or the rifle. She looked at the devastation around her. The beautiful chair, the sumptuous carpet, ruined. She didn't dare let her thoughts venture further than that. It was just an unfortunate accident. She glanced quickly at the fire and noticed that no trace of the pine cones or twig remained. She let out half a sigh.

Frankie was the first to return with a dangerous new glint in her eye, elated, determined to root out Jessica.

'I checked the firewood store and that whole side of the house. It doesn't look like it's been tampered with.'

Clemmie also returned, shaking her head, then India, glaring at the others hungrily, hoping they had something better to offer.

Clemmie lowered her gun and looked at India.

'You can put that down. It's ancient. It's only good for scaring someone, giving them a nasty bump on the head at best.'

India looked at the antique weapon in her hands and lowered it.

'Well, what the hell is that?' she asked, pointing at the gun Clemmie was holding.

'Hunting rifle. Security. Last resort. We keep it locked away.'

They looked out one more time into the darkness, all three of them reluctant to give up the hunt. Frankie eventually slung the poker back into its holder in frustration.

Clemmie walked towards the burnt carpet and took a closer look.

'What actually happened?'

Frankie joined her, inspecting the damage carefully. Joni stepped forward too. She shook her head and looked at their guns. 'Probably best you put those away,' she said grimly.

Frankie nodded and India and Clemmie acquiesced. They turned and walked out of the room. Yaz and Ayesha loosened their grip on each other. They were both still trembling. Yaz looked at Ayesha with genuine fear in her eyes.

'I need to clean up a bit,' she said pointedly to Ayesha. Ayesha nodded.

'Good idea.'

CHAPTER SIXTEEN

MAY 2018

'I'd be careful, is all I'm saying.'

'You don't need to worry.'

'Well, I do. Try to at least have something of your own going.'

'I do. Kind of. Well, I'm working on it.'

'Good. It can be all-consuming. This ... gang. Sorry, collective. Which is a wonderful thing for a while. You go from feeling completely isolated and alone to being at the heart of it all. Drawn into the bosom. Frankie's stiff little bosom.'

'Jessica!'

Jessica chuckled, sighed.

'I do miss that bit. Belonging somewhere. Joni's cuppas. God, she makes a good cup of tea ...'

They considered Joni's tea-making skills in quiet awe for a while.

'I worry about her too,' *Jessica continued.*

'Who, Joni?'

'She's young. Younger by a fair amount.'

'Younger than Frankie?'

'Yep, by at least ten years. I'm afraid that's one area I am definitely conservative about.'

'Joni's hard as nails.'

'Except she's not.'

Ayesha didn't argue.

'I know she must be livid that I upset Frankie,' Jessica continued, 'but I do worry . . . I worry for us all.'

'So how does this . . . collective work exactly?'

Ayesha took a sip of cold, crisp white wine and looked at Lynne Lexx across the lacquered table in the lounge of the members' club just off the main Soho drag. She had concluded that Lynne must have made separate arrangements to meet with India and tried to let the beginnings of any guilt she might have been feeling wash down with the wine.

'It's just a group of us that have got together to support each other really,' she replied.

'Great. So, it's a mutual thing. You all found each other.'

Lynne looked at Ayesha with a gentle intensity. She seemed to genuinely be trying to understand. Her fine blonde hair was cut in a short bob and swept back off her face, which was fresh with warm smile wrinkles at the edges of her eyes. Her bright red lipstick was the same shade Ayesha remembered her wearing that night after the show, when Lynne had first approached her.

Ayesha glanced around the plush room, taking in the leather armchairs, the soft lighting, the other members exuding quiet importance, leaning back, talking warmly, but discreetly. She tried to remind herself she belonged.

'Well, Frankie did the heavy lifting,' Ayesha conceded. 'She kind of got in touch. Got me in touch with India, with the others.'

'So, it's Frankie's thing?' Lynne's eyebrows raised slightly.

'No, it's not like that,' Ayesha explained. 'India's the one that got us the recording studio. Joni's tech, roadie and guard dog so . . .'

'So, you make the decisions as a collective?'

'Yep, pretty much.' Ayesha took another sip of her wine, conscious of how she was holding the glass, even more conscious of how many times she had been told by the others what was happening after it had been decided.

'And who came up with that term? The collective?' Lynne pressed.

Ayesha faltered.

'I'm . . . not sure. I guess it was Frankie? We kind of always called ourselves that. Because that's what it is,' she concluded.

Lynne nodded.

'And what do you pay yourselves?'

'Pardon?' Ayesha paused mid sip.

'How does the money work?' Lynne enquired gently.

Ayesha thought for a moment.

'Well, there isn't any really.'

'From the ticket sales. Downloads. Patreon. That sort of thing,' Lynne elaborated.

Ayesha shrugged.

'It kind of just gets pumped back into the collective?' she guessed.

'Okay.' Lynne paused, then pressed on. 'And the media appearances? You did lots of those for a bit. Did you negotiate a fee?'

Ayesha tried to keep up.

'I don't think . . . The thing is, it's not really about that. It's activism,' she explained. 'We're speaking out. Trying to raise awareness. There's so many people who . . . When you see those young women at the end of the show . . . They're so . . . inspired, grateful. They've never had anywhere to go to talk about this stuff.' Ayesha caught herself, realized that she was quoting Frankie word for word. Parroting her inflections even. The young woman's desperate, hurting face from the trip to Edinburgh flashed across Ayesha's mind. She sighed sadly, smiled bravely.

Lynne nodded sympathetically, she took a breath and smiled back at Ayesha.

'Yes. It's very impressive what you've created,' she said.

They both took another quiet sip of wine. The afternoon sun shone gently on the table between them. Lynne tried again.

'Tell me about the writing. Where do you get your ideas from?'

Ayesha put down her wine glass.

'Well,' she began. 'We started out brainstorming together and then I'd go away and write it up into some sort of loose script and then the others would come in and add a few flourishes, put it in their own words. That sort of thing. But then the turnaround for episodes and content got tighter so I just kind of started doing it myself.'

'That's impressive, Ayesha. It's a lot of content you've generated.'

Lynne seemed genuinely appreciative of Ayesha's work. Ayesha sat forward in the cushioned chair.

'I love it,' she enthused. 'And the others are great. India's really great. Did you hear about her latest project?'

'I did hear her mention it.' Lynne acknowledged. She gave it a fraction of a moment then continued. 'So how many hours do you reckon you work on each script?'

Ayesha shrugged.

'No idea. Until it's done. But then sometimes something comes up on the news and I'm literally writing it into the final version on the bloody bus on the way there. That's happened a few times.'

'Wow.' Lynne sat back, giving Ayesha her full attention.

'Well, there's a fair bit happening in the news at the moment. You blink and suddenly your material feels outdated,' Ayesha quipped.

'It takes quite a mind to keep it all so fresh. What do you get paid writing-wise?'

'Sorry?'

'Is it word count or by the hour? Is it on delivery of the script or ...?'

'It doesn't really work like that. We all just sort of pile in. Everyone grafts. That's just my bit.'

'Ah okay. So, what about income, if you don't mind me asking?'

'Income?'

'Well, it sounds like this is all part of the activism that you do, and that it's not about the money. I appreciate that. It's an incredible investment of time and talent. So, are you gigging too? Is that what pays the rent?'

Lynne's eyes searched Ayesha's, her gentle pressing suddenly hitting the spot.

Ayesha felt the nausea she'd been trying to hold at bay for months threaten to rise up and regurgitate all that lovely, expensive wine right back out and onto Lynne's exquisite cream jacket.

The truth was, she couldn't seem to slow down the increasing four-figure number that greeted her whenever she had to use her online banking. Four figures growing exponentially. With a tiny minus sign next to it.

There was always so much to do. And no time for gigs. No agent to set them up or be on her case. She just assumed that this new gig would eventually pay. They were selling out every event. The focus was always on being as accessible as possible and they put out messages every week letting everyone know that cost was not an obstacle, but most people paid and often sponsored a seat too. It was part of the ethos of this new community. Of the collective. No one else in the group had ever brought up pay. It didn't seem to be an issue for anyone else, which baffled Ayesha because that's all she thought about, in between edits and write-ups. It even dominated her dreams. Numbers plummeting, viewings soaring, likes, shares, five-star reviews – all overlapping and spinning in a perpetual spiral as she slept fitfully. And the overdraft increasing, and Ayesha knowing that one day, any day now, it would be blocked. And that would be it.

Frankie had referred to expenses a few times, like when she had booked them a last-minute flight back from Edinburgh. Ayesha had got so desperate she almost asked if she, too, would at least be able to claim some of those.

But Ayesha would rather have eaten the cardboard box her last bit of cereal came in than be the one to bring up money.

'Yes, I squeeze a gig in when I can,' she said quietly.

They both took another quiet sip, Lynne regarding her carefully. She put her glass down gently but firmly onto the lacquered table.

'Ayesha, you should be paid – well – for what you do,' she said steadily. 'You should have been paid from the start. However worthy the cause is.'

Lynne continued looking at Ayesha with a steady gaze, mirroring Yaz's gaze. And her words.

Ayesha struggled, squirmed slightly, then composed herself, looked Lynne in the eye, and held it.

Yaz raised her glass.

'To representation,' she declared.

'To representation,' Ayesha echoed and they drank their rum and ginger beer.

They were in Ayesha's local. The Earl Spencer. A pub that had witnessed dramatic changes in the decades it had stood watch over the neighbourhood. Ayesha could still remember what the area was like growing up. Despite being moved from one foster home to another, social services had managed to keep her in the same borough at least, the same school for most of her formative years, which was why she had the gift of those precious memories with Yaz and the gang.

She remembered the old Earl Spencer, or the Trinny pub as it was called then. A haven for the Trinidadian community that had settled there in the Fifties. Across the road had been the Half Moon, or the Irish pub. Both were now under new management. She looked over the road at what was now an exclusive restaurant surrounded by high hedges, with a menu that didn't have prices on it.

Ayesha remembered her and Yaz being out with their school friends on this very street, not long after she'd got her flat. One of their friends was arguing with an old Irish man and it was threatening to turn into a full-blown fight. The girl's uncle sauntered out of the Trinny pub, pint in hand, to see what the trouble was. When he saw his niece involved in the altercation, his strides became more decisive, his face set to defend her. But when he stood next to her and looked at the man she was exchanging heated words with, he broke into a gold-toothed smile.

'Relax,' he told his niece, putting his arm around the man, 'he's all right. I used to fight him.' To the girl's bemusement, the two men embraced and then sparred playfully before walking into the pub arm in arm.

Now that same pub served rum in jam jars and chips in mini goldfish bowls, but the lovers' rock classics were still playing, perhaps in homage to the original establishment, perhaps because they were so old they had become retro. Who really knew?

Yaz and Ayesha drank awkwardly from the jam jars as Lord Kitchener's 'London Is The Place For Me' played gently around them.

'So, it's official then. Lynne Lexx is your new agent.' Yaz beamed at her friend. 'It's certainly a step up from that Simon dude.'

Ayesha snorted.

'D'you know my first call with Lynne was longer than all the calls with Simon put together?'

'The bar's set so fucking low you're actually grateful your agent spoke to you,' Yaz said.

'He wasn't that bad. I didn't make it easy for him,' Ayesha protested gently.

Yaz frowned. 'Why, because you walked out of a gig you'd just been fired from for being too brown? Shit girl, that is some diva behaviour right there. No wonder he lost his shit,' she said sarcastically, cutting her eye at Ayesha.

Ayesha watched her friend's face as she tried to negotiate her rum and ginger beer. A wave of love surged through her, as it often did when she was around Yaz – especially when she had her back. Hanging out with this funny, frank, no-fucks-giving woman was still her favourite thing to do.

GODDESSES

'I could get Lynne to come see you do a gig. Put in a good word,' she suggested.

Yaz looked back at her friend and smiled like a Cheshire cat.

'Actually, I've got some news of my own,' she said enigmatically. 'You ain't the only one with fresh *representayshun*.' She laid the London accent thick on the last word.

Ayesha looked at her with surprise.

'What? You got a new agent? When?'

'Couple of weeks ago.' Yaz shrugged nonchalantly. 'He approached me after a gig in town. Gave me his card. I played it cool. Looked him up. Turns out he's a big deal.'

'Really? Who is he?' Ayesha asked.

'Will Thomson.'

'Shit! He's part of . . . Yaz, that's massive!' Ayesha gushed.

'Yeah, it's pretty sweet. Turns out it makes quite a difference having a posh white Oxbridge graduate on your team. My guy is *co-nnec-ted*,' Yaz exclaimed.

'No shit,' Ayesha replied.

'And he's so terrified of speaking over a queer brown woman he leaves these long silences after I've spoken in case I've got more to say. I had to tell him, *Bruv, I was done five minutes ago, what's the hold-up?*'

'Ha!' Ayesha chuckled. 'So has he hooked you up?'

'Sis, my pager's blowing up,' Yaz bragged. 'I've got meetings and gigs booked in till next year and you best believe he's negotiating hard for the cash money.'

'Yaz! That's amazing.' Ayesha beamed.

Yaz remained cool. She watched Ayesha for a moment, deciding whether to continue, and then she did.

'There's something else. He's also Jessica's new agent.'

Ayesha looked at her in surprise. Jessica hadn't mentioned a new agent in their calls.

'Really?'

'Yeah. You cool with that?'

Ayesha thought for a moment.

'I mean, sure,' she replied thoughtfully. 'Have you seen her?'

'No,' Yaz shook her head, 'I just saw her on the website. She's pretty high-profile at the moment. Will's kept busy managing all that.'

Ayesha thought of the articles and interviews that had only intensified over the last few weeks. The political controversy that had ensued and the wider discussion about how this scandal could bring down the whole paper, the media organisation it belonged to, the entire Opposition party.

She recalled her last conversation with Jessica. Another two-hour marathon. She wasn't really surprised Jessica hadn't mentioned the new agent; she had been anxious, distracted, but also resigned to the rollercoaster ride she was now destined to see through to its messy end. Ayesha had listened with sympathy and then finally, sleepily, they had said goodnight.

The opening bars of 'Silly Games' lilted through the sound system.

Ayesha snapped herself out of her reverie to find Yaz watching her with concern. She leaned forward.

'Hopefully this means we'll all get paid now. With a capital P,' Yaz said meaningfully.

Ayesha tried to meet Yaz's eye, failed. She had no idea how she was going to balance Lynne's expectations with Frankie's. She just hoped that it would somehow mean she would find a way to get her finances in order, pull herself out of this hole, keep her flat. That sort of thing.

'Damn right,' she exclaimed in what she hoped was an assertive tone.

'Because that's what we deserve,' Yaz pushed.

Ayesha felt herself stiffen.

'Sure,' she replied.

'All of us.'

A wave of irritation surged through Ayesha.

'I can take care of my own finances, thank you,' she said defensively.

'You sure?'

'What's that supposed to mean?'

Yaz remained fixed on Ayesha.

'I just don't like anyone taking the piss out of you, that's all.'

'No one's taking the piss!' Ayesha flushed a hot red. She didn't need this on top of everything else. Everyone else.

Yaz backed down.

'Okay, okay. I'm sorry, yeah? It's cool.'

She raised her jam jar once more.

'*Representayshun.*'

CHAPTER SEVENTEEN

JULY 2018

Saturday 10.00 p.m.

Yaz and Ayesha hurried up the staircase and up again to
their comparatively cosy room on the top floor. Yaz sat on
the edge of one of the beds, elbows on her knees, head in
her hands, trying to think straight. Ayesha perched on the
bed opposite.

'Are you okay?' Ayesha ventured.

'Not really, Yeesh. This is getting less and less fun and
more and more like a bad dream.'

'You look great,' Ayesha offered.

'I look like a character in one of those bad dreams. So do
you. Yeesh, these women ... this crew ... it's fucking weird
mate. They're all a bit ...' Yaz struggled to find the right
words, to hold on to a thought.

'Some of it's a bit out there, but so what?' Ayesha tried.

'There's brownies, champagne . . . You've got to broaden your horizons a bit, Yaz—'

'No, I don't, Yeesh. My horizons were fine where they were,' Yaz pushed back. But she softened almost immediately. 'Look, I get that this has opened some doors—'

'No Yaz. It's not that.'

'Okay, well, I get it's been good to meet other people who have been through some of the stuff—'

'It's life-changing,' Ayesha insisted. 'To be able to . . . to even be in a room with people who get it.'

'I know, Yeesh—'

'No, Yaz, you don't.' Ayesha snapped.

Yaz flinched, the hurt showing on her face, and then she nodded and tried again.

'Do you really feel that they get it? Do you feel they get you?' She looked hard at her friend.

'Yes, actually. I do,' Ayesha replied.

'Yeesh, the shit they're wearing. The fucking blackface. The *guns*. They just tried to hunt someone down for fuck's sake—' Yaz reasoned.

Ayesha shook her head. 'I knew you'd be like this,' she said.

'Like what?' Yaz frowned.

'Looking for any little thing to make an issue out of. It was just a bit of fun. And it's not blackface. It's a couple of Fenty shades darker than—'

'A couple!' Yaz retorted, incredulous.

Ayesha refused to acknowledge that she had thought the

same thing. Instead she doubled down and let all the frustration and tension out at Yaz.

'Why are you being like this?' Ayesha fired back.

'Yeesh, are you actually having fun? Have you stopped
to check? Or have you been too busy shoving your nose up
their arses—'

'Shut up!'

'No, you shut up!' Yaz shouted. 'What the fuck, Yeesh?
We're in some duchess's house who's literally got a room full
of appropriation, you keep looking around for Jessica like
she's the Second Coming, and everyone's acting like they're
Krishna resurrected or his number one disciple. You're massaging some white woman's feet while she aims a gun at you
and acting like it's the rave of the decade! Get me the fuck out
of here. I beg you.'

Yaz glared at Ayesha and then looked down again with a
frustrated sigh. She massaged her temples, her eyes darting
one way then the other trying to get a handle on the situation. Ayesha could see her battling the high now, desperate
to anchor herself in some kind of reality.

'Something's not right, Yeesh. I think ... I think I saw ...
some weird shit going down. Weirder than the rest of it—'

'Oh come on, Yaz—'

'No, hear me out. Jessica ... It's not right. Someone's messing with you. She's not—'

'Are you starting on Jessica now, too? Are you jealous?
Is that it?'

Yaz looked at Ayesha, incredulous.

'Are you joking? Of what? Of your I-Went-To-Rhodesia-On-My-Gap-Year coven? Of some bloodthirsty white bitches who wanted to shoot someone down for jokes? Of your Frida-Glasto-floral nightmare get up? The vibe's dead. The party's dead. Let's bounce.'

Ayesha frowned.

'What did you say?'

'You look like Glastonbury died on you.'

'No. You said dead. It's dead . . .'

'Well, I'm sorry to break it to you, Yeesh, but it stopped being fun a while ago,' Yaz countered.

Ayesha observed her friend with new suspicion.

'That's what Jessica's message said,' she accused. 'She said I was dead to her. Jessica doesn't talk like that.'

Yaz shook her head.

'Exactly. That's what I'm trying to tell you. The messages . . . You were outside, on your own, right? You tried to call her—'

'What's going on, Yaz?' Ayesha demanded.

Yaz looked up at Ayesha, an urgency in her eyes.

'I don't know. I don't know, Yeesh. And I don't care. Let's just get out. Enough, man,' she pleaded.

'We can't go,' Ayesha reasoned. 'Jessica might come.'

Yaz frowned with confusion.

'She's not coming, Ayesha—'

'She might, and I need to be here if she does.'

Yaz shook her head.

'Fuck that. She's not here, fam. What is it you lot don't get? She's not here! But I am,' she said loudly.

269

'You *are* jealous!' Ayesha accused.

Yaz reeled back in shock.

'What now?'

'Is that what all this is about? Are you that jealous that you would—'

'ARE YOU THAT MENTAL?' Yaz shrieked in exasperation.

The word reverberated around the room, around Ayesha's head and body.

Mental.

Back over the decades it echoed. Over the years that word had chased her, thanks to the public knowledge of her mum's sectioning, and here it was, coming out of her best friend's mouth.

Ayesha didn't realize what she had done until the numbness and shock gave way to pain. A throbbing in her hand that was still balled into a fist. Yaz's face, forced sideways by the blow, turned back to her in shock and pain. Then it morphed into rage and she came at Ayesha. They fought ferociously. Like sisters. Something crashed. Something else cracked. Ayesha heard shouting and then someone pulled them apart. Frankie held on to Yaz and Ayesha felt Joni's strong grip on her arms.

'Shit, you two. What the fuck?' Joni loosened her hold and tried to make Ayesha look at her.

'Yeah, Ayesha. What the actual fuck?' came Yaz's furious voice. 'Did you actually punch me? Bitch, are you crazy?'

Ayesha felt the rage surge through her once again and she lunged for Yaz. But Joni was close enough to pull her back in time.

'Call me that again. Go on,' Ayesha spat at Yaz.

'Okay this is hilarious, I literally don't know anyone who is closer than the two of you so just stop it.' Frankie's voice was calm but firm. They froze, catching their breath and staring furiously at each other.

'Now we're going to let go and all four of us are going to go straight to the drinks trolley downstairs and neck a good portion of that whisky. Are you with me?' Frankie demanded.

Ayesha was breathing angrily, glaring at Yaz who glared back, a fierce glint in her eye and a desperate desire to say more. But Frankie's tone made Yaz hold her tongue and the rage Ayesha had felt dissipated almost as quickly as it had materialized. She nodded grimly. Ayesha felt Joni's grip loosen once more as Frankie did the same with Yaz. The two friends watched each other, waves of intense emotion passing between them as they were led back downstairs.

In the library, Frankie poured four healthy measures of fifty-year-old single malt from a delicate crystal decanter into weighty crystal tumblers and handed them out from the tray. They all took a swig, Ayesha and Yaz still seething, Frankie and Joni watching them closely. Joni looked like she was about to cry. She gulped down a good measure from her own glass and looked at the two of them hard.

'It breaks my fucking heart to see you two like this. It's not right. You're like sisters. What the fuck?' Joni pleaded.

Yaz and Ayesha both fought back tears too. They clenched their jaws, not taking their eyes off each other.

'We've got to stick together,' Joni continued, 'Jessica's already tried to mess things up. And now this? Come on man. We're family. This is better than family. And it's so fucking beautiful. We've got to fight for it. Nothing's worth this. Nothing … Ah, fuck it.' She turned away as the tears threatened to overwhelm her and took another shaky gulp. Ayesha did the same. Yaz didn't move.

A rush of fabric and India swept into the room, Clemmie close behind. India was wearing the crumpled dashiki, Clemmie still in her traditional African attire, the headdress only slightly askew despite recent events. India stopped, scrutinized the four women closely, and homed in on Yaz and Ayesha.

'Hmm. The energy is dense in here. Has there been trouble, sisters?'

Frankie kept her eyes on the two friends. 'Nothing a good drink and a boogie won't fix.'

India wasn't convinced. She looked again from one woman to the other, hesitated briefly, then,

'Yaz, can you help me with something? Bring your glass.'

Yaz looked at India with surprise. India had already turned and was heading out of the room. Yaz took one more look at each woman and then moved quickly. She grabbed a bottle from the drinks tray and followed India.

Clemmie regarded the other three carefully, before hurrying out herself.

Ayesha stood with Frankie and Joni and watched Yaz leave, a piece of her heart leaving the room with her.

But also, fuck her.

She downed the last of the Scotch then grabbed the decanter and topped up Frankie and Joni's glasses too, clumsily sloshing it about.

'Easy!' exclaimed Joni, trying to make light of the mess Ayesha was making. Ayesha slammed the decanter down on the countertop causing the other two women to jump.

'Right. How about that rave in the car park then?' she demanded, bitterly.

Frankie and Joni looked at her in silent bewilderment. She tried again.

'Come on! Who's with me?'

Frankie looked at Joni. Joni raised a hand, opened her mouth to placate Ayesha. But Ayesha jumped in first.

'No? Cool. Cool. Cool. No problem!'

She spun around and the other two women watched in silence as Ayesha stormed past them and out of the front door, grabbing her phone from the ledge.

She jabbed at the screen clumsily as she stomped into the night.

'Jessica!' she screamed into the phone. 'You're right. This party's dead. This whole scene is stale as fuck. Fake as fuck. I don't blame you, they don't get it. None of them. They don't fucking get it, do they? Not really.'

Tears of rage and pain threatened to overwhelm her. But she pushed them down and shouted even louder.

'In the end, it's just you and me, J. Just you and me,' she added bitterly into a beeping, disconnected line.

Jessica remained unreachable. Ayesha huffed in frustration. All the things that had happened in such quick succession raced around her frazzled mind. The fire in the lounge, the guns, the fight with Yaz.

Something didn't feel right. None of it felt right. They had never fought before. In all their years of friendship there had been nothing but fierce, frank love between them. How had it got to the point where she had hit her best friend? She had actually hit Yaz? Ayesha shook her head violently, drunkenly, trying to push the image of Yaz's shocked, pain-filled face from her mind's eye.

But there was something else. Something that felt even less right. What was that knot in her stomach? The thing that had bruised her so much she'd had to get out, get away from them all, shout and scream because she felt so stupid, so betrayed.

'Jess—'

She stopped shouting for a moment, just long enough to hold on to one thought until it solidified in her foggy head. The image that came was India beckoning Yaz, Yaz turning to follow her. That was it. That was what hurt so much. It hadn't been her who had asked India if Yaz could come; it was India who had instructed Ayesha to invite Yaz. It wasn't Yaz who should have been questioning why she'd been invited, it was Ayesha.

Because that was the real reason she was here. It was clear to her now, crystal clear, that she had only ever been invited by India so that she would bring Yaz. The knot in her stomach became a lump in her throat, the pain and rage, the betrayal and manipulation, the frustration and helplessness of being stuck here alone was too much.

'JESSICAAAAA!' she screamed desperately.

'That's enough. Jessica doesn't care about you, Ayesha.'

Ayesha jumped. She hadn't noticed Frankie approach and her tone alone slapped the scream out of her. Stopped her short. She was using her righteous voice now. The strong, resonant one she used when she was going head to head with politicians, journalists, giving impassioned speeches to dewy-eyed students at the front of protest marches, or on graduation day.

'Jessica doesn't care about anyone.' Frankie glared sternly at her.

'How do you know that?' Ayesha spat back. It was an accusation. Not a question.

'Because Jessica only looks out for herself. That's the cold hard truth of it. It's a hard fact to face up to, especially when you've supported someone so intensely. But sadly, Jessica only cares about one person. And that's Jessica.'

'You don't know that,' Ayesha protested.

'Yes, I do,' Frankie replied firmly.

'No. You don't get it. None of you get it . . .'

'She made you look like a fool on live TV, Ayesha. She tried to destroy the collective,' Frankie insisted.

'No, she didn't, she just wanted to find a way to . . . to . . . she couldn't see any other way.' Ayesha tried desperately to defend her one remaining friend.

'She's sending confusing contradictory messages, she's playing games, and she's trying to ruin this for all of us,'

275

Frankie countered. 'Why would you show any loyalty to someone like that?'

'Why are you hating on her so hard?' Ayesha yelled back.

'Enough! Don't you dare throw this back in my face. After everything I've done for you,' Frankie shouted. Her anger took them both by surprise. They stood glaring at each other, Ayesha's heart racing wildly, her breathing coming in angry pants.

They were all snakes. All of them. There was nowhere safe. Not even here, out in the night. She was stuck here, in the middle of nowhere, on her own. Even Yaz had abandoned her – Yaz.

Yaz.

How could she? The worst thing Yaz could have accused her of was being mental. Ayesha had trusted her. Opened up to her about her mum being sectioned when she was a child. She'd told her about the bullying, how it spread around the kids in care that her mum was mental, which meant it probably ran in the family, which meant Ayesha was probably mental too. Every home Ayesha had ended up in, the label followed her there, carried along the network of kids being moved from institution to institution. It was used as a way to torment her, abuse her even, and then deny anything had happened, that it had all been in her crazy little head.

The shock had quickly turned to hurt, then to rage, and then, before she knew it, her fist had made contact with Yaz's cheekbone.

Ayesha felt a wave of shame and regret. She rubbed her

eyes, sighed. Felt the buzz of chemicals and adrenaline swirl around her body, her head. They'd never fought. Never so much as exchanged a bad word. What the fuck had happened to them? These bitches. That's what. These weird-ass women with their mad rituals, brews and costumes.

Ayesha blinked, then spun around. She left Frankie glowering at her as she marched back into the house, kicking a stray Birkenstock that found itself in her way.

Ayesha stalked through the house, first heading into the kitchen and then, finding it empty, along the hallway to the side that led to the room where they had donned their costumes. It was dark and silent. She growled with frustration.

'Where the fuck are you?' she called into the darkness. A new determination channelled her pain, honed her bitterness into a point. She would find Yaz. She would get them out of here, take her away from these slippery bitches, from India's clutches. If India thought she was going to give Yaz up without a fight, she was wrong.

A creak came from somewhere outside the room. Ayesha turned and tried to follow it, tracing her steps back. Back along the corridor, Ayesha found herself next to the entrance of the kitchen once more. From this angle, with the kitchen to her right, there was another door directly in front of her, smaller, inconspicuous, tucked just under the main staircase, painted the same colour as the wall which surrounded it. And it was ajar.

She stepped through and found herself in another

narrower corridor, with a different flight of stairs at the end of it. As she crept up them, Ayesha tried to keep her bearings clear in her head, but now there were no windows, the walls and steps seemed to waver and undulate and she wasn't sure which direction she was travelling in. Her mind drifted from her present location to Jessica's sullen face, then to Yaz, a surge of unbearable guilt now rising in her.

Maybe Yaz was right. Maybe Ayesha had gone mad. Just like her crazy-ass mum.

No.

Ayesha shook her head once more. These women were playing games with them and it had made her turn on her best friend.

Her jumbled thoughts were interrupted by voices ahead of her.

Ayesha crept up the final few steps and was met with another small wooden door, identical to the one at the bottom of the stairs. Like that one, this too was ajar. Warm, bright light escaped through the opening and illuminated the top of the staircase.

Ayesha stayed well back, out of the beam, but peered through the gap and saw it opened into one of the large bedrooms on the first floor. It wasn't one she had been in on the tour earlier, and this staircase seemed to serve as a secret entrance, or exit, to that particular room.

Ayesha blinked as spots of purple clouded her vision for a moment, adjusting from the darkness of the windowless staircase to the brightly lit room. She squinted and once again tried to get her head straight, keep the room upright. She glimpsed an enormous marble fireplace, the corner of a king-size sleigh bed with white sheepskin furs draped diagonally across it, a plush carpet with thick rugs on top of it. Every surface soft and voluptuous, perfect for relaxing in, difficult to extract yourself from its depths once you were in.

From the lavish outfits sprawled across every surface, and more on the floor, Ayesha tried to figure out if this was India's room or Clemmie's, but she couldn't tell.

Ayesha watched as India stepped into her line of vision and then turned around, her long, dark braids draped down her back. Her crumpled dashiki was a little higher on the thigh, just revealing the first streaks of paler skin. She looked at someone beyond Ayesha's sightline and smiled mysteriously.

'I've been meaning to talk with you properly for a while,' India crooned. 'You're a tough nut to crack, Yasmin. Hard to pin down. But I've finally got you to myself.'

Yasmin. Ayesha's heart pounded. Yaz hated being called that. It was a privilege only permitted to the elders in her family. Ayesha adjusted her position and looked through the gap between the hinges of the door. Yaz stood at the other end of the room. She returned India's intense gaze with a quiet calm. Ayesha started, ready to charge into the room and grab her friend. But then another creak and Ayesha turned to see Clemmie step forward and stand next to India. India nodded once and Clemmie walked over to a large oak wardrobe standing at one edge of the room. From somewhere in the folds of her brightly patterned headdress, she produced a set of small keys. She used one to open the doors of the ward-robe. Ayesha could just make out rows of fur coats inside. Clemmie pushed them aside and stepped in. She disappeared into its depths. A scraping sound seemed to indicate she was feeling around for something at the back of the wardrobe. A jangle of keys, a click, a push and the sound of a door open-ing, deeper beyond the wardrobe.

Ayesha blinked several times, took a long quiet breath. A door in a wardrobe? Was this real? Yaz's words ricocheted around her head.

Are you that mental?

Another click brought a cold glow of light emanating from inside the wardrobe.

India remained facing in Yaz's direction. She inclined her head.

'After you,' she said.

A long pause, Ayesha saw Yaz move towards India, then past her to the wardrobe, stepping carefully inside. Her friend raised her hands and drew the furs aside, then dis-appeared into its depths. Ayesha watched silently as India turned and followed her in.

CHAPTER EIGHTEEN

MAY 2018

'Travel writer. That was the big plan. But my parents insisted I study journalism, have a proper career. I thought maybe I could do some kind of blog or programme that explored how languages and music and food evolve as you travel further east. Flamenco into Kathak, Greek into Hindi. Or maybe it's the other way around ... Anyway. Turns out travel writing is pretty much a closed shop. Only a small, elite group of guys get to write about the world. Probably for the best. I'd melt into a messy freckled puddle if I was anywhere hotter than twenty degrees.'

'You'd be great,' Ayesha insisted. 'It's a great concept.'

'Yes. It is,' Jessica agreed. 'A concept that won't see the light of day.' She sighed, gathered herself. 'What about you?'

'Hmm? Oh, well, I don't know. Nothing really. I just want to make a few people laugh.'

Jessica's silence was sign enough that this would not suffice. Ayesha tried again.

'Actually . . . I kinda thought I'd be quite good at those TV panel shows . . . Maybe even host one of my own . . . Silly really.'

'You'd be brilliant at it. I've seen you. I don't know how you do it. The collective's lucky to have you. They're really lucky Ayesha. Never forget that.'

Ayesha felt her cheeks grow hot. A discomfort in her stomach. She'd reached her compliment threshold. Yaz had said something similar and inevitably followed it up with a comment about pay. Jessica didn't seem too concerned with that. She wondered if now they might be able to talk more honestly about the collective and money – or the lack of it – but she had no idea where to start.

'Anyway,' Ayesha said quickly. 'Like you said. Closed shop and all that . . . Good job you've got the journalism to fall back on, eh?'

'Oh. No. That's done with. I could never . . . I don't think I could ever . . . I don't really know what I'm going to do now.'

Rafting, that's what Ayesha was doing. A new word for when you choose – *choose* – to work from the comfort of your bed. Spread all your work out and sit in the middle of it being creative. It was totally a thing. And she was doing it.

Ayesha balanced the phone between her ear and shoulder, tried to sort through sheets of paper with one hand and reach over to the foldout table at the foot of her bed to take a sip of lukewarm tea.

'I'm calling it,' said the voice at the other end.

'I'm fine,' Ayesha protested, holding up one sheet, then another, the tepid tea sloshing dangerously in her other hand.

One meeting. Ayesha had missed one meeting. Just one. It

had clashed with her appointment with Lynne. And Ayesha had lied to them, said she'd felt a bit run-down. Needed to work from home. And they'd jumped on it.

'Nothing is more important than your well-being, Ayesha. The show will go on,' Frankie insisted.

'How? I mean. Of course. But ... the thing is ... it's quite hard to ... host a live ... I wouldn't want to put you in ... expose you to something you're not ...'

'India is thrilled to be hosting,' Frankie's voice said through the phone, 'I'm thrilled to remain firmly on the panel.'

'Oh. I see. Well, that's great. Mixing it up. It's good. Just the two of you?' Ayesha tried to sound encouraging.

'Two and a half,' Frankie replied. 'We're going to bring Joni in from behind the sound system. Get her to add a few cheeky asides. She can be pretty feisty when she wants to be.'

'That's a great idea,' Ayesha responded weakly.

And she *was* exhausted. She hadn't had a day off in months. Her bank balance was terrifyingly in the red, there was no way she could see of paying it off any time soon – or ever. And now the thought of the call that would inevitably be made by Lynne on her behalf to discuss money made her feel weak and dizzy. Although that could also be due to being down to one meal a day.

It had only taken a glance in the mirror to conclude she was worn-out, and thinner than she'd ever been. She grieved the increasingly diminishing curves she'd had since adolescence, that she had cultivated and maintained and shown off. An older, paler, gaunt-looking self looked back at her from every reflection now, and she cringed, avoided it and kept even busier.

But still, India? Doing her material? It was so quintessentially *Ayesha*. She ran through the lines in her head, like she'd practiced several times that day in between writing up the next script, and tried to imagine India's slower, decadent vowels delivering the punchlines. It hadn't worked when she'd taken it upon herself to steal her lines in the previous show, Ayesha remembered with resentment. It wouldn't work this time either.

Ayesha caught the phone as it dropped from her ear, steadied the cup which sloshed its contents onto the script. She swore, picked up the phone again.

'Hello? Can you hear me? Are you still there?'

She tried to salvage the pages, using her sleeve to wipe them down, and balancing the cup back on the table beside the plant that was looking increasingly dry and depleted these days.

'I'm here,' Frankie confirmed.

'Ok, phew! I had a bit of a mishap. Just putting the finishing touches on the next ... the next ...' The print on the pages started to blur. Ayesha blinked, trying to force it back into focus.

'A good dose of R & R for you missy,' Frankie's voice was firm. 'We've got everything we need here and I look forward to welcoming you back when you're ready.'

She ended the call.

Ayesha leaned her head into her hands. She felt empty.

Cast out. The thought of the show happening without her seemed too surreal to fathom.

But what could she do? It had been decided.

She pulled a piece of paper towards her and tried to jot down some ideas she could work up for the next script. She was soon out for the count, though, head slowly coming to a rest among the sodden pages, drool dripping gently onto them too.

'It's bigger than any one person. That's the point,' Ayesha protested wearily into the phone. She wasn't sure how long she'd been asleep, at what point she had been woken by another call. She wasn't really sure what her point was any more either.

'Sure. Cool, but if it's your material why do they get to butcher it?' Yaz's challenge came through the speaker clear as crystal.

'They're not butchering it, they're just … putting their own unique spin on it,' Ayesha insisted.

'Yeesh, I've heard them both try to be funny. They couldn't land a joke if they had the whole of Heathrow at their disposal.'

'Stop it, Yaz.'

'Stop what? Speaking truth? Why are you letting them play you like this? Why do they get to decide who's in and who's out?'

Ayesha lay on her bed staring at the ceiling, the traffic outside making patterns that swept across it every few seconds.

She sighed. She knew she shouldn't have brought it up, but that's what happened with Yaz and Yeesh's conversations. Yaz was the only other person she knew that worked the same odd hours as she did and was therefore available to chat indefinitely at 11.30 a.m.

'It's just one ep. It's good to mix it up a bit,' Ayesha argued.

'Have a word, Yeesh. Put your foot down for once,' Yaz replied. 'And for fuck's sake sis, when are you gonna get paid?'

'That's none of your . . . You don't need to worry about that,' Ayesha said faintly.

'Well, I do, Yeesh. Cos I'm your friend,' Yaz insisted. 'Look, do you need me to lend you some—'

'No! No . . . I don't need any—'

'Cos I just got paid,' Yaz explained.

Ayesha was suddenly angry. Why would she throw that in her face? She'd watched Yaz's latest TV appearances with a confused mix of joy and resentment on the bus to and from Frankie's. Yaz was smashing it. A regular feature now on the quiz shows, panel discussions and stand-up specials on the many channels across multiple streamers and platforms. She looked great too. Her skin shone with wellness and good moisturizer. Her clothes were still understated and black, but Ayesha had clocked her wearing more than one limited edition pair of trainers that would have been a healthy investment. She didn't need to spell it out too.

'Yaz! Enough! I don't need a lecture from you, ok? This is a movement, a global movement and I am—'

'I beg you, stop quoting that Frankie woman.'

'I'm not! I'm just—'

'You keep switching voices like you're doing an impression of her, except you're not. It's weird.'

'No I don't! I just appreciate her. And I ... This is the best gig I've had.'

'In what way—?'

'Yaz!' Ayesha's voice trembled with desperation. She was at her wits' end.

'Okay! Okay. Fine. I'm getting on board. I'm here. It's all good,' Yaz reassured her.

'Okay.'

'Okay.'

Ayesha took a breath, rolled onto her front. She rested the heavy weight of her head in one hand and tried hard to push away the exhaustion that came in nauseating waves now.

'So,' she began again, resolutely. 'I'm thinking maybe the problem is that I was giving myself too many of the punch-lines anyway. Like, maybe the reason it became a bit of a free-for-all was that I was writing material like I used to when it was just me on stage doing my thing. But now there's three of us. Three different personalities, three different voices. That's the thing that makes it so strong.'

'So ... ?' Yaz tried to sound supportive.

'So, it's a chance for me to expand. Upskill,' Ayesha continued. 'I'm gonna start working differently. Factor in everyone's strengths. Make the most of Frankie's rants. Make them witty, punchy, give her some material that works for her.'

'All right. I see you . . .' There was a hint of a suggestion that Yaz might be budging, maybe half an inch.

'Same with India. Make the most of . . . of . . .'

'—of her head-girl-does-tantra vibe.' Yaz concluded helpfully.

'Well, yeah. Basically.' Ayesha conceded.

'Seen . . .'

'I honestly cannot wait to hear the new episodes. It really is a fantastic idea to mix it up, keep it fresh. It can only be a good thing for the show. And the collective. And it's in keeping with the ethos of the collective that I want to talk to you about it maybe being time to clarify what the collective actually is? Like, maybe a manifesto of some sort that we could all work on together? Just so we're all on the same page . . . Literally! Ha. So that no one else gets confused . . . Puts a foot wrong . . . Says the wrong thing. And perhaps then we could talk together about things like official roles . . . who actually does what . . . work distribution . . . decision-making . . . even profit and investment. Pay . . . That sort of thing. Just to make it sustainable for all of us.'

She'd practiced it all last night. The tone, the words, the key message, just like Frankie had trained her to do. And how Lynne and Yaz had coached her to approach the conversation today. Lynne had offered to email Frankie directly, but Ayesha had insisted she talk to her personally first, certain that their strong friendship, their special bond and sisterhood deserved it. All the way to the pub in South London she had practiced. And now she was there, and Frankie's familiar mousey crew cut hovered over the pint of ale in her hand and she grinned as she saw Ayesha come towards her.

Ayesha's stomach lurched but she kept her smile steady.

The signature awkward hug.

'Let's get you a drink.' Frankie turned and nodded to the woman behind the bar who deftly started pulling another pint. It was soon placed beside Ayesha who sipped it nervously.

'You were missed, Jones. The vibe's just not the same without you.' Frankie said.

Ayesha blushed slightly despite herself.

'Ah well. Good to mix it up though,' she replied.

'Is it? I'm not sure. It was a bit of an experiment but to be honest it mostly just made me appreciate you even more.' Frankie grinned warmly.

Ayesha smiled, relieved but also surprised. She took another sip.

'I'm glad you suggested a meet-up,' Frankie continued, 'I know it's only been a week or something, but it feels like ages since Team Frankie and Ayesha, Team Freesha, or is it Ayekie, met last.'

'Ha! They're both awful.' Ayesha relaxed a little more, felt the ground beneath her become more solid.

'Yep. Pretty bad,' Frankie admitted. 'I'll work on it. Or maybe just hand it over to the professional.'

Exactly, Ayesha thought. She took a breath.

'Speaking of—' she began.

'Speaking of ... I've been thinking.' Frankie moved her pint slightly to the side, leaned in. 'What do you think of having a few special guests on? Mixing it up a bit?'

Ayesha tried to keep up. Had Frankie not just said that it had been a bad idea to mix it up? She also tried to keep a grip on the well-practiced speech in her mind, the key message you should never deviate from, whatever questions they threw at you.

'I mean, the thing is ...' she tried again.

'How about starting with your friend Yaz?' Frankie interrupted.

'Yaz?' Ayesha blinked with surprise.

'Sure.' Frankie grinned wider.

'As in, Yaz on the podcast?'

'Yep.'

Ayesha looked carefully at Frankie, trying to read the clues, make sense of what she was suggesting, her foothold feeling less secure by the second. She wasn't sure how much Frankie knew about Yaz and her success, other than the involuntary gushes of praise for her bestie that Ayesha offered up regularly to anyone who might be listening.

'What, like, presenting an episode?' she asked.

Frankie tilted her head to one side, looked out across the bar.

'More like an extra feature, alongside the usual team.'

Ayesha frowned.

'Like, the two of us actually on the same bill?'

'The same stage at the same time, actually.' Frankie replied, 'You reckon England is ready for that much cool?'

Ayesha raised her eyebrows and tried to picture it. Her and Yaz. On the same stage at the same time. Finally.

'I mean, the world might implode at the very concept, but sure . . .' Her mind was racing, trying to keep up with this new curveball, 'What does India . . . the others . . . think about this?'

'It was India's idea actually,' Frankie revealed.

Ayesha blinked again, shook her head gently. Had India seen Yaz perform? She was sure she remembered India proclaiming proudly that she didn't own a TV. Why would she be the one to recommend Yaz join the podcast? Ayesha had a lot of questions. She tried to put them in some kind of order in her head, but Frankie jumped in first.

'Do you reckon she'd be up for it?' Frankie asked.

'I mean, I think so.' Ayesha shrugged.

'So, what's the rate?' was Yaz's first question.

'Yaz, you know it's not paid,' Ayesha replied.

'Still?' Yaz said incredulously. Ayesha bit her tongue. She hadn't meant to reveal that to Yaz. 'Yeesh, man, I thought you were gonna have a word.'

'I was! I am,' Ayesha insisted 'But . . . then your name was in the mix and I want so bad for us to do our thing in front of a decent audience. It'll be so great, Yaz,' she pleaded.

'Exactly,' Yaz retorted. 'We're a quality act. So show us the money.'

They were sat on a bench just outside the street market eating falafel wraps with everything. The vendor had seen them coming and winked. Without a word he started loading them up. He always put extra chilli in for them. Yaz would lead with the banter, ask how his knees were this week. He never cracked a smile but there was always an ironic, warm sparkle in his eye when she spoke to him. He'd smear a generous dollop of hummus on the end of each wrap and, with a flourish, hand them over. Yaz and Ayesha took hungry bites out of them as they watched the market vendors tempt the tourists with their loud sing-song holler.

'How do they know me anyway?'

'Well, mostly through me, but also probably your videos, maybe they've come to a gig or two.'

Yaz didn't look convinced.

'Please, Yaz,' Ayesha begged, 'Just this once. You and me. Doing our thing. No one can deny it then, they'll have to pay for quality like that. Besides, Frankie reckons England ain't ready for so much cool.'

Yaz looked up in alarm.

'She used that word?'

'What word?'

'Cool? She said we were cool?'

Ayesha shrugged.

'Sure. What's wrong with that?'

Yaz pursed her lips.

'Well, firstly, I love you sis, but you ain't cool. Like, you might be the least cool person I know, despite your brown skin.'

'What? Oh Yaz, come on now. You know she didn't mean it like that. Please,' Ayesha said.

Yaz sighed. Shook her head.

'These people, man.'

But the following Friday she was there. Ayesha opened the show as usual, brought on Frankie and India with a flourish, and after a bit of lukewarm banter with the two of them, she had the privilege and joy of introducing her favourite human onto the stage beside her.

It was silly how elated she was watching Yaz run on. A cheer from the audience and they were off. They'd been rehearsing all week, but in the lights, with the adrenaline pumping, the live crowd before them, they really came into their own, effortlessly adding asides and extras to the carefully honed script, making each other corpse to the delight of the audience who were under no doubt they were watching two besties riff off each other with a warmth and connection rarely witnessed. And they all felt part of it somehow, invited in on the joke. And it was a good joke.

It was a resounding success. The audience, already engaged and enthusiastic, gave them a standing ovation and a roar of delight at the end. And then that moment when Ayesha looked into the crowd and spotted those few faces of colour dotted around the room, beaming at the two women at the centre of the stage, flanked by Frankie on one side, India on the other, as they took their final bow. India beaming at them too, at Yaz especially, Ayesha so grateful to her she let out a quiet sob. A highlight in a night of highlights.

'Well, that was magical,' India crooned backstage. 'I just knew it would work.'

'You smashed it,' Joni gushed. 'Yaz, you're an utter don. You had them eating out the palm of your hand like it was effortless.'

Frankie nodded with approval.

'Welcome to the collective, Yaz,' she said solemnly.

Ayesha watched her friend move around backstage, still buzzing from sharing a stage with her, still marvelling at the reality of being with her here, now, finally sharing that after-show high in this space, this moment.

Yaz seemed pretty nonplussed by the others, despite their obvious adoration. She was pumped, a gorgeous glint in her eye that seemed to need no affirmation from the others to sparkle. But she did look at her friend, share that glint with her, express her wordless approval and appreciation of the magic they had created together, and also a sense of vindication of the years they'd known that, if they'd just been given the chance to share a stage, magic would have manifested a lot earlier.

India watched them too, a quiet fascination at their connection, a hunger growing.

And the numbers spoke volumes.

As Ayesha sat quietly at her modest dining table a few days later, looking at the downloads of the two episodes she had missed and listening to them with trepidation, the difference was clear. Even the live audience's reactions were distinctly quieter when it was India and Frankie delivering the punchlines. Ayesha had written Frankie a generous and rousing speech to end the first of the episodes and that received the biggest applause, helped along by Joni doubling up the audience track in the edit. The listeners dipped sharply in the second episode, though, a strange mishmash of Ayesha's script edited to shreds and delivered in a confused fusion of content added by Frankie and India, each vying for more mic time than the other. Ayesha pulled up the original script and tried to follow it. It was all over the place. The sections where Joni was enlisted were cut considerably as she sounded permanently horrified to be in the limelight. It was Joni who'd cut them.

But the numbers soared for Ayesha and Yaz. Shares, comments, likes and reviews came flooding in.

'Looks like you two are a roaring success.' Frankie's voice was full of approval. 'India's instinct was right.'

'I haven't thanked her properly. I'll call her. Take her out maybe.' Ayesha gushed.

'Well make sure you call Yaz first and tell her she's officially part of the collective, whether she likes it or not. Although she did seem to be enjoying herself.'

Ayesha giggled, thinking of the two of them being their silly selves, this time not just in her poky little flat, but in front of an audience who also got the joke, got their friendship, their magic.

'I'll let her know,' Ayesha responded.

'Good. And get her booked in for the next one asap,' Frankie insisted.

Ayesha called Yaz straight after, but Yaz was her chill self.

'Yeesh, man. Let it marinade. Like a good chicken. What's the rush? Keep it quality. Anywayz, I've got a bunch of gigs coming up. Paid gigs. So you lot need to find some moolah if you want me back.'

'So she's part of the collective now?'

'Yes! Well, kind of. The jury's still out ... Oh God, sorry. I didn't mean ... Oh God.'

A tinkle of laughter. Ayesha realized it was the first time she'd heard Jessica laugh, properly. It was a beautiful sound. There was an innocence to it, a purity.

Relief washed over Ayesha, so intense it made her laugh too. For a while they both laughed, stopping to catch their breath only to begin again when one set the other off. Ayesha felt them both shedding months and months of stress. Maybe even years. Tears streamed down her face, her stomach loosened, her shoulders dropped. They both sighed.

'Very good,' Jessica managed. She took a breath. 'So who do you think will get the cull this time?' she enquired, darkly.

'What do you mean?' Ayesha asked with alarm.

'Well, there's fresh blood now, so ...'

'Jessica. It's not like that. There's room for everyone. The whole point of the collec— the group is to expand. Frankie said that herself.'

'Is that what she said?' Jessica asked bitterly.

'Yes.'

'Then watch your neck.'

'Jessica.'

'And your back,' she said coldly.

'Jess—'

'And if you need a right-wing politician to be your new bestie, I've got a few spare ... Because even they seem to have more backbone than—'

Jessica caught herself, stopped abruptly.

'Than ... ?' Ayesha tried.

But Jessica remained silent. A heavy, loaded silence this time.

A long silence.

Ayesha had watched the footage of her standing outside the Houses of Parliament beside an MP who spoke in a series of soundbites about how the war on women was about to reach a turning point in this country. That he, personally, would be leading the campaign to ensure that all those in positions of power who had harmed or abused women would be named and brought to Justice. That the rings and networks of the Left – be they union leaders, politicians, or even leaders – would be exposed for the good of womankind and for everyone's safety. Jessica hadn't spoken, hadn't been given the option to speak. She seemed like she'd checked out – there, but not really there.

The headlights of a car made an arc of light across Ayesha's ceiling. Another dry, dead leaf brushed past the others as it fell from the parched plant onto her small table.

'We can talk about something else if you prefer?' Ayesha tried eventually.

'Hmm?'

'I said we can ... You seem ... quiet.'

'Do I?' Jessica said sadly. 'It's just ... so ... complicated, Ayesha.

It feels like the whole world is full of . . . snakes . . . And the deeper I get, the more snakes there are, and they're all connected in this complicated twisting, writhing mess, and I can't, I'm not allowed to talk about it. I can't even tell you because . . .'

Ayesha heard her gather herself, make an effort.

'Anyway! You're right. Let's talk about something else.' Jessica took a breath. 'What kind of school did you go to, Ayesha?' she continued, more upbeat this time.

'Huh? Oh. Well, just a normal one, I suppose. Like a local comp. We had a few famous musicians come out of it. Have you heard of Steezy?'

'No.'

Another silence. Jessica's pillows rustled as she adjusted her position.

'How about you?' Ayesha asked.

'I went to boarding school,' Jessica replied. 'With India.'

Ayesha sat up in surprise.

'Really? I had no idea. So you were friends since you were—'

'Friends is a strong word,' Jessica interjected coldly.

'Oh.' Ayesha stopped short.

'Although I did receive an invitation to her nuptial celebrations yesterday,' Jessica added.

'You're coming to the wedding!' Ayesha gasped.

'Well, let's see if I get over the shock of being invited. And there's this goddess thing first . . . Not sure I'll survive that.'

Ayesha felt a wave of emotion rise in her. The thought of them all hanging out together, having fun, with everyone included, forgiven, made her want to sob with relief and gratitude.

'See?' she said. 'Your old schoolmate cares about you after all.'
Jessica scoffed.

'I'm not sure that's how India operates,' she replied. They both
fell silent for a while.

'It was a ruthless place, that school,' Jessica continued eventually,
'It had a particular culture, shall we say. Honed over decades. They
kept a pane of each window broken so the cold air hit you throughout
the year as you slept. No hot water. That sort of thing. Character
building, they called it.'

'Shit.' Ayesha replied. 'Sounds like some of the homes I lived in.
How much did you pay for all that . . . character building?'

'Too much.'

Ayesha pictured a little red-haired girl shivering in a dark dorm
room while across the country a little brown girl lay shaking in
her bed too.

'It did the trick though,' Jessica said. 'It built a certain character.
India and several of her peers are a good example. She appears to
reject everything the school stands for, but she is in fact the epitome of it.'

'What do you mean?'

'These . . . moguls I'm surrounded by now. These MPs and Lords.
They're cut from the same cloth. There's a cold ambition to them that
cuts through any sense of humanity. India's like that.'

'She's not,' Ayesha protested, 'Jessica, she might have been like
that once, but honestly if you could see her—'

'I don't need to.'

'Jessica,' Ayesha insisted. 'Everything she does is to raise awareness, uplift us all, give a voice to—'

'Be careful, Ayesha,' Jessica warned. 'Trust me. There is a ruthless-ness to her political correctness.'

'But she's invited you,' Ayesha reasoned. 'She wants you to be a part of it all. Of her special day.'

'Yes,' Jessica mused. 'A clever play.'

Ayesha sighed with frustration, couldn't bear being pulled in so many directions.

'You must think me a paranoid wreck.' Jessica laughed miserably. 'A minute ago, it was Frankie, now it's India. Or maybe I'm just bitter.'

'No, you're not. Paranoid or bitter. Or a wreck.'

'I am a bit of a wreck.' Jessica's voice wobbled ever so slightly. 'I'm in really deep now. No turning back, that's for sure.'

'Would you want to?'

'I don't know what I would be returning to, really,' Jessica said sadly.

Ayesha's heart broke at her words. She understood all too well.

'Not the collective, that's for sure,' Jessica said resolutely. She sniffed, pulled herself together. 'They want me to start naming names,' she said.

'Really?'

'Yep. They've got lawyers and advisors and we've had endless meetings and there's a whole plan about who's going to be outed and when. It's quite an epic operation. And I seem to be at the heart of it. Little old me.' She gave a small, unconvincing laugh.

'How do you feel about that?'

'I don't know. I haven't known what I'm feeling for a long time.' Jessica mused. 'But if it means I get to name him, finally, then ... that's something.

CHAPTER NINETEEN

JULY 2018

Saturday 11.00 p.m.

Ayesha swore under her breath, angry at herself for not step-ping forward earlier. She steeled herself and rubbed her face, trying to get her head as clear as possible. Then she walked into the room.

She headed straight to the wardrobe and, not stopping to think about how bizarre it all was, stepped into it as quietly as she could.

The fur coats to either side of her caressed her face and shoulders. They were impossibly soft, but smelled stale, dusty, dead. She moved past, trying not to disturb them as they hung lifelessly around her. Beyond the coats Ayesha found a narrow doorway in front of her, flung wide open, a cold light emanating from it. Her bare feet felt the oak bottom of the wardrobe turn into frigid stone. Clemmie came into view and Ayesha took a step back into the wardrobe, concealing herself behind a weighty pelt. A creak echoed from beneath her as her feet made contact with the wood once more. She froze, but Clemmie had mercifully started talking at the same time.

'Welcome to Narnia,' she announced, throwing her arms wide. 'Our most exclusive of spaces. Where our darkest and most fertile secrets live. We only bring our most trusted of collaborators here,' she divulged.

Ayesha peered carefully around the part of the room visible to her. Large, windowless and self-contained, it was the strangest room she had ever seen. Stranger even than the costume room that was somewhere downstairs in this confusing, labyrinth of a house. She vaguely surmised they must be somewhere at the very centre of the building, which was why there were no windows. The walls were papered with a pattern of palm leaves, trimmed with gold. There were several framed photos on the walls. The ones nearest her showed Clemmie and several other white people standing in a crowd of black people; Clemmie arm in arm with an African woman dressed in traditional clothes; next to a newly built well in a dusty desert; sitting with a group of African women all waving mobile phones. That one made Ayesha take a second look. She'd seen it before. But how could she have? She'd only met Clemmie today, this afternoon, which seemed years ago now. Time seemed to be behaving strangely this weekend ... And she'd definitely never been in this room before, except perhaps in her nightmares, which seemed increasingly real these days.

Ayesha couldn't quite make out the other pictures, the ones at the far end of the room. What she *could* make out clearly were the animals placed around the space. The head and neck of some kind of exotic deer with majestic spiral antlers stared lifelessly from the top of the far wall. Below it, to the left, was an entire zebra standing motionless on the stone floor. To the right, Ayesha could just see the front half of a full-sized lion lounging on the ground, a tiger to her near left, and beside her, by the doorway, a bear on its hind legs, its teeth bared, towering above her. Life-sized and motionless, caught and preserved forever in frozen action, they must have all once been very alive, and then killed, stuffed and transported to this secret mausoleum.

A movement to her right made Ayesha crane her neck uncomfortably. Yaz appeared at the edge of her vision, her back to the entrance, facing India who had stepped towards her and was gently teasing the whisky bottle from Yaz's hand. Ayesha saw her friend instinctively grip it harder and then, with India watching her carefully, insistently, Yaz let go, and allowed India to ease the bottle from her and take a long, deep swig.

India paused to savour the rich liquor, shivered with pleasure as it burned her throat on the way down, then focused back on Yaz. She reached out her hand and caressed Yaz's cheek.

'You're a special one,' she said huskily. 'Such a talent, such a natural. You're loyal, you're independent and you're strong. Ayesha's lucky to have a friend like you.'

Ayesha tensed at the sound of her name.

India took another long swig, never taking her eyes off Yaz.

'You've always stood out, Yasmin,' she continued. 'Stood alone. Above the clique of the collective, above the petty squabbles for space, limelight, punchlines. I know you don't need us. And I find that fascinating.'

Ayesha could see only the side of Yaz's face. She seemed to be watching India carefully, but it was impossible to read her expression. Ayesha was also aware of Clemmie nearby. She darted a look in her direction and then let her eyes wander once more around this strange space. She strained to see if she could make out the pictures on the far wall, but it was no good. They were too small and too far away. But there was a print just behind India that her eye was drawn to again and again. She couldn't quite figure out what it was, but something about the design, the shape and pattern, also seemed familiar. She took a few quiet, deep breaths trying to clear her mind, fighting the chemicals in her system, trying to focus on where she'd seen that design before. She craned her neck even further, a spasm of pain shot up it.

'I'm going to be frank with you, Yasmin, because I know you're too clever for anything else.' India's assured voice cut through her line of thought. 'I think you're being wasted. I think you're playing small. This gigging, this rushing from venue to venue, the brief TV appearances, the banter with Ayesha. It's cute, it's really cute, but you're better than that. You know and I know, deep down, that you are destined for much bigger things. We both are. The podcast is a lovely hobby, but there's a whole world to conquer. And I want you with me.'

Ayesha gritted her teeth, fought back the wave of rage that suddenly surged through her. She stared hard at Yaz, waiting for a response, retaliation. But Yaz kept quiet. Ayesha looked back at India's cool expression, but then her eyes were drawn again to the frame on the wall just behind and to the right of India's neck. The oblong shape. One end straight, the other curved. The small dark lines decorating its interior, one after another after another. *Think straight. Think.*

'So, what do you say?' India's voice forced Ayesha's focus back onto her.

Ayesha looked from India, back to Yaz and then blinked. And there it was. She knew what she'd been staring at that whole time. Of course. It wasn't a strangely shaped oblong; it was a ship. Those weren't small dark lines, they were people. Hundreds of them. Slaves.

And then she knew where she'd heard the name before. Clematis Rhodes-Woodhouse. Woodhouse. Cyril Woodhouse. The infamous philanthropist who had made his millions in Africa. Who had donated so much money to so many worthy causes. Built schools and hospitals and railways. Whose statue stood proudly outside Oman College at Oxford University. Who had made his fortune buying and selling, trading and bartering hundreds of thousands of human souls.

She looked again at the stuffed animals. All from the African continent. And Asia. And now she noticed the strange chains they were wearing. The iron around the neck. The spikes in soft places. The head vice, the foot locks, the metal mouth guards. She peered intently at the photos at the far end of the room and now she could make out dark figures sitting in chains, lighter figures standing above them, rifles in hand. Very similar to the rifles she'd seen Clemmie and India wielding earlier.

Her eyes darted back to the first picture she'd seen. The one of Clemmie sitting among the black women waving mobile phones. *Rhodes-Woodhouse. Rhodes-Woodhouse Foundation . . .*

Clemmie stepped forward to stand at India's side, blocking the picture behind them, interrupting Ayesha's train of thought again.

'I have been so very privileged, Yasmin,' Clemmie began, 'to grow up here, to bear this name, to be called to help so many. It is a complex, complicated world with so much pain and sickness and I just want to help. And I want you to help me help. You are a strong, modern, Indian woman. You are the epitome of what that great nation should be. We, as a family, have helped so many in Africa over the centuries, but I truly want to make *my* mark now. It's *my* turn.' She had a fiercely single-minded expression that chilled Ayesha. 'It is no coincidence that you came here today,' Clemmie continued. 'It is no coincidence that a living goddess came into my life bearing the name of that great nation. The jewel in the Empire. The message is clear. It's time to help the women of India.'

Yes. She had seen it before. Large and looming on the front cover of a broadsheet just a couple of years ago.

Mired in Controversy ...

The article was an exposé on the work the foundation had been doing in Africa, referring to its historical connection to slavery and then giving accounts of the women in Malawi who had been helped by the foundation to set up their own textile business. They were offered training, accommodation, food and a crèche. They were also provided with medical care. Each woman received a mobile phone as an incentive to undergo a small procedure. For their own good. To help with the health of the nation. None of them realized they were being given a full hysterectomy.

These women are enslaved by the many children they bear.

They have no recourse to contraception.

They are raped by their husbands.

They spread AIDS and give birth to children who are HIV-positive.

They are simply not educated enough to understand their choices.

We estimate that we have reduced the AIDS epidemic in this country by at least 30%.

There was outrage. A petition. A brief internal investigation. And then a week later a little white girl went missing and every media outlet was filled with her small, pale face. The national horror, the collective grief, the search, filled every minute of news. And the Rhodes-Woodhouse story faded from memory as the women of Malawi nursed their scars somewhere far away.

'Help us help them,' Clemmie persisted. Her gaze was hard, determined, fixed on Yaz, as was India's.

'I'm from West London,' Ayesha heard her friend finally reply.

India inclined her head. 'Of course you are,' she acquiesced, 'and it's that directness, that rawness, that ... spirit of yours that we want on our team.'

'And who else are you planning to have on your team? Ayesha? Joni? What does Frankie have to say about it?'

India kept her gaze steady.

'Frankie is a consummate politician,' she said, a hint of amusement in her voice. 'She chose me to join the collective for her own self-serving purposes. I knew this from the start. Nothing wrong with that. It benefitted us both. But I owe her nothing.'

The final statement was delivered almost as lightly as the others. Almost.

'Is that why you brought me in? Why you invited me here? For your own self-serving reasons?' Yaz countered.

India giggled.

'Yes, of course, silly,' she admitted enthusiastically. 'I want you, Yasmin. But I also know I'd be very, very good for you.'

Ayesha gritted her teeth.

'Win-win,' India concluded.

India watched Yaz intently. Ayesha also watched her friend, held her breath.

Yaz looked from one woman to the other, a smile forming on her face.

'I'm good, thanks,' she said simply.

Ayesha almost cheered with pride. Yaz could see what she

could finally see, was surrounded by the horrors of that family's legacy. Ayesha wanted to burst in and pull her friend out of that bizarre trip of a room. But something kept her rooted there, behind the musty fur, in the dark, as the scene before her played out.

Clemmie and India both continued to watch Yaz carefully. A smile spread across India's face too. For a moment, Ayesha watched as Yaz and India stood face to face, smiling broadly at each other. Then India finally spoke.

'It's a big decision. You should take your time. Weigh up the pros and cons.'

Yaz continued to smile.

'I'm good,' she said again.

India also kept smiling. She held Yaz's gaze and then took a breath, tilted her head.

'Is this about Ayesha?' India asked lightly.

Ayesha tensed once again.

'The same person who just attacked you so viciously?' India continued. 'You see, this is the thing, Yaz. When you do the kind of work we do, take on projects all over the world, use our privilege and power to help, to raise up our sisters in all sorts of ways, you find yourself working alongside a variety of other people with all sorts of agendas. I know you might find this hard to believe, but the charity sector is full of very strange people out to get what they can for themselves and then exit. It's disgusting. And over the years I've got very good at clocking them. Jessica is an obvious one . . .'

Ayesha sobered further at the mention of Jessica's name.

'In many ways she's a damaged little soul, but ruthless too. We went to the same school, and even then she was ... calculated, shall we say.'

Clemmie smirked.

Ayesha suddenly recalled Jessica telling her they'd been at the same school. She hadn't thought much about India's connection to Jessica. There had been moments, during those few occasions when they were briefly both part of the collective at the same time, where Ayesha noticed them share a look of knowing, and not a warm one. Looks that seemed to let the other know that she was on to her, knew what game she was playing. She realized now that much more had been going on between them than she had known. Why had India invited Jessica then? Surely she'd known it would make Frankie angry? Now that Ayesha understood the way India worked, she could think of only one reason: it would benefit her somehow to have Jessica here.

Ayesha began to realize how much she hadn't challenged or questioned until now, how she had been so desperate to be accepted, to be included by these women that she'd held her tongue and held it some more, until it seemed so very important to speak up, and maybe too late.

India shifted slightly and Ayesha caught another glimpse of the picture hanging behind her. It seemed so clear now. And the ones beyond, the white mens' rifles sticking out above the crouching dark figures.

The rifles.

Where were they? Ayesha's eyes darted helplessly around,

but there was no sign of them, and no reason why they'd be in this part of the house instead of somewhere else, anywhere, in this vast place.

'Where is Jessica?' Yaz's question cut through the tense silence. She kept her tone light, but Ayesha knew that she too must have a hundred questions about these women's connections and motives racing through her mind.

India shrugged.

'Exactly,' she said. 'Where is she? I invited her here, despite everything. I genuinely thought she deserved a second chance. To be completely transparent, I'm impressed. She's made some powerful allies and I actually thought she could be a valuable asset to us.'

Ayesha nodded to herself. Of course.

'But where the fuck is she?' India delivered the curse lightly, dangerously. 'She's not hanging out with friends because she doesn't have any; she's done a great job of ejecting herself from the collective; she's not here, in the fucking circle, like I expected her to be. She's not in the house, she's not in the woods. So where is she ... hmm?'

India held out both hands in a dramatic shrug.

Clemmie giggled.

'Nowhere,' she replied. 'Jessica is nowhere.'

CHAPTER TWENTY

JUNE 2018

'It was inevitable, really. I always knew my days were numbered.'

'What do you mean?' Ayesha turned cold at Jessica's words.

'In the group. It couldn't have lasted.'

'You were one of the originals. A founding member. You could have stayed as long as you liked—'

'Wrong and wrong,' Jessica countered. 'I was nothing of the sort. There were many, many iterations of that group before us. All of them discarded. All of them rejected in the end. Found to be wanting in one way or another. Or simply ...' She sighed, tried again. 'And no, I couldn't have stayed much longer. Not if I really wanted to speak out.'

Ayesha was at a loss. Again. Just when she thought she had a grasp on the complicated web of associations and history between these women, she found herself even more confused.

'Jess, I don't understand. The whole point of the collective is to speak out. To help you speak out.'

'Come on, Ayesha, you know it's more complicated than that,' Jessica reasoned. 'I have a whole team of the most expensive legal heads in the country on my side right now and even then we have to tread very carefully. Frankie isn't given free rein to rant to her heart's content, encourage anyone and everyone to name names just like that. She's worked at this for a very long time. Covered her back, placed herself in the right circles, the right company so that she is protected, supported, untarnished. But that means allegiances, compromises, complicated agreements with complicated people. Men. In positions of power. And that means that every now and then a sacrifice needs to be made. I just wasn't willing to be that for her.'

Ayesha wanted to cry with frustration. She had no idea what Jessica was talking about, and she suspected strongly that her friend had got to that stage where she saw danger and exploitation on every side. It broke her heart, because she'd teetered on the edge of that abyss so many times herself, had no idea who she could trust, was certain everyone around her had the potential to hurt her, abuse her, mess with her head. It took a friendship like Yaz's – and now Jessica's – a solid, honest, rock of a friendship, to pull her back, anchor her. She wanted to be that for Jessica too.

'Jess,' she tried. 'I know there's so much I don't understand, but I want to. I really want to. I'm not very good with all this ... politics stuff, but ... why is Frankie so dangerous to you?'

There was a long silence. And then, to Ayesha's shock, a deep sob echoed down the line.

'Actually,' Jessica said grimly. 'I think I'm more dangerous to her.'

* * *

Joni had bought them a copy each. They were at Frankie's house drinking tea and planning the next few episodes when she let herself in with a big grin on her face and dropped a heavy load of papers onto the dining table.

Front page. National paper. Broadsheet.

VETERAN ACTIVIST FINDS HER SQUAD

Ayesha gasped as she looked at the photograph of Frankie and India leaning into each other which took up a third of the cover. The article began below it and continued on page eight. She took her copy from the pile and leafed through the large sheaves eagerly. Page eight greeted her with another large picture, this time of Frankie's face alone, followed by several stills of her over the years, speaking up, speaking out, receiving her honorary degree. On page twenty-seven, the final section of the article, Ayesha was elated to see a small picture of herself, not much larger than her thumb, mic in hand, addressing the live audience at the podcast recording. Beneath the picture the caption read: 'Host greets audience for Frankie's hit show'.

Ayesha scanned the article. The interview with Frankie was interwoven throughout the piece, where she spoke eloquently and passionately about the cause, but not about the collective. The 'squad' seemed to be the wider movement, all those speaking out and speaking up, a new global gang that had made Frankie's message trend again.

Ayesha flipped to the front of the paper once more and

looked more closely at the picture of Frankie and India. It was an awkward position. But then that was a signature look of Frankie's. Looking again, Ayesha noticed two things. The awkward lean into each other was because the photo had been shopped. Cropped. The outfits they were both wearing were the same outfits they'd worn for the last show – the one with Yaz. And this was a picture of the final bow, the one with Ayesha and Yaz in the middle, between the two other women. And they'd been cut out.

Ayesha went still, the others chattering excitedly around her. That night had felt so sacred – the one show she'd had with Yaz, and *they* had lit up the venue. How could all traces of that – of them – be so coldly and systematically photo-shopped out? She gritted her teeth and tried to control the rage she was feeling. It was selfish. This moment wasn't about her or Yaz. It was Frankie's moment. And she deserved it.

A ring of the bell and Joni jumped up.

India swept in. She rushed straight over to Frankie and embraced her warmly. Then India held her at arm's length.

'My sister. What an honour to share in your glory. So well-deserved.'

Frankie beamed.

'It's about bloody time. Only taken the best part of twenty years,' she quipped.

'How did you … When did you have the interview?' Ayesha asked, trying to sound enthusiastic. 'This is huge. How did you manage it?'

'Because she's the real deal,' Joni jumped in passionately.

'Simple as. Frankie was talking about this stuff way before it was trendy. Decades of commitment. All those women speaking out now? They're all standing on her shoulders. She gave a voice to all those who couldn't speak for themselves. She made it possible for this all to happen.' She turned to Frankie, barely able to look her in the eye, so intense was her feeling. 'You should be on every bloody front page, every channel, every platform going ...' She gripped the top of the chair nearest her, overwhelmed with emotion.

Frankie basked in the praise for a moment.

'It helps to know a few people in the right places,' she conceded with a shrug. 'Once you've been around for long enough, some of your peers inevitably make it to places of influence and if I've taught you nothing else, I've at least helped you learn how to work the system to our advantage.' She finished with a sly grin.

Ayesha nodded. Of course. It wasn't just India who moved in the right circles. Frankie too had gone to the right schools, been in the right scene from the beginning. In the end, it always paid off.

'Politics, politics, politics,' India exclaimed with a shudder. 'How incredibly impressive you are to navigate all that. I must admit I don't understand it at all.'

'But your work is so powerful, so political—' Joni protested.

'Thank you, my sibling,' India acknowledged. 'Powerful, yes. Representative of the zeitgeist, sure. But I pride myself in identifying as apolitical. Never voted in my life. Couldn't tell

you who stands for what because they're all steeped in patriarchal self-interest. Frankie, on the other hand, is a master of
political manoeuvring. Friends in all the right places—'

'I prefer colleagues. Comrades, perhaps,' Frankie corrected.

'... and the chief of this paper is one such comrade.
Correct?' India finished with a conspiratorial raise of
her eyebrow.

Ayesha looked from one woman to the other, trying to
digest these new levels of connectedness she hadn't pre-
viously been aware of. She knew Frankie had followers
and some influence, but this was beyond anything she had
imagined or understood. She couldn't fathom what it would
be like to have associates in your phone contacts you could
ring up to get you on the front page of a national newspaper.
Ayesha looked at Joni who seemed to mirror her awe.

'Jack has been very supportive,' Frankie conceded.

India's eyebrow rose.

'Jack Vine?' she asked.

'Correct.' Frankie grinned.

Ayesha had no idea who he was, but India's expression
told her everything she needed to know. She could see her
brain working, making connections and assessments and
readjusting Frankie's standing even in her mind.

'Very impressive, Roberts,' India gushed. 'That is clout
right there.'

'That's just the tip of the iceberg,' Joni said proudly.

'You are a regular guest at the House of Commons, I
believe?' India added.

Frankie shook her head.

'God no. I couldn't think of anything worse. I've petitioned a few select VIPs at a few dos who were sympathetic to the cause, got them to push forward the agenda in the next debate, that sort of thing. But that was years ago. No real standing now. Not with these new Etonian clones. That's more your circle, isn't it?' Frankie raised her eyebrows at India.

'I did indeed have the misfortune of attending the same school as some of them,' India conceded. 'Clones indeed.'

'That's why you are such a breath of fresh air,' Frankie grinned. 'You managed to come through that system with your humanity intact.'

India beamed.

'There were a few of us who kept close. Clemmie, for one, was a godsend.'

Ayesha waited for India to mention Jessica too. She didn't, but something flashed across her face momentarily. A quiet acknowledgement of their absent mutual friend. She shook it off with a flourish.

'You've inspired me, Frankie Roberts,' India announced suddenly, pointedly changing the subject. 'I've decided to double down on my commitment to be the voice for the voiceless ones.'

She paused, letting the suspense grow. She took an indulgent breath.

'You're not the only member of our collective being spotlighted today.'

She turned to the rest of the group.

'I just got a call congratulating me on the front-page picture and offering me a gig at the Modern Gallery this Saturday.'

Joni whooped.

'India, that's fantastic. Where?' she asked.

'In the main foyer,' India confirmed.

'Oh my god. That's huge,' Joni gushed.

'Yes, it is,' India agreed. 'A month-long residency where I take over the main foyer, and I've been thinking. They want *The Bloody Truth* – my last piece – to be revisited. And I'd be happy to do it as I usually do, to tell the stories of all those anonymous survivors, but I want to give them *The Bloody Truth: Part Two.*'

India moved around the room, pulled back a chair next to Ayesha and sat down with determination. She looked intently at Ayesha who was struggling to keep up.

'Ayesha,' she said quietly, 'We have heard Jessica's story over and over. She has been given every platform possible. Because she is a white woman. Because of her privilege. You, on the other hand, and so many like you, have had to resort to social media to vent your pain. You have had to cover your pain with humour. But we have all glimpsed the tragedy behind the comedy. We are, after all, sistren.'

She took Ayesha's hand in hers. Paused. Ayesha froze.

'I want to write your story on my body in blood,' India said quietly.

'Sorry?' Ayesha looked around in alarm.

'What happened, Ayesha?' India pressed.

'What happened? When?' Ayesha's heart was thudding in her chest. She cast about wildly at the others and wanted desperately to pull her hand away from India's.

'You tell us. When, how, what. Who, even,' India pressed.

Ayesha could hardly breathe.

'The thing is, I don't really ... talk about ... I think maybe it might be better to ask someone else to ... Joni? Maybe ... ?' Ayesha tried desperately.

India shook her head sympathetically.

'We don't identify as survivors. We have all, of course, experienced the numerous violations of a patriarchal society on a daily basis. But you are our sister survivor, as was Jessica. But she's not here now. I am the voice, and Frankie is the expert.'

Frankie and Joni nodded.

Ayesha felt all three pairs of eyes on her. She wondered vaguely when those titles had been agreed upon. Where she'd been.

They waited expectantly as she tried to stop herself from upending the furniture and bolting through the door. She tried to make sense of India's definitions of each of them. She had wanted clarity on their roles, she had asked for that, or at least was planning to, and this made things very clear. Crystal clear. So why was she experiencing the very real symptoms of a panic attack?

The three women looked at Ayesha with a pity she found unbearable.

'Talk to us, your sisters. It's safe here. Tell us,' India encouraged.

Ayesha tried to swallow.

'The thing is,' she began quietly, 'I don't want to.'

CHAPTER TWENTY-ONE

JULY 2018

Saturday 11.30 p.m.

Jessica is nowhere.

Ayesha watched them both giggling at their own little joke, as India pretended to look around for Jessica. She suddenly felt cold, the memory of the icy stone floor her feet had touched reverberating up through her body. India sighed.

'You seem to have taken her place in this ... collective,' Yaz challenged.

India raised her eyebrows in surprise.

'Oh! I thought that was you,' she shot back.

Ayesha saw Yaz start to protest. She could feel her friend's desire to distance herself from any connection to the collective. But Yaz stopped herself, said nothing.

India waved a hand.

'I'm not really into politics,' she continued. 'I think it strays way too far from the sacred feminine and the masculinization of the few women who are allowed in those circles is very disturbing. No, we don't vote.' Clemmie shook her head in agreement. 'But I was sickened to hear Jess had been aligning herself with those ... Tories.'

'Sickened,' Clemmie echoed with disgust.

Ayesha looked from one woman to the other.

'Do you know the son of one of those men left his Labrador in the car in this heatwave and it died?' India said incredulously.

'Monsters,' Clemmie spat. 'They should be shot on the spot.'

Ayesha couldn't help but glance at the majestic animals around her, reduced to immobile ornaments with a single, fatal bullet. She suddenly felt very, very tired.

'Hear, hear,' India said with glee. 'But,' she suddenly held up a finger in front of her face, 'I admire Jessica. I really do. And I'm impressed by her game plan.'

Ayesha gaped. She thought of Jessica, trapped into a corner, running out of options, allies, safe spaces, making allegiances with people who she knew couldn't care less about her, just so that she had someone on her side. It was all she could do to keep herself from shouting out, defending her.

'I mean, if we've learned anything, it's that the criminal justice system is not fit for purpose,' India continued. 'Sometimes you have to take justice into your own hands, at any cost.'

Clemmie let out a low, ominous laugh.

Ayesha's stomach sank. Her mind was swirling with confusion. It couldn't seem to hold on to anything tangible. India ploughed on.

'And then there's Ayesha,' India sighed. Clemmie sighed too, shook her head. Ayesha's heart began to thump loudly in her chest.

'We tried so hard with her. Were so generous. Me, Frankie . . . and still it wasn't enough. She just takes and takes. Manages to find a way to make it all about her. Resorting to spitting, fighting, stealing even.'

Ayesha frowned. *Stealing?*

India looked at Yaz. 'But I don't need to tell you that, you know that better than any of us. You've done so much for her, shown such loyalty and love, and then she turned on you, viciously and violently out of nowhere.'

Ayesha tried desperately to read her friend's expression from the little she could see of her. She was so very sorry.

India lifted a finger to Yaz's face and pressed on a bruise. Ayesha involuntarily flinched.

'Does it hurt?'

Yaz pulled her head away, said nothing.

India gazed at Yaz intensely, 'How dare she hurt you? How dare she,' she said through gritted teeth. 'No one has a right to touch you, do you hear? No one.'

Yaz stared back, their faces now just a few inches from each other. India's hazel eyes had darkened. She seethed with rage. Ayesha's attack on Yaz seemed to be a personal affront to India, but only in as much as it had damaged her property. It seemed so obvious now that she regarded Yaz not with empathy, humanity, but like she was a possession of hers that had been mishandled. They were all just possessions to her. Artefacts she could collect and arrange into a pleasing, multi-hued tableau, allies that helped her climb the rungs, perfectly balanced circles that looked lovely with the right filter. The royal event birther with the handy country home; the veteran lesbian activist and her working-class partner; the old school peer with powerful connections; the ethnic survivor; her charismatic brown queer friend . . .

Ayesha felt herself solidify somehow, begin to become less human, more the object India regarded her as. Her soft insides, her pliable dark olive skin, her ever pulsating organs, the flowing systems they served within her – all congealing, hardening, cooling into something lifeless, empty. Just like the furs. Just like the stuffed animals.

They had never been her friends. None of her thousands of followers were her friends either, Ayesha saw this now, and understood what India had coveted from her: Yaz, yes. But also her friendship with Yaz. Their precious, invaluable connection. Something India had never known and wanted to have for herself now. To possess. So she divided. And then conquered.

India's anger seemed to dissipate as quickly as it had formed. A smile curled at the side of her mouth. She tilted her head.

'How's the high treating you?' India seemed happy again. Playful, flirtatious. Ayesha was struggling to keep up. She wasn't sure if it was her own confused mind, or whether these two women were jumping from one extreme emotion to another. Turning on a sixpence that was making Ayesha dizzy again.

'Hmm?' India continued, moving even closer to Yaz. 'Your pupils are dilated. You're blinking slower than usual. And your mouth. Your mouth, when it's not smiling at me so deliciously, is busy moving, pouting, chewing.' She ran her eyes over Yaz's face.

'As is yours,' Yaz returned.

Ayesha had noticed Clemmie and India chewing and gurning in between their eloquent and persuasive speeches. Working their jaws like hungry predators preparing for their next feast.

India giggled playfully, loosened her jaw, 'You must have been watching me as closely as I've been watching you.' Yaz let that one slide, continued to watch her carefully. 'It's potent stuff.'

'Does the job,' Yaz replied with a slight shrug.

India's eyes glinted with flecks of gold. She looked up, took a long breath through her nose, savouring her own high. 'I don't know about you but it's like there's a kind of euphoric feeling mixed with something a bit more trippy, but also just mellow, y'know?'

'Sure,' Yaz said.

India beamed. 'I knew we were on the same vibe. It's fun.' She ran her tongue along her teeth, her eyes flashing daringly. 'Shall we take a bit more? See what happens?'

Yaz's eyes darted momentarily to Clemmie, then back to India. Ayesha's did the same. India leaned in slightly.

'I have a very sensitive system,' India confided. 'No gluten, no dairy, and definitely nothing manufactured or processed in any way.' Clemmie nodded solemnly at this. 'I've been hospitalized several times because the menu at a restaurant did not clearly stipulate the hidden evils in the garnish. That's why Clemmie has been so brilliantly careful with all the ingredients, the décor, the guest list. It had to be perfectly balanced you see. Everything and everyone playing their position very precisely.'

'Purity and precision,' Clemmie added. 'That should be our coat of arms.' The two white women looked at each other, giggled.

'That's why it is so dangerous when people don't play by the rules,' India was serious again. 'If they set out on their own selfish little agenda when we've been so generous in including them. It has to be nipped in the bud,' she concluded.

'Any impurity must be eradicated swiftly and completely,' Clemmie added coldly. 'This is a safe space. Nothing that is a threat to our person, our circle, will be tolerated.'

'What does that mean exactly?' Yaz asked calmly.

India turned back to Yaz but did not elaborate further. Instead she held out her hand towards Clemmie. Clemmie sprang into action, rummaging around her person before producing a small silk purse. She opened it and took out a tiny parcel wrapped in paper. Ayesha watched as she slowly unfolded it like the petals of a flower and in the middle was

327

a dense, brown powder. Clemmie held it out and India took a generous pinch between three fingers. She raised the whisky bottle in her other hand and dropped the powder into it, swirling it gently.

'This is not a drug,' Clemmie clarified. 'It's sacred medicine.'

Yaz looked from India to Clemmie.

'Sure,' she replied levelly.

'This goes beyond anything you can read in a book, discuss intellectually, politically,' Clemmie continued. 'This heals us, rids us of our imperfection, our sins. Forgives us for what we have done out of hate, anger, revenge.'

'Or what we may yet do,' India smirked playfully. She brought the bottle to her lips, took a deep drink, then held it out to Yaz.

Yaz looked from India to the bottle and back again.

Then a smile spread across her face.

To Ayesha's shock and despair, Yaz reached out and took the bottle from India's outstretched hand. She raised it in her direction.

'To new collaborations,' she said, and drank.

CHAPTER TWENTY-TWO

JUNE 2018

'Hey. It's me. Are you okay? Did I fuck up? I always fuck up. It's inevitable really. I'm sorry if I did. I'm not sure what I said, or . . . Did Frankie say something? Because ages ago I said this stupid thing and I didn't mean it at all. I was just . . . well, talking. Just to . . . well, talk. Fill in the . . . Anyway. It was really stupid and I didn't mean it and if that's what it is then I'm sorry. I'm really sorry Jessica. Please call back. I . . . miss you? Is that okay to say? And it's getting a bit weird with the others. I could do with talking it through. I'm not sure what to do . . . I hope we're cool.'

'It's a life-changing experience. Essential really. I did it once five years ago as a single entity. But to experience it with Hassan has been truly transcendent.'

There was a pause as they sipped their tea and contemplated the course Ayesha had found herself agreeing to go on. India had mentioned it the day she'd announced her engagement. Swore that this was the one thing that had transformed the trauma she had inevitably experienced just by living in this masculinized world and made it possible to be open to the kind of transcendent connection she and Hassan shared. Ayesha had gone to the website afterwards, desperately keen to see if she too could share in the secret to India's success, that effortless way she moved in the world, the career, the connections, the relationship. It seemed such an exhausting process for Ayesha to just keep up with herself and the modest circle of people around her. To keep her head up when she walked through Grove, to keep breathing as the walls of her tiny flat edged in. But how to really break out, to finally be thriving? She had to work on herself. That was the key. She had assumed for too long that she could just coast along being her flawed self, but *that* an India Baxter-Wright did not make.

It was an awe-inspiring website. The course was world-famous and women across the globe swore by it. Many associated it with the turning point in their lives and Ayesha wanted that too.

And then she saw the price. Four figures for the first instalment. A number very similar to the one in her bank account, but without the minus sign next to it. She had quickly logged off.

But India had pressed her on it, and Ayesha was desperate to keep India happy, felt that she couldn't possibly say no to her a second time, not after refusing so brazenly not to be a part of her art installation. Something had hardened in India after Ayesha had declined. And yet a few days later, Ayesha had reached out to her, keen to reconnect, and was relieved to find India sympathetic, almost pitying of Ayesha. Of course she didn't have to do it. Of course it was okay to say no. In fact, India was relieved to see Ayesha finally practicing some boundaries. It was a small start, but a start nonetheless – something for them to build on.

So Ayesha found herself promising to seriously look into the course, then promising to sign up, then India had so kindly made a call to her contact on the team and then, as they were waiting for their food, got her a discount which meant the price was still well into four figures, but with slightly lower digits. India had never been so warm with her, had never looked at her so closely for so long. Ayesha couldn't bring herself to say anything that would ruin that.

So it had all been agreed. Just like that, Ayesha would be starting the course as early as next week.

India took another sip of her nettle tea, picked at the vegan plate she had discussed in detail with the waitress, asking to check the special ingredients menu that all establishments should be able to provide when requested and scrutinizing the contents at length. It took them a full half hour to order.

Ayesha had ordered some sweet potato fries and held off on the burger she'd been planning to have. She had invited India for lunch at India's favourite ethically sourced restaurant in Hackney Wick. Located on a floating platform attached to the bank of a canal, she'd had to book a week in advance. It was the first time they were hanging out just the two of them. It felt like a moment, one that Ayesha was keen to get right. This was a thank you, really. For so much. For suggesting Yaz be a part of the podcast. For bringing her to so many fabulous parties, introducing her to so many of her amazing contacts, including her in her Instagram posts, and, of course, inviting her to the wedding of the year.

It was also a sorry. It appeared that Lynne had no interest in meeting with or representing India. Up until now, Ayesha had managed to avoid the others discovering the news of her arrangement with Lynne, mostly because India and Frankie didn't seem very concerned with the workings of Ayesha's life beyond what she did for the collective. But it was only a matter of time.

She tried not to look at the prices on the menu, felt she should definitely pay for them both, had no idea how she would.

'It sounds amazing,' Ayesha gushed, picking at a fry, trying to make them last. 'I can't believe I didn't know about it before. How was it different with Hassan?'

India smiled again, considered her reply.

'The first time was all about building a deep intimacy with my own being,' she began. 'And I did. Body, mind and third eye. When I sat staring into *his* eyes, both naked, both stripped of our armour, it was transcendent in itself. But then he was encouraged to go deeper, because I already had. To shed the patriarchal conditioning and learn how to best serve the goddess in his presence.' She picked at a chickpea. 'He's doing very well. To be perfectly honest, there are still times where the old conditioning comes back in, but he's good at checking himself now. I hardly have to say anything at all.'

'That's amazing,' Ayesha exclaimed. 'You're both amazing. Together, the two of you are just goals. Honestly, to be part of witnessing you guys take this to the next level is just awesome. I can't wait.'

India smiled. Agreed.

Ayesha picked up another fry, nibbled at it. 'Thank you so much for the personal reference. The discount made a huge difference.'

'You're very welcome,' India replied.

'No, really,' Ayesha insisted, 'you didn't have to. And you did. It just means so much that you would share this experience with someone else. With me.'

Ayesha had absolutely no idea how she was going to pay for it. A minor detail in the grand scheme of keeping up with these women.

'I'm merely sending the elevator back down. The patriarchy aren't going to do it, so we uplift each other. Literally.' India beamed.

Ayesha laughed. Long and loud. 'Very good.'

India carefully selected a forkful of gluten-free, non-dairy, raw goodness and brought it to her mouth. Ayesha hesitated a moment.

'Do you have to do the naked part?'

India smiled kindly.

'It is the most important part. Vulnerable, exposing and essential.' She sat up straighter, looked at Ayesha with authority. 'What I will say is this: try to follow it as closely as possible. Adhere to the strict schedule of the course. Don't short-change yourself. Because it really is yourself you will be cheating,' she warned.

Ayesha nodded earnestly.

'It's what you need, Ayesha. Desperately,' India said lightly, but forcefully. 'You can't have any sort of meaningful relationship with anyone until you have built it with yourself,' she continued. 'Until then, all relationships are built on very shaky foundations. They are toxic because they are based on need. Do you follow?'

Ayesha nodded again. India cocked her head to the side, looked at Ayesha with pity.

'I say this with love but to be frank, I have been deeply concerned by what I have witnessed of your friendship with Yaz,' she continued.

Ayesha paused mid-chew, blindsided by the mention of her best friend.

'You cling, Ayesha, you cling like a baby bat to someone who is clearly outgrowing you, on her way up and out of here.'

It landed like a blow to the stomach.

'Let her go. Because she's letting go anyway,' India advised. 'Let go and let love. And then focus all that desperate attention on yourself,' she concluded with a sad smile.

Ayesha was speechless. The chips congealed suddenly in her belly and throat, clogging her voice inside her. Is that what India thought of her and Yaz? Is that how people saw them? She looked back over their friendship and could suddenly see now how imbalanced it was. She had nothing to offer Yaz, so she went to Yaz's family dos, watched Yaz's gigs, followed Yaz to the club, begged her to do a free gig just so they'd keep her in the collective. It was pitiful. She was pitiful.

'Anyway, you'll have no time for anything or anyone else over the next few weeks because you'll be busy seducing yourself.' India's smile turned into a wicked grin.

Ayesha giggled sadly, desperately. She wished so hard this was true. What even was her sexuality? She couldn't remember. She knew that India often looked at her with such pity as she carefully tended to herself in the dressing room; as she kissed Hassan; mentally, physically and sensually prepared herself for a performance. When it came to sex, Ayesha's first instinct was to crack a joke, several jokes, and then change the subject.

'Yes, I guess so,' she mused.

'So don't worry, we've got the shows covered for a while. And everything else,' India said reassuringly. Ayesha's stomach sank further. They were the same words Frankie had used just a few weeks earlier. Once again Ayesha was being forced to take a sabbatical from the collective, except this time it seemed that Yaz would very much be a part of it. Were they planning to get rid of her permanently? Phase her out like they had with Jessica? Did they get Ayesha back just long enough for her to provide them with her replacement?

India was scrutinizing Ayesha even more closely.

'I really do recommend you immerse yourself in it,' she

insisted. 'It changes everything, if you allow it to. All your relationships. Especially those with whom you are most intimate.'

Ayesha clenched at the word *intimate*. She struggled to
maintain eye contact. Several nervous jokes almost exploded
out of her. She swallowed them down with another precious chip.

India tilted her head coyly, her fork flirted with her food.

'What do you think Yaz will make of this newly transformed Ayesha?' she asked lightly.

Ayesha blinked, trying to keep up with the turns in conversation, desperate for India not to analyse their friendship
any further.

'Yaz?' she said helplessly.

'Hmm,' India said.

Ayesha shook her head.

'I dunno. I guess she'd think the daily baths and ... self-
pleasuring was a bit ... excessive. And I think she'd find the
price a bit ... I mean, obviously with the generous discount ...
I mean ... she would ... I'm not sure really.' Ayesha concluded
in confusion.

India smiled.

'Is that a part of your life that you share with each other?'
she asked, calmly yet directly.

Ayesha's face flushed hotly.

'Yaz? You mean, like ... sex and stuff?'

'Yes, I mean sex and stuff,' India watched Ayesha closely.
'Are you friends with benefits?' Ayesha felt like a mouse being
slowly batted to death by an overly-playful paw.

'No. We don't . . . We're just mates.' Ayesha managed.

India sat back. The mood lightened.

'I see,' she said.

Ayesha reached for another chip. To her surprise, India took one too. She didn't so much eat it as wave it around suggestively.

'Do bring her to the weekend,' India said.

Ayesha paused.

'To your hen do?'

'Goddess retreat, yes.' India confirmed.

Ayesha's heart swelled. Relief flooded her nervous system.

'Yes, of course. Thank you. I'd love to.' Ayesha replied.

'Good.'

India smiled.

CHAPTER TWENTY-THREE

JULY 2018

Saturday 11.45 p.m.

Ayesha stood, shocked and transfixed, her body registering the heartbreak, the betrayal, before her mind was willing to fully fathom it.

She looked on as India broke into a beaming smile at Yaz's words and watched Yaz drink from the bottle with glee. Then, with one swift movement, she took Yaz's face in her hands and kissed her, forcefully, hungrily, on the lips.

Clemmie gasped and laughed with delight. Ayesha also gasped, appalled.

India held Yaz's face with both hands, her tongue exploring Yaz's mouth deeply, ravenously. Yaz's hands moved slowly upwards from her side. She put her hand on the back of India's neck, brushed the bottom of the cane row with her fingers and kissed her back.

Ayesha backed out of the closet, through the confusion of furs. She stepped onto the carpeted floor and paused, breathing rapidly, her mind blank with shock. She made her way numbly back down the secret stairway, not caring who heard or saw her now.

She found herself back in the hallway and headed straight through the front door towards her car parked in the driveway with the others, fumbling around in her dress for her car keys as she went. There was enough light coming from the windows of the house to illuminate her way, but beyond the parked cars the night was solid, impenetrable, pitch black. Ayesha tried not to think about that.

She also tried not to think about how high or sober she might be beyond the shock and distress that dominated her body and thoughts. And she tried not to think about whether she was fit to drive anywhere. She had to get out of here, that was all. Leave them all here and go. She saw now that she had played her part perfectly, and that there was no further need for her. So she would leave.

She reached the car, still struggling with her outfit, trying to make sense of the layers of fabric covering her. It took a while of mindlessly wrestling with it to finally realize. No pockets: no keys. She stopped, defeated, and looked forlornly at her scruffy, loyal little car. So close to being free of this nightmare. So very stuck here. Her mind raced back through the painful events of the evening, the whole thing a horrific series of episodes she wanted to distance herself from. Run away from. Drive away. But she couldn't think where her keys might be. She couldn't leave. The reality hit her like a slap. She contemplated simply walking out of there, barefoot, but the solid iron gates suddenly loomed high and vast in her mind's eye, and before and beyond them, that unforgiving, all-encompassing darkness.

She had to escape somehow. If not physically, then she would draw on a lifetime spent cultivating a rich selection of skills to check out, deny, distract herself from the horrific realities of life. She peered once again into her beloved car, the speakers inside promising hours of Lauryn, Beyoncé, Missy, Simz at full volume, exactly what she needed to drown out this nightmare. Then, jaw set, she spun around and headed back in.

Joni and Frankie had moved into the living room and Joni had begun to sweep the burnt pieces of fabric from the chair into a dustpan, Frankie watching her. They looked up as Ayesha marched in through the door, searching feverishly around, her naked feet stomping through the ash, making a mess of angry, blackened footprints through the room.

'Watch it!' Joni protested.

Ayesha glared down at her. Then, gritting her teeth, she kicked ash into Joni's face, once, twice, three times.

Joni flinched, looked at her in shock.

'Get the fuck up off the floor, Joni,' Ayesha shouted at her. 'Stop crawling about begging for her approval. It's pathetic. You're pathetic. All of you.'

Her foot hit something solid and she looked down to find

the row of little India effigies they had made out of the forest bits at her feet. She picked one up and threw it angrily. It hit the back wall of the fireplace and fell into the still-blazing fire. The fire crackled for a moment and then settled again. So Ayesha picked up another, and another, and chucked them into the fire too. Another ravenous crackle as the flames made light work of the mini-Indias.

Joni gasped. Frankie stepped in.

'Hey! Hey. That's enough,' she warned.

'Or what? You'll tell on me? You'll report me to the clique? You won't let me do any more podcasts? You won't choose me to be your skivvy on your next trip? You won't let me write you shitloads of material for free? You won't let me line up the next brown girl to take my place when you've squeezed me dry? Fuck that. Fuck you.'

'How dare you speak to me like that,' Frankie bellowed. 'After everything I've—'

'PAY. ME. BITCH!' Ayesha bellowed back into her face.

Frankie gaped at her. Ayesha looked around and spotted Clemmie's portable speakers lying discarded on the sofa. She grabbed them and headed back out into the country night. She snatched her phone from the window ledge and carried it all to the roof of the car. It was not quite cool outside, but there was at least some reprieve from the heat of the day and the stifling, unbearable interior. She fumbled with the equipment, trying to find a way to connect the phone and the speaker.

She kept pressing buttons, desperately turning the speakers over in her hands, looking for a signal on her phone, something. She cursed Clemmie for not sharing the Wi-Fi and gritted her teeth, determined to find a way.

'Come on,' she willed the jumble of wire and expensive metal. 'Give me a fucking break, I beg you.'

But the mess of technology before her showed no mercy. Ayesha screamed in frustration.

'Fuck it!' she shouted. 'Who needs the fucking music anyway?' She waved her silent phone in the air, took in a lungful of night air and bellowed out the lyrics to Beyoncé's 'Hold Up' like she was chanting at a football match.

She shouted it into the night. Something didn't feel right. Because it most definitely wasn't right. And she felt jealous. Or crazy ... Or was it jealous *and* crazy?

She shook her head violently. Tears of rage and pain threatened to overwhelm her. But she pushed them down and shouted the lyrics even louder.

It didn't feel right.

The image of Yaz lifting her hand to India's head.

Because it wasn't right.

Kissing her back.

Jessica tossing her red hair as she laughed and laughed at them all from somewhere nearby.

Jealous ... Crazy ...

India's piercing gaze, Clemmie's commanding presence, Frankie yelling in her face. She whirled around, desperately trying to fight the images that crowded into her frazzled, exhausted, bewildered mind.

Just then, a tinny sound escaped Ayesha's phone and her

eyes lit up. Incidentally finding a patch of reception, it came to life, Beyoncé's voice cut through, and Ayesha joined in, singing loudly into the night.

'*Jealous,*' she shouted. '*Crazy!*' she wailed.

It didn't feel right … It wasn't right … None of this was right.

Waving the phone in the air, she sang the words over and over until her throat was raw.

Then suddenly her voice was drowned out by an even louder sound. The speakers had come to life. A sitar whined as a tabla beat kicked in over it. Ayesha tried to keep going, shouting over the music until it hurt. But the speakers overrode her.

With a defeated sigh, she finally gave up.

The external lights switched on and Ayesha turned to see Clemmie appear through the front doorway, holding her phone which had automatically synced to the speakers. She walked into the centre of the light and stopped. Her hair was covered in a rich, dark material. Matching fabric draped across her mouth and nose. Her eye make-up was painted on thick and dramatically, accentuating the one part of her face that was still on show. She turned as two other figures walked out. This time India wore her hair slicked back in an androgynous style, and was dressed in a man's ornate oriental suit with the buttons undone on the jacket, revealing flashes of flesh and cleavage. She walked arm in arm with another. It took a long time for Ayesha to recognize who it was. Her face was framed by a fuchsia silk hijab, several bright flowers pinned on top. Her floor-length dress an explosion of hot pink florals, her eyes heavily ringed with khol, pink blush on skin paler than usual, bright lipstick. A living doll.

Ayesha strained her eyes, trying to make out who it was, and then reeled back.

'Yaz? What the fuck?'

CHAPTER TWENTY-FOUR

JULY 2018

Saturday – midnight

If anyone comes near me with anything pink or floral, I will deck them.

Yaz's words echoed around Ayesha's confused mind.

If you try to put me in a dress, you will die. Alone. I promise.

They had laughed. On the drive up. They'd laughed and laughed at the thought.

Ayesha stared hard at her friend covered in pink, floral. In a dress. She seemed to be teetering slightly, unstable. She looked so much more fragile in that get-up. And paler. Her expression hard to read under the heavy make-up.

What had they done to her? Her awesome kick-ass friend who had fought so hard to be unapologetically, fully herself? Ayesha's rock. Her family. Her bestie. The funniest, strong-est person she knew. The one who had dropped everything to come here to be with her. What had she done? What had they done?

Something deep inside Ayesha snapped. There it was. The line, the boundary that had been crossed which, even for Ayesha, was unacceptable.

Fuck. These. Bitches.

Clemmie turned the music down and loosened the fabric covering her face.

Joni and Frankie stepped out behind them and stood in the doorway.

'Sisters. We have an announcement to make.' Clemmie looked to India, who was still holding on to Yaz possessively. India nodded once. Clemmie turned to the other women.

'A new collaboration has been birthed this very evening in this anointed place,' Clemmie began. 'As you know, both India and I are passionately committed to uplifting the women who are left in the margins. And of all the charities I have birthed, the refugees I have sponsored and the projects I have witnessed bear actual fruit in barren lands, nothing excites me more than India's new commitment to bring *The Whites of Their Eyes* to the world. But it would be wrong for two white women to assume we have the right to tell this story, even with India's Traveller ancestry, even with India so wholly connected to her soulmate of colour, Hassan. That is why I am elated to announce that the Rhodes-Woodhouse Foundation's strict ethical guidelines have now been met and we are able to fully fund a world tour of the upcoming project *The Whites of Their Eyes*. Together, we will bring high art into the darkest, most deprived, rural corners of the globe, where they need it most. This has been made possible because we have been blessed with another goddess and a woman of colour joining us on this exciting journey. Sisters, it is my pleasure to introduce our executive consultant, Yasmin Khatri.' With a flourish, Clemmie gestured to Yaz.

They all clapped. Yaz remained still, but she smiled weakly.

'What the fuck is this?!'

The women turned to Ayesha as she glared at her friend. The sitar whined in Ayesha's ear and the tabla disrupted her line of thought with every thump. She let out an exasperated growl and turned around, grabbing the speakers off the car and fumbling to find the off button.

'Shut this crap off.' She found it and the music stopped abruptly. Ayesha dropped the speakers and they hit the floor with an expensive clatter.

Someone gasped.

Ayesha looked around at the staring faces.

'What the fuck are you doing? What are you wearing? What is this?'

She turned to Joni, Frankie, appealing for some support. They stared back coldly. She turned back to her friend.

'Yaz? What the fuck? You almost quit this whole thing because of what they were wearing. And now look at you.'

Yaz's face remained neutral. A blank doll shrouded in layers of paint and fabric.

'Is that it then?' Ayesha appealed to her friend one more time. 'Are you just gonna blank me?'

Clemmie stepped forward, blocking Ayesha's view of Yaz. She glanced at the expensive speakers on the ground and then back up at Ayesha.

'You seem hell-bent on being the centre of attention once again,' Clemmie said sternly. 'Well okay then.'

Clemmie took a deep breath and locked Ayesha in a penetrating stare.

'Ayesha, what do you have in your car?' she demanded loudly.

Ayesha frowned in confusion.

'What do you mean?'

'What do you have in your car, Ayesha?' Clemmie's eyes remained trained on her. 'A little bird told me that you brought your own ... accessories.'

Ayesha's stomach sank. She looked at Joni who glared back at her defiantly.

'Pink hen costumes?' Clemmie said with disgust. 'What are they made of? Whose children were forced to sew them by hand for us to prance around in for a day? Some kind of pink cake? What's in it? Do you even know? Did you make it? You do know India is acutely allergic to dairy and gluten. You know that. And goddess forbid if there's even a trace of nuts in there,' she threatened, her voice wavering slightly with the promise of her wrath. 'And then there's the large, inflated phallus.'

Clemmie pursed her lips together, paused for a moment as if she hardly knew how to go on. A wave of shame washed over Ayesha, but then she shook it off. She had nothing to be ashamed of.

'What part of goddess retreat don't you understand?'
Clemmie continued with indignation. 'Women's circle. The
clue is very much in the name. And the guidelines were
clearly written out and sent to you in advance. Are you so
conditioned, so psychically enslaved that you can't go one
day without a penis?'

'What about *your* fucking clothes?' Ayesha shrieked.
'Where do you even get this stuff you've covered us in?
You've covered *her* in? Who made *that?*' Ayesha gestured
towards Yaz who looked back at her, her gaze still impossible to read.

Clemmie paused, trying to conceal her surprise at this
counter-attack. Then she gathered herself once more.

'I'm glad you asked,' she replied reasonably. Clemmie
stepped back to include the others. She took a breath.
'Celebrating the textiles and handicrafts of the women of the
world is a passion of mine. I've spent most of my lifetime col-
lating this collection. But many of the pieces we are wearing
actually come from the same source. There is an initiative.
In Malawi. One of the poorest countries in the world. I personally oversaw the establishing of it. We train women there,
single mothers who are HIV-positive, to make finely crafted
pieces such as these and then we ship them to Europe where
they are sold. All the profits are pumped back into the project, the crèche adjacent to the factory where their children
are looked after, the free bicycles each woman gets and the
free meals they and their children receive, medical care, even
mobile phones.'

Clemmie paused. This time it was India who started the applause. Passionately and loudly, she clapped her friend and the others joined in, including, to Ayesha's dismay, Yaz.

When the applause died down, Clemmie turned to Ayesha again.

'I hope that answers your question, Ayesha, and alleviates some of your concerns.'

'You're sick. The whole thing is . . . is . . . Your family should never . . . never . . .' Ayesha was overwhelmed by the injustice, the horror, the violations that were so numerous she had no idea where to begin. She took a moment, channelled her feelings just like she did when she stepped onstage. 'I know what you did to those women. What your real legacy is. It's not just textiles and fabrics you've taken from them. It's their humanity. Their pleasure. *Their womanhood.* And now, what? You're gonna do the same in another part of the world? Haven't you done enough damage?'

Ayesha glared at Clemmie who met her gaze levelly. Ayesha turned desperately to Yaz again. She tried to lock eyes with her.

'Yaz, man. Please. We've got to get out of here. This place, this family . . . You don't know what they did.'

Yaz remained unreachable. India gripped her firmly.

'Yaz. Step away from her. She's evil. They're all evil. They built this house on slave money. The property and the land and the antiques and that fucking flag. The schools, the hospitals. All of it. Built with pain and horror, on the backs, the lives of—'

'Be careful, Ayesha,' Clemmie said quietly, 'before you speak against my family. Our mission is a complex and complicated one and there are many, many things you do not understand. What *is* crystal clear, however, is that you have been more than happy to avail yourself of our hard-earned abundance.' Her eyes were azure pebbles fixed hard on Ayesha.

Ayesha looked desperately at the others, and then she landed on Yaz once more.

'Are you listening to this? Look at the fucking state of you. Say something!' she pleaded.

Yaz watched her, unmoving. Ayesha waited a moment longer for something, anything from her friend. She gave her nothing. Ayesha shook her head, hurt and frustration hardening into something closer to fury.

'You're a fucking sell-out, Yaz,' Ayesha said bitterly. 'You sell out your nan every night for a cheap laugh so I don't know why I'm surprised—'

'Enough. Don't you dare speak to her like that.' India's clipped voice rang out as she stepped purposefully between Ayesha and Yaz. Ayesha felt a surge of rage at the audacity, the possessiveness. She struggled to keep her voice under control.

'What is this, India? What game are you playing?' Ayesha growled. 'Why did you invite her here? Why did you invite me? Just to get Yaz here for you? So you can add her to your little collection? What's this fucking obsession? D'you know what you two look like? You look like a groom and a bride. Is she your bride, India? Your colourful little mail-order bride? Have you forgotten you're about get married. To a man?'

'You really are very angry, aren't you?' India said calmly. 'You are being extremely aggressive and I, for one, feel attacked.'

Ayesha looked at her with incredulity, India's detached serenity tipping her over the edge.

'Good!' she replied wildly. 'Because I'm just warming up!' Ayesha's words were accentuated with a weak flop of the Union Jack flag above them. Ayesha looked up.

'And this shit? Are you kidding me? Did your African workforce make this too, Clemmie? Fuck that.'

Ayesha ran at the flagpole and started to yank at the rope. At first it didn't budge, but then she pulled the other way, hard, and something gave. The Union Jack descended in fits and lurches and as soon as it was within reach, Ayesha grabbed at it and pulled it down. She wrestled with it angrily and managed to rip it half off and tangle herself in the rope. She screamed in frustration and then felt a pair of hands drag her off it. She fought back.

'Get off me!' She turned around to find Joni gripping her shoulders with surprising strength. Ayesha pushed her off. 'You. It's always you doing their dirty work, isn't it? At least you're not crawling about on the floor this time.' She spat the words at Joni.

'Enough. That's one too many things you've broken,' Clemmie said threateningly. Ayesha rounded on her.

'Who even are you?' she yelled in frustration. 'What do you

actually do apart from skip about making announcements and licking India's arse? You want maid of honour? Have it. Who the fuck else is there anyway? Does she actually have any other friends?' India glared at Ayesha angrily, holding Yaz's arm tightly.

Ayesha looked from one face to another. It was crystal clear to her now that none of them meant anything to her. Not without Yaz. They'd taken the one person away from her she really cared about. She'd lured her own beloved friend, sister, to this living nightmare and they'd got into her head, taken the essence of Yaz somehow and it was all her fault. Well, fine. If Yaz wasn't going to call this shit out, then she would do it for the both of them.

She would be the Yaz for them now.

Ayesha squared her shoulders, channelled the rage into one seething final pronouncement.

'You're all fucking dead to me. All of you. I. Am. Done.'

Ayesha tried frantically to rip the lopsided flowers out of her hair and throw them on the floor in a final act of defiance, but managed only to loosen them slightly, painfully yanking a patch of her hair from its roots in the process. She gave up with a frustrated growl and settled for kicking the speakers on the floor.

'You're all fucking sell-outs. All of you,' she shouted, 'The only decent one out of all of you is Jessica and I don't know where she is. What have you done with her? Why did you shut her out like that when she needed you most?' she screamed, her eyes finding Frankie's face.

353

'Don't you dare.' Joni stepped in front of her, glared in her face.

Ayesha focused back on Joni and laughed bitterly. 'And you, following *her* about like a stray dog.' She gestured to Frankie. 'Tell me something, Joni, is it only raging narcissists you get wet for?'

Ayesha saw the blow coming, closed her eyes tight. Then nothing.

Her face hovered above, looking down. She was trying to tell Ayesha something, but her words made no sound. Ayesha fought the grogginess, the deep longing to go back under, to that peace, that darkness, the nothingness. But the face insisted, her expression more urgent now. Her words tumbling out faster. The same phrase repeated intensely but silently. Her pale skin paler. Jessica's vibrant red hair framing her face like ... like a fire. The fire was burning now, dangerously, spitting, hissing, consuming. Jumping from the furnace to set fire to it all. All around her. Her skin dark now, her mouth wide with terror ... Dark eyes reflecting the flames, looking for the way out that wasn't there ... And the heat ... the excruciating heat ... Stifling, burning, melting ... She looked back at Ayesha. Tried one more time to tell her. But then she changed again. Morphed into another face. Skin a sickly, unnatural beige. Layers of make-up caked onto brown skin. Black pencil drawn around each eye like a child with a crayon. Messy, smudged, hiding the expression of the woman underneath who stared back at her. And again a change.

354

Ayesha was tired now, wanting more than anything to slip back under. But now she saw a hard face. Cool blue eyes watching her carefully, coldly. Ayesha took a sharp intake of breath and forced her eyes wide open.

She was still trying to focus, but she could make out Clemmie sitting back, watching her. Ayesha struggled to sit up and felt someone's hot, strong hands help her. She felt drunk. Too high. Unable to shake it off. The left side of her jaw ached. She was inside now, and she looked around the room for Jessica's telltale red hair. With a jolt, she saw her, there on the floor, just out of reach. Why was Jessica lying on the floor? In this room? What had they done to her?

The fire blazed on. Her tongue was thick and dry; she wanted desperately to escape into the cool night air. Waves of nauseating intoxication washed over her followed by moments of acute sobriety. She tried to keep her eyes fixed on Jessica but then Clemmie shifted forward, blocking her view.

'That vintage liquor is pretty potent. Not everyone's palates and constitutions are built for it. I'd go easy on the hard stuff from now on.' Clemmie paused, still watching Ayesha carefully. When she could see Ayesha was indeed conscious, she continued.

'Where is Jessica, Ayesha?'

Ayesha's head was still swimming. She didn't understand the question. Jessica was right there.

'Where is she?' Clemmie repeated. 'You were screaming her name out into the dark and now, just now, even in your ... sleep, you were calling for her. It's obvious you both planned this. And now you want her to come save you. So where is she?'

Ayesha tried to make sense of what Clemmie was saying. She tried to move so that she could see Jessica again, but something, someone was holding her back.

'And why on earth would you both work so hard to destroy my event?'

Clemmie glared at Ayesha with seething rage. It was hard enough trying to comprehend the present situation. What had happened in the past, what existed somewhere else, was beyond her capacity to recollect.

'You rain your filthy saliva over my priceless collection that I so generously shared with you; you disrupt every ritual I curated so carefully; you start a brawl in my home; you fill your deathtrap of a car with cheap allergy-ridden tack that could have serious consequences for India's health; you shout and scream and attack us all; you say the most horrific things about Joni's love for Frankie, Frankie's lifelong cause; you accuse and insult my family; and you may well have helped your crazy little friend set fire to my property. Are you completely insane?'

This wasn't fair. Ayesha wanted so much to explain, to defend herself. But words seemed to fail her completely. Her tongue stuck to the roof of her mouth, too thick to form words. She stared helplessly at Clemmie trying to keep her bearings, sober herself up. She suddenly remembered Yaz and looked around desperately for her. But a firm hand continued to hold her down from behind and she couldn't see her friend anywhere.

'Is nothing sacred to you Ayesha? Does none of it, no one, mean anything to you?' Clemmie continued. 'I can only assume you were planning to sabotage the whole weekend and I have no idea why you would do such a thing.' Her voice rose dangerously in indignation. She sighed deeply, lifted her chin. 'You have a very big apology to make.'

Clemmie turned away to reveal Jessica once again. Ayesha tried to reach her, but her body seemed incapable of moving. Then Clemmie brushed Jessica's hair as she moved and it folded over itself limply, no body attached. A wig. It was a wig. Joni's bright red wig, now discarded. Ayesha's heart sank. It wasn't Jessica.

Clemmie's movement also revealed India sitting behind her. She had changed again. Her hair was scraped back into a tight ponytail high on her head and it fell long and dark down her back. Around her throat was a metal choker with a single chain link attached to the front. From there two thinner chains ran to metal handcuffs on her wrists. A leather bodice was pulled tightly around her torso, forcing a brutal, unnatural hourglass shape. Leather shorts gave way to black fishnet tights. A harsh, smoky eye. Nude lips. She sat regally on the floor of the lounge. The fire blazed in the immense hearth, the burnt furniture still visible in Ayesha's periphery.

'Why, Ayesha? Why does it all have to be about you?' India asked, her tone wavering dangerously. 'Why couldn't I have just one thing, one day that was for me? What is it about me that you hate so much? Why would you work so hard to ruin this for me? This night? This sacred space. Of all nights. Of

357

all spaces.' She paused. The firelight danced on her face, now blazing in her eyes, now glinting off the metal around her throat, her wrists. Accentuating the jet-black hair that hung down to her waist. Someone else's hair. Now hers.

'I've been so generous to you. I've embraced you and invited you in. Made you a part of my inner circle. My friendship womb. But it's never enough, is it? *You* have to have the last laugh, the biggest laugh. *You* have to be the centre of attention, always in the spotlight. It doesn't matter how hard I try, you have to snatch it all for yourself. Taking centre stage, taking the trips to Edinburgh, the best lines, the agent.'

Ayesha blinked. *The agent.* She knew about Lynne Lexx? She'd known all this time and she had still invited her. Why? Had she been planning to punish her for it this whole time? Is that why she had done this to Yaz?

Yaz.

Where was Yaz?

'You think I don't know? You think I'm that stupid? I've been seducing her for months. Courting her slowly, gently. And then, after that show, she went completely cold on me. And in the same week you disappear for two days, come back and won't even look me in the eye. Why would you take that from me too?' India demanded.

The heat was suffocating. Why was it so hot? They were going to burn. They were burning. They had to get out ... The furniture, the charred remains ... Ayesha tried to focus on one face: India's.

'And the course. The course I so generously got you on. Did you ever show up? No, you didn't bother.'

Ayesha vaguely remembered her bank account finally being frozen just before she could make payment. Just before she came here.

'Why would you make me go to all that effort to raise you up, just to humiliate me?'

In the changing light of the fire Ayesha thought she could see India's chin tremble. Clemmie watched too.

'I don't know what I've done to deserve this, Ayesha. I've never met anyone who wanted to hurt me as much as you do.'

Ayesha looked around. Three faces glared back, morphing continually in the dancing light. India, Clemmie and Frankie.

'And then there's Yasmin.' India's voice was harder now. 'What on earth makes you think you have exclusive rights over her?'

Ayesha's heart leaped at the sound of her friend's name, but her mind couldn't make sense of what was being said about her. Where was she? She tried to look around, but still the hands held her firmly in place, limiting her movement.

'Is it just you who gets to be with her? Just you who gets to have her in your life? Who gets to love her? Is it my fault there's a connection between us? Everyone has noticed. Everyone except you. I just have so much love to give.' Clemmie nodded solemnly at this. 'And all I wanted was to extend that to Yasmin, to bring her in to my intimate circle. But you throw a tantrum like a spoilt little brat and smash things because I took your girlfriend from you. It's just so pathetic. So tragic really.'

Clemmie shook her head in disgust. There was a loud sniff. They all looked to India in alarm. The tears were back in her eyes, they danced like a threat in the firelight.

'Sometimes . . . sometimes I feel like . . . you don't cherish the spaces I create,' she sobbed.

A single tear rolled slowly down her perfectly contoured face and was caught unmistakably in the flash of the fire-light. A gasp from behind Ayesha. Joni. It was Joni's hands holding her.

For a moment, Clemmie looked with horror at India's pain-filled face, at the tear. Something in the atmosphere changed. Ayesha fought the drowsiness with everything she had. She had so much to say, so much that needed to be put right, but the change had chilled her. She sensed that she was in very real danger. She swallowed. Tried to speak clearly.

'I do. I do cherish your spaces. India, please—' she begged.

'And my dolls. What did you do with the dolls?' India interrupted. 'You threw them – you threw *me* – into the fire?'

The tear continued to trace a terrible course down India's face. Clemmie turned to Ayesha, a new level of rage and indignation twisting her features horribly.

'No, please I—'

Joni's hands gripped harder. Clemmie let out a piercing scream and came at Ayesha head-on.

Joni held her down as Clemmie screamed and scratched. Ayesha tried as best she could to shield herself from the sharp nails that went for her face again and again. Pure terror raced through her as the scratches tore at her skin, her hair, the heavy hands on her shoulders keeping her from escaping. It was relentless. She was helpless. Just like that time long ago. Exactly like that time. It couldn't be happening again. Please no.

'Please,' she whimpered quietly. As the hands pulled and clawed, more hands pushed her down, bearing the weight of another's body onto her shoulders.

'Okay. That'll do.'

One more swipe and the attack subsided. Ayesha remained with her arms covering her face, her heart beating wildly, her breath coming in gasps. She opened her smarting eyes slowly to see Frankie pulling Clemmie off her. Joni's grip loosened. India wiped her tear away and watched with cold satisfaction.

'Just kick her out,' Frankie suggested. 'She can find her friend. They're cut from the same ungrateful, cheap cloth. Good riddance to them both.'

'And have them join forces? Destroy anything that's left of my special weekend? I don't think so,' India countered.

'Fine, then she can lead us to the other one and we can round them both up,' Frankie said with excitement in her eyes. 'Kill two birds with one stone.'

Something about Frankie's tone and expression made Ayesha's breath catch in her throat. As Frankie looked at India meaningfully, Ayesha recalled the hunger with which they had searched for Jessica after the fire – their wild elation and how they had justified their reason to be armed. The disappointment when they hadn't had the chance to use those arms. And how much more paranoid they seemed now, convinced Jessica had started the fire. They were high, drunk, not themselves. Or perhaps more themselves now than they had ever been.

Ayesha shook her head. This was crazy. Killing birds with stones. It was a phrase, a common proverb. This was Frankie and India. But the scratches and blows throbbed across her body.

'You will not ruin this sacred night,' Clemmie spat at Ayesha, still wild with rage. 'You will not contaminate this sacred space with your hatred. We will cleanse the circle of you. We will cleanse you of this hate. Cleanse her. Cleanse her. Cleanse her. Cleanse her,' Clemmie repeated, and soon India took up the chant, as did Joni from behind Ayesha.

Ayesha's eyes darted from one twisted pale face to another. Something had taken over. They were drunk on their own rage, the chant fuelling their collective high, justifying their euphoria, their lust. They weren't themselves anymore but a single, pulsating mob, united in their cause. She wasn't herself anymore but the focal point for their fury. The target. The sacrifice.

As the chant rose in pitch, Clemmie's scream pierced through them all.

'Take her to the lake! Drown her like the witch she is.'

Ayesha looked around wildly as they began to scream 'Lake! Lake! Lake!'

She found Frankie, who was watching the others quietly, and locked eyes with her, appealing desperately for her to intervene once more. But Frankie ignored her, walked to the door and calmly opened it.

Ayesha's jaw dropped; she was devastated.

'No, no, no.' She tried to push and pull and wriggle as India stepped forward and more hands took hold of her. They began to half drag, half carry her towards the doorway. The terror rose inside Ayesha once again. For the second time that night, she fought the hands that forced her, invaded her, gripped her. Except this time they weren't just planning to hurt her.

'Wait. WAIT!' The women paused momentarily in their apparent mission to drown Ayesha. They looked at Joni who was still gripping tightly onto Ayesha and looking at her with hatred. 'Frankie's right. She's had enough attention as it is. Don't let her gang up with Jessica and take this whole night over. The lake's too good for her.'

Clemmie looked at Ayesha's terrified face and smiled.

'Fine,' she concluded, 'Put her in the boot of her putrid old banger with the rest of the rubbish. She can have some quiet time in there. Think about what she's done.'

'Where's the key?' India's voice demanded from above Ayesha.

The women began to search Ayesha frantically. She pushed their groping hands off her, the panic so complete that she could hardly see, hardly breathe, the lump in her throat growing as numerous hands pushed, grabbed, fingered her, the tears and terror, the familiar helplessness.

'Please stop,' she whimpered.

They didn't. But then, over their probing heavy breaths, a

light jingling cut through. They froze. Looked up. Across the room Yaz had appeared. She held the car key in her hand. Ayesha watched, devastated, as her friend raised her hand blankly. What had felt like a horrible dream suddenly felt as real as cold, hard marble. Several thirsty screams. Two of them lunged for the key. And then Ayesha was lifted again, dragged towards the doorway, past her painted friend who she looked at with shock and a heartbreak she'd felt only once before, looking back at her dad as the social worker had led her away.

Ayesha looked desperately from one woman to the other as they gripped her tightly and dragged her outside. Joni's wiry arms were around her torso. Clemmie held steadfastly to an arm and leg and moved resolutely towards the car. India had grabbed the other side and watched her with a cold thrill. A fresh wave of terror and nausea swept through Ayesha as she fought even harder against the six pale hands.

Despite the mild night, Ayesha was trembling violently.

Frankie was at the car. She clicked the key and the locks popped up. Standing by the boot, she opened it just as the writhing mass of women arrived.

Several things happened almost simultaneously.

A moan escaped Ayesha in the shape of a desperate *No!* A blast of hot air that had been trapped in the boot hit them like the gates of a metallic mini hell opening, infused with the sickly-sweet smell of molten pink icing. Six hands attempted to push her in. A flash of shiny pink latex rising from its depths. A loud bang. Multiple screams. The loosening of six hands. A moment of stillness and shock.

And then Ayesha ran.

CHAPTER TWENTY-FIVE

JULY 2018

Sunday 1.00 a.m.

Ayesha pelted away, around the side of the house, running parallel to the odd extension that seemed like a solid dark tumour attached to the grand old main building. Across the stones of the garden patio, cooler now with the turn of the night. Her mind raced from the terror of being held down by so many hands to the shock of the bang and suddenly being free, her body breaking into a run, her brain only now catching up. She'd glimpsed the bright pink of the objects in the boot and then another brighter, shinier pink had glided out of the heat, knocked the corner of the metal boot and instantly disappeared with a loud bang. The balloon. It had exploded. They had let go. And she had run.

Her bare feet hit the lawn and soon the field beyond. If there were thistles in her path, she didn't notice them. Her feet barely touched the ground. She ran without a plan, but her instinct was leading her to the dark of the woods ahead.

The shouting came from behind her. Screams of outrage aimed in her direction. A pack of angry women hot on her scent also galloped across the cold stone, the tamed grass and then the wild.

She reached the edge of the trees and hesitated. It was so completely dark in there. Beyond the first line of trees, she could make out very little. Despite having been there earlier that evening, nothing seemed familiar. Another shout from behind her, louder, closer, forced her on, but more slowly, the darkness requiring her to feel her way more carefully.

'Ayesha! Where are you?'

'We're coming for you.'

A laugh. A scream. More laughter.

She faltered for a moment. Was this a joke? Is that why they were laughing? Was she completely overreacting? The thought of this all being some kind of awful misunderstanding gave her a surge of hope.

But then she remembered Clemmie's rage. Her features twisted with hatred. The scratches still stinging on her face. The feeling of the hands all over her. The euphoric, savage chants. Yaz's outstretched arm holding her car key. Her heart sank. This was real.

She hurried on, trying to quieten her breathing which seemed appallingly loud. She stumbled over dry leaves and twigs, felt her way through damp, cool earth, leaning then pushing off against one tree then another. Then she stopped dead. She'd suddenly lost all sense of direction. She looked wildly about, trying to make sense of the surroundings in the darkness, but she was completely disoriented.

'Please, please ...' she whispered urgently, looking from one identical dark column to another.

A flash of light from between the branches behind her. Then another. The beams swung dangerously across the forest, searching hungrily for Ayesha. Their phones; they were using them as torches. Ayesha's heart thumped harder in her chest.

Then a crack made her jump. It echoed in the darkness. Too loud to be a twig. Maybe a stone being thrown against a tree. Not a gun. Surely?

A whoop sounded to her left, so she fled to her right.

This time she didn't stop to even contemplate the thick darkness that met her like a wall at each turn. She ran recklessly at it. Gradually, it seemed to thin somehow. A few more feet and a chink of something, an opening in the air, and she ran onwards until the relentless canopy subsided, gave way to a starless sky, but sky nonetheless. She slowed but forged on. Then her feet felt damp. Then wet. Then a small splash. She paused for a moment, confused and unsure how to continue. She realized she must be at the edge of the lake she had glimpsed through the trees. The lake they had threatened to drown her in. Instinct moved her feet forward, further into the water, knowing somehow that a hunted creature's scent is hard to track in water, that the pack would at least hesitate, falter before trudging in. She waded and waded, the water reaching to her ankles, her knees, then her waist. She pushed on through the chilly resistance, but soon found that the water seemed to be levelling out, then getting shallower again. She stopped, confused, standing waist-deep in the shallow black lake. It seemed somehow lifeless. No moss or weeds or creatures moved in it. The bottom was gritty and clay-like. A man-made feature, she concluded vaguely behind the fear. Superficial, ornamental. Providing little sustenance or shelter. Nowhere to hide.

Another crack. Another whoop. Coming closer, also finding the edge of the forest, the sky, the opening. Cold beams of light swinging left to right and back again. Ayesha took two steps back to what she thought must be the deepest part of the lake and started to lower herself down into the water. She had got as far as her shoulders when something brushed her arm. A lacy, gentle, chilling caress. And then a hand, unmistakable, clawed at her and she let out a scream as she hauled herself out.

CHAPTER TWENTY-SIX

JULY 2018

Sunday 1.30 a.m.

Ayesha pulled herself out of the water and stood shaking and gasping. She could still feel both the strange, soft underwater caress and the claw-like grasp on two different parts of her chilled, mottled skin. That, along with the tepid, stagnant, lifeless water suddenly made her heave. Bile rose involuntarily up her throat and she fell onto all fours retching and retching. Her body shook as waves of acidic liquid poured violently out of her.

She waited for her body to calm down and wiped her mouth as best she could, shaking uncontrollably. Then she paused. She sensed the change in the air before she heard it. She had made too much noise. She had given away her location. The whoops and jeers had stopped. They'd caught her scent, locked on to her location, and she knew they were coming for her, methodically, hungrily, intent.

She crouched down and tried to slow her breathing. She shivered once more and her body began to settle. The violent vomiting had sobered her up. She realized how drunk she had been. But it was more than that. Something else had been eliminated from her body. She was clear-headed for the first time in ages. The last few hours flashed across her mind in a nightmarish series of images, all of them crazed, animalistic, intense and illogical – herself included. How had it got this bad? She thought back to the hazy infernal scene in the living room and could recollect clearly the widened dark pupils staring, deranged, into her own. She had been high. They had all been high on something strong, chemical.

Terror and the instinct for survival sharpened her mind further. She listened and could sense their approach. Ayesha waited until she could make out the dark figures beginning to emerge from the wood, flashes of light dancing with every step. They stalked towards the water and then hesitated. A disturbance of droplets, a hurried whisper and someone retreated from the water's edge. To Ayesha's relief, they kept together and made their way keenly around the edge of the lake.

Ayesha kept low and crept slowly around the other side, keeping in time with their progress. Her soaking body trembling uncontrollably, her teeth chattering violently, she tried to calm her panicked breathing and keep herself concealed in the darkness of the country night. When they were just over a quarter of the way around, there was a chilling scream of triumph. Ayesha froze; her stomach sank. She could just make out the silhouette of a finger against the night sky pointed directly at her. A beam of cold light locked on to her. Then another. Someone ululated. More voices joined in and then they ran at her.

Ayesha pelted away, back into the thick darkness of the trees. But they were much closer now. Two figures sprinted with intense determination in her direction. She didn't need to look behind her. She felt their intent and heard their rhythmic breathing as they closed in on her. What would happen when they caught her? How far would they go? She had no idea anymore where the line was. She knew they weren't fully themselves, but even as themselves she was now terrified of what they were. How had she got them so wrong? How could Yaz do that? Join them? Help them hurt her? Surely there was some mistake. She thought of turning, trying to reason with them, snap them out of this savage intoxication. But she didn't dare slow down. Instinct told her to keep running. Maybe for her life.

Ayesha looked around wildly as she sprinted, desperately trying to think of a plan as she strained with all her remaining strength to keep the distance between her and her hunters from closing. But her body was weaker now, the violent expulsion had taken it out of her, and all she could see was layers of darkness in every direction.

They were close now. And she was running out of strength. And options.

And then a flash.

Another flash. Two flashes up ahead.

Ayesha's heart sank. They were surrounding her and flooding her out. But the voices were coming from behind her, and the lights ahead were moving together. Two lights, bouncing up and down in perfect synchronicity, unlike the disjointed dancing of the phone torches. A hum. Then a rumble.

A car.

It was a car.

CHAPTER TWENTY-SEVEN

JULY 2018

Sunday 1.45 a.m.

The vehicle bumped up and then down over the uneven ground at an almost comically cautious speed as Ayesha sprinted towards it. The increasingly loud growl of the engine overrode any other noise so that she had no sense of how close the others were now, just that she had to get to the car, despite not knowing who was driving and what would happen when she reached it. She was out of options. Something about the powerful headlights felt important. These layers of darkness, the heat, the smoke and fire of the interior had facilitated this nightmare. It needed light. Light needed to be shed on them all, a starkness that would wake them out of their dark trance and expose the insanity for what it was. Ayesha ran towards the light.

They were further away than she had anticipated. She felt

her body begin to tire, the lactic acid seize in her muscles, the shaking return, her breathing becoming unbearably laborious and she wanted so much to just stop, for it all to stop. But she pushed on, through the fatigue, willing the car to move faster towards her.

And then suddenly she was in front of the headlights. She waved frantically and threw herself at the bonnet. The breaks screeched, the sound of a handbrake being hurriedly pulled. A moment of stillness as the engine turned over, exhaust fumes cloaking the forest in an unnatural haze and red light. Then the driver's door opened and a figure stepped out.

'Shit, are you okay? Are you hurt? Why did you jump out like that? I could've ...'

His voice trailed off as he saw the wild terror in her eyes, the trembling body, as he took in the soaking clothes, the dirt smeared across her face, the scratches up her legs, on her face, the bleeding.

'Please. Help me. Get back in the car. They're coming,' Ayesha gasped.

'What? Who? Woah, woah, what's ... I'm just ... I'm just here for the—' the man stammered.

'*Get in the fucking car!*' she screamed.

The man stood, shocked and completely confused. Ayesha pushed past him and stumbled into the driver's seat.

'Shit,' he exclaimed again and jumped into action, trying to reach the car door before she slammed it shut. He ran around and managed to scramble into the passenger seat even as the car started moving.

'What the hell are you doing? What's happening?' he asked
desperately.

Ayesha's face was set with a new determination as she put
the car into gear and took the handbrake off. She ploughed
forward as quickly as she dared, trying to make sense of
the track they were on and the quickest route out. The front
gate was made of iron. It was controlled from somewhere in
the house. And she had no idea which direction to drive in
from here.

'Where are you going?' the man asked helplessly.

'How did you get in?' Ayesha demanded.

'What?'

'How did you get in! Tell me!'

'The . . . the phone map. It sent me to some . . . some random
gate. Back there.'

Ayesha looked to the side of the steering wheel and saw
the glow of the phone attached to a holder; the same familiar
expanse of green that she had seen on her drive to the house
filled the screen. She remembered the first stop they'd made
at the strange old gate and the overgrown track beyond leading to the forest.

'Where is it?' she begged. 'The gate. Please!'

'B-back there! I think,' he indicated behind them. 'I've been
driving around for ages. I couldn't find—' Ayesha immediately swung the car around, narrowly missing the thick trunk
of an ancient oak that would have budged not an inch as the
metal vehicle wrapped itself around it.

'Shit,' he said once more as he gripped the dashboard.

376

Ayesha shoved the gearstick into reverse with a sickening rasp and completed her one-eighty. As she slammed it back into first, the man in the passenger seat let out a startled scream.

'Who the fuck is that?' he shrieked looking with horror behind him.

Ayesha looked up to see Clemmie in the rear-view mirror, her face illuminated from below by the red rear lights, a rifle in her hands. She swung at the back window and the butt of the gun slammed into the glass with a sickening thud. The man ducked. Another swing and a large crack appeared. She swung the rifle back a third time, ready to smash the glass clean off. Without thinking, Ayesha slammed the car back into reverse and pressed down on the accelerator with all her might.

Clemmie deftly spun to her right and narrowly avoided being mowed down. But her smouldering glee quickly turned to pain-filled rage and she let out a blood-curdling scream.

'Oh my God. What did you do?' The man looked at Ayesha incredulously. Ayesha glanced behind her to see Clemmie cradling her foot gingerly.

'My foot! She broke my foot!' Clemmie screamed.

Ayesha once again slammed into first and pressed down hard on the accelerator. A smash to the window right beside Ayesha sent shards splintering into her face. She flinched and then looked up to see India scream with rage as she turned the gun around in her hands and aimed. Ayesha swerved to the left and looked away from the pointed gun just in time to catch a glimpse of Yaz appearing in front of the car. And then a sickening crunch as her beloved friend flew over the bonnet, her face smashing into the windscreen right in front of Ayesha.

CHAPTER TWENTY-EIGHT

JULY 2018

Sunday 2.00 a.m.

Ayesha stumbled out of the car and rushed over to her friend, who was lying crumpled on the ground.

'No, no, no, please,' she begged as she held Yaz's hand and searched her body for injuries, trying to figure out how bad it was. Yaz's eyes were open just a fraction, her breathing laboured. She groaned weakly.

'Yaz, I'm so sorry. Talk to me. Where does it hurt?' Ayesha begged.

Yaz's eyes wouldn't focus, but for a moment her mouth seemed to form a word. Then again. She was trying to say something. She made a strange convulsing sound as she tried to speak.

'Yaz babe, tell me. Try,' Ayesha pleaded desperately.

Her friend didn't respond. Instead, her gaze, which had

been focused on Ayesha so intensely, weakened until her eyes rolled away, her body limp.

'Please, Yaz. No,' Ayesha sobbed, holding her friend tenderly.

'Oh my God. Is she okay? What's going on?' The man had climbed out of the car and stood over the two women with his hands on his head in shock.

Ayesha rocked her friend gently, desperate for a sign she was still with them.

'Who the hell are you and what are you doing on my land?' a cold clipped voice demanded suddenly.

They looked up to see Clemmie pointing a gun at the man and India pointing a gun at Ayesha. Ayesha's eyes darted from one woman to the other. Clemmie's clothes were torn and muddy. Her left foot was cocked at a strange angle behind her, but she stood resolutely on her right leg, holding the gun perfectly steady. Ayesha oscillated between utter relief and complete dismay that she hadn't injured Clemmie further.

'Woah woah woah.' The man put his hands out in front of him.

'Put them back where they were!' Clemmie screeched.

'Okay, okay. I'm doing it,' the man stammered. 'I'm putting my hands up. Please, just don't—'

'I am terrified right now. Absolutely terrified,' Clemmie screamed, her rage making the gun shake in her grasp. The man watched it with horror. 'You've violated my space, you've contaminated the circle, this women's circle, uninvited—'

'Hold on, hold on. I *was* invited. I'm here for the party. The hen do.' He tried to reason with her and at the same time kept his arms firmly above his head.

'The *what*?' Clemmie shrieked. 'How dare you. This is not a ... a ... This is a goddess retreat—'

'Sure! Sure! Yes, that's right. And I'm the ... I'm Juan Carlos. I'm the, the ... the stripper,' he stammered.

There was a moment of confusion, and then the penny dropped.

Ayesha gasped. 'Oh shit.'

'What?' For an incredulous moment, Clemmie forgot herself and lowered the gun a fraction. Juan Carlos watched it carefully, but he tried to keep his voice steady, calm.

'I'm the stripper you ordered. Remember? I'm just here to ... to ...'

'How dare you,' Clemmie seethed. 'How dare you. We did not order a ... a ... stripper. Oh my God. I feel violated. This is violence. This is violence!' she screeched as she raised the gun once more.

'Please!' the man begged. 'I've got the print-out in the car. If you let me just get it—'

'Stay where you are!' Clemmie screamed.

Juan Carlos froze.

'I'm sorry I'm late. I got lost ... I ... Please,' he begged again.

'Enough!' Clemmie bellowed, 'This is a safe space! A safe space!' She steadied her hand, focused her rage. 'You will never desecrate another space again. You will never force your unwanted sexuality onto another woman, and you will never, ever leave this place.' A calm determination settled across Clemmie's face; she took her aim. Juan Carlos braced himself to be shot, liquid beginning to seep through his trousers.

'Clemmie, no!' India shouted.

Clemmie spun around to look at her.

'He is a sex worker. He is a brown man. As brown as my Hassan. I will not let you harm him,' India stated.

Clemmie looked at her incredulously.

'He has broken into my property, run me over with his car and helped this traitor ruin the whole thing. The whole ceremony. I spent weeks organizing this. Weeks planning every detail, for you, and now you side with this piece of shit?' she spat back.

'You will not harm him.' India's voice was firm.

Clemmie suddenly spun the gun around to face India. There was a gasp.

'Don't you dare tell me what to do,' she said through gritted teeth. 'This is my land. This land is sacred to my family. Generations of us. I will defend it at all costs.'

'I will not be party to this,' Frankie suddenly bellowed. 'I cannot condone this violence and I am not a witness to this.'

Clemmie trained the gun on Frankie now, who froze.

'Who the fuck do you think you are, Frankie? Who are you but some washed-up old dyke? You come here and you stomp around my property with your filthy boots, you take and take and then tell me you are not party to this? Where would any of you be without my charity? My philanthropy? You are nothing! Nothing without me,' she spat.

A bloodcurdling scream emanated from behind her and Joni came out of nowhere. She ran at Clemmie, grabbing at the gun and trying to kick wherever she could. Clemmie held on tight, but Joni's squat frame housed a formidable strength fuelled by even stronger outrage. She gave a final yank and the gun pulled free. It went clattering to the ground behind her and, without pausing, she jumped on Clemmie and pushed her to the floor.

'Don't you ever, ever point a gun at her again. You could have killed her, you stupid, stupid bitch.' Joni punched and punched until Clemmie's attempts to defend herself grew weaker and weaker and she finally lay there, bloody and still.

Ayesha watched with horror as she knelt by Yaz, who remained unresponsive. She was desperate for a moment, an opening where she could get her some help, or somehow quietly carry her away from this, far, far away from this nightmare to somewhere safe, somewhere where she could be tended to, saved, as the others turned on each other.

Frankie stood perfectly still, watching her girlfriend tire of hitting Clemmie, who was now unconscious.

Then a movement at the side of Ayesha's vision. She saw India slowly drop the gun she was holding and edge towards the gun that Joni had flung from Clemmie. Instantly, she understood. It was the real one. The loaded one. The one India had been holding was the ornamental gun.

Ayesha leaped forward and reached it a millisecond too late. India snatched it from the ground and with terrifying mastery placed it, cocked it and aimed it at Ayesha before Ayesha fully understood what was happening. Then she pulled the trigger.

CHAPTER TWENTY-NINE

JULY 2018

Sunday 2.30 a.m.

The gun clicked. There was no bang. Everyone stood frozen as if in an absurd picture for several seconds before Ayesha realized she was still very much alive. This time she was the first to move. She lunged at India with all the strength she had left and they both came crashing down, the gun once again clattering to the forest floor. Ayesha was on top of India, but India fought back and they struggled messily as one tried to overpower the other.

Ayesha screamed in frustration and caught India in some kind of awkward lock.

'Stop! Please just stop fighting me!' Ayesha begged.

India faltered for a moment. Ayesha tried to keep eye contact with her.

'This is fucking crazy, India. You tried to kill me. What the fuck?'

India hesitated for a moment, the crazed rage seeming to dissipate before she gritted her teeth once again and started to struggle against Ayesha. Ayesha held on desperately.

Then India spotted Yaz lying behind Ayesha and a surge of determination passed through her as she flung Ayesha aside and strode towards her. She dived to the ground and pulled Yaz towards her in a greedy embrace. A weak cry escaped Yaz, her head lolling at a dangerous angle. Ayesha rushed forward, then stopped abruptly as India pulled Yaz closer.

'Be careful! You're hurting her,' Ayesha cried.

India turned on her with venom.

'Stay away from her, you evil bitch,' she hissed. 'Look what you did. Look what you did to her. My Yasmin. My Yaz ...'

As India tried lifting Yaz towards her, there was a painful crack and Yaz let out another stifled cry. Ayesha felt bile fill her mouth. Yaz shouldn't be moved, she was very badly hurt and any movement could make it worse, much worse.

'India. India. Listen to me. Look at me. Look at me!'

But India continued to cradle Yaz possessively.

'I'm sorry,' Ayesha said. 'I'm sorry, okay? I fucked up. I ruined your night and I'm so, so sorry. But please, be careful with her. Please let me just—'

'No!' India spat.

Ayesha fought the desire to run over and pull Yaz out of her grasp. Yaz's eyes remained closed, but a tear fell down the side of her face.

'You're right, India,' Ayesha continued desperately. 'Yaz should be with you. You can take much better care of her. You want the agent too? Have her. You want the fucking punchline? It's yours. You're so beautiful, and successful and lucky. You're so fucking lucky ... and I'm so jealous.'

India paused her pawing of Yaz. She looked up at Ayesha with clear, piercing eyes. Ayesha continued.

'Look at you. You've got it all. The connections, the talent, the beauty, the drive, and the most beautiful man I've ever set eyes on, who clearly loves you to bits. I just can't compete. I never could. I just wanted to be your friend. Your sister. And I fucked it all up.'

India slowly began to loosen her grip on Yaz who slumped gently back to the ground. India tilted her head and listened intently. Ayesha had no idea what to do, no plan, so she kept talking, and creeping slowly towards her.

'We were never in competition. That's hilarious. Me in competition with you? Please. I'm lucky enough that you called me Sister. I'm lucky to be invited into your circle. Your beautiful, perfect circle. Our collective. I've got no idea how it got this bad. Why we thought we were in competition with each other. It's silly really.'

Ayesha was in touching distance of India now. And Yaz, who lay quietly beside her. She wanted so desperately to reach out to her friend, but instead she crouched down and held her arms wide.

'India, I—'

India suddenly lunged at Ayesha. For a moment, Ayesha's

heart stopped. She had let her guard down and India had taken the advantage. Her luck had run out. Then she realized her arms were still free. India was hugging her.

'I knew it,' India sobbed. 'I knew you loved me, really, deep down. Everyone does, don't they? I just feel so fucking crazy right now. It's all got so out of control . . .' India laughed. Laughed and laughed as she held on to Ayesha.

Ayesha let herself be held and laughed on. They swayed from side to side in merry glee. On the third sway, Ayesha lunged to just beyond Yaz and grabbed the metal barrel. She swung around and in one movement slammed the wooden handle against India's head. India flew to the right – away from Yaz – and stayed there.

'Touch her again and I'll end you,' Ayesha snarled.

She hurled the gun away from her and rushed over to Yaz, barely touching her now that she had been so horribly manhandled.

'It's okay, it's okay,' she whispered over and over. 'I'm gonna get you out of here, I promise.'

Ayesha looked around wildly and saw Juan Carlos standing open-mouthed by India's fallen body.

'Help me!' she yelled, but he stood transfixed, looking at India.

'What— What did you do?' he asked breathlessly.

'Pull it the fuck together and help me get her out of here!' she shrieked.

A crunch of leaves and then another person appeared beside them.

'It's okay. It's okay,' she said breathlessly, 'It'll be fine. It's over now. I've called the police and they're on their way.'

Ayesha looked into Frankie's face as Frankie crouched down and put her hand on Ayesha's trembling shoulder. Then she looked down at Yaz and let the sobs of terror and relief finally come.

'Those fucking guns. What the hell were they thinking? Pointing those things at us, shooting. What the fuck?' Frankie said as Ayesha sobbed.

Ayesha looked at Frankie, intense relief and gratitude mixed with a confusion of thoughts. She remembered her stopping them from dragging her to the lake. Or was that Joni ... ? But then Frankie had also unlocked the car, opened the boot for them to ... But that was when Ayesha had managed to make her escape. It had all happened so fast. She hadn't been able to make sense of who was where, who had said what. All she knew was that it was over now. Another arm around her and she looked up to see Joni hugging them both, also crying.

There was a groan and they looked down at Yaz. She was trying to focus, trying to pull herself up. She managed to get halfway up and then collapsed again. Ayesha turned to her.

'Yaz, it's okay. It's over. Relax. Don't try to move. The police are on their way. They're going to help you.' She tried to calm her friend who seemed determined to move, straining to speak. Ayesha put a gentle hand on her chest, her leg. Under her hand she felt something solid, square.

Ayesha gently lifted the floral dress, now ripped and smeared with blood and dirt, and found Yaz's old costume underneath. The teal leather trousers were oddly pristine in comparison to everything and everyone else at this hideous scene. Wedged half in, half out of the front pocket at her waist was a phone.

Ayesha pulled it out. It was her phone. She fumbled with it, trying to unlock it and cursing as her shaky, filthy fingers failed over and over. Finally she managed it. The screen lit up. She stood and waved it desperately in the air. Faster than she had hoped, a loud, clear ping announced a sliver of reception.

'She needs an ambulance,' Ayesha said. 'We've got to call them back. Tell them to—'

But she was momentarily distracted by the message that had just come through.

> I'll never ruin another moment for you
> again. Goodbye.

'Jessica. No!'

Ayesha pressed the button almost automatically and put the phone to her ear. Flashes of their phone conversations raced through her mind. What had she missed?

Actually, I think I'm more dangerous.

I'm scared I'm losing myself.

Don't worry. I'm not going to jump.

They'd all been calls for help. The acceptance of the invitation, the rejection of it, turning up after the recording, hoping to be let into the circle once more. All of it had been a stoic but quietly desperate plea. And she'd missed it.

A pause. And then, mercifully, a ring tone.

'Come on. Pick up. Where are you?'

'Wait. Who are you calling?' an alarmed voice demanded.

And then a moment of confusion. She took the phone away from her ear, could hear it still ringing faintly in the earpiece, but she could also hear another sound, a faint buzz, then a pause, then another buzz. She looked around wildly trying to locate it, and then she saw that same faint rectangular glow in the side pocket of the woman in front of her. She looked at her, confused.

'Why have you got Jessica's phone?'

CHAPTER THIRTY

JULY 2018

Sunday 3.00 a.m.

Ayesha let the hand holding her phone drop to her side. Eventually, both phones stopped ringing and she stood in confusion, staring at the woman in front of her.

'Why have you got Jessica's phone, Joni?' she demanded again.

Frankie looked at Joni too. Joni glared at Ayesha with defiance and then turned to Frankie, her expression melting into a pleading, desperate one.

'Where's Jessica, Joni?' Ayesha watched her closely and racked her own brain at the same time. Thinking back to the messages, the moments they'd come through on the phones. Had Joni sent them?

Joni looked only at Frankie.

'Joni?' Ayesha demanded more urgently.

'Shut up,' Joni snapped at her and then turned immediately back to Frankie, her eyes searching her face desperately. Frankie looked back, a slight frown on her face.

'I found it,' Joni tried pathetically. 'I just found it. Honest, I . . .' Her voice trailed off. She seemed unable to continue, to lie to Frankie's face.

'What's going on, JJ?' Frankie asked gently.

Joni continued to look at Frankie, her breathing quickening as she built up the courage to speak.

'They just don't get it. They don't. None of them do. They don't get what it takes. The commitment. The years of work, of sacrifice. You bring them in, broken, desperate, alone. You take them under your wing, give them somewhere to belong, a voice, and they just snatch and grab and take and then fuck off.'

Her face contorted for a moment in rage, then recovered quickly.

'See, I get it,' she said defiantly. 'I get it. I do.'

She paused, her face like a whimpering dog's staring at her owner.

'Don't I, Franks?'

Ayesha watched Frankie stare back at Joni. Joni's face broken, desperate, waiting for her judgement. Frankie's harder to read.

'What happened?' Frankie asked quietly.

'I didn't mean to, Franks. You've got to believe me. I'd never, ever do anything to ruin what you built. You know that. But she . . . she . . . said . . . she came . . . to our house. Our house,' Joni sobbed indignantly. 'After everything she did, she just rocked up. That's not right.'

Frankie's gaze remained steady.

'I didn't mean it. I swear,' Joni repeated desperately. 'I didn't mean to ... You know what I get like. I don't know my own ... my ... my ...' Her face flushed pink. She swallowed.

'She barged in, demanding to see you. But you weren't there. You weren't there,' Joni went on. 'And she kept demanding to see you, and I told her you weren't in, but she didn't believe me. She started searching the house, saying you were a rat, a leech, a fucking ... a, a ... she said horrible things, Franks. About you. But I kept my cool, even though I wanted to ... I didn't ... I didn't touch her,' she said proudly.

Then her eyes clouded over and she shook her head bitterly.

'She called me your skivvy. Said I was just another one of your projects and when you were done, you'd move on like you did with the others. She said she'd seen it all before.' Joni looked at Frankie once more. 'Even then, I didn't touch her, I swear.'

Joni paused, searching for Frankie's approval, for an acknowledgement of how restrained she had been. Frankie stared back blankly. Joni deflated a little.

'She said she'd seen that article in the paper. She knew you were friends with that man. The perpetrator. The man who she accused of ... doing all those things to her.'

Frankie raised her head slightly.

Ayesha took in every word. The papers. Frankie's interview. Jessica's warning. She'd realized that Frankie knew her attacker. The head of that newspaper ... Ayesha couldn't remember his name ... John somebody ... or Jack?

'Jack Vine,' Joni confirmed.

Ayesha's heart sank as she thought of Jessica realizing Frankie knew him. Imagined what it must have felt like when she'd seen the front page spread in that newspaper of all newspapers. No wonder she hadn't answered her calls. But then, maybe Joni had already ... Ayesha couldn't bear to think about it. Hoped desperately that her friend was okay, even now. If Joni just stopped talking now, maybe Jessica would stay okay. But Joni's voice went on.

'She said that tomorrow she would be naming names. That she had been given the green light to take him down and bring down anyone associated with him. That she had a list. And you were on that list.'

Joni paused, trying to read Frankie's face. Frankie's jaw tightened, but she remained quiet.

'I just laughed,' Joni said, and she did again now. Joni laughed desperately, hoping Frankie would join in, but she didn't. 'She started shouting then. Ranting on about bringing the whole collective down. The family ... Bringing you down.' Joni's voice was now trembling with rage.

'She rushed up the stairs, started screaming your name again, saying you owed her an explanation or she was gonna name you. I followed her up, trying to calm her down. I told her she was part of the family, that we were the same, but she twisted it, said we were both just pawns in your game. That we were both disposable to you. She kept twisting everything

I said ...' Joni frowned, remembering her own confusion. 'She said you were the worst kind of hypocrite.' She swallowed, paused, summoning the courage to tell Frankie the rest. 'I told her how grateful she should be for all you've done for her. I tried to remind her that without you, there'd be no interviews, no exposure. She wouldn't get to tell her story anyway. She had to get back in line, play her position like the rest of us, and then we would all win. I was calm, I swear, Franks. I just wanted the family back together. That's all ... But she just came at me. Out of nowhere she started scratching and slapping me, pulling my hair, saying she wouldn't let you treat her like a piece of shit, let you get into bed with that monster. She called you a ... a ...' Joni couldn't bring herself to say it. Her face contorted with disgust at the thought of the word. Ayesha wished she would stop this strange babbling speech, but still it continued. 'You know how I get,' Joni implored desperately. 'I don't know my own strength, that's what you said, especially if someone talks dirt on you. I just pushed her off me. I swear. She hurt *me*.' Joni started to sob. 'I don't even know what ... She must've lost her ... balance or something ... She fell ... down the stairs. I swear I ... I didn't mean it, Franks. I ran down. I tried to ... But she wasn't moving.'

Frankie bristled slightly. Her head raised a fraction away from Joni. Ayesha felt sick. *Jessica. Oh god, Jess.* She didn't dare move. She saw Joni's fist clench once and then loosen. She could see Clemmie's motionless, battered body in the periphery.

Joni continued.

'I kept calm though. I swear, Franks. All I could think was that I had to keep you well out of it. I knew I had to find somewhere to hide her, hide the ... Far away from ... you. I remembered this place. Drove up. At night. Sorted it.'

Joni waited for something from Frankie. Frankie remained quiet. Joni breathed heavily, desperately, trying to think of what to say that would make Frankie understand, forgive her.

'We would have got away with it. Everyone would have just forgotten about her if that stupid bitch hadn't gone on and on about where she was, that she was ruining the fucking circle.' Joni jabbed a finger at Clemmie. 'I had her phone,' she continued. 'I was gonna dump it, too, when the time was right. Far away so they wouldn't ... No one would be able to ... I had a plan, Franks, honest, to keep you out of it ... But I had to make a few changes. Improvise a bit. Send some messages, get everyone to leave her alone, think she was still ... still ... Y'know ...'

Alive, thought Ayesha incredulously.

'And then I was gonna make it look like she ... did it to herself.'

Ayesha felt the a wave of nausea.

'See, Franks? I had a plan,' Joni pleaded.

'But that stupid idiot kept looking for her, mentioning her.' She looked at Clemmie once more. 'And then *she* had to go and call her phone.' She locked eyes with Ayesha for a terrifying moment and Ayesha froze, but Joni soon turned back to Frankie. 'It wasn't meant to happen like this. I had a plan.'

Frankie stood still, her face neutral, passive. Joni's anger subsided. She tried again.

'I was just trying to make sure nothing, nobody fucked up the plan. You've worked so hard, *so hard* to get here. We're gonna change everything, for everyone. And they can't fucking see it. I see it, Franks. I see you. I get you. And I'd do anything for us, for you. I'm different, aren't I? It's not true, what Jessica said. She doesn't get it because she's never had what we have. That's why she behaves the way she does, only looks out for herself . . . Looked out . . .'

Ayesha's stomach sank.

'I did it for you,' Joni said imploringly into Frankie's face, 'I did it all for you. Please, Franks, I'm sorry. I'm so sorry. I didn't mean any of it.'

Ayesha could hardly breathe. Joni watched Frankie carefully. Frankie returned Joni's gaze. Eventually Frankie spoke.

'I called the police—'

Joni cringed.

'Why? Why did you do that? The pigs? The fucking pigs? Fuck the police, you taught me that. Fuck the fucking police, they're in on it.' Joni spat the words out. 'This is a war, you said, a war you've been fighting for decades. I remember. I listen, don't I? To every word you say. And wars are a dirty business, that's what you said. You've got to get your hands dirty, get in bed with the right people, do the deals, make the allegiances, the sacrifices. This goes right to the very top, you said, and also deep, deep underground.' Joni's voice took on a deeper, more resonant tone as she quoted Frankie, a gleam of adoration in her eyes, 'The networks, the abuse, the covering up. You spent years negotiating, years building up connections, making a name for yourself, building your profile step by step so you could actually change the fucking system. Get to the root of the poison. To save us. To save all of us. I just wanted to protect that. To protect you.'

She waited desperately for Frankie to say something, couldn't bear her silence. 'Frankie?' she pleaded.

Frankie shook her head slowly.

'You silly girl,' Frankie began in a low, cold voice. 'You silly, silly girl.'

Joni's face crumpled, devastated.

'What have you done? What on earth have you done? I told you. I told you to take it easy, to rein it in, didn't I? Didn't I?' Frankie snapped. Joni jumped, so did Ayesha. Then Joni nodded weakly. 'And now look what you've got yourself into. I can't help you. No one can.'

Joni looked up, imploring. 'Don't be angry, please. I can't bear it.' She began to cry, all the time watching Frankie. 'I'm sorry Frankie. I'm so sorry. Please,' she whined.

She stood, limp and helpless, crying in Frankie's face. Frankie, stiff as ever, looked on.

'The police are on their way,' Frankie said loudly, officially. 'You can explain what happened yourself. I wasn't party to any of it. I wasn't there and I have multiple witnesses to prove it.'

Joni stood speechless for a moment. She tried again.

'Don't talk to me like that,' she cried desperately. 'It's me, Franks.'

Joni leaned towards Frankie who took a step back and held up her hand.

'Keep away from me,' she warned. 'I will have nothing to do with you.'

Joni's mouth dropped in disbelief. Frankie's jaw remained set resolutely, her eyes already disengaged, devoid of any affection or affiliation to Joni.

'You can't,' Joni said quietly.

'Yes, I can,' Frankie explained almost pityingly.

Joni shook her head.

'No, you can't,' Joni repeated.

Frankie looked at Joni as if she finally realized she was talking to a mad person, a bewildered smile beginning to form. She looked behind her, into the dark of the forest, anticipating the sirens she knew were coming.

'Not me, Franks, you can't get rid of me.'

A hint of fear began to form on Frankie's face.

'What are you going to do?' she demanded.

Joni let out a shocked trill of laughter.

'I'm not gonna hurt you, Franks. Fuckin' hell,' she exclaimed, as if the thought was completely outrageous. 'But you can't get rid of me,' she insisted again.

Joni took a step forward and this time Frankie didn't move.

'I know too much,' she said meaningfully.

Frankie sobered at the words.

Ayesha tried to follow each new revelation. She strained desperately to hear sirens that weren't there, remained glued to Yaz's side.

'Cos it's not just Jack Vine you've been doing business with, is it? He's nowhere near the worst,' Joni said darkly. 'I know everything, Frankie, everything about you. All the meetings and deals and favours and back scratches.'

Frankie's face had gone very pale.

'And there have been a couple of really bad eggs. Really stinky ones. High up – but stinky as,' Joni continued. 'You had to do it. Course you did. It's a war, after all. You gotta do what you gotta do. I'd be the last to judge you, Franks. I'd never judge you,' she said meaningfully. 'And it was a long time ago, wasn't it? But it's all come out now, hasn't it? Just how bad those eggs were. You weren't to know. At least, I don't *think* you knew ...'

She delivered the last few words as clearly as if they were made of glass.

'So, you see? You can't get rid of me just because of a silly mistake.'

Ayesha watched Joni point awkwardly behind her. It was a strange gesture, and Ayesha tried desperately to comprehend it. There was so much Ayesha was struggling to understand, but the last two words echoed around Ayesha's head.

Silly mistake.

And suddenly she knew where Jessica was.

Our phone map sent us to some random gate at the other end.

You must have ended up there too if you put in the same postcode?

Random gate?

Our trip was pretty smooth ... No wrong turns for us.

Joni had known where to go because she'd driven here before.

I had to find somewhere to hide her.

Far away from you.

The lake's too good for her.

'I did it for you, Frankie, I did it all for you.'

The tepid water. The brush of hair. The groping hand.

We all mess up at some point.

'Oh god,' Ayesha whispered.
She'd accused Yaz. Attacked her. And now she was unconscious on the floor. Badly hurt, or worse, because of her.
She looked down at her beloved friend, limp and motionless.
Yaz had known. That was what she had been trying to say to her, trying to get the words out before she'd passed out, badly injured at Ayesha's own hands.

In the distance a faint wail.

Joni looked at Frankie, a new determination spreading across her face.

The wail was louder now. A siren, Ayesha realized.

Joni held her breath. She watched Frankie.

Frankie looked back at Joni with new eyes. She was almost smiling, almost impressed.

Without taking her eyes off her girlfriend, she lifted her phone and dialled three numbers.

'Please,' Frankie cried into the phone suddenly, 'help us. I called earlier, from the mansion. My friends are hurt. We're in danger. I know who did it and they're here now. You have to get to me as soon as you can.'

Joni shook her head, speechless and heartbroken. Frankie continued, her voice rising higher, her face morphing, twisting into a mask of terror and desperation.

'I can hear your colleagues. They're almost with us, but you need to know something. There are two men here, foreign-looking. They've attacked us. Shouting things in some strange language. I think it's Arabic. We think they might be friends of the groom. He's from Syria. We fled into the woods. Some of us are missing. They've got guns. One of them was injured.' She glanced at Yaz, still, on the ground. 'The other looks like he's got something attached to him. Around his waist. I think it might be ... an explosive of some sort ...'

She slowly turned her gaze to Juan Carlos. Juan Carlos stared back, his eyes widening in disbelief.

'What? Me? You can't be serious. I didn't ... I haven't ...'

Frankie wailed into the phone, covering up Juan Carlos's words. Ayesha shook her head, dumbfounded, looked from him back to Frankie, to Yaz, whispered, *no,* as it dawned on her.

The siren had become several sirens.

'Please, it's just me and my girlfriend. We're very scared. Help us,' Frankie cried into the phone. Joni beamed.

'No!' Ayesha shouted, 'No! It's not true. They're not the ones who—Don't hurt them!'

'Help us please!' Joni shouted madly over Ayesha's words.

'And there's another woman. She's with them. She ran over our friend with a car. And she beat the other one with a gun. I think she killed her. Oh God!'

'No!' Ayesha made a desperate grab for the phone. Joni swung round and shoved her hard to the floor, stood over her and punched her in the face. Ayesha heard the crack as the fist made contact once again. A numbness and a darkness threatened to overwhelm her. She stayed down.

The sirens were loud now and multiple. There were several cars. And they were close.

'Yes, I'll stay on the line. I'll try ...'

A sound of screeching. Car doors opening, closing. A radio.

'We are walking towards them now. Please tell them who we are. Don't hurt us. They're armed. Help us please. We just want to be safe. For this all to be over ...'

Frankie's voice trailed off as she and Joni rushed towards the police cars.

There were shouts. A dog barked. Torchlight flickering among the trees.

'Oh fuck.' Juan Carlos looked around wildly. He made to run towards the lights, stopped, started running in the other direction. Two more dogs barked. He stopped, came back, looked wildly from side to side. 'Fuck!' he cried. He turned to Ayesha desperately.

Ayesha tried lifting her head; it felt like it weighed a ton. Bright sparks exploded in her eyes as she pushed herself shakily from the floor. She tried to breathe deeply. Another flash of light. She fought the dizziness and nausea, the heavy weight of her limbs. Through the blur she saw Yaz's prostrate body a few feet away. She crawled to her, her head and face smarting with pain. As she reached her friend, she saw that her eyes were open and she was fighting to keep them that way. Yaz reached for Ayesha. Ayesha reached for Yaz. The shouts, mingled with the barks, came ever closer.

'I'm so sorry, Yaz. I'm so, so sorry.' Ayesha held her friend's hand, stroked it, touched her beloved face gently.

'Yeesh,' Yaz tried weakly. She took a deep breath and with more conviction, more focus, 'Yeesh, it's my fault. I should have said something . . . I was trying to protect you. I knew they wanted to hurt you . . . I . . .'

Ayesha sobbed as Yaz fought to stay conscious. They held hands tightly as the torchlight came ever closer. The stomp of footsteps, twigs breaking and hungry yelps were almost upon them now.

A torch swung onto them and mercifully passed over. Ayesha and Yaz fixed their eyes on each other, squeezed each other's hands tighter. Then Ayesha shook her head.

No.

She let go of Yaz's hand, hurled herself up and ignoring the searing pain in her head, she stumbled forward towards the car parked nearby. Juan Carlos watched incredulously as Ayesha fell into the driver's seat once more, found the key in the ignition, turned it, and with a final glance at her beloved friend on the floor in front of her, slammed the car into reverse.

'What the fuck?' came the confused cry from Juan Carlos who stood terrified with his hands already high in the air. Ayesha only paused long enough to switch on the lights and get her bearings. The torches were coming from that direction, so they must have found the back gate. That meant that she needed to go right. She swerved the car away from them and drove off, past Juan Carlos who stood, mouth agape. She drove as fast as she dared back through the trees and after a few seconds she slammed the heel of her hand hard against the horn. The sound filled the car and cut through the night. She hit it and hit it again. The forest abruptly opened up into a frozen starless sky and Ayesha pressed down on the accelerator, all the while beeping the horn as hard as she could.

The water appeared faster than she had anticipated. Her reactions were slower than usual. By the time she slammed her foot on the brake, she was already skidding into the water. The car lurched forward and down and thudded into the lake. It jolted to a stop. Ayesha's head slammed onto the steering wheel and stayed there, her eyes closed, her cheek pressed up against the horn.

I hope it was enough, she thought.

CHAPTER THIRTY-ONE

JULY 2019

Ayesha stepped out of the solid grey brick courthouse into a street refreshed by a recent downpour. The sky was sombre, as sombre as the halls and courtrooms had been, despite the people filling them. But out here the air was fresh, invigorating, soothing.

It was over. Weeks of hearings and counter-arguments, retelling and recounting, cross examinations and paperwork. It was messy, confusing, often frustrating and ultimately dissatisfying. But it was done.

She breathed deeply, thought of that night one more time. The night she'd had to describe over and over.

She remembered waking to hands on her, searching her body, a voice confirming she was unarmed, then they had gently but firmly pulled her from the car. Her half-open eyes had registered the sea of uniformed white faces, barely visible behind the strong lights trained on her. Frankie had been right. They would have come out shooting.

She had fought against the tiredness, the heaviness in her limbs, the desire to go back to sleep, and gripped onto the arms carrying her, followed them up to a face and told them clearly and firmly as they carried her out that there was no bomb, no armed foreigners in the woods. That there was only one dead body and it was in this lake and she knew who had killed her.

They had found Jessica soon after. Frankie and Joni had already been driven off in an ambulance, but a police car was sent after it, a radio call put out. India and Clemmie were next to be brought out, sent away for treatment. They had both made a full recovery.

It turned out Clemmie's firearms certificate had expired years ago, though. She and her family were in possession of a gun illegally. Ayesha had tried to ask the investigating officer what charges she would face, but each time the answer seemed vaguer. The guns hadn't been used to kill anyone and that was their main priority. Clemmie maintained that she had felt her own life was under threat and anything she or India had done was in self-defence. Although, after some legal advice, the two of them seemed to distance themselves from each other as the case progressed. Ultimately, they were cleared of all charges.

Ayesha still noticed the family name pop up every now and then. Their projects in Africa seemed to be progressing nicely. Their seat in the House of Lords safe. Their statue standing ever proudly outside the great halls of learning.

* * *

The police hadn't seemed so sure about what to do with Juan Carlos that night. He had dropped to the floor next to Yaz with his arms high over his head where they could see them. The police had approached with caution, shouting for him and the other brown person not to move. They hadn't. Mercifully, the police paused long enough to check that they were unarmed.

Ayesha had watched the dark blue uniforms march him out of the forest and then seem to hover around him. It looked like they were about to put him in a police car and drive him away. He'd looked terrified, trying to keep his voice steady, co-operate with everything and everyone, keep his hands where they could see them at all times. Ayesha stepped forward, grabbed his shoulders. She made a fuss, checking him, asking where it hurt, walking him over to the ambulance and insisting they both be driven to the hospital to be checked out, just like the others had. Mercifully, the paramedic agreed, and the police grudgingly conceded.

'You're shaking,' Ayesha had said to Juan Carlos as they had waited in the back. Juan Carlos looked over to Ayesha.

'So are you.' Ayesha looked down and realized her hands were trembling as much as his. She tried to laugh. Failed.

'I'm so sorry. I'm so, so sorry, Juan Carlos. It was me. I booked you. I never thought . . . You could have been . . . They were going to . . .' Her voice faltered.

There was silence as they sat looking out of the back doors into the dark country night.

'My name's not Juan Carlos.'

Ayesha looked up.

'It's Raj. I'm Raj,' Juan Carlos said. 'I'm not Latin American. I'm from Birmingham. My parents are Indian. I just realized a few weeks into the job I got triple the work if I shaved my chest and put on a Cuban accent.'

Ayesha's mouth fell open. It stayed that way for a long time.

They hadn't let Ayesha back into the forest. She had to wait helplessly until they finally emerged with Yaz on a wheeled stretcher. She had rushed forward then, ignoring the pain in her own body, the protestations from the paramedics, and sobbed as she held her friend's hand in hers and helped them transfer her to a waiting ambulance. Even then she had refused to let her go. So she sat by her as she was checked and made comfortable.

In faltering words, Ayesha told her that she was safe now, that they were going to get her to hospital and make her better. And that she was so, so very sorry.

In faltering words, Yaz explained to Ayesha what had happened that night, deep inside that cursed house.

Yaz had stood silently in the driveway watching Ayesha's rage and pain as Clemmie announced to the group the new collaboration, said her name, applauded. India's firm grip on her arm, the trace of that alcohol-infused kiss, the demanding tongue snaking ever further into her mouth, the strange texture of the silky hair in cane rows brushing her hand as she had kissed India back. She had wanted desperately to spit on the floor. Knew she couldn't. The layers of make-up helped. She watched them all closely, using the mask of the costume and paint to cover her, keeping her expression neutral. Blending in. She even pulled the headscarf further over her face.

She watched Ayesha attack the flag, fight Joni, insult them all, turn her rage directly at her for a moment. Then the final blow from Joni and her friend fell to the floor. It had taken everything she had not to race forward and deck Joni there and then. But she had stayed where she was, tried to steady her breath as she looked helplessly at Ayesha unconscious on the ground. She saw Joni shake out her punching hand, turn around to look at Frankie who looked back with approval.

And then Clemmie was giving orders, Frankie and Joni began to tend to Ayesha, pick her up. Clemmie took India by the hand and led her away, back into the house.

Yaz had waited a few moments, watching Joni and Frankie clumsily try to carry Ayesha. She looked to where Ayesha had been lying and saw her phone discarded on the floor. Yaz grabbed it and pocketed it. She kept one ear on the sounds in the house, heard the other two women rush down the corridor. Then Yaz had slipped back inside.

She took the main staircase to the first floor and tried to get her bearings. This place was a fucking labyrinth. Eventually, she found the bedroom that she'd followed Clemmie and India into. She crept in, leaving the door ajar for some light, the vast windows offering no illumination at all, even with the curtains still open.

411

She made her way swiftly to the wardrobe, hoping she was right. She had been the last one out. No one had locked the door behind her. If she remembered rightly, she'd glimpsed it as she'd kept her eyes open, as the alcohol-infused tongue had snaked deeper into her mouth, the fingers pushing at her over the layers of clothing she was so grateful had provided some form of defence. She'd kept her eyes wide in order not to scream, not to push her off, to panic. And as she cast about wildly, she'd caught a glimpse of it, just as India had pulled back and led her out.

Keeping the door open, Yaz crept back through the fur coats and stepped back into Narnia.

She tried to keep her mind off the huge dark figures of the stuffed animal cadavers looming in the windowless dark. She avoided the pictures of the chained humans on the walls. She turned sharply to the right as she entered and faced the bear that towered several feet above her, its bared teeth just visible in the darkness. She steeled herself and reached to its side, brushing the dusty lifeless fur of its sturdy right leg and then her hand felt the solid metal she was looking for. She grasped the rifle and pulled it to her.

She turned it over, its steel bulk heavy in her hands. She gave it an awkward yank, but nothing happened. She tried to remember back all those years. The one other time she'd held a rifle, something similar to this. She was sixteen and had been picked by her school to join a citywide scheme to get kids living in London out into nature. Outward Bound it was called. They'd spent a week being woken at dawn, jogging five miles before breakfast and ending with a dip in the freezing lake nearby, before spending the day climbing trees, building fires, launching arrows and finally trying their hand at rifle shooting. She hadn't been great; the other kids cussed her for her lack of skills. How was she gonna survive *On Road* if she couldn't handle a weapon? But they'd taught her how to load and unload it. How to aim, release the safety catch, and pull the trigger. And that was what she tried to recall now.

She turned it over once more, tried again and with a bit of a fumble, an alarmingly loud snap and then a thud, the bullets fell to the floor.

Yaz placed the empty gun back behind the bear. She picked up the bullets, reached up and placed them gently in the back of the cavernous, perpetually snarling mouth. Then she tiptoed out.

Yaz slipped out of the room and back down the stairs. The door to the lounge was ajar and Yaz could feel the heat from the fire radiating out of it. She tried to listen for Ayesha's voice but heard nothing. Clemmie and India had rejoined them, in their new outfits.

'Still sleeping?' she heard Clemmie's voice ask darkly. 'Typical. She'll wake up soon enough. Sit her up. Bring her nearer to the fire . . .'

Yaz couldn't bear the thought of them manhandling Ayesha. But there was one more thing she had to do.

She headed back down the corridor to the costume room. Messy piles of colourful fabric lay scattered on the floor mixed with darker, plainer clothes left where they'd been discarded as the women had transformed into goddesses. She picked her way through it all, searching. She groped around, picking up a dark piece of clothing, discarding it immediately on feeling the light richness of the fabric, until she finally felt the familiar heavy roughness of her own black denim. She almost dropped it with relief, but then quickly fumbled about until her fingers touched something cold, ridged: the car key Ayesha had given her when they put the pink stuff in the boot. They were getting the hell out of here.

Yaz made her way back down the corridor. Again the voices in the lounge reached her as she landed in the hallway. Once again she paused outside the lounge door and listened. Clemmie giving orders, reassuring India. And then a figure passed the gap in the door towards the fire. This time the woman used her foot to snap a thick branch in two, then leaned over and fed it to the flames. And something clicked. The phone messages . . . A flash of two phones sticking out of tight jean pockets as she leaned over the pot in the kitchen; a glimpse of her texting from two phones when she thought she was alone – an image that had troubled Yaz but she hadn't known why, that she hadn't been able to share with Ayesha, so she had focused on getting as plastered as she could just to get through the night till they could get back to London.

Yaz's head was swimming once more. These women, they were all fucking dangerous. Every one of them. And now, if she was right, she knew who had really been sending Jessica's messages.

Her heart was racing but she tried to keep her mind cool, her breathing steady.

She had planned to creep back into the lounge, wait for the right moment to grab Ayesha and run, get in the car and bust their way out of here. But then they started chanting, shouting, screaming, scratching. Yaz had burst into the room and saw them groping wildly at Ayesha, Joni pinning her shoulders down while the others searched her body. She found the car key still in her hand and swung it round her fingers so the sharp end was facing out of the fist that she was about to bring down on those bitches feeling up her terrified friend. But they heard the jingle. Stopped. Turned around and went for her. And before she knew what was happening, they'd snatched the key right out of her hand and she watched helplessly as they dragged Ayesha to the car.

Ayesha had listened to Yaz's account in quiet shock. She'd sobbed as she realized what her friend had been through to save her, held her hand even tighter until the paramedic had pulled her gently away.

The time of Jessica's death had been hard to ascertain due to the exceptionally hot weather and her prolonged immersion in the water. There was little for the forensics team to go on. No one had seen Joni attack her.

It was her own words that got her in the end.

The most important piece of evidence turned out to be on Jessica's phone. When Ayesha had called Jessica in the woods and her phone had rung in Joni's pocket, it had automatically gone to voicemail. But Ayesha hadn't hung up, just dropped her arm. Jessica's phone recorded Joni's words and most of Frankie's just before the police arrived. When Joni attacked Ayesha in the woods, it wasn't just Ayesha who had dropped to the floor. Jessica's phone had landed nearby too. It was retrieved, along with other evidence, by the team soon after.

Frankie was given a suspended sentence. She seemed almost disappointed not to do some jail time, something that would have added to her credibility and kept her in the limelight. Joni's prison sentence was significantly longer and, despite her threats to use her knowledge of Frankie's questionable connections against her, Frankie distanced herself from Joni during the court case. Frankie's friends were indeed many and powerful. Any dirt or stink Joni had on Frankie somehow didn't quite land. Her claims were twisted into the ramblings of a deranged, bitter ex-lover – someone so unhinged, they were capable of killing someone. Frankie held a fist up as she was led out of the courtroom, unfolding her rousing new speech for the waiting journalists as she went, her new entourage of young women already surrounding her. Joni glanced once at her then back down and kept her eyes on the floor as she was walked out of the hall in handcuffs.

Standing outside the courthouse, under a muted sky, Ayesha let her thoughts turn once more to the person whose name had dominated the trial. Jessica. She noticed that the image of her that appeared in her mind was different now. Ayesha no longer saw the haughty, cold expression she'd seen so many times; instead she saw a softer, more serene Jessica. A Jessica she had never really seen in real life, but she liked to imagine that maybe sometimes in their more relaxed telephone conversations, Jessica might have looked like this.

A lump formed in Ayesha's throat. She let out a sob.

She was weary. She had felt deeply weary for so long now. But there was something more now. Not exactly peace – the justice system was far too complex and archaic, too flawed and biased to offer that – but perhaps a new-found strength, a voice and a power she had discovered within her – had *had* to discover. She had spoken up, clumsily and falteringly, but she had done it. She had challenged those women. She had protected her friend. She had taken action and been the only one to tell the truth that night, and again in court. She had helped get justice for Jessica – this time at least. Jessica's face appeared once again on all the front pages, alongside that word, *Justice* – even in her original attacker's broadsheet, Ayesha noticed grimly. As she stood outside the imposing building on this fresh afternoon, she thought of that terrified, silent little girl she had once been and wondered what she would have made of this new Ayesha – clear and true and stronger than she had ever known she was. She wondered briefly what it would feel like to have justice for herself, for that little girl who had been wronged so badly, so many times. What it would have been like to stand in court and be questioned and examined and to have told *her* truth, spoken up for that little girl, and been believed, heard the judge pronounce the sentence – a concrete number that represented the gravity of what had been done to her. She smiled sadly. That's not how it worked. She knew that. Not for her. She also knew that she couldn't go through that process again. So she held on to the victory she had helped win for Jessica – the one person who had listened to her disclosure. Because that was something.

Ayesha breathed in the fresh air deeply.

A single footstep and Yaz was beside her. She turned to her friend.

'Come,' she beckoned.

EPILOGUE

AUGUST 2019

It's a scorcher. One of the few good-weather days this summer. It has rained and rained, a complete washout, but Ayesha doesn't mind. After the sweltering furnace of last year's hell, this year seems to offer some reprieve. The heavy rains feel right. Cleansing. Washing away the old, bringing the fresh scent of quenched earth, lush greenery and shimmering concrete. And now the sun drying it all up, making way for the new. Just in time for Carnival.

Yaz and Ayesha clang their cans of Red Stripe together and take a messy sip. They bought them out of a bucket full of icy water on a shopping trolley one of their old school mates was pushing around the streets. He'd given them a discount and chucked in a whistle.

They drink to their success. To their bright, booked-and-busy future. It's only now that either of them is ready to begin to fathom what's next, but their agents have been busy working through, and lining up, the many opportunities these bright, gifted women have been offered – both as individual acts and together, as performers and as writers.

And they're getting paid – well.

They stand shoulder to shoulder in the crowd watching the brightly feathered costumes go by and feel as much as hear the booming bass from the sound systems on the floats in their chests, their cells, their whole beings. The rich musicality of the steel pans, the impossible dexterity of the players competing with the collossal speakers. The flash of gold tooth, the shake of foot, the liquid whine a stark contrast to the stiff, beanpole policemen stationed in the corners, regulation earplugs firmly wedged.

Carnival in West London. As far as Ayesha can remember, she remembers Carnival. It signifies the final flourish of late London summer. The coming together of all types in the biggest street festival in Europe. Founded by the immigrant community who settled here so long ago to keep their culture alive on these chilly shores, it is a riot of colour, tastes, sounds and joy. Face painted as a butterfly, a rainbow, a superhero, she has stomped these streets shaking and shimmying until she could no longer stand. Year after year.

And once again, Yaz and Yeesh hit the streets of West London. Together. This time she's even managed to get Yaz to wear some glitter.

She remembers all too well how every year there has been some kind of drama. They have tried to move it out of the area, rebrand it, contain it with a fence, make it a festival in Hyde Park, make it illegal, sue it, arrest it, and push the people out of the area, price them out, burn them out.

And still they come. For one weekend a year. They come and come, wave after colourful wave, and reclaim their neighbourhood, fill the streets, for one weekend a year. Communities commune again. Old faces find each other. New faces take up the mantle, the flag. Sweet bread is broken. Chicken and goat consumed. Plantain and patty munched. Green smoked, rum sipped and Red Stripe slurped. Backside whined and foot shaken.

Ayesha wears green this year. Yaz has a green scarf wrapped around her arm and a single green ribbon wound around her walking stick. Raj wears a T-shirt with a green heart on it.

Green.

For Grenfell.

They wait for the 72-second silence. The entire carnival comes to a standstill. Sound systems stop. Heads bow. They remember. All of them. Each precious soul. Lost.

Ayesha feels for Yaz's hand. It's already searching for hers. They find each other and stand like this, in silence.

And then a single song plays through the speakers. They all listen as 'We Shall Overcome' by Toots and the Maytals plays clear and loud across the crowd. They stay quiet and begin to sway. The DJ plays the track till the end and then a whole festival applauds sombrely. A hoot and they look up to the train bridge crowning this infamous street. A tube driver has stopped his train in respect. He waves a green scarf from his window. Thousands wave back.

The sound systems start up again, the dancing begins anew. They rave like they always do, like they always have, in each other's faces, syncing with each other, and this time with everyone else. Then a body comes between them. She shakes and winds her curves in Yaz's direction. Yaz at first looks surprised, glances at Ayesha, lets herself be danced on.

Ayesha grins, turns around, surveys the crowd of heads bobbing to the music and sighs.

'Right. I'm ready for a chill-out. Anyone up for heading to the park?'

Yaz turns to her, a smile flickers across her face.

'I reckon I'm gonna hang here for a bit,' she replies, 'check out the local talent. See what it's saying.'

The woman smiles up at her, continues dancing.

Ayesha looks at them both.

'Seen,' she says, raising her eyebrows.

'I'll come.'

She turns to see Raj smiling nervously. She smiles awkwardly back.

'Sure,' she says and leads the way through the crowd, taking his hand gently so as not to lose him.

As they head away from the procession, Ayesha takes one more look back at her friend, standing tall and dark, all in black apart from the green armband and the occasional sparkle on her face, before she disappears, enveloped in the multicoloured mass.

ACKNOWLEDGEMENTS

To Hannah Weatherill, who has been my companion on this long writing journey and a cool, calm, level-headed rock throughout – thank you.

To James Carroll, who saw the potential when this was not much more than an anecdote over a cuppa – thank you.

To Sabhbh Curran, who has taken up the mantle with such enthusiasm and warmth – thank you.

To my editors Bethan Jones and Judith Long, for loving Ayesha and the gang as much as I do and helping to hone their voices and story – thank you. To the whole team at Simon & Schuster, including Jess Barratt, Harriett Collins and Amy Fulwood, thank you for believing in *Goddesses* and treating this new novelist with such care.

To my GCP crew – Martin McGuigan, John Robert Lee, Darren John Travers – you're the best creative allies a gal could have. Thank you for the years of meetups and notes. And to my wider writing community – the Rogue Playwrights, Criterion

New Writers, School of Hightide and my 4Screenwriting fam – thank you for making this solitary thing we do feel like family.

To the wonderful individuals who took the time to read sections of the book and to consult with me on issues as diverse as hen dos, gentrification, asbestos, growing up in care, housing associations, the criminal justice system, sexual violence, sexuality, gender, race and class – thank you. Genevieve Pottier, Jade Swaby, Dana McDonald, Anthony Moriarty, Katrina Mayhew Taibe, Rayen Salgado Pottier, Dani Tagen, Anna Reeve – your expertise and lived experiences are sewn into the fabric of this story.

To Greg Mosse, for being an unofficial mentor to so many of us and a tireless encourager of writers – thank you.

To dear Francoise, whose generosity gave me the space to heal and live and write – thank you.

To Kaash, for the hundred daily kindnesses, for truly walking the walk and for being the kind of man who makes it easy for a woman to thrive – thank you.

To my chosen family, for being there through it all – I am here because you were there.